ARENA

"Stunning . . . fast-paced, action-packed, with an interesting romance and a compelling yet flawed heroine . . . Read this book. You haven't read anything quite like it, and you don't want to miss it."

—Ilona Andrews, #1 *New York Times* bestselling author
of the Kate Daniels novels

"Blistering action right from the first page, but it's Jennings's brilliant characters that kept me logged in to *Arena* . . . Thrilling."

—Jason M. Hough, *New York Times* bestselling author
of the Dire Earth Cycle series

"Serious nerdcore entertainment. Gamers, get ready to plug in!"

—Chloe Neill, *New York Times* bestselling author
of the Chicagoland Vampires novels

"Subversive and tricky, just like the best games . . . Fascinating."

—SFcrowsnest

"Depict[s] the action and excitement of virtual gaming that made Ernest Cline's *Ready Player One* such a hit . . . Readers seeking more fast-paced SF about virtual reality will be pleased."

—*Library Journal*

"A nuanced and complex novel with a strong, imperfect heroine and a different approach to the 'rebel in a dystopian society' trope."

—*RT Book Reviews*

continued . . .

Jul 17

"Action-packed . . . will appeal to fans of science fiction like Ernest Cline's *Armada*." —*Booklist*

"Kali Ling is truly a fascinating character." —The Bookbag

"A solid coming-of-age story." —Smart Bitches, Trashy Books

ACE BOOKS BY HOLLY JENNINGS

Arena
Gauntlet

GAUNTLET

HOLLY JENNINGS

ACE
New York

ACE
Published by Berkley
An imprint of Penguin Random House LLC
375 Hudson Street, New York, New York 10014

Copyright © 2017 by Holly Jennings
Penguin Random House supports copyright. Copyright fuels creativity,
encourages diverse voices, promotes free speech, and creates a vibrant culture.
Thank you for buying an authorized edition of this book and for complying with
copyright laws by not reproducing, scanning, or distributing any part of it in any
form without permission. You are supporting writers and allowing Penguin
Random House to continue to publish books for every reader.

ACE is a registered trademark and the A colophon is a trademark of
Penguin Random House LLC.

ISBN: 9781101988954

An application to register this book for cataloging has been submitted to the
Library of Congress.

First Edition: April 2017

Printed in the United States of America
1 3 5 7 9 10 8 6 4 2

Cover illustration by Larry Rostant
Cover design by Adam Auerbach
Book design by Kelly Lipovich

To my dad.
Thanks for the video games, and everything else.

PRESS THE START BUTTON TO BEGIN . . .

LEVEL 1:

THE WALL

CHAPTER 1

O
nly the top gamers in the world were invited to the most exclusive spot in all of L.A., and no one knew what was inside.

Not even me.

"The heat coming off The Wall is huge," one reporter crooned, emphasizing the last word until he sounded like a mooing cow. Huuuuuge.

With a name like The Wall, you'd think everyone was talking about a nightclub. But no. It wasn't a boutique or a restaurant, either. Sure, any of those would have made perfect sense. Throughout history, those were the kinds of elite establishments marked "Invitation Only" for the Hollywood glitterati. It was expected.

A tradition, if you will.

But the year was 2055. Virtual reality had permeated every aspect of society, and pro gamers were the top celebrities in the world. So, let's just say tradition had taken a long-needed vacation and was a little too drunk on coconut margaritas to give a shit about what was to be expected.

I cranked up the volume on the celebrity-gossip channel, where a drone-camera feed hovered over a single house located in the Pacific Palisades district of Westside Los Angeles. Okay, to call it a house would be an understatement. A compound. Or maybe an estate. Fifty thousand square feet of guarded walls, high-tech security, and absolute mystery. Any gamer who got invited past the armed guards and steely gates never talked about what happened inside. So, after weeks of endless speculation, I'd pulled in a professional on the matter.

"*This* is why you called me in here?"

Dr. Renner sat in a guest chair across from my desk, though it had been turned to face the oversized screen in the far wall. She glanced back at me with a curled lip.

"You're a psychologist—" I began.

"A psychiatrist," she emphasized.

Potato. Po-tah-toe.

"Whatever. You can read between the lines. What do you think is inside?" I nodded at the screen, where the paparazzi camped outside the house in droves, hoping to catch a glimpse of the latest gamer let through the magic gates. Drones hovered above, snapping as many pictures as the people below did. The Wall had so many of those UAVs buzzing around, it must have looked like a beehive from space.

"Kali, I specialize in virtual psychiatry. I study the effect of virtual stimuli on a person's mind and body. How am I supposed to figure out what's inside some random house?"

I already knew what she specialized in. A few months ago, I was on a pro gaming team under different management, and Dr. Renner was the mental-health expert on staff. Since then, I'd bought out the team, and Dr. Renner followed. She believed in me and my dream to erase the corruption in pro gaming. But currently, my concern over problems in eSports had taken a backseat to figuring out what was going on in that damn house.

"Why is everyone calling it The Wall?" she asked. With a high ponytail, buxom lips, and chunky glasses resting on a perfectly straight nose, Dr. Renner looked like someone who paid her way through med school by modeling, then ten years into her career, forgot how beautiful she was.

"It's short for The Invisible Wall," I said.

She glanced at me and blinked. Twice. "I'm afraid I'll need a little more than that."

I sighed. "It's a retro video game term. When you reach the edge of a map in a game, you run smack into an invisible wall. It's a way of keeping the player inside a set area."

"But why bother? Can't a player tell where the end of the map is? Isn't the landscaping just grayed out or something?"

"No. Usually the landscape continues on. It's seamless. The area beyond the wall looks like it's accessible, but it's not."

A wave of understanding washed over her face. "So, everyone's calling that house The Invisible Wall because—"

"You can see it but can't access it. It's off the map. Unless you're invited in." I opened the television remote app on my tablet. "Here, watch this." I brought up an old video of a pro gaming team entering the house. It didn't matter which one I chose. The rundown was always the same.

It starts at the airport.

The television screen went black for a second as the video loaded up. LAX appeared on the screen with the video's title superimposed over the image.

ANOTHER GAMING TEAM VISITS THE WALL.

Paparazzi and fans were camped out around the airport's pickup/drop-off zone. More were inside, and a few had even bought tickets to the cheapest flights to get past security. From baggage claim to the getaway vehicle was one long line of cameras, flailing arms, and screaming admirers.

The team exited the terminal, and the crowds erupted in

cheers. The team members wore hoods, pulled low over their faces, so no one knew who they were. It didn't stop anyone from losing their mind. Airport security and private guards cleared a path for them through the airport as they clung to their sunglasses and filed into an SUV with tinted windows.

Sunglasses. Tinted windows. As if pro gamers could conceal their identities nowadays. But they tried. Some of them even succeeded.

The video cut away, and the same vehicle from the airport (verified by license plate) appeared at the house. More fans and paparazzi assaulted the car, pounding on the windows. The gates opened, and the SUV slid through. Armed security at the gates kept the riffraff out. Once the SUV rounded the driveway and stopped near the door, the team piled out, hoods still pulled low over their eyes until they disappeared inside.

Dr. Renner crossed her arms and leaned forward in the chair. Her brow furrowed. "Why are they hiding their faces?"

Even she sounded interested now.

"Exactly."

Dr. Renner pressed her lips together and adjusted her glasses. "How do we even know these are gaming teams?"

"A few have been revealed. Either a fan pulled their hood off or the paparazzi got close enough to snap a picture of their faces."

Dr. Renner considered it and sighed.

"What do *you* think is inside?"

Ah, flipping the question around on me. Psychology 101. Oh, excuse me. Psychiatry 101.

"Drugs," I said. "That's why no one's talking about it and why everyone is hiding their identity. I think they've cooked up something more addictive than HP."

HP was the ecstasy of the gamer world. It makes you feel

invincible, just like the game. And just like a game, you'll hit it. Again, and again, and again.

"Kali," she began. "If you had relapsed, you'd tell me, right?"

"I'd whiz into a cup for you and put a bow on it."

Her lip curled again. "Please don't relapse. And not just for your own sake." She eyed my mug. "How many cups of coffee did you drink today?"

"This, plus one."

In a Big Gulp.

"Really?" She raised an eyebrow. "You seem a little jittery."

Raise the threat level to Defcon Four. She's onto me.

"Look," I said, holding up my tablet to distract her, secretly hoping my hands weren't shaking as badly as I thought they were. "It's in all the tabloids. Read through them. I'm sure you can wade through the bullshit."

Dr. Renner took the tablet in her hands, flipped through it a few times, and peered over the edge at me.

"You hate these magazines."

I only hated them when they screwed around with my love life—when I had one. Funny how actors, rock stars, and heiresses used to constitute the fodder that fed the tabloid cows. Now they came second, behind gamers. Since the mystery of The Wall, nearly every article centered on the virtual elite.

And yes, I used to sneer at these magazines. Now I had a subscription to every one of them. The mighty fall sometimes, okay?

Dr. Renner eyed me again.

"Kali," she began. "I know this must be fascinating to you, but I'm not completely comfortable encouraging you to indulge in this compulsion—"

"Interest," I emphasized. "It's a healthy interest."

"I'm not so sure."

"Oh, come on." I pointed at the television screen. "If there was something this interesting going on in the world of psychology—"

"Psychiatry."

"—wouldn't you be intrigued?"

Something interesting in the world of psychiatry. Pffft.

She considered it, shrugged, and flipped through the magazines on my tablet a few more times.

"Any idea who owns this place?"

"Tamachi Industries. A Japanese company that specializes in artificial intelligence."

"So it's about technology."

"No."

"Why not?"

"What does artificial intelligence have to do with pro gaming?"

"There are chilling towers." She pointed to a picture of the house, holding up the tablet for me to see. "Are you sure it's not tech related?"

"Nah." I dismissed the suggestion with a wave of my hand. "That's just to throw people off."

"Why are you so sure it's a drug house?"

"Everyone knows it's something I stand against."

She studied my expression for a minute with narrowed eyes and slightly pursed lips. I hated when she looked at me like that. It felt like she was reading my mind.

"Oh," she began with a smile. "That's what this is about. You don't care what's in the house. You just want to know why you haven't been invited."

Well, her psychic powers hadn't failed her. Actually, I did care about what was in the house. If it was drugs, I wasn't interested. Not anymore. But I did have a bit of a reputation in the gaming world. I was Kali Ling, the warrior. Holder of three Virtual Gaming League records and the undisputed queen of the RAGE tournaments, the VGL's most brutal fighting game. Didn't that at least merit an invitation? You know, delivered on a platter. Maybe silver.

"Can you give me any other clues?" Dr. Renner asked, eyeing the television screen, which had gone dark at the end of the airport video.

Hook, line, and sinker. From doctor to detective in less than five minutes.

I flipped the television back to the celebrity-gossip channel. "They're always debating it on Hypnotized."

Hypnotized was the biggest gamer-celebrity news channel in the country. Lately, debates over The Wall took up nearly all of their programming. When the channel popped up, a group of reporter-journalists sat on a couch, talking about . . . guess what?

"Okay, let's talk about who hasn't been seen at the house."

"What about Kali Ling?"

Well, look at that.

The volume went up.

"I mean, she won a championship last season and was the first female captain in the VGL. You'd think she'd be at The Wall."

See? Invitation.

"You're out of your mind. What's she done since then? Nothing."

Nothing?

"Hey, three words. Youngest team owner in history."

"That's five words."

The cell phone wrapped around my wrist buzzed. I tore my

gaze away from the television screen long enough to glance at the caller identification. Speaking of my love life . . .

James Rooke

My heart clenched, and I forced myself to read the name several times. No, that couldn't be right. He hadn't talked to me in weeks. So what was with the sudden phone call?

Since we'd won the RAGE championship last fall, I'd left the team to build up resources, sponsorships, and—most importantly—money, in order to take over ownership of Defiance. Rooke had stayed with the team. But when I bought out our former owner, Rooke immediately bowed out and just left. No explanation. No phone call.

Until now.

I let a slow breath pass through my lips and tapped the IG-NORE button.

"Why are you ignoring him?" the doctor asked.

"How did you know—"

"Body language."

I frowned. "How come you can figure out who's calling me, but you don't know what's inside that damn house?"

"Your exterior is a little more expressive than the house's."

Was that sarcasm? I was rubbing off on the good doctor.

"You might not feel like talking to Rooke," she began. "But maybe talking to me or someone else about it will help."

"He left. What is there to talk about?"

The words left my mouth in such a way I might as well have chewed them up and spat them out. Dr. Renner repeated her pursed-lips, narrowed-eyes, mind-reading pose for a minute. She opened her mouth like she was about to say something when a reporter burst into the scene on the TV screen.

"We've got the latest footage," he announced. "And we know who it is this time."

The reporters bristled, exchanging glances with each other.

"There's another team at the airport?"

"No. But there's a team about to go through the gate."

"If they weren't spotted at the airport first, that means—"

"It's an American team."

An American team? Interesting. None so far had been seen at The Wall.

The volume went to maximum.

The journalists turned to the screen between them. The shot showed a black SUV rolling through the gate and stopping just in front of the house. A security guard exited the car, along with five figures clad in black, hoods pulled low, same as usual.

"How the hell can you tell who that is?" one reporter protested. "They're dressed just like all the others."

"The scans from the survey drones are telling us that this individual"—the new guy pointed at the screen, and the camera zoned in—"is a woman who's five-foot-five."

"Lots of women are five-foot-five."

"Sure, but how many have a crescent tattoo on their calf?"

The camera zoomed in on the woman's calf muscle, where the edge of a crescent tattoo peaked out from beneath her pant cuff.

"That's Jessica Salt of Team Legacy!"

"Legacy is at The Wall? This just went epic."

My heart stopped.

This *was* epic. For two reasons. One, Legacy was the first confirmed American team to appear at the house that we knew of. All the other teams seen at the house, identified or not, had arrived on international flights through the airport.

Second, Jessica Salt was *the* female gamer. Nine-time

championship winner and overall goddess-on-Earth. If she was there and this was about drugs, what did that mean?

Dr. Renner grabbed my arm and shook it.

"Are you okay?"

Am I okay that the number one female gamer in the industry was just seen at the biggest drug house in all of L.A.? Uh, no. Really, really not.

My tablet pinged in Dr. Renner's hands. When she tapped the screen, her face fell.

"Kali," she began. "We have a problem."

Those were never good words but were considerably worse coming from our resident psychiatrist. When she handed me the tablet and I gave it the once-over, my mouth fell open. Spelled out in the upper-right corner of the test results was a single word that turned my stomach to stone.

FAILED.

Speaking of problems with drugs . . .

The taijitu pendant around my neck gained ten pounds. I gripped it, swinging it from side to side as my teeth gritted. For the moment, my Taoist studies and anger-management techniques vanished.

I narrowed my eyes at Dr. Renner over the screen.

"Which one of them is it?" I asked, pushing the words through my teeth.

She shifted in her chair. "I'll give you four guesses, but you won't need any."

That stupid fucker.

I bolted out of my chair and toward the door.

"Kali," Dr. Renner called out. "Remember to stay calm."

Sure, calm. I'm sure I've felt that once. There was a reason why I meditated every morning. Or at least, tried to.

As I made my way through my home, calmness took over on its own because of the house itself. I loved this place. Hardwood floors, granite countertops, and trickling ponds in the backyard. For most people, they were selling points. For me, they were requirements. Because they were natural.

Because they were real.

The renovations to turn the house into a gamer's dream had only taken a few weeks. With machines now actively working on construction sites, productivity had tripled over the last few decades. Several single-purpose drones could be left running all day and night under the supervision of one or two humans. Go to bed with no floors and wake up to gleaming marble. Like the shoemaker's elves, just the updated, electronic version.

I followed the sound of the clashing weapons of my team-mates and stepped into the training room. It had been the pre-vious owner's gym. I'd kept the concrete floors and free weights in the gym area. But I'd added a few touches so it looked a little bit like a traditional dojo. If I didn't mind sleeping on the floor, I could have lived in this room alone. Bamboo flooring covered the weapons and sparring section. Shoji sliding doors, their wooden frames inlaid with glass in place of translucent paper, opened to a Chinese garden outside and a pond with trickling waterfalls and free-floating stones.

A Japanese dojo with a Chinese garden, where I'd practice my Korean martial art, in Los Angeles, California. Boy, it's a small world after all.

All four of my teammates were there. Derek and Hannah sparred on the mats. Cole, our newest member and replacement for he-who-had-left, watched from the sidelines. Lily leaned against the wall near the doorway, nose pressed to her tablet. No trainers today. In the off-season, we only worked with trainers once a week to keep us on track. Trainers cost money, and if money really did equal happiness, then not even Dr. Renner could have talked my bank account off a ledge. It would be too easy just to jump.

Lily looked up from her tablet when I entered the training room.

"Hey, Kali," she called. "Did you hear that Jessica Salt was seen at The Wall?"

I wasn't the only one obsessed with the videos.

Lily blinked at me, waiting for my response. She had impossibly blue eyes, like the color of the ocean where it meets the sky. I'd always wondered if she'd done something to permanently enhance the color. It wasn't unusual in this day and age, especially for pro gamers. But Lily was a private person, so I hadn't asked.

My stomach turned into knots over the mention of Jessica's appearance at The Wall. I frowned, but Lily didn't seem to notice.

"Yeah. I heard."

"I can't believe an American team is finally there. Do you still think this is about drugs?"

I wasn't sure, but I had my own problems with drugs at the moment.

"I . . . don't know," I finally said.

I excused myself from Lily, crossed the training room, and stopped in front of Cole.

"Can I talk to you for a minute?" I nodded to the side.

He shrugged. "Sure."

Once we were out of earshot of the rest of the team, I turned back to him and lowered my voice.

"You failed your drug test."

He pulled back and folded his arms. He was dressed in a sleeveless training shirt, and the muscles in his arms bulged almost as much as the veins running over them. Cole Wilkinson, a real-life Hulk.

He glanced at the rest of the team practicing on the mats, then back at me. "Marijuana is legal." He kept his voice low. "Besides, you said you don't care if we smoke a little."

"No, I don't care if you smoke once in a while, or if you get a cold and have to take medicine—as long as it's all outside of the tournament."

"So what's the problem? The RAGE tournament is months away."

"Because of all the *legal* drugs you could put in your body, steroids isn't one."

He went a little rigid then, as if he was holding his breath. Did he really think it wouldn't show up on the tests?

Cole studied my face for a minute. "Why did you even bother with running a test? It doesn't mean anything outside the tournaments."

"Because the VGL is considering running random tests in the off-season."

He laughed. "Oh, yeah. The drug tests in the VGL. Because those are so official. Are you serious?"

"I am."

He looked stunned. His mouth opened and closed a few times before he found the words.

"This isn't a joke?"

"Nope."

"But . . ." His voice trailed off, and he glanced around the training room. Man, he was having a hard time processing this. Couldn't blame him. Most team owners would have covered up the tests results.

"Why do you even care?" he finally asked.

Why did I care so much? Because a former teammate had died right next to me from an overdose. Because I'd taken one too many pills myself just to escape the pressures of reality.

Because, at the end of the day, this was supposed to be a game.

It was supposed to be fun.

But when I stepped a little closer to Cole, a completely different answer came out, and it was equally true.

"Because I care about my teammates. I want what's best for all of you."

"How else am I supposed to look like this?" He nodded down at his arms.

"You don't have to look like that," I told him. "Look, you're new to the team, and you don't really know me yet, but I'm running things differently than most owners in the VGL. Image isn't everything."

At least, I was *trying* to run things differently. But if I was getting this much pushback from him alone, I couldn't imagine what it would be like to deal with the sponsors and everyone else who expected him to look like an Olympic god.

"Look, Kali. This *is* how I want to look. What does it matter, anyway? I'll be clean in time for the tournament."

I didn't know what to do. Too many team owners in competitive gaming tried to control every move their players made. Told them how to act and dress. I didn't want to do that with my team. Still, this was drug use, on a different level than dictating wardrobe and hairstyle choices for photo shoots.

"Kaliiiiii."

Hannah bounded up to me, her ponytail bouncing like a strawberry blonde spring. Hannah was a walking contradiction. With model height, unbelievable curves, and a picture-perfect face, she belonged on the cover of a swimsuit magazine. Instead, she used her perfectly manicured nails to grind her opponents to a pulp in the virtual arena.

She tugged on my arm and pushed her bottom lip out into a pout.

"Can we go out tonight?" she asked. *"Please?"*

"You don't need my permission. Go out whenever you want."

"No, I mean as a team. I want to hit the gaming clubs."

I sighed inwardly. So much for steering clear of drugs and alcohol. I'd been away from the club scene for months, ever since I'd left the team and prepared to take it over. But we'd have to hit the clubs sooner or later. With my recent acquisition of the team, the sponsors would want us in the spotlight and showcasing our new lineup. Might as well start reimmersing myself in the celebrity-gamer lifestyle.

"Fine," I agreed. "After we plug in."

CHAPTER 2

The sword was heavy in my hand, the weight of it both foreign and familiar. I pressed my back against Cole's as we stood in the center of a stone tower, wearing armor that revealed more of our body than it protected.

Can't make it too easy, now.

We were surrounded. A gladiatorial opponent stood on either side of us, muscles straining against their armor, wielding swords as tall as I stood.

They charged. Their footsteps pounded into the tower's stone floor. Cole and I held our ground, still back-to-back. The gladiator rushing for me was a behemoth of a man.

And he was all mine.

I smiled. Come to me, darling.

He did.

He swung as he reached me. I slid under his sword, delivering a swift kick to his ribs. He grunted and stumbled back. His eyes went wide, and his hand lingered over the spot I'd kicked. I stood tall and crooked my finger at him. Get back here.

His face set into a grimace, and he charged. Behind me, Cole's elbow jammed into my back. I stumbled forward and narrowly missed my attacker's sword. I sucked my gut in as the blade slid so close it whispered along my skin. I spun, ended up at his back, and slashed my sword across it.

He gasped. Blood sprayed out of the gash stretching from shoulder blade to kidney. He sunk to his knees and planted face-first onto the stone floor. A red puddle formed around his lifeless body. It thinned at the edges and slithered through the gaps between the stones. Beige stones, black armor, and ribbons of blood.

This was the arena.

The biggest high. The greatest thrill.

I sighed. My insides simmered somewhere between "blah" and "good enough."

Yeah, what a thrill.

Cole turned to me and glanced down at his elbow. His own opponent was facedown like mine, gagging into a pool of blood.

"Sorry about that."

"We just need more practice." I shrugged, trying to look casual. Really, I felt empty, like my passion for the game had evaporated. I still loved a good fight, but I had wanted to take over the team so badly, I'd never really thought about the consequences of doing so. Leaving Los Angeles. Traveling for weeks on end. Not having time to check in with my friends. It was like building a business, in a way. I'd been away from gaming and the team for months.

Knowing we'd all be back together eventually had kept me motivated, but now that I was back and had taken over the team, it just wasn't what I thought it would be. I'd hoped it would be fun, playing games with my friends and kicking ass in the arena. Instead, Rooke was gone, and the rest of us felt like disjointed parts of a whole that had been assembled by a three-year-old, forced together in ways that didn't quite fit. Something was off, and now my hope was that we'd bond together again before the next tournament.

A female voice echoed overhead.

Simulation complete.

With a jolt, I opened my eyes to the virtual pod's shadowy innards. Cords detached from my skin and trickled away. I sat there for a minute, blinking. My head was clear, my stomach calm. I surveyed my hands. No trembling. No adverse effects at all.

Good. That was good.

The virtual world and I had a rocky relationship. There were times when I liked it better than the real world. Okay, more than liked it. Honestly, looking back now with a clear mind, I was addicted from the first time I'd plugged in. For some, that's all it takes. There, I'd felt alive. Here, not so much.

It was only March now, but the RAGE tournaments would be starting up by late summer, and I had to prepare myself for the intensity of the training period. The last time I'd gamed at the pro level, I'd been named the first female captain in the VGL, led my team to a championship, told the team owner to shove it, and vowed to create my own team. Now I'd done exactly that. Still, it hadn't turned out how I had expected.

The pod doors hissed and opened around me.

"Good practice, guys," Derek said, as I climbed out of my virtual pod. He glanced between me and Cole a few times. "You're getting smoother when you're together."

I exchanged looks with Cole. I wasn't feeling it, and he didn't look too sure himself. But when I'd first joined Defiance, we hadn't been much of a team then, either. Talented, for sure, but forging us into one unit took time, and now it seemed like I was starting from scratch all over again.

Hannah rushed up to me, brimming with excitement. "We're still going out, right?"

"Yes, yes," I said. "Everyone shower and get dressed. We'll leave in an hour. But no one has to come if they don't want to."

They did.

My teammates were out the pod-room door before I even finished speaking. Around the pod room, the programmers began packing up their things. All of them, except mine.

Elise sat in the workstation behind my pod, typing madly on her screen. Like Dr. Renner, she was another one with glasses even though they were nothing more than a fashion accessory anymore, given that corrective surgery was so accessible nowadays. In the last few weeks, she'd dyed her hair, so blue chunks were woven throughout her brown locks.

I waved a hand in front of her face. "You know the simulation is over, right?"

She didn't even blink at my hand. "Just analyzing some stats here."

"Elise, go home. I'm glad you have a job you love, but it's Friday."

"Just another five minutes."

I shook my head. Knowing there'd be no deterring her, I turned toward the door.

"Have fun at the club," she called out.

I wasn't counting on it. I might have enjoyed the clubs and the parties a few years ago. But since then, I'd been focusing on the business. Late nights. Paperwork. Figuring out how to take over the team. I'm sure to most people that sounded boring, but to me, it was invigorating, like I'd stumbled across my purpose in life. Suddenly, nightlife became a whole lot less . . . fulfilling. Oh God, look at me. I'd aged ten years in one. Am I a grown-up now?

I glanced back at her and smiled anyway.

"Thanks."

As I headed to my room to change for the evening, I let a long, slow breath pass through my lips. The clubs. The nightlife.

The crazy, high-pressure world of the celebrity gamer.

Here we go.

The sun had set on L.A.'s S Hill Street, the cool air bit at my bare arms, and the crowd was something fierce tonight. I stood with my teammates in front of the club, posing for some pictures and signing autographs for the fans.

"Have you been invited to The Wall?" one of the paparazzi called out.

There was no escaping it. Everyone had become obsessed with that place.

"If we had," I began with a wink, "you'd never know."

The crowd erupted into a bunch of "oooo's" at my little tease. This is what they want.

The cameras flashed, blending in with the surrounding lights of L.A.'s nightlife. Although we were there as a team, most of the cameras were on one person.

Lily.

Just a few weeks ago, she'd been sporting blond pigtails as part of her image, a character the team's previous owner had created for her. But now that I'd bought out the team, she'd chopped off her hair. Hadn't asked me or anything. Just came home one day, and it was gone. Part of the reason I'd bought out the team was so they could look however they wanted, create their own image. But when I saw Lily's hair for the first time, my stomach went knotty. Her pigtails had been her trademark. What would the crowd think of that? Luckily, they'd loved it.

She'd had her locks sliced into an asymmetrical bob, starting near the edge of her hairline in the back and growing longer in the front. One long chunk hid her right eye. That was Lily now. Edgy and a little mysterious. Couple that haircut with her petite features and striking eyes, and her image had gone from cheap porn star to smoking-hot Bond villain.

"Love that hair!"

Funny how team owners create images for their players in an attempt to max out their marketability. Ever since Lily had cut her hair, the media had gone crazier than they ever had before. Her new look had landed her on the covers and blogs of every hairstylist magazine this side of the Hollywood hills.

Eventually, we made our way to the club's entrance, and the bouncer waved us through. It was off-season for us, but we still got in for free—the perks of being a pro gamer. Fight and die on-screen for the fans. Free drinks at the club for your efforts.

Inside, a hostess greeted us and motioned for us to descend a set of stairs. A basement club. I preferred those, for some reason. Something about them just felt that extra bit private. Just a little more VIP.

Oh, look at me. Kali Ling, the snob.

When I reached the bottom of the stairs and stepped into the club, my breath caught in my throat. The place had class, I'd give it that.

The décor was all deep blues and ice whites, with a punch of dark-leather seating and wall panels. The floors gleamed, reflecting every light, so they, too, looked as if they were glowing. Jazzy lounge music flowed from hidden speakers at a comfortable volume, one where you wouldn't have to shout to hear the person standing right next to you but loud enough to wrap you up in its hypnotic beat.

Cage-like chandeliers hung from the ceilings, with thousands of lights wrapped around the bars. Within the cages, virtual dancers, naked silhouettes of men and women, swayed and ground to the music. There were four circular bars throughout the club, with pillars in the center to showcase the countless bottles of various liquors. About ten feet up, a seamless television screen circled the entire pillar, giving a 360-degree view of the action if you walked around the bar. The screens always displayed the latest gaming tournament, and currently, a virtual car raced over a digitized cityscape. With the 360 screen, one loop around the bar gave you a front-to-back view of the vehicles as they raced through the streets.

"Hey, boss," Hannah called out. She rushed up to me, bouncing like usual. "Have we been seen together enough as a team? Because the dance floor is calling my name."

I was hoping to have a little more time together than this. We still felt disjointed, and not just inside the game. Then again, we'd already spent the day together, training and grinding in both the real and virtual worlds. I sighed.

"Fine. Make yourself scarce."

My teammates scattered, leaving me alone near the front of the club. At least, so I thought. Cole circled around to face me.

"Can I buy you a drink, captain?"

I had to chuckle. Looked like he was trying to put our earlier disagreements behind us, and I was more than willing to oblige.

I motioned with my hand.

"Lead the way."

I followed him through the crowd, hoping to go unnoticed. But as I passed a table of male pro gamers on our way to the bar, one of them called my name.

"Hey, warrior," he shouted, dredging up the nickname I'd earned in the minors, when I'd taken out an entire simulated team by myself. "Glad to see you're coming back. I've got a teammate who needs a good ass-kicking."

I grinned. "Make a line, gentlemen."

I was met with applause and general appraisal as I walked away. I think I even heard a marriage proposal in there somewhere.

Cole glanced back at me as we continued on.

"They love you."

"They're just teasing," I told him. I got it a lot. Fighting guys all my life, both in reality and in the virtual worlds, I'd learned that, at times, they disguised their respect with verbal pokes and jabs. Luckily, I was good at jabbing back. With my fists.

"Well, yeah," Cole began. "You're strong and beautiful. I guess it's expected."

Beautiful? Cole had never said something like that to me before. I drifted back a few feet as we shouldered our way through the crowd. Maybe I was reading too much into his words, but the space felt more comfortable.

As I followed him, snippets of conversation floated over to me before being swallowed up by the music. Like bubbles, they drifted along with the breeze, snagged attention, then disappeared in a burst.

"Did you hear?" one voice said, punctuated by the slow, lounge beat. "Team Legacy got invited past The Wall."

"No shit."

Yes, yes. Jessica Salt had been spotted at the magical land beyond The Invisible Wall. Everyone was buzzing with the news that an American team had appeared at the estate containing gaming's biggest mystery. I pushed farther through the crowd, passing by another table.

"Oblivion did, too," someone else said. "And Syndicate."

More American teams making it past The Wall? Interesting.

"It's a drug house. Everyone knows it."

"That's just a cover-up. It has something to do with the Illuminati. You know they control the paparazzi, right?"

Oh, dear God.

We reached the bar and leaned against it, waiting for the bartender. I glanced around for my teammates. Hannah and

Lily danced together in the middle of the floor. Lily wasn't one who typically danced or sought attention, but I think she was secretly digging all the raves over her new look.

At the bar closest to the front of the club, a cluster of ladies had already appeared around Derek. He leaned against the bar, drink in hand. Though I couldn't hear anything he was saying over the music, the women all leaned toward him, hanging on his every word and laughing the same practiced laugh at just the right times.

Sometimes, it wasn't just gamers who played their parts.

As I turned back to the bar, I found the bartender in front of me. He grinned.

"The famous Kali Ling."

"No. Just Kali Ling."

He laughed. "Famous again soon enough. You're coming back to the pro circuit this year, aren't you?"

I nodded. "Yeah."

"That's good. The fans really miss you."

It was nice to be missed. The fans were the reason I kept going. That, and giving my team the life they deserved.

"What can I get you?" He folded his arms on the bar and leaned toward me, giving me a sexy grin. You want some sexy back? Here it comes.

"H_2O, on the rocks."

"Water?" He scoffed. "Don't tell me you have to drive yourself home."

Cars had been autonomous for nearly two decades now, so, ha-ha, what a punch line. But no, the problem wasn't driving myself home. The previous year, during the 2054 RAGE tournaments, I'd gotten a little too caught up in the celebrity-party lifestyle. Okay, scratch *gotten a little too caught up in* and insert *nose-dived right into*. After time away from the spotlight,

I was more than happy to put a fifty-foot chasm between me and that way of life. Besides, as team owner, I had the extra responsibility of looking after my players and having to crawl out of bed at the crack of dawn—something I already had enough trouble with when I was sober.

"You know drinks are free for the pros, right?" he continued. "Along with anything else."

He nodded behind the bar. I leaned forward and spotted several Pac-Man-shaped bowls filled with hits of HP. I recognized their distinctive colors immediately, combinations of red, blue, and yellow from the classic Dr. Mario game. They sat behind the bar like they were nothing more than mints. Most gamers treated them that way, too. A shot of tequila and pop a hit. Or was that the other way around?

I pressed my lips together.

"I know. Water is fine, thank you."

The bartender shrugged and handed me a glass. Water with ice. Somehow, it hadn't been too difficult for him. He turned to Cole.

"And you?"

"Scotch."

The bartender grinned. "A scotch man, nice." He filled a glass and handed it to him. "Anything else?" He nodded behind the bar. Cole glanced over the edge and gave me the side-eye.

"No. Thanks."

Had he only turned down the HP because I was here or because of the drug test earlier? I'd run the tests because I was trying to do what was right for the team, but I was starting to feel like an overprotective mother.

I sipped my water, letting the ice-cold liquid fill my mouth. It grounded me in the moment, and my gaze flicked up to the screens circling the bar, still featuring the racing events. Racing had been one of the less popular divisions in eSports, until this year. For more than a decade, it had been extreme off-road races. Up mountains. Across glaciers. It was interesting, sure, given that the liability meant no one could do that in real life. But this year had introduced a version that was more like street racing in the most exotic cities around the world.

People loved it.

Really, it played more into the celebrity-gamer lifestyle. The super expensive cars, the foreign, upscale cities. Currently on the screen, a Lamborghini, a Bugatti, and a Viva—the virtual-only line of vehicles—all battled for first place. They weaved around each other, slipping between other cars and oncoming traffic, all accented by different shades of neon, glowing against a midnight setting.

A building began to crumble, casting bits of brick-and-steel debris onto the road, and time slowed. They'd mastered the slow-mo cuts now, where the action would phase in and out of slow motion, specifically designed to allow the viewer to watch a particularly intense action scene in immense detail. As the building collapsed sideways onto the road, time slowed, and the drivers slid through a volcanic rainfall of debris. Concrete smashed. Tires screamed. Colors blurred.

Beautiful.

"So," Cole began, reminding me of the moment and other things he'd called beautiful. "You were gone for a while to buy out Defiance."

I pressed my hip against the bar, wondering where he was going with this. "Yeah. I missed a few months."

"What were you doing?"

"Touring, doing interviews, whatever needed to be done to buy out the team."

"Was it hard? I mean, most team owners in eSports are multimillionaires."

While his question wasn't the most appropriate, he wasn't wrong, either. Buying out the team from the former owner, personalizing the house into our own facility, renting the virtual pods, all cost more than I had expected. A lot more. Like, add-a-couple-extra-zeros-to-that more. But it was worth it. I had my team, and I was going to do things right. No corruption. No falsified drug tests. With me, they'd be safe.

I smiled. "You worried about the money?"

He glanced down at his drink. "It's not my business."

Yeah, it wasn't his business. But if he was worried about the money, he wasn't alone. If the current status of my bank account was represented by some sort of facial expression, it would have been snickering at me.

"You used to be with Rooke," he said, meeting my eyes.

My fingers tightened around my glass. I wasn't sure if that was a question or a statement. Yes, I used to be with Rooke, our former teammate. While I had been away, Cole had taken my spot on the team, so he and Rooke would have practiced together during the time I was off. Which possibly made them friends. Which possibly meant he was . . . checking he wasn't making a move on his buddy's girl?

"And?" I managed to ask, struggling to keep my expression neutral.

"And now you're not?"

I supposed we weren't together, but how was I to answer that?

"We . . . haven't talked in a while," I said. It was the best I could offer him.

"What happened?"

My stomach tied itself in a knot, then twisted some more. Looks like Cole was nudging the night in a certain direction. One that ended with the two of us as more than just teammates. But the answer to his question was, not only had I not spoken with Rooke about the situation, I hadn't talked with anyone. Mostly because talking about it felt worse than getting a knife through the gut. I knew. Literally.

I had suspicions of what might have gone wrong. Was it too much space? The struggle to maintain a relationship long-distance while I was traveling? Business trips. Conferences. Planning and more planning. Rooke had been practicing with the team, grinding away. Every spare second we had was going into the game, and none was going into each other. Considering we were both putting so much energy into the same thing, we'd never been further apart. And, at one point, he just cut me off. Backed away when I bought out the team. Never spoke again.

I mashed my lips together, as if that would dull the sudden pain in my chest. "It didn't work out."

"Was it all just bullshit for the cameras?"

That day we kissed during a match flashed through my mind. Pretty easy to remember when you're on the receiving end. Or had I kissed him? In a way, Cole's question was justified. My relationship with Rooke had started as bullshit until it became something more. And now it was nothing at all.

"Why are you asking so much about him?"

Cole shifted his weight a few times and glanced around the club. "Look, I don't mean to butt into your love life . . ."

His voice trailed off, and he didn't say anything more. This was going right where I didn't want it to. What was that old saying about watching a train wreck in slow motion? Here comes the crash.

"Because I was wondering . . ."

Don't ask me. Just don't ask.

"If it's all right with you . . ."

Oh shit. He's gonna ask.

"Maybe that . . ."

Here we go. Incoming disaster . . .

"Rooke could step in as your fifth?"

What?

Seriously, what did he just say? Apparently, the train had derailed and slammed into me instead. I blinked several times before I managed to spit out a couple of words.

"Excuse me?"

"Listen, Kali—"

My heart sunk as I realized what was happening. I pushed myself off the bar. "Are you leaving the team?"

The words came out much louder than I expected, and a few heads swiveled my way. I glanced down the bar, bit my lip, and turned back to Cole. He fidgeted with his drink, staring hard at it. "I don't want you to be screwed."

Funny how just a second ago, that's exactly what I thought he wanted to do to me. There was an edge in his voice now, and he wouldn't meet my eyes, either.

He was leaving the team.

I lowered my voice and leaned toward him. "Is this about the drug test?"

"No." He stood up straight and turned to face me head-on. "I want to be the best."

So did everyone, but what did that have to do with leaving? I tried to follow his line of reasoning. "And you don't think you can be the best on our team? Defiance took the championship last year."

"Under different management."

Ouch. So his problem was me.

"You don't think I'm good at this," I concluded.

"I think you're just getting started, and it'll be a while before you get there. In five years, you'll be destroying everything you touch. But I don't want to wait five years."

That I could understand. He was hungry for greatness. We all were, or we wouldn't have gotten this far. Most people think talent and skill is what takes you to the top. And it helps, sure. But what really takes you from zero to a hundred is motivation. Drive. An attitude where "not possible" doesn't exist.

He wasn't entirely wrong, either. I was asking a lot of the team to stand by me while I made this move. I had some learning to do, and it was true I was just getting started. And money. I didn't have the money. Cole hadn't said it directly, but hey, a girl can read between the lines.

"Look," he continued, "if it's going to affect the team too much, I'll stay."

Why did he have to be so professional? It made it hard to get angry at him. Not *impossible*, but harder.

"When would you be leaving?" I asked.

"As soon as possible."

Yikes, he really wanted out, and fast. What the heck had I done to him?

"Look, if I offended you in some way—"

He held up a hand. "I got an offer from another team. They need to know by tonight."

That explained the urgency. Sort of.

"Why so soon?"

"They have a tournament starting up, and they need a fifth."

"Can I ask what team?"

He hesitated before answering me.

"Oblivion."

Huh. Well. There's a name drop if I'd ever heard one. One

of the best teams in the league. Typically, they specialized in the Ops games, but rumors were they were looking to expand this year. Guess whatever game they'd be playing was something that needed hand-to-hand combat experience. That would explain why they were looking for RAGE players to join them.

Then something started nagging at me. Something I'd heard earlier while we'd been making our way through the club. My stomach clenched. Hell, every muscle clenched, and my mouth nearly hit the floor.

"Oblivion got invited past The Wall," I gasped. Cole pressed his lips together and took half a step back. He'd been hoping I wouldn't make the connection. I marched up to him. "I'll let you out of your contract if you tell me what's inside that house."

"Uh . . ." he stuttered, shaking his head a few times. Guess this wasn't the reaction he was expecting.

I hounded him. "Did they tell you? Have you been there?"

"No."

"What do you know?"

"Nothing."

"Bullshit."

"I don't know anything. I honestly don't know what's beyond The Wall. Okay? They're not going to tell me unless I sign a contract with them, and even then, I have to sign an additional confidentiality agreement about the tournament."

My eyebrows went up. "Tournament? What tournament?"

He froze.

I pointed a finger in his face. "You do know something."

"Kali, please."

His eyes went soft, pleading with me. He was worried about blowing his chance with one of the best teams in the States. I pursed my lips. Damn it.

"If you want to go, go," I said. "Our tournament isn't for

months. We'll find a fifth by then, so don't worry about us. This is an opportunity you have to take."

He let out a small sigh of relief and smiled. "Yeah, I know. That's why I'm doing this." He glanced at the club's exit. "I really have to go meet with them. Sign some papers."

I waved a hand toward the door. "Fine."

He left his drink on the bar and started heading for the door. He didn't get more than a few feet away before he turned back to me.

"Kali, thanks for understanding."

His face looked like he was trying to hold back a smile. He was excited about Oblivion, The Wall, and where he was heading. It tugged at my heartstrings a little. What kind of teammate was I if I wasn't happy for him?

I smiled.

"Good luck. Go kill it."

At my word, he let his excitement show through, and a grin took up his entire face. And with that, he turned around and disappeared into the crowd, leaving me standing at the bar. Alone.

The rest of the team figured it out pretty quickly when Cole didn't ride back with us. Derek and Hannah sat in the front and had turned around to face Lily and me in the back. Given the car's automatic responses to traffic and objects, no one really had to keep their eye on the road.

"So, what did he say exactly?" Hannah asked.

A lot of things. That he didn't believe in me as team owner, that he was worried about the money, and that he didn't think playing with Defiance equalled being the best. And then there was the whole situation with The Wall. I shook my head. Best to keep things simple.

"He got an offer from another team," I explained. "It's a better fit for what he wants to achieve in his career."

Derek nodded. "That's understandable. So what do we do? Hold tryouts for our fifth spot? Maybe scout out the other teams and see if anyone is unhappy?"

It went silent in the car, and everyone was staring at me. Rightfully so. I was team owner now, and it was up to me to decide the best course of action. But with only weeks' worth of experience, I didn't know what to say.

"Yeah," I said, trying to force a confident tone to my voice. "Tryouts. Scouting. Sounds good."

"You know," Lily began, leaning toward me. "Technically, we have an alternate player."

Somebody had to say it. But in my book, that definitely was not the right course of action. Rooke had left, and it wasn't just about me. He had abandoned the team. No explanation. No reasons. Just gone. How could I ask the team to count on someone like that?

On the other hand, our history as a team with him was great. When the five of us were together, something just jibed. We balanced each other. Whatever weaknesses one had, others made up for it. We were harmony. A perfect chord.

But my personal history with him was, well, not so solid.

Our relationship had never been perfect. In fact, it started out as fake, just a way to get us onto the cover of every tabloid and magazine on this continent and the next. Our previous team owner, who to call an asshole would be an insult to assholes, had created the whole thing. We screamed more than we talked, and every matchup, no one knew if we'd fight our enemies or each other. We'd fought, and made up, all on the screen. Even now, our relationship was still occasionally gossiped about in the tabloids or online. I couldn't entirely blame them. It had been a hot mess, a manufactured lie.

And then it became something more.

Because when Rooke and I had finally managed to crawl away from the cameras and all the bullshit disappeared, what we were left with was so raw and ugly that all we could do was make it beautiful. We were both addicted to the virtual world. The celebrity-gamer lifestyle. The pills and the alcohol.

Together, we'd healed.

"He hasn't called?" Lily asked.

I bit my lip. Yes, the tables had turned. He had called, and now I was the one ignoring him. If he wasn't going to be there when I needed him the most, what was the point of keeping him in my life at all?

I never answered Lily. Just gave her a look that said "back off." She got the message and left it alone for the rest of the trip.

After we arrived home, I went straight to my room, flopped down on my bed, and covered my face with the duvet. What a night. Lost our fifth player, and now my options were to either start scouting or contact our elusive backup. And that was on top of contacting all the sponsors and informing them that any photo shoots done in the last few weeks would need to be reshot. I could just hear the screaming now.

Ugh.

Double ugh.

I rolled over, bringing the blanket with me. Maybe my bed could be our fifth. I certainly wouldn't mind bringing it with me through the day. At some point, sleep's heavy fingers pulled my eyelids shut, and I drifted in and out of consciousness every few hours as the stress from the day leaked into my dreams.

The club. The sponsors. Cole. Rooke. They say not to bring your problems to bed with you, but looks like I'd missed the memo.

At some ungodly hour, my cell phone buzzed on the nightstand. Who the hell would be calling so early? Probably a sponsor. Must have heard that Cole was leaving and was ready to chew me out. My fingers crawled along the nightstand until my hand closed around my phone. I snatched it up and pressed it to my ear.

"Hello?"

An unfamiliar voice came through the phone.

"Good morning, Ms. Ling."

Are you sure it's not still yesterday? I took a breath and exerted as much kindness and professionalism as pre-coffee-Kali could muster.

"How can I help you?"

"My name is Mr. Tamachi."

All the air in my lungs left. I knew exactly who he was and why he was calling. Mr. Tamachi, of Tamachi Industries. Owner of the house featured on every gossip channel and tabloid. We were about to be invited in on the most coveted secret in all of gaming. A secret that any gamer in the world would give their playing hands just to find out what it was. So I did the only sane and logical thing.

I hung up the phone.

CHAPTER 3

Yes, I hung up. On the guy who was inviting me past The Wall.

I panicked, okay?

I dropped my phone on the bed like it was a stick of dynamite and recoiled, cocooning myself in my blanket. The phone started to buzz. Incoming call. I curled up in the corner of my bed, pressing myself as far away from the phone as possible, as if it were some critter that had wandered into my sleeping quarters. Ironically, it scuttled closer with every ring.

Two more rings to voice mail.

Do not pick it up.

One more.

DO NOT PICK IT UP.

Half a ring.

I picked it up.

"Hello?"

"Ms. Ling, sorry. We must have been disconnected."

Ah, sure. That's what happened.

"No problem," I said, trying to sound aloof.

"As I was saying, I own the facility that's been on the news lately. Well, more on the gossip channels than anything, but I'm sure you know what I'm talking about."

I clicked my tongue against the roof of my mouth. "I've heard about it."

I was good at this aloof thing even while my insides were going *squeeeee.*

"I'm calling to extend a formal invitation for this evening."

This evening. The Wall.

Was this really happening?

Given the ridiculous hour of the morning, this evening was still years away, and there was a very good chance this was a dream. Still, despite the mental cloudiness and lack of coffee in my veins, I had the presence of mind to keep calm.

"Look, Mr. Tamachi," I began. "I'm not sure what you're offering my team, but we like to keep our drug tests clean."

He chuckled softly. "Despite some of the rumors, there are no drugs involved, Kali. I can assure you."

"Then what's with all the secrecy?"

"It's something that has the potential to change professional gaming forever. I don't want my competitors finding out."

I got a little jittery then. This was sounding more and more like it actually was tech related. *Something that would change pro gaming forever.* The last time that was said, it was about combining competitive gaming with immersive virtual reality. Put these two things together and watch them explode.

"How do you stop people from talking about it once they've been inside?" I asked.

"I require all gamers who enter the house to sign a confidentiality agreement. If any of this is a problem, you're welcome to bow out at any time. We do ask that you at least attempt to conceal your identity. We can't make it too easy for the paparazzi."

The paparazzi. I'd forgotten about them, trying to catch a glimpse of the rock stars of the gaming world. But the more I thought about it, the less this made sense. There was no reason for my team to be invited past The Wall. We'd just gone through a change in management and had yet to prove we could still take championships under my lead. We'd been through several player changes in just a short time, between Rooke, Cole, Nathan, and myself, so we lacked the stability of some veteran teams that had been together for ten-plus years. And, so far, only the virtual elite had been invited to that place. We were talking the undisputed best teams in the entire world. What did he want with Defiance?

"Why are you inviting us?"

"Well, your team, while young, does have a fierce reputation in the gaming world. Especially you, Ms. Ling."

Little did he know, Kali "the warrior" Ling was currently hiding under her duvet.

"You were the first female captain," he continued. "Now you're the youngest team owner in history. Some people aren't taking that lightly and have a close eye on you and your career."

He had a point. I'd made ripples in pro gaming. People knew my name. In Los Angeles, at least. *Maybe* across the United States. Was my reputation really getting that big?

"I think this will have special appeal to you," he finally said. "You really need to see what I've done with the game."

Now, I started shaking, and my insides matched. I had to know what was in that house.

But this wasn't just about me.

"This is the team's decision, not mine," I told him. "I need to talk this over with them first."

He paused, and I could almost hear him smiling through the phone. "From you, I'd expect nothing less. Please call me back at this number, whatever you decide."

I pressed the END CALL button.

I sat in my bed, blinking, staring at a spot where the wall met the ceiling. If the events of that phone call were supposed to be sinking in, my brain didn't get the memo. This wasn't real. It was a prank. Or a dream.

Must have been.

I glanced at my call history. Nope. That really happened. Now I had to figure out what the hell I was going to do about it.

After deciding I'd never fall back to sleep—and that takes a lot—I wrapped my cell around my wrist until it clamped in place and switched over to watch mode, displaying the time. Then I crawled out of bed, got dressed, and tromped down to the kitchen. With a brimming cup of coffee in hand, I sat at the table.

I'd just gotten the call every pro gamer had been dreaming about. I should have been running around the house screaming, jumping on my teammates' beds. But I wasn't.

We were only a team of four. I hadn't started on a replacement yet, because first I'd have to make the phone call to the guy I'd rather forget about but couldn't. Technically, I could just replace him without the phone call. But as team owner, I was trying to do the right thing, and the right thing was to call him first even if it was just to tell him we were looking for someone else.

The team would have been fine, either way. My heart would have been . . . something else. Either way.

If whatever was going on beyond The Wall really was tech related and Tamachi was expecting a full team to show up tonight, he'd be disappointed. Should I have told him that on the phone? Maybe. Still, we had an invitation on the table. Tamachi had hinted that this would change pro gaming forever, and I doubted he was exaggerating. This was something that had the potential to revolutionize our careers, and possibly our lives. Funny how fast things can change in a matter of minutes.

At some point, dawn crossed over to actual morning, and

my teammates started buzzing around me, chattering and preparing breakfast. I must have looked like one of those videos
where a person is sitting in a chair in current time while everything else moves around them in fast motion.

"Kali, what's wrong?" Hannah asked, snapping me back to
reality. All three of my teammates were there with plates, bowls,
and glasses full of the various yet common edibles of breakfast.
Toast, cereal, juice, tea. Hannah pointed at my mug with her
spoon. "You haven't touched your coffee."

My coffee. I dipped the edge of my finger into the liquid. It
was cold. I'd let my coffee get cold. In the history of my entire
life, or at least since I'd discovered these God-given java beans,
I didn't think I'd ever let my coffee go cold. Okay. Don't panic,
people. We've trained for this.

"I'm just distracted," I said.

"Is this about Rooke?" Lily asked. "Is he going to be our
fifth?

I pressed a hand against my forehead and groaned. I knew
it was inevitable, but something about saying it out loud made
the situation all too real. Seconds ticked by, all of them empty
and quiet.

Hannah leaned toward me. "We know you probably don't
want to talk about it much."

But?

"But—"

There it was.

"Watching you and Rooke together, there was something
special there."

Yes, okay. Rooke and I had been good together once we'd
figured all of our shit out. I'd never given the team much of an
explanation over what happened. Hell, I didn't even have much
of one myself. But they'd given me space so far, and I knew it

would only be a matter of time before they started asking questions. But before I opened my mouth, Derek spoke for me.

"If it's not going to work out with Rooke, we can recruit someone else to be our fifth," he said, shifting in his seat. I don't think he was too comfortable pressing me on the matter. "Maybe we should start scoping out other players—"

"We've been invited to The Wall," I finally said.

The room froze, as if I'd hit the PAUSE button in real life. Hannah had a spoon half-lifted to her mouth, Lily gripped a cereal box in midair, and Derek just stared. Several seconds passed by, again, all in silence. Finally, Derek managed a word.

"When?"

"Tamachi called me early this morning. He wants us to go there tonight."

"What did you tell him?"

"That I'd talk to you guys first."

"What the hell did you think our answer would be?" Hannah exclaimed, nearly shouting.

Everyone else laughed, but I held up a hand. "I understand it's exciting. I'm excited, too. But I'm not making decisions like that without bringing it to you guys first. That's the whole point of my being team owner. I'm not deciding your life. You are."

"Did he give you any clues to what this is all about?" Derek asked.

"It's nothing to do with drugs, apparently, and it's something that will revolutionize pro gaming forever, according to him."

I spoke slowly and calmly, trying not to induce a near-manic reaction from my teammates. But with words like "revolutionize pro gaming forever," it was pointless. They looked like a trio of cartoon characters just before they explode.

"Kali," Derek said simply, the calmest one of the group. "We have to go. What's the harm, really?"

There wasn't any. Tamachi said if we weren't interested in whatever he had to offer, we could leave at any time. I looked around the table at everyone. "You do realize that not everyone has to come if they don't want to—"

They all nodded feverishly. They wanted to.

"Okay."

I pulled my cell phone from around my wrist and made the call.

"This is Tamachi speaking."

"It's Kali Ling. We'll be there tonight."

"Excellent." His enthusiasm came through the phone, like I could hear him smiling again. "I do ask that you dress in black and wear hoods."

Judging by the countless hours of footage I'd studied myself, the mystery of it all was part of his marketing plan, I'm sure.

"That won't be a problem," I assured him.

"Excellent. I'll send a car to pick you up at five p.m. tonight."

"We'll be ready."

I hung up the phone and turned to the team.

"It's set."

After that, hardly anyone ate breakfast. We decided to spend the day in training, the morning working out in the real world and the afternoon in the virtual, trying to make the hours go by. I'd like to say that it helped, but really?

Longest. Day. Of. My. Life.

Seriously, physicists could have tested space-time theories in the hours between breakfast and 5:00 p.m. At four forty-five, we were all gathered by the front door. We'd dressed in black, head to toe, complete with hoods to hide our faces, as Tamachi had requested. I don't know why we bothered. If the Hypnotized crew was telling the truth, and their drones could analyze body stats to tell who was who, there was a good chance they'd figure out which team we were. Still, it was kinda fun.

The door buzzed. The car was here. I pushed myself off the wall.

"Finally."

When I pulled the door open, what stood on the other side was not a vehicle to whisk us off on our magical journey to the house, but James Rooke, our former teammate.

There were suitcases in his hands.

"I heard you need a fifth," he said.

He had one of those I-forgot-to-shave-all-week-but-damn-this-looks-good kind of beards. His skin was pale, as if he hadn't seen the sun in a month, and the circles under his eyes were a little dark. Besides that, he looked good.

Too good.

My chest tightened, but I smiled anyway.

"You know what? We're fine. Thanks for stopping by."

I slammed the door shut in his face and marched away. Hannah grabbed me as I passed.

"Kali!"

She managed to wrangle me back into the front hall. Lily opened the door and invited the bastard in, suitcases and all.

Hannah gripped my shoulders.

"Since he's here, maybe you should deal with this. You know? Get the bad blood out of the way and see what's left."

I was way too far into pissed-off territory to process much of what she said, but I was pretty sure she mentioned something about spilling blood.

Sounded like a plan to me.

I marched up to Rooke, steam coming out of my ears.

"What are you doing here?" I demanded. "Let me guess. You found out we lost a player and thought you could just show up."

Lily got between us. "I called him."

She *what*?

I must have stood there blinking for several seconds as I tried to process that information. Lily wasn't the type to stick her nose where it didn't belong and meddle in other people's affairs. In fact, she was the last person I knew who would do such a thing. Where did she get off calling Rooke and inviting him here behind my back?

"That wasn't your place," I told her, straining the words through my teeth.

"And it's not your place to let your love life affect the team. If you hadn't been in a relationship with Rooke, you would have called him the second Cole left. But you didn't because there's history there. That's not fair to the rest of us. Either put Rooke on the team and deal with your shit, or find someone else. For your team's sake."

I blinked. Did Lily just school me?

I didn't think I'd ever heard her speak that many words in one day, let alone strung together like that in a single speech. Derek and Hannah took a step back and, for once, said nothing. Honestly, she was right. If Rooke and I hadn't been together, I would have already reached out to him about taking Cole's place. I was being selfish and putting my own problems above the team's needs.

"Lily's right. I should have called," I said. I glanced up at Rooke. "If you want to come in, we can discuss the team's situation."

Rooke glanced around, taking in our appearance. "Why are you all dressed like that?"

Our invitation to The Wall. I'd completely forgotten.

"We got invited past The Wall," I told him. His eyes went wide. He knew about The Wall. Of course. What gamer hadn't heard of it?

"The car's here," Hannah announced, peering out the front door. She glanced back at me. "Are we *all* going?" Her gaze flicked to Rooke, then back to me.

Well, this put me in a jam, didn't it?

On one hand, he knew the team, and we knew him. We already had chemistry and hundreds of hours of training and practice together. I wouldn't be able to find that with anyone else even if I managed to recruit one of the top players in the league. On the other hand, he'd left, and I had no way to know he wouldn't do it again. I glanced around at my other teammates. They stared back, waiting for my answer. To them, Rooke was a friend. A teammate. He always would be, no matter what.

"So," I said slowly, drawing it out. "Does this mean you're interested in rejoining us?"

"Yes."

"And how can we know you're not going to leave again?"

"I won't—"

I stepped toward him. "Because as team owner, I need to guarantee consistency to my sponsors. We're already reeling from Cole's leaving, and you don't exactly have the greatest track record."

He stepped toward me and matched my tone. His expression went serious. "I want to come back to the team. What do I have to do to prove that to you?"

"Sign a contract. I won't let you out of it until the end of the season, under any circumstances. It's only fair to everyone else. Can you manage that?"

I met his eyes. He stood there blinking for a minute as he processed my words. Rooke wasn't one to show a lot of emotion, but I knew him. He was surprised I'd made the offer.

Eventually, he nodded. "Uh, yeah. I'll sign."

"Good. Get dressed. Dark clothing with a hood."

"Guess I'll get changed then," Rooke said.

"Here." Derek held out a hand and took one of his suitcases. "Let's get these in your room."

As the guys passed by, heading back into the depths of the house, Rooke leaned toward me and lowered his voice.

"We need to talk."

Ya think?

"We'll talk later," I muttered back, under my breath.

Talk. For us, that would be new.

As I watched Derek lead Rooke to his room, I knew one thing for sure. No matter what our conversation entailed, my combo points would be huge.

Whatever the current definition of "awkward" was in the dictionary, it should have been replaced by a screen capture of the scene inside the van. A guard sat in what would have been the driver's seat and explained he was there to make sure we complied with Tamachi's request to keep our identities hidden. He was also there for our protection and security though that seemed a little tacked on. Derek climbed into the front beside him while Lily and Hannah crawled into the back, leaving the middle seats open for me and Rooke.

Yippee.

I moved as far away as I could, nearly pressing myself against the window. As the car guided itself through the streets, Derek chatted with the guard, while Hannah and Lily listened to music through earbuds. There was movement beside me, and I felt Rooke lean toward me.

"I tried to call you," he said in a hushed voice.

Really? We're doing this here? This wasn't my idea of "later."

I gritted my teeth, still looking out the window. "I've been busy."

"Look, I know you're pissed that I left the team."

"Oh, you know that? But you still did it anyway?"

"We had six players," he reminded me. "Only five can be on a team."

Yes, yes. I'd left the team for a few months, and our previous owner had replaced me, never thinking I'd actually come back with the money to buy him out. So, when I actually did, we were left with five players plus me. The sponsors expected me to play, so it left us with six gamers and five spots. But no one thought Rooke would back out without so much as a word.

I turned to him but kept my voice low. "And how come you bowed out so easily? Remember when you said you'd be there for me through all this? That you'd support me in what I'm trying to accomplish?"

"I do support you."

I scoffed. "By leaving, then not calling? Excellent support."

"You still had five players. The team was more than okay."

The team? *The team?*

My chest turned to ice, and I fought myself to keep from screaming. "The team was fine," I said through gritted teeth, "but *I* wasn't. Did you ever think of that?" He pulled back from me, and his face went solemn. "Oh, you didn't know? I have these things called feelings. Yes, it's shocking. Kali Ling has a heart, and you ripped it to shreds."

He winced and turned to the window, refusing to meet my eyes. After a few seconds of silence, he spoke so softly, I barely heard him.

"Leaving you was the hardest thing I've ever done. But it was best for you, not me. Did *you* ever think of that?"

I blinked, and the ice in my chest melted. That was not the

answer I was expecting. Why would he think leaving me would be best? Did he think he wasn't good enough?

I opened my mouth to ask, but the guard cut me off.

"We're coming up on the house," he said. "Pull on your hoods and keep your heads down."

We did.

The car slowed, and the paparazzi crammed against the car even while the vehicle was still in motion.

"Who's inside?"

"Is it another American team?"

"Let's see those faces!"

I cupped a hand against the side of my face, keeping my profile hidden from the cameras. Even with the tinted windows, they could see through if they got close enough.

"Get the fuck out of the way," the guard yelled. Hands pounded against the car. Cameras clicked incessantly. The guard turned around in his seat. "Keep your heads down," he commanded again. I buried my head farther into my palms. I'd thought the obsession over The Wall and the attention from the press was ridiculous when I was watching the videos of other gamers sneaking into the house. I'd underestimated it. With the advent of American teams now getting past The Wall, it was downright insane.

There was some commotion outside the vehicle, and some commanding voices cut through the insanity of the crowd.

"Back away now, or we'll press charges."

Looks like additional security had shown up, or maybe the police.

Finally, the car inched forward. I heard the gates close behind us and the general ambiance of the crowd began to fade. The car started its long journey over the driveway up to the house.

It hit me then. We were past The Invisible Wall. We were about to find out the biggest secret in the gaming world. I took a deep breath and slowly let it out. How many people wanted to know what was inside that house, and how few ever got the chance to find out? We'd been invited against all odds. It was a weird feeling. When you start to see the fruits of your labor, when you start to accomplish all of your dreams, you have to wonder: Was it really because of hard work or talent—or was it just plain luck?

"Okay," the guard said. "You can lift your heads, but keep those hoods on until you're inside."

The high-flying drone cameras could still see us, hence the need for the hoods. The car slowed to a halt in front of the house, and we got out. I risked a glance up. The house was massive. I'd seen pictures and videos, sure, but in real life, the place was downright huge.

The guard led us to the door, opening it for us.

"Oh my God, this is so exciting," Hannah gushed.

I shooed my teammates forward. "Just get inside."

They hurried in until only I remained. The guard took up his position beside the front door. He hooked his thumb at the door, like he was signaling to me to hurry the fuck up. His mouth was pulled into a slight snarl. I didn't blame the guy. If I had to deal with this much chaos on a daily basis, I'd be pissy, too.

I couldn't help but feel that I was standing on a threshold. Out here, I was Kali Ling. Pro gamer. Team owner. Record holder. Inside that house, who knew what was waiting for me? *Something that will change pro gaming forever.* Tamachi's words echoed in my mind. My life was about to change, and whether that was for the better or worse, there was only one way to find out.

I took a breath and stepped inside the house.

CHAPTER 4

Nine figures. The house had to be worth that at a minimum. From the inside, it looked more like a luxury hotel than a home. The floors were marble tiles laid out in a spiraling pinwheel design. Hallways stretched out on either side of us, seemingly endless, as if one stomp of your foot would echo for days. In front of us was a grand staircase leading to the upper levels. It was at least ten feet wide, lined with wrought-iron filigree banisters. The only thing missing was a counter and a clerk asking for my reservation.

Speaking of which, a personal assistant appeared from around the staircase and came to greet us.

"Welcome," he said. "Mr. Tamachi will be with you shortly. Is there anything I can get you in the meantime?"

No one answered. After a few seconds, Lily nudged me, and I realized everyone was waiting for me to speak first.

"I think we're fine, thanks."

He eyed us for a minute, probably noting our stunned expressions. "You can remove your hoods now. The cameras can't see you in here."

So says he. But we did as he suggested and pulled off our hoods.

After he disappeared back into the depths of the house, I clustered in the entryway with my teammates, afraid to move forward. Forty thousand square feet, and we took up a grand total of three.

"I feel like I'm going to break something if I move," Hannah whispered, and we all nodded.

"Team Defiance."

A confident voice, one used to public speaking, boomed down the left hallway, where a tall Japanese man with salt-and-pepper hair walked toward us. Another personal assistant scampered along beside him. Tamachi extended his arms to us and smiled. "I'm so glad you've decided to join us."

Personal assistant number two handed us all tablets with a contract on the main screen.

"It's a standard confidentiality agreement," Tamachi explained. "All it asks is that you do not talk about the technology you see here today. If you'd like to read the contract in detail, I'm happy to wait, and even after you sign it, you're welcome to leave at any time."

Suspicions confirmed: This was about technology.

My teammates all scribbled their names across the tablets, but I paused for a minute before signing.

"How long is this contract in effect?" I asked.

He peered down at me, a hint of amusement in his eyes. "Until the tournament is announced."

"What tournament?"

The amusement in his eyes spread to the rest of his face and turned up the corners of his lips. "That's what you're here to find out."

Clue number two. This was about a gaming tournament. I stopped stalling, signed the contract, and handed it back to the personal assistant.

"Excellent." Tamachi clapped his hands together. "Now, if you'll please follow me."

Tamachi led the way down the hall. We followed.

"I want you to know that Tamachi Industries has had its eyes on eSports for some time now," he said. "This isn't something we just jumped into."

"And how exactly are you jumping in?" Derek asked.

Instead of answering, Tamachi turned to a door in the hallway and pressed the button beside it. The door slid open, revealing an elevator. Together, we rode down three floors in silence. What was that I said about it being awkward in the car? The tension inside the elevator brought it to a whole new level.

The doors opened behind us, on the opposite side from where we entered, to a warehouse-sized room. If the house had a brain, this was it. The whole place hummed, as if it had been plugged into one giant electrical outlet. People walked in every direction across the concrete floors, tablets in hand, some dressed in white lab coats. Tamachi's employees, I had to assume, since everyone here seemed to have a purpose and a place to be.

Throughout the room were several clusters of pods, in groups of five, all gleaming white as if they'd been buffed until they shone. The word CHIMERA was etched into the side in faint gray lettering. I glanced around to the rear of the pod. No workstation sat behind it.

"Where are the programmers?" I asked.

Tamachi leaned around the pod. "This system doesn't require any. It runs itself."

No programmers? That was different. Virtual pods used at the pro level were essentially sensory deprivation chambers encased in solid, opaque hulls. This prevented any outside force from impacting the players in the virtual world, which would be considered cheating if it helped you win or interference it if caused you to lose. Even while plugged in, a punch in the chest would send you flying back inside the game. But the pod's opaque encasing, used to prevent real-life light sources from penetrating the game, also meant no one could tell if you were having a heart attack or seizure while inside. So, for medical reasons, programmers sat behind the pods and monitored both the game and gamer for any signs of distress. They were especially handy during training sessions, since they could code new enemies and scenarios to their liking and integrate them into the game.

"How can it run without programmers?" I asked. "How is that safe?"

Tamachi smiled. "I can assure you these pods are the safest the market has ever seen. Everything is run by artificial intelligence, smarter than any programmer. Smarter than any doctor. It can tell if you're having problems inside the game far better than a human could."

I figured he was saying that as a means to comfort me, but something about that made me want to shudder. Artificial intelligence was nothing new, but the idea that the only safety net between me and the virtual world was another artificial construct just didn't sit right with me. And all that aside, I was a little disappointed. With all the hype surrounding this house, I had been expecting so much more. No programmers. Artificial intelligence. What was the big deal about that?

"Is this the big secret?" I asked, trying to hide the disappointment in my voice.

Tamachi smiled. "No. You'll be able to see once you plug in and play a round of our game."

"You want us to plug in," I repeated. "Now?"

He nodded.

He had suits for all of us, perfectly sized. I probably would have thought it was a touch creepy if I weren't so excited. We changed in private. The house had plenty of rooms.

Just as I was climbing into the pod, I caught Rooke's gaze. He stared back with no emotion. At least, to the untrained eye. But I'd become a bit of an expert on all things Rooke since we'd been together and could pick up on the subtleties of his true feelings. His bottom lip twitched, and his hands gripped the edge of the pod just a little too tightly. There were always hints about what he was really feeling, and right now, we were both thinking the same thing.

What are we getting ourselves into?

I nodded at him. See you on the other side.

I lay back as the doors closed around me. Cords crawled over my skin, attaching to the pod suit and the bare skin around my wrists and face. So far, nothing was different from the standard pods back home. Same shiny exterior. Same darkened interior. Kind of like, well . . . me. In front of Tamachi and the team, I'd kept my game face on. But now with the pod doors closed, I let my smile slide and my jaw go slack, and gave in to the uncertainty I felt on the inside.

What was I doing? I was in some strange man's house, plugging into a virtual world that we had no knowledge of or experience in. I'd dragged myself into this. I'd dragged my team into this. And why? Because of some cheesy segments on the gossip channel? This game, these pods, could be anything.

Anything.

But the situation brimmed with possibility, too, didn't it? If the pods were really anything bad, would gamers from around the world be flying in just to try them? I pushed my thoughts aside and smiled. I was probably overreacting. Besides, if it *was* something bad, then there was nothing I liked more than a good challenge.

I settled back against the pod as the last of the cords attached to my jaw and temples and waited for the ride.

Loading into a game isn't as bizarre as it sounds.

Your vision goes black at first, then flickers, like a loading screen. The pins in the cords stimulate your nerves, making you feel, taste, and smell everything. Code becomes sensory detail.

I stood in a small room with metal walls a shade halfway between beige and gray. Empty shelves lined three of the four walls. On the fourth wall was an oversized map. Must be the map of the game. A doorway stood to the left of it. The emptiness shimmered with an opalescent grid. A force field. We were trapped in here until the game began.

A clear visor covered my eyes, so just a hint of the edges filled my vision. A map blinked in the bottom left corner, same as the screen on the wall, except mine was blinking with five gray dots all clustered together—representations of me and the team. YOU ARE HERE, in virtual space.

I looked down at myself. I wore a dark gray jacket cinched closed at the waist. The edges of the front flaps were embroidered. I thumbed at the stitching, the bumps and valleys flowing under my fingers. A chill whispered up my spine and turned my skin to goose bumps. Hidden within the swirling details were a handful of Chinese characters.

Harmony. Balance. Nature. Peace.

If I had to pick four principles I lived by, or at least attempted in my better moments, those would have been it, and now they were embroidered on this jacket. But I hadn't chosen this jacket. The game had for me. I closed my eyes and took a breath. Hello, artificial intelligence. Nice to meet you.

When I turned around to find my teammates, my mouth fell open. They were all dressed similarly, in dark gray with clear visors covering their eyes. But all were outfitted in custom gear matching their personalities and tastes. Looks like we didn't need to choose our image in this game. The pods took your deepest secrets and desires and put them on display for all to see.

Pink and purple chunks streaked through Lily's blond hair, which had double the volume and edginess it did in the real world. Purple lipstick emphasized her pouty lips. She wore leather armor with only glimpses of skin showing. A hint of shoulder here. A sliver of torso there. But, for the most part, highly practical for fighting.

Hannah, on the other hand, looked like . . . well, Hannah. Skintight armor over everything that had to be covered and bare-skinned everywhere else. Her strawberry blonde hair was tinted nearly platinum white. Coupled with makeup in all shades of pink, her coloring made her look like a futuristic nymph. Opera-length black leather gloves stretched nearly to her shoulders. Tight pants spread from hip bone to feet, ending in a pair of high, platform boots.

She winked at me. "You look hot, too."

I laughed.

Both Hannah's voice and my own echoed back in my ear. I reached up and followed a line from my ear to the corner of my mouth. We had mics. Nice.

"This is all we do?" Rooke asked. "Stand here?"

Like Lily, Rooke's floor-length jacket and fitted clothing covered him nearly head to toe. A hood pulled low over his eyes turned his already chiseled face into nothing but shadows, edges, and angles.

It did nothing for me. Just saying.

Though if this was a contest in nonchalant coolness, Derek would have taken the trophy, the money, and the whole damn stage. The upper half of his body was covered in a thin sheath of armor, almost like a second skin that covered his arms and chest, and stretched up the sides of his neck. A half-zipped jacket sat on top of the armor, giving him an edge that said "I'm cool and composed." *Oh this? Just threw something together.* Combine it all with heavy boots, fitted pants, and the faint glow of his visor, and he looked like a futuristic assassin.

All around us, the room buzzed. On three out of four walls, shelves appeared, all containing an assortment of weapons. Directly in my line of sight was a three-and-a-half-foot Dao sword. In traditional gamer-gear fashion, it swirled and arched with excessive details, all curves and glimmer. A matching dagger sat beside it.

Wow. Kali likes.

"Hello, gorgeous."

When I picked up the sword, the movement produced a smoky streak of color off the blade's edge, dark gray for Team Defiance. Nice touch. I twirled the blade a few times, slicing it through the air. Gray smoke trailed behind my movements, like the ribbons of flames left from a fire spinner.

I grinned.

"This one is mine."

As soon as I said those words, a strap unfurled across my chest, wrapped around to my back, and formed a sheath running from shoulder to hip. I touched the sword to my back, and the sheath wrapped around the sword, gripping it like claws. When I tugged on the sword again, the leather bands retracted instantly. I picked up the matching dagger, and another sheath materialized, this time on my outer thigh.

Lily selected a pair of small axes. Straps formed around her legs to sheathe her weapons. As each of my teammates chose their weaponry, their outfits morphed to match, forming straps and sheaths as necessary. Okay, I had to admit. That was impressive.

The screen next to the room's door buzzed with white noise

for a second, then made a sound like a comm was clicking in. A female voice filled the room.

"Welcome, Team Defiance."

The screen flickered a few times. The map of the arena looked more structured and grid-like compared to the natural settings we usually battled in. Buildings lined every block, creating tight roads and even tighter alleys as passageways through the game.

"The game mode is capture the flag," the voice said. "A flag will spawn in front of your opponent's base to the north . . ." A blue dot appeared at the northern edge of the map, marking the enemy's base. ". . . And another in front of your base to the south." Another dot appeared in the corresponding spot. I glanced out the force field beside the map, and a flag appeared approximately ten feet away. It glowed in a bluish white and glitched a few times, code running through it.

"Your objective is to capture your opponent's flag and return to your base before they retrieve yours." The screen showed a mock demonstration of a player running through the flag. As they did, they were consumed with a faint bluish glow. So that's how we'd identify the flag carrier. Meaning, that would be the one to take out. And as a trial run, that meant we'd be playing against the computer. Computerized opponents were the norm in virtual practices. "You cannot score while both flags are in play. If your enemy has your flag, you must retrieve it."

"Standard capture the flag," Derek said, and lowered his voice. "Is this really supposed to be unique?"

We all traded glances with each other. Capture the flag in gaming was older than the competitions themselves. Really, what was the fuss about this technology?

On the screen, a thirty-second countdown appeared over the map.

"The girls and I will go for the flag," I announced. I glanced back at the guys. "You good for guarding ours?"

They nodded.

Good. I wanted to see this place.

The countdown neared its finale.

3 . . . 2 . . . 1 . . .

The doorway fizzled, and the shield dropped. I bolted out of the base and into the street. The rain hit me first, a soft, hazy mist that dampened my hair until it clung to my cheeks. The streets, the buildings, the entire backdrop of this world was a shade of gray, punctuated by neon lights outlining nearly every sign and window. Their carnival colors smeared in the haze, like melting cotton candy. Kanji symbols slid down buildings, also flashing in neon. Red lanterns were strung from rooftop to rooftop like pearl necklaces against the black neck of the open sky above.

As our footsteps pounded the pavement, a strange feeling crawled along the base of my hairline, and my breath went sharp. It was too quiet here. No cars. No people. No sound whatsoever. Just our footsteps, our huffing breaths, and the weight of the air pressing around us, so clear, yet so thick, it felt like it had a presence. And it was watching.

As we reached the northern end of the map and rounded a corner, the flag came into view. Two opponents flanked the flag. That meant three had gone for our base. Here's hoping the boys could handle themselves.

"Who's getting the flag?" Hannah asked, not breaking her stride.

I exchanged glances with Lily.

"You get it," I told Hannah. "We'll take the guards."

She fell back several steps, allowing Lily and me to take the lead so we could clear the path for her. I drew the sword from my back. Lily drew her axes.

I glanced at Lily. "You take the left, I've got the right."

She nodded.

We closed in.

I lunged for my opponent, kicking out with both feet and slammed into his chest, knocking him to the ground. I followed him down in a rolling fall and threaded my sword between his third and fourth ribs. He gasped, clawing at my face for a second, before his arms dropped, and his head rolled to the side.

Hannah slid through the flag and powered up. A horn rang out overhead. She became like the weapons, kiting a trail of white-blue smoke behind her.

Lily's attacker sliced through her neck and knocked her to the ground. Blood pooled around her, and her body contorted and rocked as it curled in on itself, and she gasped her last breath.

"Lily's out," I said into the mic.

Hannah took off down the street. Lily's attacker pursued Hannah, trailing fifteen feet behind her. Damn it. I sheathed my sword and raced after them. Corner after corner, I trailed behind, pumping my legs, cutting through alleyways. It was useless. I wasn't gaining on them. Every time I closed in, got faster, gained an inch, my opponent ran faster. Like it knew. Like it was toying with me.

Toy with this, pal.

I drew my dagger from the sheath around my thigh and whipped it like a dart. It tomahawked through the air and nailed Hannah's pursuer in the spine. His constant footsteps became a broken, tumbling dance as he lost his footing and crashed into the street, his face smearing along the pavement. Then he slid to a stop and didn't move again.

I scooped up my dagger as I darted past the body, swiping it clean from his back without missing a beat. Hannah continued her race through the streets. I tailed her, guarding from behind.

"We've got two closing in on the base," Derek informed me through the mic. "About to engage."

Two?

Two with the guys and two at the enemy's base made four. Where was the fifth?

A soft whooshing noise pulled my gaze up to the rooftops beside us. Another opponent cut through the wind, jumping between the gaps of the buildings.

Ah, there he is.

Wait a minute. The rooftops. Shit, the rooftops were as accessible as the streets. That introduced a whole new component. The RAGE tournaments were mostly fought on the ground, with few opportunities to attack from above. But here, buildings lined nearly every inch of the streets. Just like that, fights became 360 degrees.

He leapt from the rooftop, landed behind Hannah, and joined the chase.

"Look out," I shouted, forgetting I had the mic.

Hannah rolled, barely avoiding his blow as his sword cut through the air above her. Hannah scrambled to her feet and shot down the street. Her latest assailant stayed right on top of her. I whipped my dagger through the air, this time aiming straight for his head. Just before it sliced through his skull, he turned around and caught the blade. Bare-handed. I slammed on the brakes and stumbled to a halt.

He just caught the blade.

He knew. He knew I was going to throw my dagger and was ready for me. The air closed in around me, pressing down my throat, cutting off the passageway to my lungs. What the hell was going on here? First, Hannah's pursuer outran me at every turn, and now this one had anticipated my attacks.

The game was learning.

I really was being watched.

He charged for me with my dagger gripped in his hand. Panic seized my chest. I grappled for my sword across my back, but the hilt slipped across my hands. Shit, shit, shit.

He closed in.

I brought up my fists, preparing for his attack. He dodged my block with ease and ripped my own dagger across my gut. Blood spilled out, instantly soaking my lower half. The pain bowed my knees and back, and continued up my body until I even felt it in my teeth. I collapsed to the ground. My hands moved on their own, grasping at the gaping wound, as if somehow, if I could put the pieces back where they belonged, it would heal together again. Then my fingers went cold, my arms went limp, and my soul retreated to the center of my body.

Well, death felt the same in this game as any other.

My attacker's footsteps faded down the street as he chased after Hannah. She had enough of a head start to beat him to the punch.

I lay in the middle of the street, waiting to bleed out, soaking in the hazy rain and the kaleidoscope of the neon signs. Above me, the lanterns rocked on their strings, looking like kites trapped in an endless glitch, a loop stuck on repeat. The buildings loomed overhead in their dreary gray tones, their walls perfectly sleek, as if made of metal. The bluish tinge of the streetlights glossed the entire setting like a cyanotype filter.

The air pressed down on me, enveloping me in a bubble of absolute silence. I was alone here. Completely alone. Crippled, bleeding out, unable to move, consciousness barely clinging to my slowing heart. There was nothing else. No one. Just me, and the game. Like the angel of death, it sat there with me. Hovering. Waiting. Holding my hand until the last bit of me vanished.

I shuddered. At least, my soul did.

A horn rang out overhead. The end of the game. Looks like Hannah had scored.

I felt the jolt. My body jerked and my vision went black. I closed my eyes and kept them shut, listening. It was dead silent. A kind of silence that only comes from sensory deprivation. I opened my eyes. The shadowy interior of my pod wrapped around me, swaddling me in its emptiness. Strangely enough, I felt almost as empty on the inside. This technology was supposed to be revolutionary. Yes, the opponent guided by artificial intelligence meant they'd learn faster and present better challenges than the programmers ever could. And it was nice to play a new game mode with the team. But, other than that, what was the big deal?

When we exited the pods, Tamachi was waiting for us.

"So," he began. "What did you think?"

I exchanged looks with my teammates.

"I don't think the VGL has a game that combines capture the flag with hand-to-hand combat and short-range weapons," Derek said. "And the Japanese cyberpunk feel is pretty cool."

"It looks incredible," Hannah added, and everyone nodded. Then they all turned to me. I faltered. It was a cool game, and the visuals were stunning, but there wasn't much more to it than that.

"It's interesting, sure," I began. "But . . ."

Tamachi smiled and nodded, like he'd been expecting my answer. "It's not worth all this fuss, is it?"

"Frankly, no." I crossed my arms.

He circled my pod to the rear and motioned me to follow. "Let me show you something."

I walked up beside him. He tilted the screen my way. It listed several of the standard statistics, including blood pressure, pulse, an EEG report, and brain-imaging scans.

"This is an average feed from a gamer when they're plugged into the pods currently used by the VGL."

He tapped the screen a few times and a new set of stats popped up. The blood pressure and pulse were much lower, the EEG was a softer wavy line, and the brain-imaging scans focused activity around the prefrontal cortex.

"And this is your feed, Kali, while you were playing just now."

My teammates gathered around me to review the screen as well. I frowned and motioned at the screen. "So, does this mean I'm brain-dead?"

Maybe that would explain why I'd allowed Rooke back on the team.

Tamachi suppressed a smile and shook his head. "No, no. It's these pods. Our system puts the user in a much more relaxed state."

"Like sleep?" Hannah asked.

"Not quite like sleep. More like—"

"Meditation," I answered. The word left my mouth in a rush and left behind a numbing sensation. Suddenly, I felt like I was back in the virtual world. No way was this real. Had Tamachi actually managed to turn the virtual world into an oasis of peace and tranquility for the mind? There it was, right in front of me. The slowed EEG, the lowered blood pressure, focused brain activity, were all typical physiological signs of someone in a deep, meditative state.

"What does that mean?" Hannah finally asked.

I knew exactly what it meant.

"It's safer for us," I said, and glanced up at Tamachi, praying I wasn't getting my hopes up. "Isn't it?"

Tamachi answered with a smile. "And without the added mental stress, you can play the game for as long as your body holds out."

"So," Derek began, "that means we could plug in for . . ."

"Hours."

"Really?"

"You can't sprint forever, but you can jog."

Up to now, the maximum gaming time in the VGL was forty-five minutes, and that was for the dungeon raids. Of course, at-home VR sets could be played for hours. But the virtual pods used by the VGL—with their combination of real-life sensory deprivation and artificial stimuli—had always put so much stress on the user's mind that no gamer could last more than an hour continuously. These pods had the potential to change all of that. If they functioned the way Tamachi was claiming they did, that meant we could train endlessly without breaks. The VGL really would be able to run matchups that lasted for hours instead of minutes. Would there even be any concern about too much gaming anymore? Virtual addiction could be a thing of the past.

No. It couldn't be that good. Nothing ever is. But with technology evolving by the day, maybe it was only a matter of time before the virtual pods progressed toward something safer. Maybe it was time to accept that things were finally getting better. For everyone.

"One other question," Derek began.

Tamachi raised an eyebrow. "Yes?"

"You said something about a tournament?"

Tamachi smiled. "Why don't we discuss that over dinner? Are you hungry?"

My team? Always.

We were served dinner in the second dining room. Yes, the second dining room. I had no idea how many of them there were, and I never saw the first one, either, but I knew this was the second of its kind because Tamachi had to tell his staff where we'd be eating.

The center of the table was a buffet: platters of roasted potatoes and vegetables, chicken breasts, salad, pasta. Help yourself. Wine, water, and juices were served, alongside tea and coffee. Real coffee. Not that automatic, machine ground, individual cup bullshit. As soon as the server set the pot down, the sweet, roasted aroma hit me, and I breathed deep.

Help yourself. Indeed, I did.

"So, are these pods going to replace the ones currently used in pro gaming?" Derek asked.

"That's the hope," Tamachi said. "Tamachi Industries will be hosting a tournament to help promote this new technology. Some of the top gaming teams are going to compete. We've got ones coming into this from all over the world. Europe. China. South Korea."

I choked on my coffee.

"South Korea is in this?" I asked, once I'd cleared my throat.

Tamachi nodded. "A few of their teams have agreed to participate."

I swallowed down another gulp of my drink. South Korea. Practically the birthplace of eSports and competitive gaming. Over there, children were raised as gamers. If they were participating in this tournament, there went anyone else's chance at winning.

Tamachi continued talking, but I'm not sure how much I was absorbing anymore.

"We're planning a standard double-elimination bracket . . . with a twist. The championship will be the final four teams of the tournament, two from the winners' bracket and two from the losers', all to play out in an arena."

Derek sat forward. "A four-way free-for-all? That's new."

"It's all new. The championship will be a marathon round that lasts up to six hours. Since no other VR technology on the market can provide both complete immersion and sustainable gaming time, we're hoping our pods will prove to be the best on the market."

Rooke took a sip of his drink. "So, by hosting a tournament that no one else in the world can provide, you're hoping the demand for these pods will skyrocket."

Tamachi smiled. "That's the plan."

That was fair. Sure, Tamachi was looking for a way to get his pods accepted by gaming leagues across the world, and hosting a one-of-a-kind, international tournament was a brilliant marketing idea. He was a businessman, and he had to make his profit. Besides, I'm sure that "making things better for gamers" wasn't the VGL's priority over making money. But these pods would accomplish both.

"Why Chimera?" Rooke asked, and my mind flashed back to the name etched into the sides of the pods. I'd caught the reference to Greek mythology, and it was a little outdated for a virtual pod. But it was no surprise that Rooke had brought it up. He'd always been an admirer of all things historical and old-fashioned. Tamachi studied him for a minute, a look of amusement masking his face. Finally, he asked, "What do you know about the Chimera?"

"It was a three-headed, fire-breathing female beast that no one could defeat in a fight."

Derek looked up from his plate and grinned. "We already have one of those on our team."

I glared at him.

Tamachi pressed his lips together to hide a smile. "Chimera is in reference to the more modern definition. A fantasy world that can only exist inside your mind."

Well, that was the virtual world. Only exists within the mind, as much as it seemed otherwise sometimes.

I sat back in my chair. "Can you tell us a little more about the tournament?"

"For starters," Tamachi began, "there won't be a preseason. We're starting straight off with the Death Match."

The Death Match was the first round of the tournament, and it divided the teams into upper and lower brackets, depending on whether they won or lost. Though the name "Death Match" was used to describe the first round in any tournament, it had earned the title from the RAGE tournaments. RAGE was a gladiatorial-style fighting game, and the first tournament match was often the bloodiest. Times ten. Hence, the Death Match.

"When does the tournament begin?" I asked.

"Two weeks from this coming Saturday if everything works out."

"Hang on a second," Derek began. "Rumors are that people like Jessica Salt have been here. We're talking the gods of the gaming world. What do you want with us?"

Tamachi nodded at me. "Kali was the first female captain in the VGL, and you have won a championship. People still think the rivalry between you and InvictUS is one of the best in the league. So, you all have recognizable names and faces."

Derek shrugged. "Sure, but we're not ten-year veterans."

"We're going for a mixture of teams, from rookies to veterans."

"How many in the tournament?" I asked.

"Thirty-two," he said. "Standard tournament play."

"And how many slots do you have left to fill?"

"One."

We glanced at each other. One slot left, meaning if we took it, the brackets would be filled.

"This is winner takes all," Tamachi continued. "Whoever takes the championship takes the entire prize pool."

Only the winner gets paid. Yikes.

"All right," Derek said with a grin. "Now that we're to the good part, what is the entire prize pool?"

"One hundred."

"Thousand?"

"Million."

My mouth dropped open.

It went dead silent around the table, except for the sound of a fork clanging against a plate. A hundred million dollars for a video game tournament. First, an all-star tournament, and now a nine-figure grand prize. This really was history in the making.

I finally found my voice. "Did the VGL actually agree to that?"

"The VGL isn't aware of my plans at this time."

Ah, I knew there had to be a sticking point.

I smiled. "I doubt they'll fork over that kind of prize money."

"The prize money is coming from Tamachi Industries. It's a specialized tournament we'll be hosting, so the prize comes from us."

"So the VGL isn't in on this?"

"We didn't want to present them with the opportunity to air the tournament until we had a full roster. We need one more team."

I exchanged glances with my teammates. They all stared back, wide-eyed. Mr. Tamachi picked up on the tension.

"I'll give you some privacy to discuss it."

He wiped his mouth with a napkin, left it on the table, and exited the room.

"This is a big opportunity," Derek said as soon as the door swung shut and we were alone. "Scratch that, it's huge. Virtual gaming's first all-star tournament?"

"Can Tamachi really offer that kind of money?" Lily asked.

"This guy invented the latest AI chip that's in every phone and tablet in the world. He's a billionaire a hundred times over. He's got the money."

Rooke leaned forward. "And if this works, and gaming leagues around the world start using his pods, he'll make a hundred million back in no time."

I sat back in my chair, letting my teammates discuss the issue.

"This will be the biggest tournament in eSports history," Hannah said.

"It's more than that," Rooke pointed out. "Even the World Cup tops out at ninety million. It'll be the biggest prize in all of sports. Period."

Hannah gasped. "You're right. Plus, it's ten times the prize pool for the RAGE tournaments."

"It's ten times the level of competition, too," I said. "In the RAGE tournaments, we're one of the highest ranked in the league. We're almost guaranteed a spot in the championship. But in this, compared to the top teams in the world? The prize pool doesn't matter if it's winner takes all. What are the chances that it would be us? We're much more likely to make money if we stay in the RAGE tournaments."

"Kali, you're loaded," Hannah pointed out.

I held up a hand. "Yes, I got money from touring and sponsorships as the first female captain. But that all went into making the house into a personalized facility. The ongoing costs of staff and maintenance alone are staggering."

"Yes, and imagine never having to worry about that again."

"This is the opportunity of a lifetime," Derek added. "We can't just walk away."

No, they really couldn't just walk away.

I didn't have the money that most team owners did, who typically made their fortunes elsewhere, then invested in eSport teams for fun. Everything I had came from competing, and if we didn't win tournaments, I didn't know how I'd keep us afloat. But this *was* the opportunity of a lifetime, and I wasn't going to ask them to sacrifice that. Even if we lost in this tournament, they could each move on to other teams. With a RAGE championship under their belts, they'd get picked up elsewhere.

Plus, if these pods really were safer for gamers, that's what I was fighting for. That was the big picture. How could I not be a part of this?

Mr. Tamachi walked back into the room and surveyed each of our faces.

"Well?"

I glanced back at my teammates. They all gave a subtle nod. I turned back to Mr. Tamachi, and revealed our decision.

"We're in."

"Excellent. With the last team added to the roster, we'll be able to go to the VGL with the proposal." He pulled out the chair next to me and sat. "Kali, I'd really like for you to come with me."

"What?"

"These pods were inspired, in part, because of you. You helped to expose some of the corruption in competitive gaming and the trouble gamers can have with plugging in too often. My pods actually make things better for the user. I think they're the answer gamers have been looking for. The VGL is taking what you did very seriously, but not in the right way. They're worried about marketing and profit. Crisis-management mode, they call it. They're not looking to help anyone but themselves. And they're also worried about what you'll do next. So, if I have the top gamers from around the world in on this, yourself included, I doubt they'll say no."

The VGL was worried about little old me? Looks like I had made some ripples in the competitive gaming world. If these pods were best for gamers, and that's certainly what they seemed to be, then I was willing to do just about anything to make that happen.

I smiled, though I'm sure it faltered at the edges.

Me. The VGL. There's a hell of a mix.

"When are we going?"

CHAPTER 5

The VGL head office looked exactly how I pictured it: a stark white lobby with harsh lines and too-bright lighting, like one of those dreams where you wonder if you're dead. Everything was Plexiglas and plastic. The letters V-G-L glowed in the wall behind the reception desk, just slightly off-white, so they barely appeared on the wall.

Tamachi and I sat across from reception on white acrylic chairs shaped in a way that was probably meant to improve posture but only gave you a butt-ache instead.

"This office is too plain," Tamachi said, as if we had one mind. He glanced at me. "Neon lights would be nice."

I laughed. "You're a big fan of Japanese cyberpunk, huh?"

"How can you tell?"

We shared a smile.

Clicking heels pulled my attention down the hall. A woman walked toward us, wrapped in a business suit and gripping a tablet in her hands. She was light-skinned with blond hair cut bluntly at her shoulders. A man trailed half a foot behind her, also dressed in a suit, though his skin was dark and his hair was short.

The blond woman promptly stopped in front of us and extended her hand.

"Hello, Mr. Tamachi," she said, shaking his hand as he got

to his feet. "I'm Diana Foote, Director of Programming for the VGL. This is Farouk Nasser." She motioned to the man standing next to her. "He's our New Games Coordinator."

Farouk and Tamachi shook hands as well. Farouk Nasser was a Middle Eastern man with a warm smile. If he didn't work for the VGL, I'd think it was genuine.

Tamachi turned to me.

"This is—"

"Kali Ling," Diana finished for him. "I think we all know who she is."

Diana Foote, Director of Programming, was also a magician, apparently, since the temperature in the room dropped about ten degrees with her tone of voice alone. She narrowed her eyes at me. Hell, her whole face pinched, like she was trying to use telekinesis to pin me to the wall and cut off my air supply.

I smiled back.

And winked.

"Ms. Ling has played the game I'm proposing," Tamachi explained. "I've brought her along to answer any of your questions and give her opinion as a pro in the industry."

Mr. Tamachi, so formal. Let's break out the teacups and doilies.

Diana raised her chin slightly, still pinning me with her gaze.

"I admire you, Ms. Ling."

Yeah right.

"Please, let's have a seat in our boardroom."

Diana and Farouk lead the way down the hall into one of the many boardrooms. This room wasn't as stark as the lobby. The ceiling, walls, chairs, and table were all still white, but an oversized screen on the far wall displaying game highlights added a punch of color, and glass windows to the outdoors allowed for natural sunlight and a view of downtown L.A.

We sat at the table, Diana and Farouk on one side, Tamachi and I on the other. One team against the other, not unlike the arena.

"So," Diana began, tapping on her tablet a few times before setting it aside. "You've come to us hoping we'll be interested in airing your event?"

"I'm not hoping," Tamachi stated. "I simply came to you first. If the VGL is not interested in broadcasting the event, I'm sure a general sports station will be eager to buy the rights, given that eSports are more popular than . . . anything, really."

Nice move, Tamachi.

Diana Foote didn't seem fazed by the tactic, though I'd yet to see her express an emotion on her face other than bored and evil.

She glanced at her tablet again and sighed. "I've looked over the basic course, and to be frank, I'm not impressed. This really isn't that different from what we currently have in our standard lineup."

Tamachi reached across the table and tapped the screen on Diana's tablet a few times. From the reflection in Diana's eyes, I saw a new map appear on the screen, but that's all I got to see. Tamachi rested his arms against the table.

"This is the championship course. It lasts anywhere from four to six hours."

Diana's eyes went a touch wide, and she leaned back in her chair. "Six hours? How is that possible?"

"The pods reenergize the user instead of draining them." Tamachi paused for effect. It worked. Diana and Farouk exchanged glances, their eyes another fraction wider. "I've signed up teams from around the world. If you swipe to the next page, you'll see the full roster."

Diana slid a single finger across the screen once to turn the page. Her jaw dropped. Well, not really. More just a slight unhinging, like the corners of her mouth came a little loose. I'm sure for her, though, that was as close as it got.

She flashed the screen at Farouk. Now his jaw actually dropped. I'm surprised it didn't hit the table. My stomach went right along with it. I had no idea who was on that list, but they were the competition. If the VGL was impressed, I could only imagine what names were listed there and who we'd be up against.

What the hell had I gotten us into?

"So," Farouk began, "the matches throughout the tournament will be standard length. But the championship will be hours long."

Tamachi leaned toward them. "And that championship will be the Super Bowl of gaming. A daylong event. People will have parties around the world."

"And when are you planning to run this tournament of yours?"

"Two weeks from Saturday."

Diana frowned and shook her head. "Two weeks from Saturday is the start of the Special Ops tournaments. That's our most popular game."

"Until now," he said. "You can bump it to another time slot, push it back a few months, or have it compete against my tournament on another channel. Besides, some of your most popular teams have signed on to play my game instead. I don't think your ratings will compare to last year's."

"We have contracts," she protested. "We can refuse to allow those teams to play."

"That's fine," Tamachi said. "But other leagues around the world have already signed on. Do you really want to be the only country that doesn't allow its gamers to play?"

She sat back in the chair again and crossed her arms. This

time, the move was deliberate. Practiced. "How would we get the pods installed in time?"

"The local teams could have pods installed by this time to-morrow. I have the means to make it happen. The other teams, including the internationals, have all flown in for the tourna-ment. I have more than enough pods available for their use inside my facility."

This guy had an answer for everything.

Diana considered that for a minute, studying Tamachi through narrowed eyes. When the same intense gaze flicked to me, I straightened my back to stop myself from shuddering.

"You've tried these new pods, Ms. Ling?"

"I have."

"What do you think?"

In a word? Awesome. But I was pretty sure that wasn't the answer the VGL was looking for.

"I think they're exactly what the industry needs," I finally said.

Diana drew a deep, deliberate sigh and slowly let it out. For a few seconds, she said nothing and simply tapped her fingernail against the table. Not easy to read, this one.

"This will be unlike anything the industry has seen before," Tamachi continued. "Imagine the ratings, the hype. Think of how much sponsors will pay to air their ads—"

Diana held up a hand. "Honestly, you had me at six hours."

Was that *yes*? It sounded like *yes*.

Diana flicked through the tablet a few times, glancing at Farouk next to her. He nodded. He was in.

Was she?

"We'll still need to formalize this," she finally said. "The higher-ups will need to sign off. And we'll have to rearrange our schedule for the next few months."

Here it comes. *Yes.*

"And we'll need to publicize the event," she added. "This is pretty over-the-top. The marketing needs to be that way, too."

Mr. Tamachi smiled.

"Trust me. I've got it covered."

The next day, the announcement was made.

The VGL and Tamachi Industries went public with the all-star tournament, the advanced VR pods, and the marathon championship round.

The Internet lost its shit.

The VGL changed up some of its programming, and the Special Ops tournament got bumped back by several weeks. Too many of the top teams from Special Ops were competing in the tournament, so the VGL didn't want to run both tournaments at the same time. Even if they scheduled them on different nights, there was no way any team would split themselves between both tournaments. Not when they had the chance to be crowned number one in the entire world and win the hundred-million-dollar prize.

"This Saturday night, the roster of teams will be revealed," announcer Marcus Ryan reported on the latest newsreel on the VGL home channel.

The coming Saturday night, there would be a party for the teams in the tournament at the Tamachi estate. No one knew who was on the roster. Not even me. I had no idea who would be there, and it was the first and only time we'd be meeting our competition outside the arena.

The frenzy over The Wall had hit an all-time high. Everyone knew now that Tamachi's mansion held the latest advancement in virtual reality and would be hosting a never-before-seen gaming tournament. So, based on the paparazzi's stalking from the past several weeks, people were guessing at the roster by who'd been seen at the house. You'd think that would have made things an easy guess. Turns out, not so much. Mr. Tamachi went to extremes to throw people off and keep things private. Sometimes, he'd snuck the real gaming teams through the back of the house while decoys went through the front. He'd even hired people matching body stats of other teams to enter the house in disguise to throw off the paparazzi. And there were a handful of teams that had gone to the house but had turned the opportunity down. So, the guesses were strictly that—guesses.

Sites were overflowing with mock-up rosters of possible all-star teams. The only thing that had been revealed about the roster was that it would feature a combination of teams from the highest-rated rookies up to gaming's heaviest hitters, and that teams were coming in from around the world. I could only imagine there would be fantasy mock-ups of the tournament spread as well once the teams were revealed. This was NCAA March Madness for gaming. Thirty-two teams go in, one comes out.

And just wait until the fans saw that code.

No one had seen the style of the game. Sure, capturing flags was as old as pro gaming itself. But that code, that style. Everything was so smooth there. Everything was silk. Now the VGL had a game that topped even racing in terms of style. And because of those insane visuals, there was even talk of having the tournament broadcast in virtual definition—specifically made to be watched with virtual-reality headsets, so the audience viewed the game as if they were inside it as well.

The new pods were installed in my home the next day. They gleamed like opalescent pearls. No workstation sat behind the pods. Just a single screen for choosing the game and basic setup info. It would also display and keep track of our activity once inside, fully available for review once we were out. However, these new pods came with a side effect I had failed to anticipate— until all five of my programmers bombarded me in my office.

"What's wrong?" I asked, looking up from my desk.

Usually my office was a peaceful place. I'd designed it that way on purpose. Wood ran the length of the two sidewalls, broken only by several poster-sized screens. Most people had poster-screens in their homes now since they were more afford- able and versatile than traditional art. Tired of that Van Gogh? One click, and you've got Monet instead.

In my office, the screens featured my team in their gladiato- rial battle gear. Clarence, my former team owner, had done the same in his office, back when I'd been on his team. I'd ques- tioned his motivations in owning a team on several occasions, but he wasn't wrong about everything. While he'd kept pictures of us in the office to show off his major assets, I did it to remind myself who was most important in all of this, including some- one no longer with us.

Nathan.

Our former teammate had overdosed on heroin after a par- ticularly grueling matchup. Sure, someone's choice to do drugs was always their own, but the way virtual gaming operated didn't make it easier for the players. Spending hours on end in a world where anything was possible, and there were no con- sequences, combined with riches and fame, led most pro gam- ers to believe they were invincible.

Elise took a step ahead of the other programmers and folded her arms. "Is it true what they're saying about these new pods?"

"That they're safer for gamers?"

"No. That they don't need programmers to run."

I blinked. Huh. I hadn't thought about that. Technically, no. They didn't need programmers to run. Which meant that the five people standing in front of me were no longer needed for the team. I'd have to let them go. At least, until the RAGE tournaments started up at the end of the summer—and that was only if they didn't switch over to these new pods for every tournament.

I bit my bottom lip. I'd never had to fire someone before, and the thought of sabotaging the livelihood of my programmers sunk my heart through the floor.

"It's true," I finally admitted.

Elise's jaw dropped. "Are we out of our jobs? I have $40,000 left on my student loans."

I stood from my desk and made a calming motion with my hand. "It's just for this tournament. We'll still need you for RAGE." If my money lasted that long. "Maybe after this all-star tournament, they won't use these pods again."

She scoffed. "You mean the pods that would save every team owner hundreds of thousands of dollars a year in salaries?"

"That's not what this is about—"

"No, it's about another machine taking the job of a human being."

A machine. I felt about as heartless as one right then. Maybe there was a way to salvage this.

"I'll pay you severance for the tournament," I offered.

Elise glared at me. "Do you really think this is about money? Maybe that's all the VGL cares about, but we do our jobs because we enjoy it."

"But—"

"Have fun in your tournament."

With that, they walked out of my office and out of the house.

So, I had to fire five people on my staff. Or temporarily lay off. They were good at their jobs, and it wasn't fair. I felt, frankly, like a horrible human being. Taking over as team owner, I'd only ever thought about the positive. About making things better for the team and leading the lives we wanted to lead. I'd never thought twice about the hard stuff, like firing people. Especially since it was beyond my control, and they really hadn't done anything wrong. But, at the same time, that was life. Industries evolved, and we had to, too. Moving on, being receptive to change, had gotten me to where I was now, and I'd learned it was one of the best ways to get ahead in life.

By the time Saturday rolled around, my emotions still wrestled between I-did-what-was-necessary and I-deserve-to-be-trampled-by-elephants. But I had to push it from my mind as I stood in front of the mirror in my bedroom. Tonight was the all-star dinner. The competition would be revealed—the best teams from around the world—and I'd have a whole new set of worries. If there's anything that can perk someone up (besides coffee with six sugars), it's an afternoon's worth of prepping and pampering for a night out. Even someone like me, who preferred swords to heels, liked to primp and preen once in a while.

Unlike our previous team owner, who'd dressed us up like little dolls, I told my teammates to dress however they wanted. But Tamachi had requested one specific limitation.

"Wear your team color," he'd said.

Defiance's dark, gunmetal gray wasn't the worst color in the world. In fact, it was one of my favorites.

After checking my appearance and adjusting my hair one last time, and another last time, I left my room and headed downstairs. My heels clicked along the hardwood floors of the house and onto the marble tiles of the kitchen and, at the sight of Rooke, I stopped short and nearly tripped over my own feet. I must have sounded like a tap dancer who suddenly fell down the stairs.

Smooth, Kali. Smooth.

Rooke leaned against the counter, dressed in a traditional suit except for the jacket, which extended down several extra inches to midthigh and had an oversized collar, leather inlays, and several extra zippers across either side of his chest. The outfit was still formal but, with the jacket's techy vibe, was an obvious tribute to Tamachi's game. Guess he liked his in-game image from the new virtual pods. Of course he did. We all did. The pods had created images based on our own tastes and likes.

When my feet decided to behave again, I took a step toward him.

"You look . . ." My voice trailed off as I hunted for a safe word. "Nice."

Yes, that was good. "Nice" was solidly neutral, like "let's be friends."

He glanced in my direction, took in my form, and swallowed. "You look more than nice."

He met my eyes and locked on me. So much for neutral. That look was anything but "let's be friends," unless you added "with benefits" at the end. We stood there, staring at each other, both apparently looking nice. Or more than nice.

Derek slid into the room then, and I could have kissed him for breaking the sexually charged standoff. He wore a suit, shirt, and tie, all the same shade of dark gray, with a purple rose pinned to his jacket and sunglasses that mirrored his in-game visor. Suave, much?

"The cars are here," he said. "Are we going now? Or do you two need a knife to cut the tension between you first?"

I stared daggers at him. He grinned.

"Whoa. No need to get a knife. Kali's got one in her eyes."

My teeth gritted together. If I'd had knives in my eyes before, then they must have been four-foot-long swords now.

Hannah and Lily walked into the room, both sporting dresses, though Hannah's was an elegant, floor-length evening gown and Lily's was an edgy cocktail dress. Still, they both looked like they could have walked the red carpet at the Oscars and owned it.

"We'll be in the other car," Derek said. "That way, you two can pretend to talk about whatever it is you're not talking about." He offered his arms to Lily and Hannah. "Ladies."

They each looped an arm around his and walked with him through the house, laughing as they went. At least *they* were having fun tonight.

I followed them through to the front door, Rooke in tow. When I hit the front porch, I stopped dead.

A pair of four-door Maseratis sat in my driveway, both dark gray for Team Defiance. The early-evening moonlight rippled across their glossy exteriors. Forget fiberglass. They looked like a combination of metal, satin, and ice blended together in one ultrasleek package. Now, that's one hell of a car.

Hannah, Derek, and Lily headed for the first car. Technically, I could have joined them. There would have been one other seat left. But that left Rooke to ride by himself, and that wasn't fair. Plus, it wasn't good for the team's image.

Did I really just think that? Since when did I worry about the team's image over someone's feelings? Image did matter in this sport, and putting on a show wasn't just for the crowd. It was also for our opponents, and we were about to be in a room full of the greatest teams in the world. But is that what really mattered to me now?

I steered myself toward the second car. When I was three feet from the door, it opened itself.

"Good evening, Ms. Ling," a voice said.

Facial recognition. The cars would open for us, and only us. I climbed into the front seat. Rooke sat next to me, in what was once the driver's seat, and stared out the window. The car locked itself and took off, coasting through the streets, directly behind its mate.

The interior of the car looked like a mashup of a high-end nightclub and a yacht. The leather interior lined the seats, while wood accents and a stylish blue glow lit up the dash. I traced my hand over the edge of the seat, my fingertips relishing the supple material.

"What are you doing?" Rooke asked, looking down at my hand.

"It's real," I said.

His jaw went tight, and he looked out the window again. "Have you been having trouble?"

Luckily, with his gaze out the window, he didn't notice my expression falter, or the way I bit my lip. Had I slipped back down the path of parties and drugs and alcohol? No, not even close. But every step back into the gamer-celebrity lifestyle brought with it another whisper of temptation, another ounce of stress. Stress that would be oh so easy to drown at the bottom of a bottle. But, given that we weren't on the best of terms, I wasn't about to tell him that. So I forced a smile across my face.

"No. None at all. It's easy, now."

He nodded though he kept his gaze out the window. "That's good."

He bought it. How's that for putting on a show?

Rooke said nothing else. Neither did I. Silence became the

car's sound track, the tempo kept by the whishing sound of lampposts as we drove past marking the empty seconds like a ticking clock. If things had been awkward between us in the kitchen, then being in this car was about as cringingly uncomfortable as a situation can get, like a sex scene coming on when you're watching a show with your parents.

"Thanks for rejoining the team," I said, trying to find a way to break the silence. "I imagine it's not easy." Every word came out strained and broken. I sounded as uncomfortable as I felt.

Rooke shifted in his seat but still didn't look at me.

"And I'm sorry I ignored you when you were trying to call. I was angry."

If his jaw had been tight before, it went even more so now, evidenced by the muscles tensing in his neck.

"That was wrong of me," I tried again. "Lily did the right thing by calling you. I shouldn't have let my emotions get in the way—"

"I cut you off first," he finally said. "I don't blame you for ignoring me."

Okay, he was talking. That was progress.

"I shouldn't have been," I told him. "I put my feelings ahead of the needs of the team, and I can't be doing that." I paused and studied his profile for a second. If I asked, would he answer? Might as well take the chance. "What happened?"

He answered faster than I expected, as if he'd been waiting for the question.

"I just needed space. I don't want to say that it was me and not you. But it was me, and not you."

Okay, I had to smile at that. In fact, I don't think I could have stopped the one that snuck across my face.

"Can I ask why you needed space?"

He rubbed his temple, like he was in pain. That was Rooke.

Internalized everything. Put the weight of the world inside his head and his heart.

"No."

"Okay." Even in a relationship, people were entitled to their privacy and secrets. But Rooke was the type to bottle up what he shouldn't and put way too much stress on himself instead of talking to somebody about what was wrong. Every nerve in me twitched with the desire to pull the words out of his throat myself. I practically had to sit on my hands. "I don't understand why you started calling me again."

More silence dominated the car until it felt like it was pressing up against the windows, the roof, and even me. The air was so thick with tension and anticipation, I half expected the glass to fog up.

"I missed you," he finally said. "I wanted time alone, and the more of it I had, the more I felt like I needed a friend."

Well, that was an arrow through the heart. Actually, more like an arrow tied to a cannonball that exploded on impact. What he did was a shitty thing. It was one thing to bow out politely when we had too many players for the team. But to abandon us completely when I was on the cusp of fulfilling a dream was almost unredeemable.

So, I had no idea why my hand moved toward him, but it was going, and I didn't stop it. It came to rest on top of his. Rooke went dead still.

Honestly, I knew why I'd reached for him. He was part of my team. No matter what happened to anyone on my team, no matter what they did or didn't do, I'd always care for them. Because we were a team, and that meant a hell of a lot more than a damaged heart.

"Whatever it was that you were dealing with," I began, "are you okay?"

He took a breath that came up from his toes, through his entire body. Then, finally, he looked at me. His eyes were distant, foreign. His expression was strained. But where my hand rested on his, he flipped his over, so palm met palm. Our fingers touched tentatively, whispering against each other.

A faint smile touched the corners of his lips.

"I am now."

A siren rang out.

A police motorbike swerved into the lane behind us. Another cut in front of the other car, so that the police bikes bookended our Maseratis. Their lights flashed, but our vehicle didn't slow down, meaning they hadn't sent out an electronic signal to pull us over. I tapped the GPS map menu in the center of the car's console. A message popped up.

Proceed at normal speed.
You will be escorted to your destination.

"An escort?" I wondered out loud. "Why do we need a police escort?"

I caught eyes with Rooke, but he just blinked and shook his head. I scooted forward in my seat and peered ahead, out the front window. As we rounded a corner, heading higher into the Pacific Palisades district of L.A., I realized why we needed the escort.

My eyes went wide, and all the feeling drained from my extremities as I took in the sight before us.

"Holy shit."

CHAPTER 6

The chaos started six blocks from the house.

Rows of fans lined the street, held off the road by guardrails. Policemen stalked up and down the rails, keeping the more aggressive fans on the other side. Security drones hovered between them.

"Please remain behind the guardrails."

As our vehicle continued its slow roll through the streets and started closing in on Tamachi's estate, the policemen morphed into private security, and the crowds grew thicker. Dozens of additional drones buzzed overhead, these belonging to the news stations and tabloids. Cameras clicked like heartbeats. Chants and cheers cut through the air. With all the news attention, the craziness of the crowd, and the level of security, you'd think this was a royal wedding or something.

I tapped the GPS map screen in the center of the car's console, switched it over to video option, and entered the VGL's home channel. Howie and Marcus popped up on the screen, the VGL's main announcers. Last year, they'd become surprise allies in my fight against corruption in gaming and helped announce the issues of virtual addiction to the public, specifically calling out how our former teammate Nathan had died of a drug overdose, which had been covered up by the VGL as an undiagnosed heart condition. They were the VGL's favorite broadcasters by a wide margin. It was probably the only reason they hadn't been fired.

They were both wearing suits and grinning at the camera.

"It's been an exciting evening so far," Howie said. "Let's take another look at the house—"

The shot changed to a drone camera flying over the house's two-lane driveway, where one lane was filled with designer cars. Red Lamborghinis. Gold Bugattis. Judging by the fact that our vehicles matched our team color, the cars in the driveway must represent the colors of the other teams as well.

The screen cut back to Howie and Marcus. Marcus pressed a finger to his ear, like he was listening to a producer through the headset. He beamed at the camera.

"Looks like they're about to reveal the next team."

The screen cut to a shot at the front of the house, where a pair of jet-black Mercedes-Benz SUVs rolled up, glowing ice blue beneath. Talk about lifestyles of the rich and famous. The pair of those cars cost more than what I paid my programmers and trainers per year. Combined. Though I had to admit this was a hell of a way to reveal the teams of the all-star tournament.

Security closed in around the vehicles. Screams and camera flashes from the crowd reached a crescendo. The crowd chanted on repeat.

"Open. The. Doors."

Security paused at the cars, double-checking each other and the status of the situation. Whether they were stalling on purpose to rev up the crowd or for reasons actually related to security, I wasn't sure, but I was betting on the former. Finally, security reached for the handles.

The doors opened, and five men climbed out.

Screams exploded from the crowd, reaching heights never

before known. The camera flashes turned into minibombs, like a war zone. On the screen inside our own vehicle, Howie and Marcus jumped out of their chairs.

My mouth hit my lap.

The entire team was dressed in black cargo pants and sleeveless, open vests, with streaks of war paint smeared across their faces, from temple to temple, right across their ice-blue eyes. I knew that look.

Everyone in the world knew that look.

"Holy shit," I murmured, covering half my face with my hands, like a little kid watching a scary movie. Good thing no one could see how stupid I looked through the tinted windows. I peered through my fingers at Rooke beside me. He seldom wore his emotions on his face like a mask, but even his eyes were drawn wide, and a hand covered his mouth.

I announced the team even though we both knew exactly who they were. "That's K-Rig."

The number one team in all of South Korea. Arguably, the number one team in the entire world. Looks like they were here to prove it.

On each of their chests was a tattoo of their team logo stretching from collarbone to abs. The logos glistened in the camera flashes as if they'd been covered in petroleum jelly for extra sheen. Judging by my time in the game, their clothing choice matched their in-game image. They never smiled or waved. Just gave straight-on death stares, so the cameras would capture perfect shots of their eyes.

Someone was already putting on a show.

Since they were of Korean descent, there was little chance those eyes of theirs were natural, especially since all five members of the team sported the exact same shade of ice blue. Contacts? Maybe. But if the rumors were to be believed, the black war paint smudged around their eyes wasn't war paint at all. It had been tattooed as well, just like the logos on their chests, and their irises had been altered by lasers. Even in the 2050s, tattoos were still permanent and eye-color alterations couldn't be reversed. So, if those rumors actually were true, what those guys had done to themselves for the sake of their team would be with them for life.

Was that dedication or obsession?

A few fans scaled the guardrails and charged. Security was on them in a second. Human and drone alike, they tackled the fans and dragged them away as they kicked and screamed, proclaiming their love and willingness to bear the team's children.

K-Rig never broke.

Staring straight ahead the entire time, they climbed the steps to the house and disappeared inside.

Image. These guys owned it.

Our vehicles rolled up next.

A guard walked up to my passenger door, which faced the house. A gun flashed from beneath his suit.

He pressed a finger to the outer edge of his ear.

"Defiance is here," I heard him say, though there was no actual electronic in his ear. Probably had an implant under the skin. "Are we ready for them?"

Hell no.

His hand gripped the door handle. I thumbed the locking mechanism for a second with my right hand before my left wrestled it away. At least half of me was behaving.

For months, I'd been outside this industry, this madness. Of course, I'd done appearances and gotten recognized on the streets sometimes, but lately, all my energy had gone into building the team and our home. I'd spent my time behind closed doors, dealing with businesses and potential sponsors, not in front of the cameras. My only experience with the crowd as of late had been the occasional public appearance or interview, and those were nowhere near this magnitude.

With a finger still pressed to his ear, the guard outside our door finally nodded and motioned to a few others standing around him to prepare for our arrival. He reached again for the door handle.

Game-face time.

The door opened.

I stepped out, wearing my warrior façade. The screams hit me with such a blast, it knocked my eardrums back inside the car. After the initial wave of screams and applause hit me, I caught the tail end of Howie's statement from the screen inside the car, just before the guard shut the door.

"—Kali 'the warrior' Ling is back—"

Damn right I am.

The team gathered around me. Rooke on my right, Derek on my left, and the girls beyond them. I had to chuckle. Standing together like this, we were balanced. I wasn't sure if the rest of the team realized it on a conscious level, but we'd been trained this way by our former owner.

This is how you look like a team. Image is everything.

I waved at the crowd and smiled my warrior's smile, the one I'd been taught. Inside, my nerves burned, and my chest was tight over all the screams, the infinite camera flashes, and the sheer number of people. But I kept smiling, and something inside me changed. They were cheering for me, for us. They wanted us to be here, to be in the competition, and their enthusiasm became my fire.

Defiance was here, and we were here to win.

Security waved us forward, probably desperate to get us

inside before all hell broke loose, as if there really were a level of insanity beyond this. I walked toward the house with measured, purposeful steps, like I was on a mission instead of running for cover. My teammates followed suit. Once the doors closed behind us, I breathed a sigh of relief. The noise of the crowd still pressed against the windows and walls, but in here, I felt safe.

"That was . . ." Derek began, his voice trailing off. "Surreal."

I closed my eyes and nodded, and though I couldn't see my other teammates with my eyes closed, I assumed they were doing the same thing.

The sound of clicking heels pulled my eyes open. A hostess approached us, smiling.

"Welcome, Defiance. You are the final team to join us this evening." She motioned down one of the halls with her hand. "Please, follow me. Everyone else is gathered in the main dining room."

We followed her down the hallway as she led us into the main dining room. Now I knew why we'd eaten in the second dining room the first time we were here. Having been in the house before, I didn't think I'd be overwhelmed by its extravagance again. I was wrong.

The main dining room was monstrous. It should have been a ballroom, really. It was large enough to hold weddings, and the number of people inside was enough to be one. Gamers and officials from the VGL filled the floor, clustered in groups as they conversed with each other, most with glasses of wine or appetizers in hand. Throughout the room, thousands of lights hung from the ceiling and adorned the tables, so the entire room glowed with golden tones. A buffet table stretched the entire length of the far wall, featuring three-stepped levels of seafood, gourmet cheeses, exotic fruit, delicacies from around the world—specifically from the countries competing in the tournament—all punctuated by flowers and chocolate waterfalls.

The sidewall, facing the back of the house, was floor-to-ceiling windows. Moonlight poured in and stretched across the floor, adding another layer of luminescence to the room. Sitting on a crest, the estate overlooked the other houses below, all high-end, with perfect lighting and infinity swimming pools. Beyond them lay the Pacific Ocean, lapping at the beach, which twinkled in the moonlight. I stepped up to the windows and placed a hand against the glass. My heart beat a little softer then at the sight of such beauty. This house could be worth nine figures based on the view alone.

"Hi, Kali."

I turned around to find Cole Wilkinson standing behind me, our former teammate. I blinked away my shock. Of course he was here. He'd joined Oblivion, and they'd been invited past The Wall before we had.

"I heard you made it in," he said. "Looks like we'll be playing against each other." He extended his hand. "No hard feelings?"

I extended my own and shook. "None. But we'll kick your ass in the arena anyways."

He grinned. "We'll see about that."

"Defiance," a voice called out. Mr. Tamachi greeted us with a smile, his arms spread wide.

I turned back to Cole. "I'll catch up with you later?"

"Sure thing."

I left Cole to rejoin my team. Tamachi practically beamed with pride.

"Fantastic. Everyone's here." He stopped in front of our group. "Things will be getting under way soon. You can help yourself to the buffet." He nodded toward the food, though I doubted my team would need the invitation. His gaze settled on me. "But I need to borrow your captain for a minute."

I smiled. "Of course."

While my teammates headed off to the buffet table, Tamachi took my arm and led me through the crowd of gamers and members of the VGL.

"Do you recognize him?" Tamachi nodded to a man across the room. He had dark hair that was just starting to gray at the temples, and a smile that crinkled his eyes. But his skin was tanned and smooth, and his body fairly fit. He was one of those men who could've been anything from thirty-five to fifty-five. A semicircle of the room's most important-looking people had formed around him, and beyond them were additional security guards. Yeah, I knew him. Only in pictures. Jonathan Kreger. The President of the VGL.

"Is that why you're bringing me around the room? So I can see who's here?"

"No, no. There's someone who wants to meet you."

Someone who wanted to meet me?

We walked halfway up the balcony and stopped behind a woman on the stairs, facing away from us. Her red locks were pulled into a stylish updo with tiny pearls pinned throughout. On closer inspection, the pearls had black eyes and pink tongues hanging out. The ghosts from Mario World. Nice touch.

When she turned around, I swallowed my yelp. Oh, sweet Jesus. She recognized me, too, and extended her hand.

"Hi, Kali. I'm—"

"Jessica Salt," I finished for her. "Holy shit, you're Jessica Salt."

She laughed. "It's nice to meet you, too."

Tamachi excused himself. "I'll leave you two to talk."

Tamachi continued up the stairs to the top of the platform, disappearing into the crowd. Jessica took another step toward me and leaned against the balcony, balancing a wineglass between her fingers. Good thing no one had offered me any alcohol. I would have chugged an entire bottle right about now.

"I'm glad to see you're coming back to the VGL," Jessica said. "I've missed watching you play."

I nearly choked on nothing but air. "You've watched me play?"

"You were the first female captain. Of course I was watching."

I swallowed thick, though I wasn't sure my neck was still attached to my body. Good thing I hadn't known that when I'd been playing.

"On top of everything else," she continued, "you bought out your own team at nineteen."

"Twenty, actually," I corrected her. "And my birthday is next month. So, I'll be twenty-one then. It's not as young as you think."

She exhaled and shook her head. "You say that like it's nothing. I wish I'd been that levelheaded when I was your age."

I laughed. Levelheaded? Oh, Jessica. How little you know me. "Buying out the team might not have been the brightest thing to do."

"What do you mean?"

I rested my arms against the banister and leaned closer to her. "Money is tight. Most team owners can spend whatever they want on their teams. Plus, they have management experience. I don't have much of either, and I'm asking my teammates to put their careers on the line for that."

"Your teammates believe in you," she said. "Otherwise, they would have left."

Maybe that was the real reason Cole didn't stay with the team.

Jessica moved a little closer still and lowered her voice. "If you have a dream, then you just have to do it. You can't let money, or experience, or anything else become an obstacle. Never bow down to the world. Always make it bow down to you."

"I plan on it."

She grinned. "I'm not surprised." She rested her arm against the balcony and looked out over the room. "I'm happy you're in this tournament. It's the first time we get to face off against each other."

My stomach hit the floor. I didn't know why I hadn't realized it before. If she was at this dinner, then of course her team would be in the tournament, and I'd be fighting against my idol. On national television. In the biggest tournament in all of virtual gaming.

"And," she added, "it's the last time we'll play together."

I took a step back. Did she mean this was the only time we'd be in the same tournament? Why would she say something like that?

"What are you talking about?" I asked. "I'm sure if this tournament is a success, they'll host another all-star—"

Jessica shook her head. "After this tournament is over, I'm announcing my retirement."

Now my stomach went right through the floor.

"W-What?" I stuttered. "Why?"

"I've been a part of the VGL since the beginning of full-immersion gaming. I've been at it for eleven years. It's time for something else. And what better game to retire on than the VGL's first all-star tournament?"

"But you're *the* female gamer. We all look up to you. You broke records previously held by guys and were the youngest to ever do so."

She smirked. "Sound familiar?"

I went a little numb then, as if I'd never realized that before, either. Yeah, it sounded familiar. Like, whenever someone spoke my name.

Jessica leaned toward me and lowered her voice again.

"When I was the first woman in the VGL, I figured it was something I could build my career on. I could use it to my advantage, exploit it to the nth degree. Over time I realized that it's not about you as an individual. It's about your team, and how much you can build each other up, especially when you fall."

I smiled. "Yeah. I was the same way when they named me captain."

Jessica moved even closer. "And then, once I started setting records and making history, I realized it was about something even bigger. I was forging a path for the women behind me, making their journey easier and altogether proving we deserved to be here. I know that now, and I know how important it is. It's not something I'd ever give up. Not unless I was absolutely sure there was someone ready to take my place."

She pushed herself off the railing and looked straight into my eyes.

"I think I'm ready to pass the torch."

Then she offered me a smile and walked away, toward her team, leaving me standing next to the balcony alone. As she left, she glanced over her shoulder at me.

"I'll see you in the arena, Kali."

What the hell just happened?

I could just imagine what I looked like. Run over by a car, maybe. There was no way I was ready to pick up her mantle, if I ever would be. She was Jessica Salt. I was, ugh—me. My stomach, which had sunk through the floor long ago, was now drifting somewhere near the Earth's molten core.

Clinking glasses pulled my attention to the top of the stairs. Mr. Tamachi stood at the very center, against the railing, smiling out at the crowd. Speech time. The clamor of the crowd rumbled down to a murmur.

"Thank you all for coming," Tamachi said, his voice booming across the room. Must have been hidden mics and speakers somewhere. "Since the turn of the century, eSports has grown from console games on tube televisions to fully immersive virtual reality, from local competitions in convention-center basements to the biggest sport in the world. Tamachi Industries is excited and proud to be a part of virtual gaming's evolution by introducing artificial intelligence into the pods, creating a better, safer experience for all."

The crowd erupted into applause. Even a few cheers rang out. Tamachi smiled and made a calming motion with his hands, as if he didn't deserve the praise. He spread out his arm to the side, motioning to a woman against the far side of the balcony.

"Now a few words from the VGL. Please allow me to introduce Diana Foote, the Director of Programming."

Everyone clapped again.

She stepped forward, smiling at us all. It was a genuine smile that touched her eyes this time, but I saw right through it. We were probably all dollar signs in her head. She waited for the applause to die before addressing the crowd.

"The VGL is honored to host this unprecedented event," she said, her voice stretching across the room just as Tamachi's had. "Tonight, we are joined by teams from gaming leagues from around the world. The VGL would like to thank Mr. Tamachi for the use of his home, both tonight and for the remainder of the tournament."

The room filled with applause once again.

"The American teams will be plugging in from their own facilities and the international teams will be utilizing the pods Mr. Tamachi has made available in his home. But the final championship will take place right here in Los Angeles at the Riot Games Arena. And whatever is inside that final round, waiting for you, will remain a secret until the final four teams are inside. No maps will be revealed. No clues will be given. You'll have no way to prepare, putting you to the ultimate test. You're here to prove you're the best, and you'll be challenged accordingly."

Which meant, if we made it to the final four, we'd have no way to practice for the final matchup and the life-changing grand prize. One hundred million dollars. To any athlete in any sport in the world, that was unheard of.

Diana glanced behind her and smiled at Tamachi. "I've been speaking quite a bit with Mr. Tamachi about what he has planned for this tournament. He's not saving everything for the final round. You might even find some surprises during the standard matchups."

So, even the standard gameplay would be getting more complicated. Against the best teams in the world. Could they raise the bar any higher?

"The matchups will be taking place every Saturday night. It will air during our most popular segment, *Saturday Night Gaming*, hosted by Howie Fulton and Marcus Ryan. Unfortunately, they were unable to join us tonight, as they were too busy announcing the team reveals from the studio and losing their minds."

Everyone laughed.

"Look around the room," Diana encouraged. "This is the competition."

Everyone did as she asked, scoping out the other players.

Most eyes fell on K-Rig, standing together, poised as if ready for a photo shoot. Were these guys ever out of character?

"There have been incredible matchups in the VGL and other gaming leagues," Diana continued, "but this tournament will be unlike anything anyone has seen before. We can say with almost guaranteed certainty that the entire world will be watching. Let's give them the greatest show they've ever seen."

Everyone clapped again. Even me.

Diana stepped away from the balcony, and the evening resumed as the rest of the crowd in the ballroom returned to eating and conversing. From above, the social dynamics of the ballroom didn't seem that different from those of a high-school cafeteria. It was subtle, but there were empty gaps of space between the teams, where they had divided themselves into cliques by their country of origin.

I pushed a breath through my lips and headed down the steps. Time to get to know the opposition. I descended the stairs and marched right past the American clique. If no one else was taking advantage of getting to know their opponents from the other continents, I certainly would.

I crossed the room into European territory and walked straight up to one of the teams.

"Hi," I said. "I'm Kali Ling, Team—"

"Defiance," one of them said, shaking my hand. They knew me? Looks like my skills were known outside of the States.

"I'm Erik Lager," the handshaker said. "This is my team, Eon."

The rest of Eon all nodded at me. I smiled back at them. While Erik failed to tell me where they were from, I thought I recognized his accent.

"You from Sweden?"

"Good guess." He looked honestly impressed. His gaze

flicked past me, and he nodded to the background. "I see you're back with your boyfriend."

I glanced behind me to find Rooke across the room, next to the buffet with Hannah. She was gabbing away, plucking bits of chocolate and fruit off the trays and popping them into her mouth. Rooke stood rigidly beside her, not reaching for any of the food, not talking, barely moving at all. God, he looked uncomfortable. Rooke was never one to shine in a roomful of people. He was more of an I'll-be-reading-a-book-in-my-room kind of a guy. And, there went my theory of the Europeans knowing me for my skills. Guess it was my love life that had tipped them off.

"We're not—"

"Is that a marketing ploy?" Erik smiled. "Nice."

The grin on his face wasn't a condescending one, but he didn't look like he was going to believe otherwise, either.

"What do you play?" I asked him, changing the subject.

"Intressesfär."

Even with the Swedish pronunciation, I knew the game he was talking about. Americans called it "The Sphere" or "Those Crazy Fuckers." It was like extreme roller derby, with a ball, gone virtual. It was played in complete darkness. Only the ball, the track lines, and bits of the players' armor glowed as they raced around in a 360-degree sphere, trying to score by whipping the ball with their bare hands into a tiny pocket space not much bigger than the ball itself. It was one of the most intense games in the pro circuit since players could bite the virtual death while playing. Gameplay was three times faster than real life and sometimes upside down, so falling on their heads wasn't out of the question. Neither was slamming into each other at faster than full speed. The only thing that topped it in terms of brutality were the fighting games, like RAGE, and even a few versions of those fell short on casualties in comparison.

"Have you played it?" he asked.

I shook my head. "We don't have that game in the States."

"I see." He leaned toward me. "So, it's a little too rough for you Americans."

He winked.

Oh, let the trash talking begin.

"Really?" I grinned, and stepped up to him. "Plug into the RAGE arena sometime and we'll see who's too rough for whom."

His team erupted into a choir of ooooo's.

Erik didn't back down.

His gaze swept over my face, and his grin grew wider than I'd ever seen it. He was impressed. This time, it wasn't because of my love life.

Sweden, meet the warrior.

"Well, we've got to mingle," he said, taking a step back from me. He nodded at his team, and they started to drift away. "See you around."

They disappeared into the thick of the European clique, leaving me standing alone. Although everyone was facing each other, somehow it seemed like they were also facing away from me. Well, that wasn't bad, but things hadn't gone as well as I'd hoped, either.

Footsteps walked up behind me.

"Don't let the Europeans fool you. They act casual, but they're just as competitive as anyone."

I turned to find Cole standing behind me with a drink in his hand.

"Giving me tips?" I asked. "Aren't I the competition now?"

He smiled. "Can't we still be friends?"

My heart went a little soft. He might not have liked our team or me as management, but at least he was being professional about the whole thing. I could, too. Like he'd said, sometimes it just wasn't the right fit. And he'd been a teammate, even if just for a short while. I wanted what was best for all of them, even if it wasn't with my team.

I glanced back at the Europeans. "I didn't realize my love life was news overseas."

"It's not," he said. "They know about Rooke because they've already been studying you."

Already?

I shook my head. "But the teams were just revealed an hour ago."

"Like I said." He nodded again at the Europeans. I turned and looked at them, really looked. They casually glanced at the cell phones wrapped around their wrists, as if just checking the time. But then one of them would nudge another, point at something on the screen, then at one of the other teams. As my gaze flicked from one set of hands to the next, I witnessed one player pass a small bag to another. The color combination was unmistakable. Red on yellow. Blue on red. Hits of HP.

"They're already playing the game." Cole took a sip of his drink. Apparently, he'd missed the drug exchange. "Sizing each other up."

I shrugged. "Guess that's how they became the best in the world."

"You really want to talk about the best in the world?" He motioned off to the side. I looked in the same direction and landed on black clothes, blacker tattoos, and ice-blue eyes.

K-Rig.

They stood alone, other than the security and other person-nel buzzing around them. Arms crossed, still posed like they were in a photo shoot, they spoke only occasionally to each other. Well, if I was going to meet the competition, might as well jump into the deep end. I started walking toward them when Cole grabbed my arm.

"You're not actually going over there, are you?" he asked, disbelief in his voice.

"They're just people," I said. "Like anyone else here."

Cole didn't look too sure, but he released my arm.

"Good luck."

Luck. Although I kept reassuring myself that K-Rig was just another team, something told me I'd need it. With every step, my mouth grew a little drier, my chest a little tighter, like I was in the presence of royalty and wasn't sure how to act.

Three steps away from them, a hand came up in front of my face.

"Whoa." A man in a suit sidestepped into my path. "Can I help you?"

He was Korean, only a little taller than I was, and spoke smooth English, with only a faint hint of an accent. Their translator, maybe? I glanced between him and K-Rig, who failed to make eye contact.

"Just looking to shake hands, I guess."

"So are a lot of people," he said.

Ouch. Elitist much?

The translator cleared his throat and raised his chin slightly, so he was looking down at me, despite being only a few inches taller.

"Oh, I'm sorry," I said, sounding anything but sorry. "I thought we were all in the competition together."

"It'll be a competition for some."

I clenched my fists together behind my back. It was the safest place for them.

My gaze flicked back to K-Rig, who stood motionless, staring endlessly forward. A realm beyond anyone else. They were celebrities of the celebrities. The one percent of the one percent.

How perfect.

The translator stepped into my field of vision again.

"Maybe you should go."

Maybe I should punch you in the throat.

I stepped back but kept my fists behind me, despite my nails digging into my skin. Like K-Rig, the translator—or bodyguard, whoever he was—didn't falter. He wasn't going to let me through, and I wasn't about to show him why they call me the warrior. I was calmer than that now. There were a lot of witnesses in the room, too, but that had *nothing* to do with it. I glanced once more at K-Rig, still motionless. Every stance they took was practiced. Every breath passing through their chest was rehearsed. They trained to absolute perfection, in the real world and the virtual one.

Then there was me, Kali Ling. Former party girl and tabloid fodder. Quick to anger and even quicker to overreact. If there was a way to fuck things up, I usually found it and invited it in to party. I'd accomplished a few things in my short career. But next to K-Rig, I was a low-class wannabe.

So much for getting to know the competition.

I wandered away, lost in thought. The room was a blur as I drifted through the crowd, weaving between the teams. A few of them called out to me.

"Hey, Defiance. How did you get into this competition?"

"Kali Ling? What are you doing here? Aren't there higher-rated teams in the U.S.?"

"Isn't this your first year as team owner? Are you sure you're ready for this?"

I smiled and laughed off their comments. K-Rig wasn't the

only one putting on a show. Inside, I was drowning. I moved aimlessly through the room, a fish caught in the current, until I blinked and found myself standing next to the windows again, overlooking that magnificent view. Wispy clouds stretched across the moon, splintering the moonlight into fractured spotlights over the midnight-blue landscape. Waves lapped at the water's edge, but the lazy, rippling motion did nothing to calm the storm in my churning stomach.

What the hell were we doing here? I was proud of my team, and of my own accomplishments, but we didn't belong in this room of the elite. We were five years away from this level of competition, at least. I glanced over the room again. Over the European teams already studying us. Over K-Rig not even acknowledging our existence. Then to Jessica Salt, who was expecting me to take her place. Even more than that, the VGL had promised a competition unlike anything the world had seen before, and they weren't just talking about bringing all the world's teams together. The final marathon round was created specifically to push us to our absolute limits, and even the standard matchups would be full of surprises. What had I signed up for?

What had I signed my team up for?

I pressed my forehead against the window, and the cool glass brought a chill to my entire body. I sighed. Training started tomorrow, I reminded myself. We needed it.

Double time.

LEVEL 2:

THE TOURNAMENT

CHAPTER 7

Gamer boot camp started the next morning, bright and early.

I'm neither of those things.

At 6:30 a.m., my alarm blared. I groaned against my pillow and smashed the clock until it stopped chirping. I told myself to get up. Surprisingly, I got a reply.

Fuck you.

Whether the thought was actually directed at me or the early-morning sunlight piercing my bedroom drapes, I wasn't sure. Probably both.

We had two weeks before the tournament began and one week before they announced the first round's matchups. As Tamachi had said, there was no preseason, and we'd be going straight to the Death Match. We had fourteen days to train to the max before we faced the top teams in the world.

I swore at myself again.

Well, this was turning out just like any other morning.

I dragged myself out of bed, pulled on a spandex training top and crop pants, and gathered my hair into a low ponytail. This was my battle gear. In the real world, at least. I ate breakfast with the team. Low-fat, high-protein athlete-perfect breakfasts.

Then it started.

Four fricking hours.

Four hours of cardio, weights, gymnastics, weapons training, and hand-to-hand combat. Sure, we were all already in shape and had trained regularly in the off-season.

That didn't mean jack shit.

Going into a tournament other than RAGE meant a new kind of training. I had sent our trainers some footage of us inside the game, so they could tailor workouts for us. At seven thirty they arrived, and the torture began. They'd created circuits combining weights, gymnastics, and cardio for endurance, stamina, strength, and flexibility. Nonstop running, rowing, box jumps, pull-ups, skipping, squats, dead lifts, blood, and tears. Quick, repetitive, explosive exercises that left our lungs and muscles burning. One minute rest. Then next circuit. More blood. More tears.

Especially tears.

"There are no reps," the trainers barked. "You go until you collapse. And then you do more."

Taking advantage of the two-story ceiling in the training room, they had us climbing up poles and jumping onto mats. Flipping, somersaulting, and twisting each way as we tried to land on our feet.

"This is not the RAGE tournaments," they instructed. "Those battles are fought on the ground. You have to think of this game as three-dimensional. The vertical is just as important to your fight as the horizontal."

Then we climbed walls.

"The rooftops are your best vantage point against your enemy. They're less likely to see you coming, and attacking from above gives you an edge."

The buildings in the game were all a minimum of three stories high and clung to the sides of the road, creating a tight, claustrophobic feel to the world. In the training room, Lily raced up the walls, catapulted off with pure grace, and landed on her feet every time. Looks like we'd found our MVP of the game.

There was a reason for this level of training beyond looking perfectly chiseled for the cameras. In pro gaming, your physical self *was* your avatar. The faster, stronger, or more agile you were in real life transferred into the game. So we trained to maximize our abilities until we could no longer stand up. And then some.

Whenever one of us did collapse on the mats, trembling, making mewling sounds that weren't quite human and probably preceded death, we were rewarded with a protein shake. Which, conveniently, came with a straw, in case anyone tried the excuse of not being able to lift the cup to their mouths.

Currently, that was me.

I lay flat on my back on the mats, an empty protein shake in hand. My vision blurred as I stared up at the ceiling. Were those tears in my eyes, or was I peering into the afterlife?

The mats smacked beside me as another body went down. I glanced over. Hannah lay on her back, panting heavily. Rogue strands of hair that had escaped her ponytail were clumped to her neck and the sides of her face.

A trainer appeared over her and handed her a protein shake.

"Five minutes," he told her, and glanced down at me. "Ling, your break is almost up."

I groaned as he walked away and let my limbs flap against the mat.

"Hey, what's wrong?" Hannah said, taking a sip of protein through her straw. "Exercise is good for you."

"So is sleeping."

She laughed.

One of the trainers appeared over me again.

"Get up, Ling," he said. "Or the tabloids will print that you spend more time training on your back than on your feet."

Asshole. If I could have lifted my arms, he'd be dead.

That was just the morning.

The afternoon was spent in the virtual world, running match-ups against the computer. This, too, was a whole new ball game.

It had artificial intelligence, so it evolved. The more matchups we played, the more the game seemed to understand us. Once you've played them enough times, most video games become easy to beat. The first time you try a racing game, you struggle to place in the top. But eventually you're flying through every course, even at the hardest level. This was completely different. The game was learning. There was no highest level. There was no end in sight. We'd get faster, it got faster. We learned short-cuts, and our digital opponents cut us off at the next corner.

Currently, Rooke and I stood atop a roof overlooking our flag, watching Derek, Hannah, and Lily attempt to score. Rooke and I had purposely held back, so they could fight against the maximum number of players, and we could witness the battle and offer tips. Derek fended off a single attacker, as did Hannah, who was glowing faint blue with the flag. The three remaining opponents circled Lily.

"Why is the computer ganging up on Lily?" Rooke asked as he watched the fight. He knelt to get a closer look. "She doesn't even have the flag."

I knew why. Lily had kicked ass in the previous matchup.

"She's the reason we scored last time," I said. "The game is learning."

"Learning what?"

"Us." I paused, realizing how strange that sounded. "Give it a week, and these pods will be reading our minds."

He considered that for a minute as he continued to watch

the fight below. His expression went tight, and he exhaled slowly through his nose. He didn't like that, apparently.

I sat down on the roof next to him. Well, this was familiar. Back when Rooke had first joined the team, we used to sneak off to the roof of our old facility and talk.

I glanced at him.

"So, how are you doing?"

He went still.

"Why do you ask?"

There was an edge in his voice that almost seemed defensive. Either that, or things were still awkward between us. My guess was on the latter since I felt it, too.

"Well," I began, "we've each had our problems with drugs and the virtual world, and I just thought—"

"I'm fine."

I leaned forward a little, trying to catch his eye. He kept his gaze on the fight though I was pretty sure he saw me.

"You know, it's okay not to be fine."

He was quiet for a minute. "These new pods are safer, right?"

"Yeah. Supposedly."

"Then maybe you should stop hunting for an issue where there isn't one."

Passive-aggressive much? This was all circling back to our relationship or lack of one. During the car ride to the all-star dinner, he seemed like he was coming around, and I'd seen a glimpse of my former friend. But ever since, he'd reverted back to his cold and distant self. I bit my lip to keep myself from coming back with *it ended because of you* and *you cut me off first*. Nope, I could be the bigger person here. Although if I had to bite my lip every time, I'd end up chewing it off before the end of the day.

In the fight below, Lily went down, and her three attackers

piled on. She'd be out in an instant, and that meant all three would turn on Hannah.

"Derek, get to Hannah," I instructed through the mic.

Derek ripped a sword through his opponent and slammed into Hannah's, giving her the time to break away. She lunged for the base, her hand touched down, and she scored.

Another match down. So far, we weren't doing too badly, even with the computer stepping up the challenge every round. Hopefully, it would be enough to prepare us for the all-star teams.

After running through so many practice rounds, I'd noticed something. There was a split second when someone scored where time seemed to stop. The virtual world became a visual bath of pastel neon lights against the dreary grays, where the air was still and yet animated by invisible, continuous rolling code. Mist clung to the air. Absolute silence blanketed the city blocks.

In that moment was peace.

Unfortunately, peace didn't last very long for me. After practice every day, I would return to my office to deal with owner stuff. First day was seven new calls and twenty-two e-mails. Then thirteen calls and fifty-eight e-mails. Every day the pile grew.

I started clicking through my e-mails, but soon they all started to seem the same, like: We need a new photo shoot by the end of the week if we're to run the ads before the tournament begins.

And: You're still captain, right? Because we're paying to see you as captain.

And: You were supposed to be fighting in the RAGE tournaments. You should have run the switch by us first.

With every e-mail, pressure built around my temples, and massaging them provided no relief. How was I supposed to practice with the team night and day, maintain our image, appear in public, and handle all this owner stuff on my own? I could hire an assistant to help me sort e-mails and take calls, but my budget was already straining. I wasn't used to the demands (read: didn't know what the hell I was doing) when it came to managing money on this scale. I wasn't about to add another staff member when I was already stressing about the ones I had. But maybe I didn't need to hire someone new to help out.

I sent a message to Derek's phone.

My office, please.

While I waited, I rested my head on the desk, but it did nothing for my mounting headache. After a minute, his footsteps approached and he hovered there for a minute.

"You okay?"

I lifted my head. "Not even coffee can fix this."

"What's wrong?"

"I can't handle everything. Between practice all day, publicity, coming up with strategies for the team, managing the sponsors, and all the other owner stuff—"

He held up a hand. "So, you need help?"

I offered him a meek smile. "Yes, please."

He stumbled back and lowered himself into a chair, as if I'd just said something shocking.

"What's with you?"

He put a hand over his heart. "You said 'please.' This is bad." I frowned, and he grinned in response. "What do you need?"

I let a slow breath pass through my lips. This wasn't going to be an easy thing to ask.

"Can you take over some of the captain responsibilities, like studying the other teams and coming up with strategies?"

He considered it for a moment. "Sure. I guess that makes us co-captains?"

My stomach clenched. I was worried he'd bring that up.

"Well . . ."

He narrowed his sights on me. "What?"

"I need to keep the title. The sponsors want to see me as captain. It's important to them."

He thought about that awhile longer. "Let me get this straight. You want me to be captain without the credit? As in, I do the work, but you keep the title?"

"I'm asking a favor. Just this once."

"As the team's owner?"

"As a friend."

His face went a bit soft, but he didn't look entirely convinced.

"It will only be for this tournament," I added. "Things are just crazy because of the all-stars. Plus, once we're a more established team, I'll have more sway over the sponsors. But for now, we need to do what they want. They want to see me as captain."

"Things aren't exactly the way you'd thought they would be, huh?"

In a word, no. We were only a week into the tournament, and technically the game hadn't even begun.

Derek's gaze drifted down to my desk as he thought to himself, and the expression on his face looked like he was counting his teeth with his tongue. "Okay," he finally said. "I'll take over as captain. Without the title. But it's just this once."

"Just this once. Promise. And thanks."

With that, my stomach unclenched, and my headache actually dialed back a few decibels, but it didn't stop an awkward silence from settling between us.

My tablet chimed on my desk. What did the sponsors want

now? But when I glanced down at it, I found a message from our former teammate, Cole.

Hey. You there?

I grinned and typed back.

Contacting the enemy again?

Another message popped up.

Did you see this?

He forwarded a statement just released from the VGL. My brow furrowed, and Derek noticed. He nodded at my tablet.
"What's up?"
"I don't know."
I tapped the attachment on the message. It opened.

VGL to Keep Tournament Brackets Secret for the All-Star Death Match.

Oh, fantastic. I flashed the headline at Derek. His mouth dropped open, and he sputtered a few times. "But . . . they tell us, right? I mean, we'll know."
Would we? I messaged Cole.

Is that just for the public?

Nope. Us, too. We won't know until we're plugged in.

Great. So much for prepping strategy against the other team.

If we didn't know who we were facing, we'd have to prepare for any scenario.

I messaged Cole again.

Is this for every matchup?

Nope. Just the Death Match.

I handed Derek my tablet.

"For the Death Match, no one will know. Not even us."

He studied the screen for a minute, like the words wouldn't sink in. "You mean, they're not telling us who we're up against until we're literally inside the match?"

"Seems that way."

"How are we supposed to strategize if we don't know who we're against?"

I shrugged. "Welcome to the all-stars."

"Kali?" Dr. Renner poked her head into the office. Her gaze flicked to Derek and back to me again. "Sorry to interrupt, but we have a problem."

What now?

"Do you want me to handle it?" Derek asked. "You know, as team captain?"

I frowned, not knowing if it was a bad joke, or if the favor I'd asked was bothering him more than he was letting on. But before I could ask, he traded places with Dr. Renner and left the office.

Dr. Renner stood in front of my desk, clutching her tablet to her chest, not saying anything for several moments.

"What's wrong?" I pressed.

She clicked her tongue against the roof of her mouth and glanced down at her tablet before holding it up in front of my face. My eyes traced across a single word I'd seen a little too much of lately.

FAILED.

You've got to be kidding me.

I pointed at a word longer than my finger on the screen. "What's that—"

"It's the chemical name for HP."

All the feeling drained from my body. Someone on my team was hitting up.

Dr. Renner pulled the tablet back and glanced at the top of the screen. "Did you see whose test this is?"

"Yes. I see whose test this is."

I stood from my desk and headed for the exit.

"Kali."

I turned around. Dr. Renner had clutched the tablet to her chest and pulled a breath through her teeth. If I didn't know better, I'd say the good doctor was worried.

"Please be calm."

I smiled.

Me? Of course.

CHAPTER 8

A jackhammer would have gone easier on the door.

I stood in front of the locked bedroom door, my fists pounding in rapid succession. *Thap, thap, thap.* After a few seconds, it opened.

Rooke stood in the doorway.

"What's your problem?"

I lowered my arms, panting hard, anger trembling in every nerve. But somehow, looking at his face, the rage flooded out until I felt numb. This had to be a mistake. I mean, this was Rooke.

Rooke.

Self-actualized, self-disciplined, self-everything Rooke.

He folded his arms and tilted his head as he waited for my answer. My mouth opened, and eventually, the words trickled out.

"You failed your drug test."

His reaction?

Nothing.

Well, to the untrained eye, almost nothing. His face remained blank, but he swallowed thick, and the muscles in his arms twitched.

"Okay . . ." he said slowly, drawing the word out. I wasn't sure if it was a statement or a question. He seemed confused over it more than anything else.

I took a step toward him. "Is it a mistake?"

Say it's a mistake.

"What do you think?"

I sputtered. "What the hell am I supposed to think?"

Seriously, what was I supposed to think? My brain at that moment might as well have been a screen saver of a fish tank. A couple of goldfish, a bobbing, plastic scuba diver, and some air bubbles.

"I would like to think it's wrong," I continued, "but I don't see you jumping to deny it."

And he still didn't. He said nothing and blinked a few times, then just disappeared into his room.

My heart thumped against my chest. What was happening? Why was he hiding? No, this couldn't be what I thought it was.

I glanced down at the division between his room and the rest of the house. Normally, I didn't enter my teammate's rooms. The bedrooms were designated as personal space, and I planned to keep it that way. But, in that moment, it was a threshold I knew I had to cross. I closed my eyes, and my rib cage tightened around my chest. Despite Rooke's dodging, I knew what was coming. No matter what he said, or didn't say, this was a moment that would affect the team for the rest of the tournament.

I crossed the line and stepped into his room.

Though it had only been a short time since Cole had left, the room had already transformed into something else. When we'd first moved in, I'd told my teammates to decorate their rooms however they wanted. Each was their space, and I wanted them to feel like this was their home as much as mine. Boy, did they listen to me. Shortly after moving in, they'd all created rooms that were complete reflections of their personalities. Especially Hannah.

Her room was peach-colored. And fluffy.

Rooke was no exception. He'd made the room his own. The walls were the same color, a shade somewhere between soft green and gray. A new bookshelf ran the length of the far wall, floor to ceiling, on the opposite side of the bed. Every shelf, top to bottom, was filled with books. Yes, real books made out of real paper. Nowadays, nearly everything was paperless, and real books cost more than most people could afford. At least I knew how he spent his tournament winnings.

Besides the books, a few antique swords hung from the sidewall, and a collection of relics sat on the dresser. Black sheets, gray walls. Together, it was one hundred percent Rooke. Subdued, masculine, and just a little old-fashioned.

Rooke was sitting on his bed, back bowed forward, elbows resting on his knees, like he was trying to close in on himself. His jaw was hard, his eyes were cold, and suddenly, he was that icy, barren man he'd been when we had first met.

I took a breath, crossed my arms, and forced an even tone to my voice.

"Why did your drug test come back positive for HP?"

"Kali . . ." His voice trailed off, and he shook his head.

I took a step toward him.

"Are you using again?"

Another step.

"Rooke, what the hell—"

He exploded and shot to his feet. "I relapsed. Is that what you want to hear? I fucked up."

The world stopped.

Oh, no.

I fought my knees from buckling. He stood at the foot of the bed, glaring at me, breathing hard. I, on the other hand, couldn't breathe at all. He fucked up. He relapsed. Is that what I wanted to hear? Shit, no. Shit, shit, shit. It wasn't true. It couldn't be true.

As I stood there, doing nothing but blinking for several seconds, the feeling returned to my body, and I found myself thumbing my taijitu pendant. I glanced down at it, and the sight of it reminded me of the values I strove to live my life by even if I failed sometimes.

Stay calm, I told myself. He won't open up if you aren't calm. This is just a moment in time, and you can get through it.

I tucked the pendant into my shirt.

"How long has this been going on?" I asked.

Rooke paced around the foot of the bed, back and forth. Looking everywhere in the room but at me.

"Awhile."

Well, that was completely nondescript but not unlike Rooke.

"I have it under control," he added.

Whoa. Oh, wow. This was bad. Denial overload.

"Actually," I said. "I have a drug test that proves otherwise."

"And what I choose to do with my life is my business. Not yours."

My heart sunk. I'd said the same things to him when I was in denial over my own problems.

"You're wrong," I said simply. "What you choose to do affects the team. It's not just your life. It's theirs, too."

He scoffed, shook his head, and started pacing around the foot of the bed again. As he paced, my mind drifted back over the last few days.

"When did you even . . ."

Snippets flashed across my mind. Getting past The Wall. Meeting the all-stars at the reveal.

The reveal.

"The other night. At the all-star reveal." With every fractured sentence, my voice got louder. There goes balanced and calm. "You got high at the all-star reveal?" Then another revelation smacked into me, like I'd been pelleted with a brick. "Is that why you left the team when I took over? You were hiding this from me."

He started pacing in faster, tighter circles, like he was in a cage, and it was getting smaller by the second. "I was protecting the team from my screwup. I wasn't about to let you lose everything you'd worked for because of me."

"But . . . why didn't you just tell me? I would have understood."

"Exactly. You would have understood. You would have dropped everything and put your dreams aside to help me. I wasn't going to let that happen. Not after everything you worked for."

I took a step back. I should have known it was something like this. Not the drugs. God, no, not the drugs. But if Rooke had bailed, I should have known his intentions were more noble than selfish. He'd always had a chivalrous streak, putting others before himself. Tears stung my eyes as the memories seeped in. Flashes of the nights he'd helped me overcome my addictions, stayed right by my side the entire time and helped me hide it from the world.

I swallowed thick.

"Accomplishments mean more when you get to share them with people." I cleared my throat a few times, trying to push out the next sentence. "And you're right. I'm not going to risk everything because of this. You have to get clean, or you have to leave."

He gaped at me. "Kali, I'm trying. But you can't kick me off the team. You can't replace me in the all-star tournament. You might have to forfeit."

"That's right. Like I said, this affects the whole team." I swallowed down the thick knot in my throat. "You need to talk with Dr. Renner. You need a trained therapist to work through this with you."

He said nothing but started pacing again. I closed my eyes and took a breath. I knew what I had to say next. He had to admit to everyone what he had done, and Rooke was a deeply private person. When I was struggling, he'd kept my problems a secret, but if I was trying to run my team the right way, it was only fair that they know what was going on.

"And," I added, "you can tell the team, or I will."

He froze, and his jaw went tight. I knew he wouldn't like it, but it was time to rip the Band-Aid off.

"It's none of their business," he said quietly.

"It is, even if you can't see it." I took a step toward the door. "I'm telling them now. Are you coming?"

He folded his arms and just stared.

Guess that's a *no*.

I kept my head high and headed for the exit. When I reached the doorway, he spoke.

"Are you going to report the test?"

It was my turn to freeze. What was I going to do about that test? If I reported it as is, we'd take a penalty and have to play the Death Match with only four players. Against one of the top teams in the world.

And that was only half the problem.

Once the media got ahold of it, Rooke would be on the cover of every tabloid in the States. He sure as hell didn't deserve the backlash that would follow, and given his introverted personality, it would do nothing but hinder his recovery, *if* I could even get him there.

I lingered in the doorway, shifting my weight from one foot to the other.

"I'll do what I think is best."

He scoffed. "You mean whatever's best for you."

It wasn't what I meant at all, but I wasn't going to argue with him, either. At this point, it was useless. So, I said nothing and walked out. He slammed the door shut behind me, and the sound from the impact shook my soul. My throat grew thick. Everything inside ached. Not just because of his actions or words.

Because I'd done the same to him.

Last year, when I was down this rabbit hole, I'd screamed at him. Slammed the door in his face. Told him he was an idiot. Now I knew what it was like to be on the other side. To watch someone you cared about play Russian roulette with their life, believing they were invincible, and that their actions had no impact on the people around them.

I made it to the kitchen before I broke down.

My breaths came in heavy gasps as I leaned against the counter. Tears streamed down my cheeks, and my whole body shook. The sadness inside turned to anger, and I punched the countertop. Then again, and again. I hammered my fists against the counter until my knuckles threatened to break.

"Kali?"

Hannah stood at the edge of the kitchen. "You know we have punching bags for that." She grinned, until her gaze flicked down to my wet cheeks, and her face fell.

"What's wrong?" she gasped, rushing to me with open arms.

"I just . . . I can't . . . I don't know . . ." I choked out.

Hannah wrapped her arms around my waist and pulled me into a tight hug. She hushed me.

"You don't have to say anything."

My knees gave out, and we sunk to the floor with her arms still wrapped around me. I gripped her tight as the tears just kept pouring out of my eyes. My knuckles throbbed and pulsed with little lightning bolts of pain, but I didn't care. I only gripped her tighter.

She held me, hushing me, stroking her fingers through my hair, and I sobbed in her arms until I had no more tears.

Hannah gathered up the team while I washed my face and blinked back any evidence of my sobbing.

We met in the living room. Everyone sat on the couch while I stood in front of them, wondering how to break the news.

Rooke didn't show.

My knuckles still throbbed. Nothing was broken, but they'd be black-and-blue tomorrow. I prayed they'd heal in time for the matchup on Saturday. If not, the injury would transfer, and I'd be playing the first matchup of the game with a weak grip and a weaker punch.

"Rooke's drug test came back positive for HP," I finally said. No point in sugarcoating it.

They all sat there, stunned. It was quiet in the room for several long seconds until Derek finally scoffed, like he didn't believe it. "That has to be a mistake."

"It's not."

"But, this is Rooke we're talking about—"

"He's had problems before," I reminded him. "Dr. Renner looked at the test herself, and Rooke pretty much admitted it."

"What do we do about this?" Hannah asked.

"We have to be supportive but firm with him. And on top of the no drugs on the premises rule, this house is now alcohol free, at least for the remainder of the tournament. I don't care if you drink at the clubs. Just not here."

Everyone nodded.

"And if he doesn't stop," I continued, "he's off the team."

Derek leaned forward. "But, if we try to replace a player,

there's no way we could train someone to fit in with the team. Not that fast. We'd be out of the tournament for sure."

"I know."

They all exchanged glances. I frowned at their reaction.

"It's the game or his health, guys. I hope we all know which is more important."

They all glanced down at the floor, or off to the side, guilty faces all around.

"Yeah, sorry Kali," one of the girls muttered, so quietly I wasn't sure who.

"So, he's out of the Death Match then?" Derek asked.

I faltered. "Yeah, I'm still figuring that out."

"What do you mean—"

I held up a hand. "Just let me worry about it."

He didn't. After the meeting in the living room, Derek followed me to my office and sat across from my desk.

"What are you doing about that test?" he asked.

I sighed as I collapsed into my chair. "Honestly, I don't know. We'd have to take the penalty and go four on five against one of the top teams in the world. Plus, if the media gets ahold of this, I don't know how he'll handle it or what that will mean for his recovery."

Derek was quiet for a minute as he stared at the floor, lost in thought. Then his gaze flicked up to mine.

"You have to report it."

I blinked. "I *have* to?"

"Yes."

"And if I don't?"

"Then I'm off the team. I'll finish out the tournament, but that's it."

My mouth dropped open. "What?" I studied him for a second. "You're bluffing."

"Is that what's important to you? Wondering if I'm bluffing?" He stood from his chair and leaned over the desk toward me. "You took over the team to change things. To make a stand. And now, the first time something goes wrong, you're thinking about backtracking."

"This is different—"

"No. It's not," he said simply. "You have to draw the line and hold it. It doesn't bow for anyone or any reason. Otherwise, what's the point?"

"If you think this is about my feelings for him—"

"I sure as fuck hope not because if you really cared about him, you'd report that test and not even think twice about it. Giving him a way out is enabling. Taking the stand makes the consequences real. That's what he needs."

I stood to face him, leaning across the desk, so we were only inches apart. "Is that what you want? We don't know who we're facing in the Death Match. We need him in the game."

He slammed a hand on the desk. "No. We need him in real life. That's what matters." We locked up, both breathing hard from the heat of the argument and neither backing down.

"We can take the loss, Kali," he continued. "It'll only knock us into the losers' bracket. You just said it yourself in the living room. His life is more important than the game. We have to be firm. No excuses."

It went silent again between us as we settled into our staring contest. But inside, I was wavering. Was he right?

Derek pulled back and stood straight. "You know how I feel about it. I'll leave you to it."

He walked out of the office, leaving me alone. I watched him go and stared at the door long after, until I finally collapsed back into my chair.

What was I going to do?

I could report the test, take the penalty, and go in with only four players. No matter who we faced off against, they would still be one of the best teams in the world, and we'd undoubtedly get knocked into the losers' bracket. And, on top of everything, the media would rip apart Rooke's reputation and put someone who hated the limelight right in the middle of it.

Or, I could fake the results and go against everything I was trying to fix. I'd lose Derek's respect, and any I had for myself. And I'd be giving Rooke an excuse to get high again because if I tampered with one test, I might tamper with more. But with him, we'd be full strength in the game, have a chance at the winners' bracket, and it would save him from becoming the paparazzi's latest victim.

Either way could make things worse for Rooke and the rest of the team. My stomach churned at the thought. Damned if I do, damned if I don't.

It hit me, right then. I didn't know why it took so long, but the realization slammed into me with the force of a freight train.

Their fates were in my hand.

The whole team. With every decision I made, I could make their futures or crush their careers. Their livelihoods, their dreams, all rested on my ability to lead the team on a whole new level. And, of course, instead of keeping things simple, I'd signed them up for the most insane tournament the world had ever seen.

We weren't ready for this.

I wasn't ready for this.

I rested my elbows on the table and buried my face in my hands.

What the hell had I done?

CHAPTER 9

"What should I do?"

I walked into Dr. Renner's office later that day and plopped down in the chair across from her. The words just started spilling out of my mouth.

"Rooke's drug test. I can't report it. The media will rip him apart. But I can't let him get away with this, either."

Dr. Renner looked up from her tablet and met my eyes. "I can't answer that for you."

I tossed my arms up. "Neither can I. There's no clear-cut answer here."

She said nothing for a moment, sat back in her chair, and laced her fingers across her stomach. "Is this all that's bothering you?"

In a word, no. Despite the fact that we'd split when he cut me out of his life, he was still a friend. A teammate. That meant something.

I cleared my throat in a poor attempt to dislogde the growing lump inside it.

"He was the one who helped me," I finally said. "When I was all fucked up, he was the one at my side, making it seem so easy. We could be at the clubs, around alcohol and drugs, and it didn't even bother him. That's what made me think I could do it, too. And now we're heading into this crazy tournament, and I can't know what will happen. I mean, you should have seen the all-star dinner and how insane the fans were. This is going to be the biggest tournament in the history of anything. I know these new pods are easier on a gamer's mind, but what about the pressure? The intensity of our training schedule? He already relapsed, and that wasn't inside this crazy-ass tournament. How can I know he can make it through all this?"

Dr. Renner pressed a finger to her lips for a second as she thought.

"You can't know," she finally said.

"Exactly. I can't know. He didn't admit that he was having problems until I caught him. He just pulled away. Cut me out of his life."

Dr. Renner made a calming motion with her hand. "It's normal for addicts to distance themselves when they slip. Husbands and wives do it to each other even though they've been together for twenty years. This is completely expected behavior. Deep down, he's ashamed. He's trying to hide."

"No offense, Doc, but nothing about addiction is normal."

"Relapse is." A slight smile touched the corner of her lips. "You're all still human even if the rest of the world doesn't think so."

That was the truth. To the rest of the world, we were invincible. Our daily grind of physical torture and high-protein diets wasn't just for the game. We were all supposed to look a certain way. Embody the epitome of the human physique and condition. There were Olympians, and then there were gamers.

Years ago, when pro gaming made the switch to immersive virtual reality, gamers themselves replaced the characters in video games, and our body expectations were just as unrealistic. Men with their eight-pack abs and chiseled jaws. Women with their perfect breasts and impossibly toned physiques. To the world, we weren't people. We were characters.

Objectification personified.

Dr. Renner tapped a fingernail against her tablet several times as she studied me. "Try thinking of it this way: When you have a hard decision to make, what do you usually turn to for help?"

"You."

My answer brought out an unconventional laugh from the doctor.

"And?" she asked, once her chuckles subsided.

". . . Rooke."

My heart twisted at the answer because the person I used to go to for help was now the one who needed it.

Dr. Renner chuckled again but much softer this time.

"I'm not talking about a person, Kali. I mean your spirituality," she said. I curled my lip. "And I know you don't like that word."

"What, spiritual? Of course I don't. We live in an age of science. It fixes everything. We ran into a lack of resources, and science gave us space mining and exploration. Then we had limited access to education in various parts of the world. Virtual reality now takes students to the depths of the oceans or to the Mars colony, no matter where they live."

"Science didn't invent these things. People did. They believed they could fix a problem and make life easier for someone else. And that starts with faith. I don't mean religion, necessarily, but a belief in what is right."

"But that's the problem. There is no right answer—"

She held up a hand. "There is. You need to put your feelings aside and think about what's right. Not what society thinks is right, or the VGL, or even the team. This is about you. You started this journey as team owner because you wanted to do the right thing. Now you're in a position to do exactly that." She crossed her legs, looked me straight in the eye, and took a breath. "So, what feels right to *you*?"

Nothing felt right to me. That's why I was here. But Dr. Renner was right. Asking her to supply me with the answer to my problems wasn't the way to handle the situation. And I knew how. I knew the way to clear my emotions and get to the root of my problems.

I pushed myself out of the chair and started walking toward the exit.

"Where are you going?" she called, as I left the room.

"To meditate."

I headed to the training room. This late in the day, it was abandoned. I pulled open the doors to the garden. A warm breeze brushed against my face, and suddenly, I remembered why I'd chosen this house. Despite the technology, every room had a sense of the real to it, whether it was the wood floors, the sunlight streaming through the windows, or the rich, natural tones on the walls. Some days, if I stopped long enough to just sit and listen to the quiet stillness of the atmosphere here, it felt as if the house itself had a soul.

I stepped into the garden. The cool grass weaved through my toes. I sat cross-legged next to the pond and breathed deep, inhaling the scents of azaleas and peonies. Air expanded my lungs and left again, each time taking with it another ounce of stress.

I closed my eyes.

Cleared my mind.

Let go of my emotions.

For a while, I thought about nothing. I just sat listening to the distant sounds of the city and the water as it lapped against the rocks. After a while, I'd calmed myself enough that I could actually think about the problem at hand without my insides screaming.

What was the right thing?

In Taoism, nothing was truly good or bad, and fighting against the tide created turmoil. Disharmony. Simply allowing things to be as they were created peace.

I don't know how long I sat there, contemplating. But when I opened my eyes again, the sun had set, and I knew what to do.

I calmly walked to my office, sat down at my computer, and sent in the test. Unaltered. This was why I'd fought so hard and bought out the team in the first place. This was what I'd set out to do. No corruption. I allowed the test to be what it was, a representation of the truth. It was the right thing. I was sure of it. Still, my stomach was a roller coaster, looping, flip-flopping. I was about two seconds away from revisiting lunch. I folded my arms on the table and rested my forehead within them, as if my own limbs could serve as a safety net from the reality of the situation.

I'd just handed the media Rooke's reputation and private life on a silver platter. Come morning, they'd rip him apart.

I didn't sleep.

The entire night, I tossed and turned in my bed, worrying over what would happen now that I'd reported the test. The day before, I'd been sure it was the right thing to do. But after a night of insomnia, my confidence had waned. So, before the rest of the house came to life, I'd gone straight to the kitchen and grabbed a cup of coffee, hoping somehow it would have the same effect as alcohol and give me the liquid courage I needed to face him.

In other news, the fact that I was naturally awake before the sun came up for the second time that month must have been a sign of the apocalypse.

But now I had a plan to win him over. Rooke loved three things: philosophy, martial arts, and books. So, sometime in the middle of the night, I'd ordered a hardcover copy of a Baguazhang instruction guide, complete with two sets of deerhorn knives. Before the crack of dawn, a drone had dropped it on the doorstep. I'd also downloaded a virtual instructor, which I could project off my tablet anywhere in the house. Baguazhang was a Taoist martial art, based on the philosophical concept of the Bagua—an eight-sided symbol said to represent the basis of reality. It was a martial art he'd never studied—at least, I didn't think so—and was based on Taoist philosophy about the concepts of reality. I'd have that boy wrapped around my finger by sunset. I hoped.

As expected, Rooke walked into the kitchen before any of my other teammates. He didn't even look at me seated at the table. Instead, he headed right for the fridge and grabbed a bottle of water.

"I reported the test," I said. Might as well get it over with.

He froze with his head still poked inside the fridge, but I'm sure the irony was lost on him. Slowly, he stood straight, shut the door, and turned to face me. He stared directly into my eyes, not blinking, as he processed my words. I fought with myself not to fidget or look away from his gaze. What was he thinking? Did he hate me for it?

After several seconds without a word, I spoke in his place.

"I still expect you in the training room with us."

"What's the point?" he asked. "I'm out of the Death Match."

He didn't have to say he was angry with me. His tone was enough. I had expected this kind of reaction. Not only was

Rooke someone who preferred privacy, but he also had high expectations of everyone around him—especially himself. And since he was struggling with addiction again, I couldn't really know what was driving his emotions. Him, the drugs, or the withdrawals.

He just needs time, I told myself. I took a breath and kept my tone neutral. "You're part of this team. We train together."

He stared at me a few more moments before his gaze flicked down and landed on the book. His eyebrow twitched.

Gotcha.

"What's that?"

I glanced around, like I didn't know what he was talking about. "What?"

"That." He nodded at the book and took a swig of his water. "You reading it?"

No, I'm using it as a coaster.

"Just starting it. Have you?"

He walked up to the table, eyes fixed on the book. "Actually, no." He glanced over the title a few times. "Are you learning this form of martial art?"

"I'd like to start," I said, taking a sip of my coffee. "But it would be easier with a partner."

He looked down and shook his head. He saw right through my plan and knew I was looking for him to join me. "It would be easier with a virtual simulation."

"I've added an instructor to my tablet, but I don't want a virtual partner. They aren't as easy to hurt."

I slid the book across the table.

Take it.

He remained standing at the edge of the table, but he hadn't taken his eyes off the book, either.

"It recommends studying with a real partner," I added,

emphasizing the word *real*. Last year, when we'd first been on a team together, he'd emphasized the importance of appreciating what was real instead of what was virtual. As virtual gaming stars, it was all too easy to get caught up in a superior digital world and leave reality behind.

Finally, Rooke sat at the table and pulled the book to him.

I grinned. "Wanna start tonight?"

He flipped the book open and didn't even look up when he spoke. "In the training room?"

"I was thinking the garden outside."

He nodded. "Yeah, yeah. Good idea."

Hook, line, and sinker.

After breakfast, we headed for the training room. As we walked in, Hannah was flicking madly through her phone. Lily leaned against her, eyes pinpointed on the screen. When they realized Rooke was present, the girls slid the phone out of sight.

Subtle, ladies.

I could only imagine the tabloid gossip. The media and public attention on the all-star teams was at a frenzy, and a scandal like this was seal meat in shark-infested waters.

"You know what?" I said, raising my voice over the noise of the training room. "No phones during training. Hand them over." I took Derek's and Rooke's first. Surprisingly, Rooke handed his over without hesitation. Guess he didn't want to know what was being said about him.

"You have to be one hundred percent present," I continued. "The media and the outside world don't exist when you're in this room. Understand?"

I went to take Hannah's, but she hung on.

"Uh, Kali," Hannah began as she leaned toward me and lowered her voice. "You realize this is exactly the same thing Clarence did, right?"

I halted. Clarence, our previous team owner, had also taken away our phones. But this was different. He'd taken away our phones for control. I was doing it for the sake of the team.

"This isn't the same thing. I don't care what you do after training. But in here, we focus."

Hannah glanced between me and the phone a few times and eventually let go. When I finished collecting the phones, Derek took up a stance at the head of the room.

"Since we don't know who we'll be facing in the Death Match, all we can really do is put ourselves in the best positions possible."

We all listened as Derek laid out the strategy for the first round of the tournament. The rest of the team already knew that he was taking over as captain but wasn't really captain. Man, that had been an awkward conversation.

"We have mics in this game, and that's rare," Derek said. "Use them as much as possible. Communication is going to be key."

In the RAGE tournaments, we never had mics. It would be an advantage, as long as we remembered to talk to each other. And actually listened.

"I think we've all seen that Lily is our strongest runner," Derek continued. "She should be the one to pick up our flag. At least, for this round. The other teams will catch on quick, so we can't have her in that position every time. But I think for the Death Match, we should be able to get away with it."

"Kali's our second runner. She'll guard Lily to and from the flag and will pick it up if Lily goes down. Hannah and I will guard our flag. Without knowing who we're facing, this is the best we can do. Again, remember to use your mics. Communication, people. It's key to this game."

Not just the game.

I glanced back at Rooke. He stood on the other side of the room, arms crossed, looking at the floor. The fact that he was out of the Death Match was hurting him just as much as the rest of the team.

His absence became even more apparent in the afternoons, when we ran virtual matchups against the computer without him. We had to. We had to practice fighting four on five if we had any hope of surviving the Death Match. But not having him in the game only emphasized our weaknesses. Out of ten matchups, we'd won the first and none that followed. Instead of the team getting better and more used to fighting with just four, the computer was ripping us apart, more and more each round. First our bodies, then our morale.

"It knows," I told Derek, once we'd exited the pods after the tenth matchup. "The computer knows we're only four, so it's destroying us like any other team would."

"Kali." He glanced at the girls, who remained near their pods, conversing with each other. Judging by the way their heads hung and their arms were folded tight across their chests, they weren't too impressed with our performance, either. Derek grabbed my arm and pulled me to the side. "We're not going to make it through the Death Match. Forget that we're down a player and these new pods are destroying us. We don't know who we're facing. How can we prepare for that?"

I shrugged and tossed my arms up. "Then we'll be in the losers' bracket. You said it yourself. Rooke's health is more important, and we can take the loss."

"And I still believe that. It's just . . ."

His voice trailed off, and he didn't say anything more, but I knew what he was thinking. Suddenly, he was beginning to understand the pressure and why I'd considered altering Rooke's test results. At least with five players, we'd be at full strength. Not just in the match, but outside of it. We weren't a team. Not like this.

Too late to change anything now.

"You're missing the RAGE tournament right now, aren't you?" I asked him. He nodded. "Me, too."

He pushed a breath out from his lips. "This might have been a mistake."

"Rooke, or this tournament?"

"Take your pick."

I sighed, and my gaze drifted from Derek's face to Rooke's empty pod. With the intensity of our training and the stress from the tournament, it was normal for things to be rocky on the team. Everyone's nerves and ambitions were in overdrive, so some spats and fuckups were completely expected. But Rooke's empty pod and Derek's words stood for something more. This wasn't just stress. We weren't weathering the storm. The hull was starting to crack, and if I wasn't careful, the ship would sink. This was my team. I'd thrown everything I had into this, and if I couldn't make it work, what then?

Right then, I decided we were done for the day. At least, I was done for the day.

I leaned around Derek to call out to the girls. "That's it for today." Then I pushed past him and walked toward the door.

"Where are you going?" he called.

"I have a date."

CHAPTER 10

Some people wouldn't think much of an evening spent practicing a martial art in a garden, especially with someone who, at times, was so frustrating I felt like crushing his skull. But for me, this was my element.

March nights in Los Angeles still got cold enough for long pants and a jacket sometimes, and the cool air tonight bit at my bare arms. Despite the chill in the air, I felt cozy, like I was exactly where I was supposed to be, reconnecting with my body against the setting sun. This was serenity, and I was swaddled in it.

I fisted my toes in the blades of grass, feeling the cool air beneath my feet. Rooke stood parallel to me, approximately fifteen feet away. Tonight, we were beginning our lessons in Baguazhang. The first exercise: circle walking.

Circle walking was the basis of Baguazhang, an internal martial art, and was used to train body and mind to become more stable, more balanced. At the head of the garden, I'd rested my tablet in the grass and opened the Baguazhang program I'd downloaded. It projected a virtual instructor and two circles onto the grass approximately ten feet wide. Rooke and I each stood inside our own circle, attempting to mimic the movements of the instructor. We glided around the perimeter, arms up, palms open, facing toward the center of the circle.

In a blink, the instructor turned to face in the opposite direction. I followed his movements and pivoted on the line, concentrating on my weight on my back foot and the rotation in my waist. Rooke turned too tightly, too reliant on his upper body. He tripped over his own feet and toppled to the ground, cursing at himself as he landed.

I grinned. "I don't think you're supposed to leave your circle."

He grunted as he pushed back up to his feet. "You've studied Tai Chi. You have an advantage."

I suppose to some people, Baguazhang circle walking seemed similar to Tai Chi. While they were both internal martial arts, circle walking was faster and had several sharp movements meant to condition the mind to anticipate sudden change and to remain balanced when met by an opposing force.

Speaking of an opposing force, I glanced at Rooke.

"This is a completely different form," I said as I walked along the circle's outline, mimicking the movements of the instructor. "Besides, I think it's best if you don't talk during the exercise."

"If I'd known that, I would have practiced this with you years ago."

I dropped my arms and started marching toward him. "Say that to my face."

He pointed at the ground and wagged his finger at me. "I don't think you're supposed to leave your circle."

I halted at the edge of my projected ring and snarled at him. He grinned.

Every night that week, we practiced together, against the setting sun. At some point, every night, Rooke stumbled, tripped, or fell out of his circle. I knew why he was falling. He was holding himself too rigidly, both in his body and in his mind.

"You know," I began, "in some parts of China, they practice

these walking steps for years before they ever get into the actual martial art."

Rooke dusted himself off. "Does that mean I have to stand this close to you for months on end?"

"You'd have to stop falling down first."

He stepped back into his circle and took up the pose of the instructor. After a few steps, he fell back into rhythm. "Are we really just going to walk around this circle for months?"

I chuckled. "No. We'll move on as soon as you learn where your feet go."

"I still think it would be better to do this virtually."

"Virtual isn't real. It doesn't have consequences. That's the point."

After the lesson, we sat on the grass together, listening to the virtual instructor explain the concept of Bagua and its importance to understanding the martial art. The Bagua was an octagonal figure, with a yin yang symbol in the center. Altogether, it was meant to represent the fundamental concepts of reality.

"Do you understand this?" Rooke asked, leaning toward me.

"Kind of," I said. "I think."

He chuckled. "Well, that makes one of us."

He wasn't getting it, and I knew how Rooke preferred to learn. I retrieved the hardcover book from the training room and sat on the grass with him. I opened the book to the Bagua symbol.

"There are eight sides, indicating eight interrelated concepts. Each one is represented by an element: Heaven in the south, then marsh, fire, thunder, wind, water, mountain, and Earth in the north." I pointed at the bottom of the symbol.

"Why are you saying north? You're pointing at the bottom."

"North is south," I told him. "It's reversed."

"Then why don't they just say south?"

I glanced down at the book and shrugged. "Apparently, it's easier to understand . . . if you weren't raised in the West."

"Great."

"Hey, that's me, too."

Rooke glanced down at the symbol again. "What's the point?"

"They're opposing forces. Heaven and Earth. Fire and water. In the middle, you find balance." I traced my finger over the yin yang in the center. "Baguazhang is about learning to repel external opposing forces—

"—by being balanced on the inside," he finished.

I smiled.

A distant look filled his eyes, and he glanced out at the sky. Rooke had always been an admirer of Eastern philosophy, so I didn't think it would take him long to catch on. Hopefully, he'd realize the reason he was struggling with circle walking so much was because of his own lack of internal balance.

Rooke turned back to me, flipped through a few pages of the book, and stopped on a picture of the Wudang Mountains, where Baguazhang and other forms of martial arts are said to have originated.

"Have you ever been to China?" he asked.

"No."

He considered that. "Do you have family over there?"

"Distant relatives, I guess. My father came over with his parents when he was a teenager."

He glanced down at the picture again and trailed a finger across it. "Would you like to go?"

I shrugged. "I suppose." A smile spread across my face. "Are you looking to take a girl, sometime?"

"A girl? I don't think Hannah would be interested."

I snapped the book shut and smacked him with it.

"How's this for outside my circle?" I asked, hitting him again. "You know, these exercises are supposed to prepare you for any sudden and abrasive attack."

"Abrasive attacks?" He held up his forearms to shield himself from my assault. "So, even the monks of the Wudang Mountains know about your mouth?"

He laughed as I hit him again.

I pulled back and rested on my haunches. Hearing him laugh warmed my insides. It was like his problems were retreating, and the friend I once knew was slowly making appearances again. We needed him to keep pushing, keep trying to get better, and it was important he realized that.

"This week has been difficult for the team," I told him. "Especially since you're not in the virtual simulations with us. We miss you in there. We're not really Defiance without you."

He looked to the distance again and didn't reply. I wasn't sure if he had nothing to say, or if the situation was just too much for him. It could have been either. After it was silent for about a minute, I asked, "Same time tomorrow?"

He nodded but kept his gaze fixed on the horizon. I sighed inwardly but didn't let my frustration show on my face. Rooke was a locked box at times, and getting upset wouldn't help him open up. Only patience. If anything, that's what this man excelled at. Testing my patience. At least, what little of it I had in the first place.

I pushed up to my feet and headed for the house. A few feet away from the door, he spoke.

"I feel like I'm angry all the time."

I halted. He was talking. I turned back slowly and waited for him to keep going. Instead, he turned his gaze to the ground and said nothing. If he really did have that much pent-up anger, then it, too, was contributing to why he'd been falling and tripping so much during the exercise. It also meant that if he was going to get better at Baguazhang, he'd have to learn to let go.

"All the time?" I prodded.

Eventually, he nodded. "Yeah. I mean, I smile sometimes. I laugh at things. But underneath it, there's this rage that never really goes away." He plucked a few blades of grass before finally looking up to meet my eyes. "Is that what it's like to be you?"

A hint of a grin tugged at his lips.

Testing patience 101.

"Am I angry all the time?" I considered it. "Only when you're in the same room."

He chuckled, and it left a hollow feeling in my stomach. That laughter coming from his throat wasn't genuine but merely a reaction to the situation. I did know what it was like to be angry all the time. I'd found peace by meditating, embracing everything about myself, and focusing my life on my goals and the fate of my team. Managing my temper was still something I worked on constantly, but I was becoming less and less the angry teenager I once was. I couldn't imagine going backwards and undoing all the work I'd already done to get to where I was now. That was exactly what Rooke was going through, and if he needed me, I was going to go through it with him.

"You've been here before," I reminded him. "You pulled through this before, and you will now."

He stared at the ground some more and shook his head. "It's different this time."

I took a step toward him. "How so?"

"Last time I got clean, it was because I saw someone die from their abuse. That was the ultimate wake-up call. But now I'm pulling at straws. It's like I don't have enough reason to stop." He stood and walked up to me until I could see the amber flecks in his eyes. "It's like there's this tug-of-war going on inside me, and I'm not winning."

My heart twisted, and I couldn't keep his gaze. I looked down to his chest, watching his breaths move in and out. I didn't know what to say to him. He had helped me out of this exact situation, but I never thought the roles would be reversed, and I'd be the one reaching out to him.

"How about this?" I began, meeting his eyes again. "If you can't get it under control, then it could be the rest of us watching you die."

He blanched. His jaw went slack, his eyes went wide, and all the color drained from his face. Guess he hadn't really considered that a possibility until I'd said it. It wasn't a surprise, either. Most addicts thought they had things under control, that their addiction would never kill them. I didn't think Rooke was that far gone, and I'll admit, it was a bit overdramatic of me to say. But it might have been the slap in the face he needed. Judging by his expression, the idea had frightened him more than anything I'd seen from him before.

"The team needs you," I said, swallowing thick. "I need you."

I wasn't saying it to be petty or guilt-trip him into recovery. It was simply the truth. I needed my friend. I needed the person I leaned on when things got tough. Judging by the insanity of this tournament, I'd need it a lot in the weeks to come. Part of me wondered if that was selfish, that I needed him to be okay for my benefit. But honestly, it wasn't just me. It was for him, and the team. Besides, I think when it came to matters of your friends and their well-being, it was okay to be a little selfish and hope that they got better, so you could enjoy the good old times again.

The good old times. With Rooke, that included sneaking away from the team and the clubs to train with bo staffs, geek out over classic video game sessions, and jab at each other both

on and off the mats—not all that different from tonight. Maybe
we were closer to normal than I thought. Maybe soon, things
would be back to the way they used to be. At least, I could hope.

My emotions swelled up at the thought. I backed up a step
and shoved down the lump in my throat.

"Tomorrow?" I asked, keeping my voice strong.

He nodded. "Every night."

My heart twisted a little. I was getting through to him, and
he was starting to respond. I was enjoying this, too. Circle
walking at sunset, in the middle of a garden, while reconnecting with an old friend . . .

Rooke's gaze left my eyes, traveled down my face to my lips,
and hovered there. My throat went dry.

Well, hello spark. Good to know you're still there.

I bit my bottom lip.

"I . . . uh," I stuttered, "have owner stuff to do." I backed
up a few more steps, hoping I was headed in the direction of
the house. "If you need to talk—"

"I'll come find you."

We locked eyes, and I kept his gaze until I slammed my back
into the closed garden door—so hard that the glass rattled in
the frame. Rooke pressed his lips together to keep from laughing at me. Heat flashed across the back of my neck and around
my heart. It was strange to feel both embarrassed and happy at
the same time, but the chemistry between us was becoming
more and more like it always had been, and that was worth my
making a fool of myself. If it meant things were improving for
him—and by extension, the team—I wouldn't have cared if I'd
walked straight into a brick wall.

I slid the door open and disappeared inside. As I shut the
door behind me, I glanced back at Rooke, to see him gather-
ing up the tablet and gear for the night. His movements were

calmer than they had been. The tension in his arms and shoulders was fading. Even his coloring was better than when he'd first come back to the team. He was improving, but the only people who knew it were in this house. I'd been ignoring the tabloids all week and shielded the team from the gossip as much as I could. But as team owner, it was also my responsibility to maintain our image and remain informed on what the press was printing about us every week. I'd put it off long enough.

Time to check out the damage.

I retreated to my office and collapsed into my chair. My fingernails tapped against the keyboard, and my stomach went on spin cycle. I was a few clicks away from a world of gossip and hate, where no one was who they said they were and everyone put on as much of a show as we did. Almost as if a parallel universe existed behind the screen. This was my job now. Whatever they were saying about my team, I had to face this head-on.

I brought up the gossip channel's live stream. It didn't take long to find what I was looking for. On the screen, three hosts of Hypnotic sat on a couch as usual, except their former topic of discussion—The Wall—had been replaced by my teammate.

"The tournament isn't even under way yet, and the drama is already kicking up. Reports are coming in that a member of Team Defiance failed his drug test, and that means they'll be heading into the first round of the tournament shorthanded."

The second host spoke up. "Let's talk about Rooke for a second. For any of the viewers out there who haven't heard yet—"

The third cut him off. "If you haven't heard yet? The only people who haven't heard this don't have wi-fi. That leaves . . . the Mars colony."

They laughed. My fists clenched, and I tucked them under

the table to prevent them from damaging the screen. Luckily, the whole world didn't really care about shit like this.

Did they?

The second host continued on, still chuckling. "He's the one who failed his drug test. Now, I heard he's already been kicked off the team."

"No. Our sources said he checked into a rehab facility."

I groaned and nearly smacked my forehead on the screen. Now they were just making up all-out lies. He wasn't off the team, and he wasn't in rehab. He was here with us. It shouldn't have surprised me, though. Gossip sites made up things about celebrities all the time, and gamers were just their newest source to exploit.

"Really?" the other host on the screen continued. "We just received a photo of him out at a club."

I went numb. No, no, no. Rooke was just here. Don't tell me he went out at some point. We'd been together after supper, practicing in the garden. But every moment I was plugged into the virtual world with the team was a moment I didn't know where he was. I buried my face in my hands, peering at the screen through the tiny slits between my fingers. A photo flashed across the screen of a man with dark hair sniffing something off a club table, but the face was so blurry that he might as well have been Bigfoot.

I exhaled, and my body nearly turned to jelly. Thank God. It wasn't him. But someone would think so. The Internet would be flooded with that photo within the hour.

"This is nothing but a marketing ploy by Team Defiance. Frankly, how did they even get into this tournament?"

My fists clenched so hard my knuckles could have turned to diamonds. Asshole. I'd never mess with my teammates' lives for the sake of publicity. We were in the tournament because we deserved it. We'd earned it.

Had we?

My fists unclenched, and I sighed. Hell, even I wasn't so sure what we were doing here.

"Kali?"

This time, it was my heart that clenched. Hard.

I knew that voice.

After mentally kicking myself in the head several times, I slow-motion turned to find Rooke standing beside me. Damn it. I'd been so focused on the computer, I hadn't even heard him enter the room.

He didn't meet my gaze. His eyes were locked on the screen, and his jaw was tight.

"I have to know what they're saying," I explained before he could say anything. "This is my job now."

He scoffed. "This is your job?" He nodded at the screen. "To watch the gossip channels?"

"To protect the team."

"The team." He scoffed again. "Are you sure this isn't about you? Maybe you want to know what people are saying because it reflects back on you as much as anyone else."

"That's not even close—"

"Bullshit. If you were really concerned about me, you wouldn't have reported the test."

I flew out of my chair and slammed a hand on my desk. "Do you even hear yourself? This isn't you. Last year, you never would have accepted this from yourself or anyone else. Where's the man who led me back to the straight path?"

His gaze flicked to the gossip channel, still playing in the background. "He's in front of you. Not on television."

I blinked and didn't know how to process that. There was a shade of his true self standing in front of me, and even more so when we'd been out in the garden. But what was in the media was partly true, too. He had slipped. He had failed his drug test. That was as true as anything else.

I glanced at the screen and shook my head. "Look, you can be angry all you want, but you're the one who got high. We're heading into the biggest tournament in the world with only four players, and that's one hundred percent on you."

He rolled his eyes and opened his mouth to speak, but I cut him off.

"No. You're done talking." The words shot out of my mouth like each was a bullet. Rooke took half a step back and blinked, as if I'd slapped him. "If you can't pull your shit together, you're off the team. I don't care if we have to play the entire tournament with four players. I don't deserve this, and the rest of the team sure as fuck doesn't, either."

He looked down at the floor and wouldn't meet my eyes. I raised my voice another notch.

"You hear me?"

"Yeah."

"Good. Get out of my office." I pointed out the door. "Now."

With that, he left and slammed the door behind him. I folded my arms on my desk and collapsed against it, repeatedly banging my head against my forearms. So, so stupid. I had finally started to reach him. Out in the garden, we were having fun, like old times. Everything was the way it was before. And now I'd lost my temper and screamed at him. For what? A bunch of gossip. But that was my job now. Rooke's trust was hard to gain, but so was the sponsors'. If they weren't happy with our image, we were screwed. Without them, we didn't have a team.

Without Rooke, we didn't have one, either.

Suddenly, I understood why most owners messed with their drug tests. Fake the test, and you keep the sponsors happy and the team together. Report the test as is, and the sponsors scream and the team stops being a team. Shit, this was all a mistake. I should have tampered with the test. Rooke wouldn't be out of the Death Match, and we'd be acting like a team.

But then Rooke would have an excuse to get high again and again, and we might lose him as a teammate permanently. I tossed my arms up. There was no right answer, and I knew only one thing for sure. No matter what way I turned or decision I made, I was fucking everything up.

On the day of the Death Match, the VGL introduced another new rule. All teams had to be in their pods from the start of the game. Not our game, mind you. Every game that would be taking place that night. So, for more than an hour, I'd been plugged in and standing with my teammates in our virtual base, waiting for our matchup to begin.

"Why won't they let us see the other matchups?" Hannah asked.

"They don't want us to figure out who we're facing," Derek said. "If we watch the other matchups, we might be able to guess by process of elimination."

"Could also be prep," Lily added. "For the final round. They're exposing us to extended time in the virtual world."

Hannah stepped toward the door and peered out the force field.

"It really makes you feel alone, doesn't it?"

I followed her gaze down the empty street that should have been bustling with people and noise. Honking horns. Herds of umbrellas crowding the sidewalks. Instead, it was silent. Nothing but the sound of humming fluorescent lights and steam escaping through the street's vents filled the air. Traffic lights changed on their own for the trafficless street. Other than the neon lights, everything was a shade of dark gray, emphasized by the darkness and moonlight. The buildings stood impossibly tall, and only shoulder's width apart. It all reeked with a strange, foreboding sense that creeped through my gut. It made me completely aware of everything around me. Of the sounds of my teammates' breaths and their feet scuffing along the floor. It even heightened the sense of my own body, where I ended, and the game began. And every nerve, every inch of me knew.

This place felt like a trap, except the prison wasn't the virtual world. In here, you were alone, and the real prison was your mind.

I shuddered.

Ten feet from our base, the flag flickered into view, its code glitching a few times before growing solid. Even still, it remained as a computerized image, almost pixilated in a way. It was the only thing in the game that didn't look real, so it would stand out for the viewers against the bleak gray background.

We gathered around the screen next to the doorway, waiting for the matchup stats. Within a few seconds, our opponent's name appeared.

DEFIANCE VS. K-RIG

Oh, no.

Not them. Anyone but them.

My eyes fell shut, and my chest felt like it had just collapsed in on itself. I'd never vomited inside the virtual world before, and suddenly, I found myself wondering if I'd end up puking in the pod as well. Apparently, finding out you're about to fight the greatest team in the world makes you wonder about all kinds of existential shit.

"You've got to be kidding me," Lily muttered.

The countdown started. *30, 29, 28 . . .*

"This is for real," Hannah said. "This is actually happening. We can't play them. We'll be destroyed."

I shoved down the sick taste in my throat and turned to face my team.

"Calm down," I said between my teeth. "All of you. The crowd can see us."

"Yeah," Lily replied. "Because that's what's important right now."

I ignored her comment and looked to Derek. "Any suggestions on strategy?"

He shrugged. "Pray."

I frowned. "I'm being serious."

"Me, too," he said, but I stared at him until he broke. He sighed. "No deviations from the plan. You and Lily go for the flag. Stick to the rooftops. Try to be as inconspicuous as you can. Hannah and I will guard our base."

"That's . . . pretty basic."

"That's what we came up with."

"It's not good enough. Not against them."

He nodded at the countdown. "We've got fifteen seconds. What else can we do?"

I shifted my weight a few times. He was right. It was the best we could do.

"Anything else?" I asked.

"Survive."

Oh, how quickly my hopes for this tournament had gone from thrive to survive.

We lined up at the door, waiting for the shield to drop. Lily and I stood in front, ready to bolt, while Hannah and Derek took up the rear.

The countdown continued.

10, 9, 8 . . .

I took a sprinting stance and counted down with the clock, trying to ignore the swirling in my gut. We were down a player, my team was in shambles, and we were seconds away from facing off against the best team in the world.

Survive. No kidding.

CHAPTER 11

"It has to be a trap."

Lily's voice came through the mic as we raced along the rooftops. Half a block up on the street below, K-Rig's flag shimmered against the grayed darkness of this world. The space around it was empty. Quiet.

"Doesn't matter," I said as I cleared another gap between the roofs. "We have to go for it. Don't hesitate."

"You pick it up," she huffed. "They'll be expecting me."

Lily was our fastest runner, and even though we'd never played this game live before, if K-Rig had watched any of our old RAGE matches, they would have picked up on Lily's speed and probably assumed she'd be the one going for the flag.

"Got it," I agreed.

Lily unsheathed her axes, preparing to defend. I kept my hands free and raced straight for the flag. We hit the edge of the roof together and pushed off, arcing through the air. Lily landed, axes out, ready. I touched down beside her, rolling as I landed, and cleared through the flag. A bluish flash consumed me.

I had the flag.

Step one, done.

The street remained quiet. No sign of K-Rig. Just the mist, red lanterns, and flashing neon. They had to be somewhere. I scanned the rooftops, the tight gaps between the buildings, the shadows.

Nothing.

I traded glances with Lily. She shrugged.

"We have to go," she said.

We had no other option but to start running the flag in. Just standing here wasn't going to win us any points. But common sense did nothing to calm my shaky nerves.

Something wasn't right about this.

I turned on my heel and booked it down the street, heading south. Lily flanked my left side, knowing it was my off-hand.

"I've got the flag," I said into my mic. "Lily's with me. K-Rig is MIA."

"They're here," Derek replied. "Three of them, at least."

Three. Where were the other two, and why weren't they attacking us?

As I ran alongside Lily, grunts and clanging swords came through the mic. Then Hannah's scream, which abruptly cut off.

I pressed my lips to the mic.

"Hannah? Derek?"

Nothing.

Great. Two on five already.

I ran faster.

My feet slushed through puddles, and the wind whipped my hair back as I ran. A bluish glow trailed behind me. Might as well put a flashing sign over my head. *I'm Right Here.*

We can still win this, I told myself. A spark of hope grew in my chest, and for a minute, I believed it. But halfway back to the base, the three members of K-Rig rounded a corner and cut off our path. Lily and I ground to a halt and turned to reverse direction. The missing two members of K-Rig stepped out from the alleyways, one from each side of the street. Here was the trap. They'd planned this. The whole thing. They let us pick up the flag while they took out our guards, just in time to sweep back to the runners and surround us on all sides. Perfectly timed. Perfectly executed.

Hell, it was just plain perfect.

One of them charged and plowed into Lily, knocking her back and off balance. Two quick slices with his blade, and he spilled her insides on the road. Her mouth opened to scream, but only air escaped as she crumpled into a heap on the road. Slowly, her body faded from view.

My heart thrummed in my ears. I was alone, and we were about to lose.

All five closed in.

My throat restricted with every step they took, as if their feet were tightening a noose line. No, Kali. You go down fighting. You always go down fighting.

I gritted my teeth, drew my sword, and took a stance. Out of the corner of my eye, I saw the one on my far right smirk at me. Well, dumb-ass. Why don't you just paint a bull's-eye on your forehead?

I faked a turn, like I was going the opposite way, and lunged for him, thrusting my sword through his chest. He stumbled back. His mouth opened and closed several times in complete shock, like he was witnessing an event he'd never seen before. I gripped the hilt and slammed into him. The full length of my blade disappeared into his chest. A gasping moan escaped his lips. I saddled up to him, so we were merely inches apart. He smelled of blood and sweat, and fear. His eyes went wide.

I brought my face even closer, so my lips nearly brushed his.

"Smirk at me again," I dared him.

He didn't.

His eyes grew even wider, and a choking, clinking sound came from the back of his throat, like a fish out of water. Poor baby. Can't get any air. Reeling back, I ripped my sword from his chest. He collapsed, his eyes glazing over in an instant. I turned to face the remaining members of K-Rig. For a second, just a split second, they looked impressed.

They circled me, moving in sync. Step for step.

Okay, now I'm really screwed.

I knelt low and fought how I did best when outnumbered or hopelessly outranked. Something I'd done in my first championship.

I closed my eyes.

The raindrops and neon buzzing filled my ears, then the sounds of K-Rig's shallow breaths. I focused my own breathing, calm and deep. Footsteps echoed along the pavement toward me.

I moved, sword out, deflecting every blow that came toward me. Sound became my ally, directing me where to go. The wind carried me. I was a cyclone as K-Rig came at me, all four of them at once. The sharp clanging of sword against sword created a grating techno beat, like chains smashing against steel. Looks like I had a new sound track.

For half a second, they pulled back, panting. One of them swore in Korean. At least, I assumed so. Mandarin and Korean weren't close enough for me to understand his meaning, but judging by the sharp harshness in his voice as he spat the word, it was something nasty.

I kept my eyes closed.

Another one said something else in Korean, this time not as harsh. More like a command. It went dead quiet for a second. Then they started zigzagging, tapping their feet along their pavement like they were dancing. Closing in, backing out.

Fuckers.

I rotated my stance, following the sounds, circling my sword around me.

They stepped faster. One whipped past within an inch of me, so I felt the breeze on my lips. My muscles seized, and I swallowed thick. A thousand steps echoed together, like four different drumbeats playing over the top of each other, making it impossible to tell which was which.

No choice. I opened my eyes.

Wrong move.

A sword drove into my back. I went rigid from the pain, and hot liquid spilled down my backside. My knees gave out, and I crumpled to the ground. Blood gurgled out of my mouth. I coughed and sputtered as little eruptions of the red stuff spewed from my lips. I must have looked like the little volcano that could.

A member of K-Rig knelt beside me, his eyes searching my face. He unsheathed his dagger and raised it over my head. I grinned at him, fully aware of the blood inking my teeth and spilling down my chin. Straining against my choking lungs, I spat three words at him.

"Make it count."

He faltered with his blade, like he'd hit some invisible wall. His eyebrows went up. Impressed again. And, apparently, he understood English.

Then his expression morphed into one of determination and he slammed his dagger straight down. Pain exploded in the side of my head. Blinding, indescribable pain for only a fraction of a second, then the jolt sent me hurling back to reality.

I sat up in the pod, trembling slightly. Nothing but the pod's shimmering white core surrounded me. While none of it had been real, adrenaline still seared through my veins. Dying in this game felt the same as the RAGE tournaments: like your soul was being ripped out of your body.

I shuddered.

The announcers' voices cut in and started streaming through the pod's speakers.

"And Team Defiance wipes out," Marcus said. "Wow. What a way to go. Though it's not so surprising given their handicap going in."

"I had hopes, you know," Howie admitted. "They've proven they can hold their own in the RAGE tournaments, and they've come back from handicaps before. But with that loss, Team Defiance drops down into the losers' bracket."

"You know, Ling did put up an amazing fight in the end. We've seen her fight like that before in her first RAGE tournament championship. Too bad it wasn't enough."

I knew going up against K-Rig was an almost guaranteed loss even with all five players. Still, there was a part of me that agreed with Howie. I had hopes. Like he said, we'd come back from handicaps before. We'd faced teams that had seemed invincible. But we hadn't been playing at this level of competition. Maybe we weren't ready for it.

My pod's doors opened. Around the room, my teammates all sat on the edges of their pods, staring at the floor. Finally, Derek looked up.

"Good try, guys," he said. "We fought hard. I don't think we could have asked for more." He stood. "Come on. Let's go do the press conference."

I still stared at the floor but cleared my throat.

"Right behind you," I said. Lily and Hannah filtered out of the room. Derek remained behind and knelt in front of me.

"Losers' bracket means we're against the easier teams," he said, trying to make me feel better.

"And it means we're one loss away from defeat."

"Kali, we had a rough start. It happens. We've been in this position before."

We had. In the first tournament we'd fought together, we'd been in the losers' bracket the entire time and still came back to win in the end. But the thought wasn't enough to push me out of my pod or stop the sinking feeling in my stomach.

Derek squinted at me for a minute, like he was trying to read my mind.

"You're worried about Rooke," he concluded.

"I'm worried about everything."

He studied me for a minute longer. "And what do Taoists think about worrying?"

I sighed. "That it's fruitless. That it does nothing but contribute to disharmony."

"And how do you deal with it?"

It was usually Rooke who asked me these types of questions. Looks like Derek was playing the part for my sake. I offered him a meek smile. "By accepting things as they are and carrying on anyway."

"Exactly. So, get up." He stood, offering his hand. "Let's get out there."

I used his hand to hoist myself up. We headed for the doors, and he lingered in the doorway for a second.

"What you did at the end there," he began. "Fighting with your eyes closed. I know you've done that before, but it's still pretty impressive. Even K-Rig looked shocked. Definitely all-star material."

"It wasn't enough."

He didn't push it further. He knew I wasn't in the mood for compliments. But I did kinda kick ass there, in the end.

We made our way outside to the edge of our property and through the gates encasing the house, to where an outdoor pavilion housed the media. On windy or rainy days, the outdoor pavilion wasn't ideal, but it was a way to keep our home off-limits and yet still allow the media to interview us after the matchups.

I sat on a panel with my teammates as our hired security made sure no one crossed the lines toward us or the house. I could only afford them during matchup nights, but Elise had set up a state-of-the-art security system around the house when we'd first moved in. Elise. Someone I'd fired. There went my sinking stomach again.

As I settled into my seat, I glanced at the one next to mine. Rooke's. It was empty.

The crowd snapped pictures of us and conversed amongst themselves until I pressed my lips to the microphone.

"We'll be answering your questions for the next thirty minutes. Raise your hand, and I'll choose from the audience. When I do, stand, give us your name, and proceed with your question. One of us will answer. Got it?"

Jeez, I sounded like a schoolmarm, but if I didn't set the rules at the beginning of every conference, they'd just start shouting over each other.

When I finished my little speech, a few dozen hands shot in the air, waving. I pointed at a woman in the front row. She stood.

"Tegan Fava, *Pro Gamer Weekly*. How did you feel going up against K-Rig?"

"They're an incredible team," Derek said. "It was an honor just to play against them. It's an opportunity not many people are going to get."

More hands waved in the air. I pointed to a reporter at the back. He stood.

"Jeffrey Stout, *L.A. Times*. Should we expect to see your missing teammate in the next match?"

We all answered together.

"Yes."

The crowd laughed. Lily cleared her throat and kept her lips against the microphone. The rest of us backed off. It wasn't often Lily answered questions.

"Everyone has their moments when they break down," she said. "But that's part of being on a team. You lean on each other."

Damn. Go, Lily.

I pointed at another reporter in the center of the crowd. He stood and didn't bother with announcing himself or what publication he was with. I quickly found out why.

"Now that you're in the losers' bracket, going up against the best teams in the world, do you think you even stand a chance?"

I blinked. What kind of a question was that? Yes, the competition was fierce, but why did he imply we wouldn't stand a chance? This guy was lucky we weren't in the arena.

Hannah reached across Rooke's empty seat and rested a hand against my knee. Her warmth grounded me in reality. I turned to look at her, and my other teammates beyond her. They stared back at me, waiting for my answer. But I took the moment to appreciate them. The team was important. The press was important only to the sport. Not to life.

I turned back to the reporter and smiled.

"It's always better to come back from the bottom. We prefer the challenge."

After the press conference, I found Rooke in the training room. The steady-yet-broken beat of his fists pounded a punching bag. I walked up to him and stopped a few feet away. He failed to look up at me.

"We're in the losers' bracket now, aren't we?"

"You didn't watch the matchup?" I asked.

"I should have been in there," he huffed.

"Are you saying I should have tampered with your test results?"

He didn't answer, just kept his gaze on the punching bag. *Thap, thap . . . thap, thap.* I shifted my weight a few times. "If you didn't watch the matchup, then what were you doing?"

He grabbed the bag to steady it and leaned toward me.

"What's wrong? Worried you couldn't watch me while you were plugged in?" He nodded toward the corner of the room. "I have a babysitter." Dr. Renner sat on the bench in the corner, typing on her tablet. Rooke leaned in even closer. "Do I have you to thank for that?"

I sighed. I knew why he was so angry. The hostility he was directing at me was really what he felt for himself. I knew Rooke, and he'd blame himself for our loss tonight. Even if he'd been in the game with us, chances are we would have been destroyed by K-Rig. He'd never admit it or see it that way. The way he was going after that punching bag, he was probably wishing it was his own face.

And yes, I had asked the doctor to keep an eye on him, and she'd willingly obliged. But I wasn't about to admit that to him.

Rooke continued to pound the bag.

"I thought on your team," he huffed, "we were entitled to our privacy."

"Privacy is earned," I said, crossing my arms. "This is still my house."

"Privacy is earned." He scoffed. "Even our rooms?"

"Yes. And I will search them if necessary."

The next punch he threw missed the bag, and he whirled around. "You wouldn't."

I nodded. He sputtered.

"Kali, you're out of control."

I really wasn't. His reaction to the thought of my searching his room was just another sign of his addiction coming through. This was for his benefit, not mine.

"Deal with it," I said. "I'll run my team the best way I see fit."

He pressed his lips together in a tight line, as if he was trying to hide a sneer. He left the punching bag and pushed past me toward the door, but not before he muttered, "Sure thing, Clarence."

My muscles clenched. Every one of them. It was bait, and I wasn't going to bite. Instead, I let him leave without another word. Dr. Renner's footsteps padded along the canvas mats and bamboo flooring and stopped behind me.

"You're doing the right thing," she said.

I turned to face her. "It doesn't feel like it."

"You have to be firm. He has to know there's nowhere to hide." She watched him leave, hugging her tablet to her chest.

I glanced between her and the exit Rooke had disappeared through. "How can we know we're doing the right thing?"

"Human behavior can be hard to predict," she admitted. "We can know people for years, and one day they'll just do something completely unexpected. Not just against their character, but even against statistics and studies that say they should be behaving in every other way than what they are." She took a breath. "But addicts tend to need a lot of the same things. They need love and understanding, but also a firm hand and rigid guidelines. You're doing that for him. You're giving him what he needs."

She kept saying that. Hell, I even kept saying it myself. But it still felt like I wasn't doing the right thing. I pushed out a heavy sigh. "It's harder than I thought it would be."

"Dealing with an addict—"

"That's not what's rough. Not really."

She circled around to face me.

"Last year, I was acting the exact same way with him, and now I know how hard it is to be on the receiving end of it. And despite that, he stayed. He fought for me. I was a miserable hothead and chewed him apart every chance I got, and he still stayed. And when I finally broke, he picked up the pieces. He held my hair back whenever I got sick from withdrawals. He was by my side every minute I needed him to be, even when I didn't realize it myself."

Dr. Renner considered that for a moment.

"He saw himself in you," she concluded. "When you were dealing with your own addiction, he was just getting through his and saw the opportunity to help someone else like him."

"Maybe that, or maybe that's just the kind of person he is. Maybe he would have helped me anyway." I sighed. "I know this might sound hard to believe because of the way he's acting, but now I understand what he did for me, and I respect him more than I ever did. Now it's just a matter of digging the real him back out."

Dr. Renner looked a little surprised by my statement. "That's a really positive way of looking at things."

"I owe him that much."

She studied me for a minute and shook her head. "You can't be blaming yourself for the media reaction—"

"I made a choice, and he's the one who was out of the Death Match. The whole world just saw us play without him, and they all know why he wasn't there."

"Do you have a plan to handle that?"

It wasn't just handling Rooke that I was concerned about. That last matchup made us look terrible, and I knew the sponsors would be screaming as soon as I picked up my phone. There was only one way to handle the situation.

Damage control.

CHAPTER 12

"**Y**ou saw K-Rig at the all-star dinner, right?" I asked Hannah when I jumped on the treadmill next to her. It was morning workout time, and she was already some distance into her run. Still, she had enough breath to laugh.

"Of course. Who didn't see them?"

"Can you create something like that?"

She slowed her pace on the treadmill and looked at me with her head tilted. "What do you mean?"

"I mean, I'm not going to tattoo and laser-alter my team, but we need some kind of look. Something instantly recognizable. You have experience in modeling and fashion. I want your input."

"Let me get this straight," Hannah said, drawing a deep breath, as if to stop herself from getting too excited. "Are you saying I get to dress up the team?"

". . . I guess?"

"Kali Ling, I think I love you." She started up her pace again, and her gaze traveled across the training room to land on Rooke. "How's things with you-know-who?"

"Rocky."

"One-word answer. You almost sound like him."

"Fuck you. There. That's two words."

She laughed. "You know, this seems a little familiar. You

and Rooke at odds, you and me talking about it. I think I'm having flashbacks."

I almost told her to shut up but figured she'd make another joke about my limited vocabulary. Instead, I watched her as she watched him. She glanced him over and got a knowing look in her eye.

"He looks good," she said, "with that five-o'clock shadow."

Rooke was usually clean-cut, and his scruffiness lately was an unexpected treat. But when her words really sunk in, I shook my head. "How do you do that?"

"Do what?"

"You date women, but you admire men's looks and bodies all the time."

"So? I don't actually feel anything for him. I'm just playing around. Besides, gay men do it to straight women. Why can't I?"

"Well . . . some people think it's weird."

"Some people have a stick up their ass."

I laughed.

"I mean it." She pressed a button to stop the treadmill and mopped the sweat from her brow with a towel. "People find out I'm gay, and they have this little box in their minds that says, 'This is what a gay woman is supposed to be.' And when I don't fit inside it, they scream."

I blinked as I processed that. "Wow, that . . . sucks."

"Actually, it's fun. I love the sound the box makes when I rip it to shreds."

I laughed again, but Hannah leaned toward me, and her face went soft.

"To me, beauty has no gender. If someone looks good, I'm going to tell them. If they've worked hard to lose a hundred pounds or tone the shit out of themselves, whether they're a man or a woman, I'm going to compliment them on it and

hopefully make their day. Because, really, what's more important? That I fit into someone's dumb-ass stereotype, or that I
made someone feel good about themselves?"

I just stared at her, and it took me a minute to realize I had
stopped running on the treadmill. "Look, Hannah, I'm sorry
you've had to deal with—"

"Don't be," she said. "I can handle it. It's just something I
had to learn. The more people find out about you, the more
they try to change you. Not because your heart isn't pure but
because you don't match their stereotypes. People like their
boxes, and they don't like anything that doesn't fit inside them."

I stared again, at a loss for words. How do you react when
someone you've always thought to be carefree and even a little
superficial suddenly says something deep? I guess that meant
I'd stuck Hannah in a box of my own.

After a moment of awkward silence, Hannah broke it by
looking me up and down. "You didn't bring this up because
you're jealous, did you?"

There she was. Right back to her usual self.

I held up a hand. "I'm good."

She smiled. "You sure?"

This was even more awkward than the silence. Luckily, Lily
walked by and gave me a way out.

"Hey," I called. "Your girlfriend is hitting on me."

Lily circled back to us. "What else is new?"

Hannah beamed at her. "Kali is developing a new look for
us. She says I can help."

Lily shook her head. "You just unleashed the beast."

Indeed, I did. By the afternoon, she'd already put together a
few samples for me. She presented her tablet to me and flicked
through a few mock-ups.

"This one I particularly like," she said, as she swiped the screen.

The picture showed a model wearing various pieces of clothing Hannah had incorporated and manipulated right on the screen. He wore a leather suit, all gray with a nude shirt underneath. The finishing touch was the visor he wore over his eyes. The whole outfit was similar to our in-game look but also more edgy and unique.

"I spoke with the designer," she continued, "and already sent him our measurements. Since the tournament has such a big audience, he's willing to see us this afternoon. That way, the clothes would be ready by tomorrow."

"He can do that within a day?"

"With the right technology, yeah."

I handed the tablet back to her and smiled. "Tell him we'll be there. Good job."

Hannah left to call the designer, and I went to the pod room to meet with Derek. He stood behind one of the pods, powering it up for afternoon practice.

"No virtual practice today," I told him. "We've got to get fitted."

"For what?"

"New clothes. If we're in the all-stars, then we need to look it."

His expression fell. "Are you kidding me?"

"Really?" I tilted my head at him. "A nice new suit, I thought you'd be happy." I leaned toward him and grinned. "You're gonna look cool."

"I always look cool." He shot me a flash of his signature million-dollar smile. I laughed. But then his smile faded. "Do you think dressing us up will make the problems go away?"

"Honestly, yeah. If we look all shiny and new, and together, the media might back off."

He actually made a *hmmmm* noise as he thought about that before he said, "Yeah, you're probably right."

He turned back to the pods and started shutting them down.

"We've got photo shoots tomorrow with the new look," I added, "and we're going out tomorrow night."

Derek halted and turned back. "Wait a minute. So, we're cutting into our practice time for two days? We have less than a week until the next matchup."

"This is part of it," I insisted. He didn't look convinced. "We'll get back to training right after this, okay?"

"Kali—"

I took a step toward him and gently squeezed his arm. "It's for Rooke."

With that, his reluctance faded. I could see it diminishing right on his face. Eventually, he sighed and nodded.

"Fine."

That afternoon, we were fitted with our new clothes.

Gray leather jackets, some longer, some shorter, all to match our personalities. All were done halfway up, or secured shut only with straps. The layer beneath was supposed to be nude, but Hannah had the designer custom manipulate the color to match each of our varying skin tones. So, really, it almost looked like there was no layer there at all.

My favorite part? The glasses. We wore visors like in the game, but these had a faint tint to them. Glowing lines snaked across the edges and corners, making circuit-board patterns: squares, and diagonal lines, and small circles with empty middles.

Standing in front of the mirror, I looked down the line on either side of me, with all my teammates dressed the same. I couldn't deny it. We looked good, and we looked like a team.

The next night, we went out as planned.

In front of the club, we posed for pictures, intentionally trying to be seen by every camera that had gathered beyond the velvet ropes. Despite the five of us standing together as one team, the voices emerging from behind the cameras zeroed in on only one person.

"Rooke, any comment on your failed drug test?"

"How many times did you get high?"

"Are you headed for rehab?"

I leaned toward him and spoke through my teeth.

"Don't answer them."

He barely glanced at me. "Not planning on it."

I pushed down the anger burning in my chest and replaced it with a smile on my face. Dr. Renner's words echoed in my mind. Have patience. Be understanding. An addict lashes out. Don't lash back. But even Dr. Renner should have known that while I can take a hit like a pro, I'll only allow so much before I strike back, no matter who was on the receiving end.

With that, I turned and ushered my team into the club. Most clubs catering to the virtual elite boasted an ultramodern style to match the taste and lifestyle of the world's newest celebrities, but this place took it to the next level. I had no idea what the floor was made of. It looked impossibly glossy yet was easy to walk on, like it was made from some blend of glass and concrete. Besides the floor, there wasn't a straight line in sight. The walls curved in and out like rolling waves. Digital red lines ran through them, occasionally dancing and switching their patterns—which I'm sure was meant to entertain those who'd had more than just alcohol inside the club.

We were barely through the lobby and inside the club when we were approached by two men. The first was older, clocking in around his late forties. He looked like the kind of guy who once had a buzz cut, but his hair had since receded so far back that his haircuts should have been half-price. Stubble lined his jaw like he hadn't shaved for three days and was more white than blond. Not sloppy, though. Between his jeans, sport jacket, and days-old stubble, there was a vibe to him that was both professional yet edgy.

The second man, judging by his size and the stance he took up behind the blond man, was either a bouncer or some other form of personal security.

The blond man extended his hand to me.

"Ms. Ling?"

I met his handshake.

"Yes?"

"I'm Chip Weston, the club's owner. Can we talk?"

I smiled. "Kicking us out already? I didn't know my reputation had gotten that bad."

He laughed.

"No, no. It's a business matter."

He motioned to the side. I looked to Derek.

"I'll catch up with you," I told him.

Derek nodded and started leading a path through the club, and my teammates went with him. I followed Chip to a dark corner of the club until we were pressed against a sidewall, as far away from the music and people as we could get. The bouncer, who'd trailed behind, now stood with his back to us. What the hell was the club's owner about to offer me?

Chip rubbed his chin. "I was wondering if you would be interested in making appearances here on a regular basis. We could set up a schedule of what works for you. I'll pay, obviously."

Okay, nothing bad. Clearly, Chip walked around with a bouncer in tow to make himself look important and easy to spot in his own club. Either that, or my reputation had gotten that bad, and Chip was afraid I'd take him out with a single punch if he pissed me off. Secretly, I preferred the latter. Still, here it was. Another opportunity to make money.

Typically, we got free admission, free drinks, free everything. That was standard for pro gamers who showed their famous faces at a club in the Hollywood Hills, with or without a contract. But since the all-star tournament was under way, and the top teams from around the world had descended on L.A.'s nightlife, things were getting a little more serious. Club owners were dishing out top dollar for gamers to sign on the dotted line.

My gaze flicked to Rooke, across the club. He sat on a couch, surrounded by the team. Still, the expression in his eyes looked just a tad empty, as if he were sitting on the couch alone. How much exposure to these clubs could he handle? Tonight was damage control for the sake of our image. What about tomorrow? Was it smart to force him into this kind of environment, night after night? Still, if I didn't have enough money to maintain the team in the first place, what was the point?

"How much?" I asked.

"Well, with the all-star tournament going on, that raises your rep a little. But I gotta tell you, that last matchup—"

"Everyone has a bad night."

"Sure, sure. If it's something you're serious about, we can come up with a number. Really, it depends on your popularity throughout the year and how many appearances you're willing to do."

I nodded again, though I felt numb this time.

There was another way of wording this. How much was I willing to pimp out my team? I'd taken over as owner so no one would have to go out and make appearances if they didn't want to. We weren't milking machines or walking advertisements, and that was the point.

"I'll have to think about it," I told him.

"No problem. But I need an answer within the next few days, or I'm moving on to another team. That's business. You understand."

"Yeah," I said. "I understand."

Chip left, bodyguard in tow. I rested my head against the wall, folded my arms, and pushed a slow breath from my lips. The life of a team owner. Pimp out your team. Make more money. Do whatever you can to stay afloat.

Glamorous, wasn't it?

I started pushing my way across the club, through the throngs of people, when the cell around my wrist buzzed. I glanced at it.

Vigorade, Inc.

Vigorade. The top sports drink for athletic gamers, and one of our sponsors. Brilliant.

I pulled the phone from my wrist and pressed it to my ear.

"Hello?" I shouted over the music.

"Ms. Ling, this is Frank Deckers, Head of Marketing. We need to talk."

"I'm a little busy right now."

"You're in a club near Sunset and Vine. You can make time."

It was rare that I was speechless, but just for a few seconds, all the words fell out of my mouth. How the hell did he know where I was? Eventually, my tongue started working again.

"How did you—"

"There are pictures on the Internet. A ton of them, mostly of you and that love interest of yours. They were uploaded just a few minutes ago. I can see the club's name in the background."

I gritted my teeth together so hard I bit the inside of my cheek. What was the Internet saying about Rooke now? I pushed it from my mind.

"Why are you calling?"

"You were short a player last round, and now the media feeds about your team are nothing but this drug issue—"

"I'm working on fixing it. This isn't going to go away overnight."

"If he hadn't failed his drug test in the first place, this wouldn't even be a problem."

"I know," I said firmly. "I'm working on that, too. He had a slip-up. It won't happen again."

"That's not what I'm telling you," he stressed. "If he hadn't failed his drug test, we wouldn't have this problem."

It didn't take a genius to pick up on the hint. He was telling me to falsify the report if it happened again. My hand clenched, and my cell threatened to collapse under the pressure. I took a breath and relaxed.

"Well," I began, forcing a calm tone to my voice. "If his drug test comes back as failed, then I'm reporting it as such. What is it you expect me to do?"

Maybe if I could get him to straight out say it, I could take action in some way.

"Then maybe next season we'll have to sponsor a team whose reports don't come back negative," he said.

That wasn't enough. All he was saying was that my team used drugs, and maybe others wouldn't. Damn it.

"Most teams can't survive four-on-five matchups," he continued. "It's embarrassing, and we don't want that as the face of our brand." He paused for effect. "I'll let you think about that. Good night, Ms. Ling."

He hung up.

I pressed the phone to my forehead, despite the people in the club looking at me like it was a tinfoil hat instead. Ugh. We needed sponsors. Keeping the team afloat on prize money alone was never enough. Not unless you won every tournament you entered. So, really, money from the sponsors paid for our staff, housing bills, and ongoing costs. Problem was, sponsors tended to drop you after a season if you didn't win or gain enough attention in the media to make up for it, which drove team owners to showcase their players like puppets for the masses.

Was that me now, too? I glanced down at myself, at the sleek designer outfit, all shades of gray and hints of nude. I touched a hand to my glasses. The softly glowing lines, endlessly dancing, played tag in my peripheral. I looked like a futuristic mercenary. Like I really had walked right out of a video game. How marketable.

How perfect.

I shook my head. No. That wasn't me. I was doing this to get the heat off Rooke. That's all.

I started weaving my way through the dancers again, pinballing my way through the crowd as I bounced off one person to the next. One walk through the club, and I already felt like I'd had the shit kicked out of me, and not just because of the dancers.

Finally, I made my way into the quieter and more secluded VIP area and surveyed the club for my teammates. Hannah and Lily danced together in the corner, and more than a few eyes were turned their way. Across the room, Derek was at his usual spot: at the bar with a cluster of ladies around him. On top of being one of the most recognized athletes in L.A., Derek was a charmer, with a perfect build and a million-dollar smile. He couldn't walk two feet in public without getting swarmed like he'd stepped on a wasp's nest. Judging by the grin currently on his face, he didn't mind being stung.

"Did you hear the rumor about him?" some girl giggled behind me. She pointed toward Derek. "He slept with one of his fans and got her pregnant."

My heart stopped. What ludicrous, bullshit rumor was the media feeding to the public now? I flicked through the phone on my wrist, surfing through the latest tabloid gossip feeds.

Another member of Defiance in hot water. Derek Cooper fathers a baby . . .

Damn it.

Damn it. Damn it. Damn it.

I stalked across the club toward Derek and forced my way through his crowd of groupies, ignoring their scowls and comments, most of which ended with the word "bitch."

I grabbed his arm.

"I need to talk to you for a second," I said between my teeth.

He grinned down at me. "Of course." He lifted his head. "Ladies, if you'll excuse me." They all whined, but he assured them he'd return. Derek led the way to a secluded corner in the club. I felt the icy stares of his fans digging into the back of my skull the entire way there.

Once we'd cleared the mob, I faced him and crossed my arms.

"Anything you need to tell me?"

Derek glanced around, as if he were looking for the answer on the club's walls. "Uh, no."

"There's a new Internet rumor."

"About me?" He grinned. Great, he was proud of himself. "Let's have it."

I closed the gap between us and spoke through my teeth. "Did you get a woman pregnant?"

He laughed.

"What? No."

Then he paused, as if the thought had passed through the filters of his brain into the area marked POSSIBLE. "Wait, what's her name?"

"Jennifer."

He rubbed his chin as he thought about that.

"I'm gonna need a last name."

Great. He'd slept with more than one Jennifer.

"Talen," I said.

He thought about it some more.

". . . middle name?"

I smacked him repeatedly with an open palm. "You slept with more than one Jennifer Talen?"

"Ow— I'm joking— Ow. Stop."

I pulled back from my assault, and Derek held up his hands in defense.

"Kali, relax. It's just a joke."

"But you did sleep with a woman named Jennifer Talen."

He rubbed the back of his neck as he thought about it. "Yeah, I think."

"How long ago?"

He shrugged. "Two months, maybe."

My eyes went wide.

"Jesus, Kali. Put your eyes back in your head. It's not true."

"How do you know?"

"Because I might fool around a lot, but I wrap up the grand duke every time."

"The grand duke?" I glanced at the area below his belt and shook my head. "I'm going to fast-forward right through that." He grinned at me. All just a big joke to him. "Are you sure this isn't true?"

"No. I mean, probably not." He lightly smacked my arm

with the back of his hand. "Since when do you care what other people are saying about us?"

Since my bank account depended on it. If the sponsors didn't like what was being said about us, they could pull the plug, then I'd have nothing to fund the team. Still, it wasn't fair to put that on Derek, especially if it all was a lie.

I took a step back. "Sorry. I shouldn't have believed it."

He shrugged. "It's okay. Now, if you'll excuse me . . ."

He slid past me and headed back to his group of ladies, who all grinned and giggled as he returned. I watched him go. It bothered me a little that he wasn't taking this seriously, but maybe he was right. Maybe this was all just bullshit. What's the point of worrying about stuff you can't control, right?

Speaking of worrying about stuff I couldn't control, Rooke appeared through the crowd and started making his way toward me.

I sat on the nearest couch and waited, knowing he was headed my way. I kept my gaze on a vacant corner as I felt my stomach begin to twist. Maybe it wouldn't be that bad, and he was ready to start talking. Or maybe he was going to chew me out again. The couch sunk beside me. I braced myself and decided to speak first. If I was honest and let him know that I was beginning to see the other side of things as team owner, he might come around a little and open up with me, too.

"I still stand by my decisions, but I'm starting to see why owners are so prone to falsifying their drug test results," I admitted. "Almost no one can survive a matchup with only four players, and the sponsors threaten to leave. Plus, it hurts the team. I mean, where's the incentive to be honest?"

"Oh, is that why you lost?"

My breath hitched. That wasn't Rooke's voice. As I turned to look at the man seated next to me, my heart ground to a halt.

Black tattoos. Ice-blue eyes. K-Rig. Or one of them, at least. After my initial shock receded, I recognized him as the one who'd taken me out of the fight. The one I'd told to *make it count.*

I looked to my side and found Rooke halfway to me, but conversing with Cole, of all people. Looked like Oblivion was here, too. They were deep in conversation and failed to glance my way. No one noticed that someone from K-Rig was sitting with me.

Was this even real?

I turned back to my couch mate. His gaze wandered over the room for a minute before he glanced at me.

"American clubs are interesting."

I gawked at him, my jaw unhinging. A member of K-Rig was talking to me. This . . . this was unprecedented. I lifted a hand to my chin, snapped it shut, and rested there, as if it were planned. Smooth, Kali.

"You speak English now?" I asked.

He shrugged.

"Oh, I get it," I continued. "Since you've destroyed my team and secured your dominance in the tournament, it's okay to talk to me."

"Actually, we haven't spoken with anyone in the tournament. Or in any other tournament, really."

"Is that so?" I asked, only half believing him. "Then why am I so lucky?"

He looked out over the club again and ran a hand over his mouth as he thought for a second. "Let's just say that out of everyone we've ever faced off against, only one person tried to fight us with her eyes closed. Some people thought that was pretty impressive."

Good thing my hand was already propping up my chin, or

it would have hit my lap this time. I could tell they'd been impressed by me in the matchup, but I never thought they'd admit it out loud. Might as well take the opportunity to properly introduce myself since I didn't get the chance at the all-star dinner.

"Kali Ling," I said, extending my hand. Maybe he'd take it.

"Kim Jae."

He met my eyes, but not my hand. After waiting with it extended for several seconds, I dropped my arm.

"What do you mean by 'American clubs are interesting'?" I asked.

"Gamers in the States are like actors. This is . . . Hollywood to you."

"Hollywood? How do you mean?"

"You work out, look good for the cameras. You put on a show. But at the end of the day, the actors go home. They don't keep living and breathing their characters every single second." He turned to look at me dead on and pointed at his face. "For us, the mask never comes off."

I swallowed thick. Even when they weren't in the arena, these guys were intimidating.

"So, if gamers in the States are just celebrities, what are you back home?"

"Gods," he said. "Idols. Pop culture doesn't exist unless we define it."

I wasn't entirely surprised. Competitive gaming had always been huge in Asia, especially South Korea. When eSports took off around the world, building with every passing year, the South Koreans started pumping out their gamers the same as they did their pop stars: manufactured pieces of perfection. Everything from the way they moved, talked, and breathed was rehearsed. The Korean influence was felt worldwide when other countries adopted their idea of gamers with image, though not quite to the same extreme. Still, I couldn't help but wonder . . .

How good would I be if I'd been born over there?

"Is it just as intense in China?" I asked.

"Not quite, but almost. More than the States, for sure. Why?"

"Just wondering."

He studied me for a minute as his gaze raked over my face a few times. "You have Chinese heritage." He said it in such a way I wasn't sure if it was a question or a statement. "And you're wondering how your life would be different over there."

He certainly pieced that together pretty quickly.

"Is mind reading listed under your special abilities?" I asked. "Or am I just that obvious?"

"Being number one in the world means understanding your opponent more than they understand themselves."

Wow. So, K-Rig didn't just practice martial arts and weapons.

"Technically, no one is number one in the world," I reminded him.

"Yet." A hint of smugness settled over his expression. "Being born or raised in China wouldn't have changed anything. For you, at least. I think not having the support from family or loved ones made you want it more." He looked me over. "You seem like the rebellious type."

Well, I couldn't argue with that.

Speaking of rebellion, my gaze dropped to the tattooed symbol on his chest. His team's logo would be with him forever unless he went through the pain and cost of getting it removed.

Like he'd said, the mask didn't come off.

I felt the heavy weight of his gaze and turned my eyes up to meet his. A grin tugged at the corner of his mouth. He was entertained by watching me watching him.

"You're wondering if it's real," he concluded, sweeping a

hand from his eyes to his chest. I nodded. The grin gripping the corners of his lips slowly spread across his entire face. "Do you think it is?"

I looked at him again. Really looked. At the outskirts of his irises, searching for the edge of a contact lens. Nothing. Then to the goose bumps prickling the skin beneath the black ink of his tattoo. A light sheen of sweat coated his chest, and yet, nothing smeared. It had to be ink. Had to be laser.

Had to be real.

"Yeah," I concluded with a nod. "I do think it's real."

His grin spread even further. "Then that's all that matters."

"Is it?"

"You tell me." He nodded behind me, where Rooke was standing. "Is that real?"

He was referring to our on-again-off-again relationship that had been portrayed so much in the media during our first tournament together. Well, someone came to play. I did, too. It was my turn to grin.

"When it needs to be."

I wasn't even sure what I meant by that, but Kim Jae cocked his head to the side, and his eyebrows went up.

"Well, Kali Ling," he said, pushing up to his feet. "This is where we say good-bye. Can't be talking for too long." He leaned toward me and winked. "Have to watch my image. You know how that goes." He started to walk away, but not before he added, "See you in the arena."

I laughed. "I'll only see you in the arena again if I make it to the championship."

He paused, casting a fleeting glance at me over his shoulder.

"Like I said, see you in the arena."

My laughter snagged in my throat, and I went numb. K-Rig believed we'd make it. Now, if only *I* could believe it.

As Kim Jae left, Hannah and Lily bounded over and collapsed onto the couch beside me.

"Oh my God," Hannah squealed, full of giggles. "Was that K-Rig?"

I gave her the once-over, studying the way she swayed even while sitting on the couch and the oversized grin plastered on her face.

"Are you drunk?"

"You said we could drink at the clubs!" she sloshed, shouting much louder than she needed to be heard over the music. She nudged me and pointed at a group of guys at another table.

Oblivion sat at another table, with a round of shots between them, and more. Before slamming the shots back, they each popped a hit of HP in their mouths and downed it with a gulp of tequila. Hannah leaned even closer to me and lowered her voice to a whisper, as if she were sharing some grand secret.

"Remember when that was us?"

She laughed. I didn't.

"Remember when Nathan died?"

Hannah's carefree expression faded into one of concern. Wow. I'd sobered her up in four words. Way to be a killjoy, Kali.

I turned my sights back to Oblivion, where Cole had just downed another shot. He coughed and sputtered as he leaned against the bar, pounding it with his fist as if it would help him somehow. His teammates laughed and patted him on the back.

I sighed.

Please be careful.

Rooke finally made his way over and sat on the couch beside me, opposite Hannah and Lily. I leaned toward him, so no one would hear us over the music.

"How are you doing?"

He barely glanced at me. "Fine."

"Just . . . fine? Any issues?"

"No."

He kept his gaze fixed on a spot on the far wall and said nothing else. I sighed. Maybe I was going at him the wrong way. Rooke wasn't the type to open up easily, and in a way, I was cornering him with my questioning. Still, after all the time we'd spent out in the garden, learning Baguazhang together, I thought that his communication skills would have slowly leveled up.

I went numb.

The garden. Practicing Baguazhang. I'd cut out our nightly ritual to drag him to this club, and I hadn't even realized it. I resisted the urge to smack myself on the forehead. No wonder he was upset with me.

I moved a little closer to him. "Did you want to practice in the garden when we get home? It might be cool, in the moonlight."

He blinked slowly, still staring into the distance. His jaw went tight.

"No."

My eyes fell shut, and I sighed. I'd done this to help him. I thought that if I could get him in front of the cameras and show the world we were still a team, he'd feel the same way, too. Instead, I had set him back to where he was weeks ago. Now he was shutting down, and I wasn't sure I'd get him to open up to me again.

Congratulations, Kali Ling. You fucked up again.

The next morning, before practice, I plopped down across from Dr. Renner in her office. Back when I'd first renovated the house, I had given the doc her own office to conduct her sessions with the team.

"He's not talking to me," I confessed as soon as my butt hit the chair.

Her gaze flicked up to meet mine, but she said nothing.

"Rooke," I explained. "He stopped talking to me about what he's going through. Is he talking to you?"

She sighed. "Kali, you know I can't break doctor-patient confidentiality—"

"This is more important than that. I have to know if he's okay."

Dr. Renner simply shook her head. "I'm sorry—"

"Doesn't being team owner count for something? I pay your salary."

"Kali, I can't discuss it. You need to figure it out yourself."

"How the hell am I supposed to do that? He's gone into turtle mode."

Dr. Renner stared at me for a second, and the corners of her lips quivered, as if she was fighting back a smile.

"Turtle mode?"

"You know, buried in his shell. How can I help him if he won't open up?"

Dr. Renner held up her hand.

"Kali, calm down. You're getting out of control."

"Because I want him to be okay. I want the team to be safe. Is that so bad?"

She smiled. "It's not bad. But you can't protect the people you love from everything in the world. They're going to make their own choices and mistakes. You will, too." She looked me over as she thought it herself. "Is this because of your feelings for him—"

"That's not what this is about."

She paused, letting the silence hang between us for a few seconds.

"Are you sure?"

"Yes. You're right about a lot of things, even things I don't want to admit, but with this, you're wrong."

"How do you know?"

"Because if it was anyone on my team, I'd feel the same. And even if I'd never been in a relationship with Rooke, I'd hate this just as much." I crossed my arms over my chest and pushed back into the chair, like I was trying to bury myself inside it. "He was my best friend, and I abandoned him."

"Yes, but you did that because he cut you out first."

"Sometimes it doesn't matter who did it first. It's who did it last."

Dr. Renner tapped her foot a few times. "You can't do everything yourself. You're trying to be his manager, his teammate, and his friend. Owners have to make hard decisions. That's going to affect your relationship with the team."

"But I started this because of my relationship with the team. I want what's best for them."

"What's best for them isn't always what's best for business, and I know you feel that they are more important than money, but if you're not bringing it in, how will you even have a team at all?"

I knew what she was saying. I was letting my emotions get in the way of handling the situation. Being emotional wasn't a bad thing. It was my love of the team that motivated me to do this in the first place, and it was my epic stubbornness that pushed me to keep going every day. But letting my emotions cloud my judgement hindered my decisions as the team owner. I'd barely convinced myself to report Rooke's drug test, and I'd been questioning it ever since. I still did. But if I'd been able to put my emotions aside, it would have been easier to remember that I started all of this to do things right, and that included reporting tests if they failed.

"Okay," I said with a nod. "Thanks, Doc."

I left her office and leaned against the wall outside her door. How could I put my love of the team aside? These were my friends, and I wanted what was best for them. So, how could I know what was right for them if I didn't allow myself to judge how I felt about it first? I clunked my head against the wall. This was harder than I thought it would be. So much harder. And it became even worse when I passed through the living room on my way to the kitchen for breakfast. Hannah sat alone on the couch with an appalled look on her face, staring out into space. I stopped dead. Hannah rarely looked that serious.

I walked up to her and stopped at the edge of the couch. She never noticed. She just sat there, blinking, like she couldn't process the thoughts in her brain.

"What's wrong?" I asked.

She blinked, and her head snapped around to meet my eyes. She didn't answer. Instead, she held up her tablet for me to read. I took it from her, and when I read the headline of the latest tabloid she had opened, my chest went tight.

Team Defiance's Hannah O'Leary comes out as straight.

"It's not true." She pressed her fingers to her mouth and sniffled. "But read the article. People believe it because I'm girly, and I flirt with guys. They hate me now. They think I've been lying about who I am just to get attention."

She curled up on the couch, pulling her legs closer to her. Tears brimmed in her eyes.

"It hurts so much," she said simply. "I mean, I know I'm not supposed to care what other people think, but to claim I'm not gay just because of the way I act sometimes . . ." Her voice caught in her throat. She drew a shaky breath and closed her eyes. "It's like the media knows how to really get to us. They could say anything else about me, and I wouldn't care. But this . . . breaks my heart."

She squeezed the last word out before she broke down. Tears spilled out of her eyes. She hugged her knees to her chest and sobbed against them. Of course it broke her heart. Hannah had said it herself; she hated when people tried to jam her into a box. Now the entire world was trying to tell her that to be gay, she could only act in ways they deemed acceptable.

I didn't know what to do. I wanted to protect her. To take her pain and make it mine. To punch anyone and everyone responsible for making her feel this way. But I couldn't do any of those things. So, instead, I sat down next to her, wrapped my arms around her shoulders, and held her, like how she always held me when I cried.

"I'm just being myself," she sobbed. "Is that really so bad?"

My grip tightened around her. "Most people are afraid to be themselves, so they take it out on those who aren't. You're not afraid, Hannah. You're one hundred percent you, more than anyone else I know. The only thing that's bad is if you hide who you are because of them."

"I know. But it's not fair. How come they're allowed to print lies like that? How come they're allowed to screw with people's lives and get rewarded for it?"

I had no words for her, nothing I could say to take the pain away. Nothing I could do to change this fucked-up situation. So, I sat there with her and held her until she couldn't cry anymore.

After I'd finished comforting Hannah, she'd actually cried herself into exhaustion and fell asleep on the couch. First, the media had targeted Rooke, then Derek, now Hannah. I tried to tell myself it was a coincidence. But the top gaming teams in the world were all in L.A. Why were the tabloids only focusing their attention on us?

I plopped down at my desk in my office and sighed. It was still the early-morning hours, and I felt as though I'd been up for three straight nights. My eyelids weighed about a thousand pounds, give or take. I nearly put my head down on the desk when Derek walked in.

"Ready to go over strategy for the week?"

I lifted my head. When he glanced at me, he ground to a halt, and his eyes went wide.

"You look like a bus ran you over, then backed up again."

I frowned. "Thanks."

"Have you had your morning coffee yet?"

A groan escaped my lips as I pushed back in my chair. "Not even coffee could fix today."

He sat down across from me. "What's wrong?"

I filled him in on Rooke's and Hannah's troubles, but that was all. I wasn't about to dump all my problems onto him, about me questioning if being team owner was the right move, about the money, about everything.

I nodded at his tablet. "What have you got for me?"

"Ascension is a rookie team from China," he began. "But don't let the 'rookie' part fool you. These guys are intense."

He tapped on his tablet and accessed the screen across from my desk. Highlights from the matchups overseas played out on the screen. Ascension played the Chinese equivalent of RAGE, a fierce fighting game in its own right. Unlike the RAGE tournaments in the West, with their fields and towers, the matchup took place in a single, dojo-style room with unlimited, short-range weapons with the sole purpose of eliminating the other team as brutally as possible. There were no bases or points to score. This was total elimination, last team standing. Think Mortal Kombat, only five-on-five and much, much worse.

Even I winced as I watched the four guys and one girl who made up their team slice and dice through every opponent thrown at them. And, believe it or not, they did so with a decent amount of style and grace for such an intense, vicious game. They soared through the air, flipping and gliding around each other, attacking their opponents with combinations nearly impossible for one fighter to coordinate on their own, let alone an entire team. They moved like they were five limbs controlled by one mind. No wonder they were one of the highest rated rookie teams.

"They're fast," Derek said. "And they have amazing coordination."

"You think?"

"But their experience is limited. Being rookies means they don't have many professional matchups for us to bank on. I think you and Lily should go for the flag again. The rest of us will guard the base."

"Lily and I got the flag last time. Maybe someone else should."

He considered that. "True, but we also have to go with our strengths. You and Lily are the fastest runners."

I wasn't sure, and it must have shown on my face because he leaned toward me.

"We have to bank on their inexperience," he insisted. "If we all play where we're strongest, it's our best chance at defeating them."

"Okay. Sounds good." I took a breath and tapped a nail on my desk. "I appreciate you handling this, especially without the credit."

He shrugged. "We're a team. That's what we do. We help each other out."

I smiled, and my heart went a little soft. Even when Derek wasn't trying, he knew how to charm someone.

I started to push away from the desk when he spoke again.

"I grew up without a father."

I knew that about Derek, but I wasn't sure why he was saying it now. I sat back down.

"I mean, I love my mama, and my grandma," he continued. "They raised me. But I swore to myself that if I had kids one day, I'd be there. No matter what. So, if these rumors about Jennifer Talen turn out to be true, then I'm taking responsibility for it." He cleared his throat. "That would mean I'm leaving the team after the tournament."

I went numb. That was the second teammate I was at risk of losing. First Rooke, with his relapse, and now this. Derek was doing the right thing, though. Guess the situation was hitting him harder now than at the club since he was sober and not surrounded by beautiful women.

"I understand," I told him.

"I'm trying to get ahold of Jennifer," he said. "As soon as I know what's going on, I'll let you know." It was quiet for a minute between us. Derek stared at the now-blank screen of his tablet, absentmindedly stroking a finger across it. Geez, this really was getting to him. Another teammate in need of comfort, and not much I could do. Eventually, he shook his head, rested his elbows on my desk, and leaned toward me. "So, what's next for the team?"

More damage control. The rumors about the team were getting out of control. After seeing Hannah's breakdown on the couch, I had to do whatever I could to counter the media. If we lost our fans and our sponsors, we'd be screwed. Plus, I didn't

know how many more attacks on my team I could handle before
I lost it and killed somebody. Now, that would be a headline.

**Kali Ling loses her mind, impales tabloid editor with sword
in real life.**

"More appearances," I told him, hearing the tiredness in my
own voice. "More photo shoots."

"And Ascension?"

". . . and Ascension."

CHAPTER 13

They weren't looking up.

At least, that's what I was trying to think about as Lily and I hovered on the rooftop above the enemy's flag. Two of Ascension's players stood guard, swords out as they monitored every movement at ground level. Looks like they hadn't prepped for the vertical component of the game.

But instead of focusing on our opponents, my mind was on something else. Something that wasn't sitting right with me. The VGL had announced a new rule shortly before the round began. Just like last Saturday night, we had to be plugged in for the entire line of matchups until ours played out. But this week, they'd added another rule, and this one didn't make any sense.

If no team scores, the game will reset.

How would that even happen? If one team wiped out the other, then the remaining team would have no problem scoring. Therefore, the game wouldn't need to reset. So, what was the point?

Lily backed up several steps from the roof's edge and waved for me to follow. I took a stance at her side and drew my sword. She gripped an axe in each hand.

I counted down with my fingers, a silent signal for us both.

3, 2, 1 . . .

We sprinted.

We reached the roof's edge in sync and pushed off together. We slid through the air, our weapons trailing a blazing arc of gray fire across the sky. Halfway through our descent, Ascension turned to face us, weapons out, stance ready.

Oh shit.

They knew. They had prepared for the vertical and been waiting for us to attack from exactly that angle.

Game on.

We slammed together.

My feet hit the pavement, my sword hit my opponent's, and we started a bloodthirsty duet. We swirled and danced all around the glowing blue flag, our weapons trailing gray smoke, theirs arcing with gold.

I knocked my opponent's arm open and slammed a foot into his ribs. He stumbled back, lost his step, and crashed into the pavement. I pounced on him, reeled back my blade, and drove it straight into his heart. He seized, gripping the sword where it disappeared into his chest, and went limp.

Damn. Wasn't even winded. I grinned down at his lifeless body. Hope you took notes, junior.

I retrieved my weapon and turned to find my teammate pulling her own axe out of her opponent's skull. A pool of blood soaked the street beneath his cracked cranium and glassy eyes. Lily caught my eye and winked.

She zipped through the flag and continued her pace down the street. A flash of blue consumed her, and the horn rang out. Two down and we already had our flag. Maybe we did deserve to be in this tournament, after all.

I sheathed my sword and pursued Lily as she headed for our base.

"We're coming in," I said into the mic. "Lily's got the flag."

"No sign of Ascension on our side yet," Derek answered. "Keep an eye out. They might be planning to ambush you."

I dropped back a little and followed Lily from ten feet back, guarding her from the rear. The soft glow from the flag rippled behind her like a mermaid's tail in the ocean. We made it two blocks from the enemy's base before I heard the footsteps. Derek was right. Ascension was planning an ambush.

I unsheathed my sword as I ran. "Keep going," I told Lily through the mic. "Get as far as you can until we have to fight."

"Got it," she huffed.

I gripped my sword tight and smiled.

Bring it on.

The footsteps drew closer, closing in at a steady yet incredibly quick rate. Just how fast were these guys? Then the constant beat tapping against the pavement grew heavier, more mechanical, like our pursuer was wearing metal boots.

A digitized voice spoke out.

"Target acquired."

What the hell was that?

Lily glanced back, and skidded to a stop ahead of me. She froze, her lips spreading into a silent scream. I nearly crashed into her and jerked to the side just before a full-on collision.

"Lil, what . . ."

My voice trailed off as I whirled around, and my body turned to ice. Running down the street toward us was a seven-foot-tall mechanical beast with six-inch-long blades for fingers. Metal from head to toe, it ran on two legs and looked like an alien had mated with a cyborg.

It closed in, now twenty feet away, maybe less.

My feet were concrete blocks, refusing to move. Cold sweat slid down the back of my neck. My mouth was an open hole, and all I could do was blink.

All I could see were its blades.

It narrowed its sights on Lily. And smiled.

"Target acquired."

A chilling, high-pitched scream ripped from Lily's mouth as it drove into her, slamming its six-inch claws through her body. She spasmed and gagged. Her body convulsed, and blood spilled out of her mouth. The machine hoisted her off the ground as its blades protruded out her back. Lily convulsed once more, her legs kicking wildly, then suddenly went rag-doll limp. The machine dropped her to the ground.

The glow faded from her body.

The flag reset.

Damn it. Now I'd have to backtrack to Ascension's base just to pick it up again.

Derek's voice sounded in my ear. "What the hell just happened guys? Why did the flag reset?"

Hannah's voice followed. "Is Lily out? Why did she scream like that?"

Then Rooke. "Ascension's still not here. Did they attack you?"

Nope. Definitely not Ascension.

Lily's body slowly faded from view, and that machine, that *thing*, turned to face me. Lily's blood dripped off its claws.

I backed away as my heart thrummed in my heart. What the hell was this? Nonplayer characters, or NPCs, were common in standard games, but never in the VGL had players faced anyone but each other.

"Kali?" Derek's voice echoed in my ear again. "Kali, come in."

"Something else is in the game," I told Derek as I pedaled backwards. "It just took out Lily."

"Some*thing*?"

"Some kind of NPC. I'm looking it now."

The machine stared back, its head slightly tilted, just watching. Why wasn't it attacking me?

"Can you get our flag back?" he asked.

Good question. If I went for the flag, would that thing stop me? I halted my backwards retreat and shook my head. What the hell was I doing? Backing away from a fight? That wasn't Kali Ling, the warrior. I stood my ground. Fought every battle. The tougher, the better. Besides, ten blades against one . . .

Now, that sounded like fun.

"I'm on it," I told Derek.

I gripped my sword and charged for the machine. Come on, tinman. Let's dance. The machine stood its ground, waiting for me to come to it, if it was really waiting at all. It took no stance, made no preparations for my pending attack. It simply stood there.

As I closed in on the machine, my teammates' voices came through the mic.

"Where did he go?"

"I lost sight of him."

A horn rang out. Ascension had our flag.

"Damn it."

"What the hell just happened?"

"Where are they?"

Judging by the frantic, confused sounds of my teammates' voices, Ascension had pulled some rogue move on our flag. On my side of the game, just as I reached the machine, its head twisted around, snapping to attention elsewhere.

"Target acquired."

It bolted toward the right and soared away, never giving me a second glance. The metal thwacking of its feet clanged down the street. Uh, did it just . . . refuse to fight me? No one refuses to fight me.

I charged after it, and as my feet pounded the pavement, I had a realization about where the machine was going. It had entered the game when Lily picked up our flag and came back to life just as Ascension picked up ours.

"Guys, get back to our base," I said. "Let Ascension go."

"What?" Derek shouted. "Let them go?"

"Trust me on this. They won't make it far."

I cut west across the map, hoping to intersect Ascension on their way north back to their base. Technically, right now Ascension's flag would be unguarded and an easy take, but I had to know what that machine was up to if I had any chance at defeating it.

I rounded a corner and discovered a hodgepodge path of boxes, storefront awnings, and fire-escape stairs leading up to the roof-top. I charged for it, bounding up the boxes and taking the steps two at a time. As I hit the first roof, the distant sound of clanking metal footsteps tugged at my ears, guiding my journey.

At a major intersection, I found them.

All three of Ascension's remaining players were running the flag in. The machine was right there with them. The two players without the flag had jumped on its back and were hacking away at its metal exterior. The machine hauled them along, ignoring their attacks, its focus only on the flag carrier. He stood about five feet ahead, glowing faintly blue, shifting back and forth like he was fighting his own two feet. One wanted to run, the other wanted to fight.

Hannah's voice sounded in my ear.

"What are we doing?" She sounded panicked. "Kali, do you have eyes on them?"

I pressed my lips to the mic. "I do. The NPC is after them." I smiled as I watched the indecisive flag carrier and the NPC closing in on him. "They're about to lose the flag."

A foot away from the flag carrier, a player on the machine's back rose and swung his blade, slicing clean through the machine's neck. Its head clanged on the pavement and rolled away while its body collapsed to its knees and face-planted on the ground. The machine, in all its pieces, slowly faded from view.

Oh shit.

That machine was out. Ascension had our flag and was only a few blocks away from their base. We were one point away from being out of the match and out of the tournament. Now the only thing that stood between us and defeat was me.

Three on one. Sixty seconds from the base.

Did I say I liked a challenge? I swallowed.

Adrenaline pumped through every vein. I backed up several steps, gripping my sword, and sprinted forward. But when I reached the roof's edge, Ascension erupted in a chorus of panicked cries. I stumbled to a halt and peered over the edge. In the exact spot where it had been defeated, the machine was reappearing, only a faint outline at first but growing more opaque with every passing second.

An instant respawn.

Great.

So, that meant there was no way to defeat this thing. Good thing for us, it was about to take out Ascension's flag carrier. Bad thing for us, my only chance at scoring and winning the game was to outrun it.

As soon as the machine fully materialized, it lunged for the flag carrier, completely ignoring the other players hacking away at its back. The machine swung its massive arms, and its claws ripped through their flag carrier. Blood sprayed out in every direction, like a sprinkler system gone haywire. He crumpled to the ground, dead before he even hit the pavement. The glow faded from his body.

"Our flag's back," Derek announced. "Did you take them out?"

"Nope. That thing did. It's targeting the flag carriers."

I backed away from the roof's edge and turned north, heading for the enemy's flag. I'd have a minute's head start if I was lucky. Probably less.

"I'm going for the flag," I told the team.

"Do you need help?" Rooke asked.

"Just stay where you are. Guard our base."

"Kali—"

"Guard our base," I said through my teeth. "I've got this."

I raced along the rooftops, jumping between the gaps in the buildings. I had the advantage. The two remaining members of Ascension would have to double back and get their flag from our base. And that was if they even made it there and figured out what was happening inside the game first. So, all I had to worry about was that . . . *thing*.

Easy, peasy. Right?

My stomach spun.

I reached the northern edge of the rooftops, where their flag sat below. No one was guarding it. I glanced up and down the street. No one was even close. That machine had them scattered. Scrambling. Point for me. At least until I picked up the flag.

Here goes.

I backed up several steps, ran full speed, and jumped as I reached the end. I arced through the air, rolled as I landed, and sprang to my feet in one smooth movement. I zipped through the flag, powered up, and bolted down the street. This time, I got about halfway to our base before I heard the words.

"Target acquired."

My stomach turned into a bundle of nerves, but I pumped my legs and pushed onward. The clanking metal footsteps echoed down the street, gaining on me with every stride. Can't kill it. Can't outrun it. How the hell was I going to defeat this thing?

Clank.

Another foot closer.

Clank.

I was running out of time.

All around me was nothing but buildings and storefronts, glass windows, and neon signs. If I stopped running to fight that thing, I'd lose my lead on it. But I was losing my lead anyway.

There had to be a way. This was a game, and there was always a way to win.

What if there wasn't?

Sweat streamed down my back as I ran. My breaths came in faster and faster pants, and it wasn't just from the running. The footsteps closed in. A swiping sound cut through the air behind me, and I could practically taste its metal claws ripping through my throat.

Derek appeared from a side street and slammed into the machine. It ignored him, still moving, reaching toward me. Damn it. He was going to get himself kicked out of the game.

"It's an instant respawn," I shouted over my shoulder as I ran. "Leave it."

Derek thrust his sword through the machine's spine. It seized up, its metal bits grinding together, and it collapsed to the ground and faded from view.

Derek looked up at me. "What?"

I skidded to a stop. "It respawns," I repeated.

On cue, the image of the machine started to materialize. I scrambled backwards.

"Guard our base," I told Derek, as I turned around to bolt. "I'm bringing it in."

"But—"

"Now!" I shouted over my shoulder, as my feet pounded toward the west.

"Kali," he called. "The base is south . . ."

His voice faded as I disappeared into the tight alleyway corridors of the map's western edge. Metal footsteps clanked on the pavement behind me.

This was planned chaos. I could just picture the announcers.

". . . Both teams scrambling . . . Defiance is all over the map . . ."

I zigzagged through the alleyways, darting between corners, like a skier on the slopes. After several sharp turns, I slipped behind a corner, drew my sword, pressed my back against the wall, and crouched, listening. Counting. The thing about machines is they're more predictable than most people realize. They're like clockwork, and this one was no different. Its footsteps were a constant, perfect rhythm. Too perfect. One footstep exactly every half a second, in fact.

Clank, clank, clank, clank.

I counted. Three . . . two . . . one . . .

I lunged just as it rounded the corner and sliced through its knees. It tumbled forward and crashed against the alley floor, metal screeching against the pavement. I pounced on its back, raised my sword, and hacked off its remaining limbs. The metal monster was now a limbless heap of parts. Its abdomen and head remained intact, so it was still technically in play.

Couldn't fight me. Couldn't chase me.

Couldn't respawn, either.

I walked around the machine and stopped a foot away from

its head. Its teeth snapped at me. Like a zombie, it inched its way ever forward, still hungry, still locked on its prey.

I took a knee before it and grinned.

"Get me now, bitch."

It did.

In a blink, one of its missing arms re-formed, latched onto my ankle, and sunk its metal teeth through my boot.

I screamed.

I slammed my sword down, slicing through its newly re-formed hand, and started backpedaling, my ankle protesting with every kick. I scrambled to my feet and bolted in the opposite direction, gritting my teeth against the pain. Metal grinding against metal filled the air, and I glanced behind me.

Big mistake. Rule one of being chased: Never look back.

Parts re-formed around the machine, swirling and linking together. Its missing arm stretched into molded hands, each ending in a set of claws. It pushed itself up and was running before its legs were even fully formed, clacking on thigh stumps, then knee stumps, as more of its limbs self-repaired with every step.

"Target acquired."

Holy. Fucking. Shit.

This was a nightmare.

I pressed my lips to my mic and screamed something I'd never expected to come from my mouth.

"Help."

No one answered.

My ankle screamed, my breath panted through my lungs, and sweat streaked down my face. Lightning jolts of agony shot up my leg every time my foot smacked against the concrete. The clanking of metal footsteps grew closer.

It's not real, I told myself. The pain isn't real. That . . . thing isn't real.

The footsteps closed in, and each became another whispered promise of death. Clank. *I'm coming for you.* Clank. *There's nowhere to hide.* I pushed my legs as hard as they would go and braced myself for the attack. Waiting for the blades to slice through my body, pierce through my abdomen, and spill blood down my body. I went weak.

My vision swirled.

Ankle gave out.

Knees buckled.

I slammed into the wall and crumpled to the ground. My hands slapped the pavement as I fell. My skin burned as it slid. Grunting, I pushed over to my back and looked up.

It towered over me, seven feet tall, glowing in the moonlight, like some mechanical god. Or a demon.

It closed in.

It reached for me, its blades glistening. I backpedaled, ankle howling with each kick. It stayed right on top of me and slammed a foot down on my bad ankle. Bones crunched and snapped. I cried out. The taste of vomit burned the back of my throat.

It reeled back, its claw aiming for the final strike.

I cringed, waiting for the blow.

A flash of blond-red hair soared past me. Hannah slammed into the machine just inches from me and sliced its head clean off. It faded from view.

I shoved down the sick feeling in my throat as Hannah helped me to my feet.

"It's an instant respawn," I told her.

"I know. Can you run?"

The machine started to materialize. With a snarl, Hannah chopped off its head again just as it fully materialized.

Could I run?

My foot throbbed and pulsed, and any weight on it sent a shock wave of agony up my leg. So, of course, my answer was . . .

"Yes," I said through gritted teeth. "I can run."

"Good."

The machine faded into view again. Hannah blocked its path, her massive battle-axe turned sideways, stretching the width of the alleyway.

"Derek and Rooke are guarding the flag," she said over her shoulder. "I'll give you as much time as I can."

The machine solidified into the virtual world.

"Go!" she shouted.

I took off in a limping run, but this time, I didn't look back. Judging by the sounds of metal clanging off the brick walls and Hannah's grunts, it sounded like she was ripping that machine apart with her bare hands.

Funny, usually I'm the one with anger issues.

I pushed myself through the streets, gritting my teeth against the jolts of blinding pain that shot up my leg every time my foot smacked the concrete. Come on, Kali. Footballers play on broken feet.

Footballers.

The glowing hue of the flag rippled behind me as my reflection slid through the glass windows and bus shelters of the street level. The sky opened up, and the rain poured down, pounded against my battered body, slapping every bruise and tear. Kick a girl while she's down, why don't you?

Finally, I rounded the corner to our base, where my male teammates stood at the end, guarding it.

I limped faster.

Derek met me halfway down the street and reversed directions when he reached my side, running beside me to protect the flag to the base.

"Where's Hannah?" he huffed.

"In berserker mode."

Twenty feet from the base, the remaining Ascension players stepped into our path from a darkened alleyway. Ugh. With the fight against the machine, I'd forgotten about the other team. Now it was two-on-three for the match and the game. I glanced down at my battered body. Well, two-and-a-half, maybe. Still, it was an interesting scenario. We were split. But they were surrounded.

Derek waved Rooke up and drew his own sword.

"Get to the base," he said to me. "We'll hold them off."

He charged for Ascension. Rooke did the same. They crashed together in a broken, harsh melody of clashing swords, heavy grunts, and thick, crunching punches.

I bolted for the base. Actually, I more or less limped like a dying gazelle around the skirmish.

Just as I passed the fight, Rooke's opponent broke away and lunged for me. Rooke tackled him to the ground, but not before the tip of his sword caught my knee, slicing a gash across my good leg. I stumbled and hit the pavement. Blood dripped out of the wound and swirled with the rain to form a puddle beneath my legs. Perfect. Between my ripped left knee and shattered right foot, I couldn't run. Hell, I couldn't even push myself to standing.

Fuck it.

I crawled along the ground, pulling myself toward the base. My hands and knees scraped along the pavement, and tiny bits of gravel dug into my skin like needles. But I dragged myself onward. Ten feet from victory.

Now nine.

"Target acquired."

Clanking footsteps pounded down the street toward me.

My body turned to ice, and my stomach lurched, shooting acid up my throat. For the second time in the tournament, existential vomit became my biggest concern.

Crawl faster, damn it.

Eight feet away, seven, six. The footsteps descended on me, and a metallic hand clamped around my good ankle and pulled.

Uh-oh.

I slid backwards. Six feet, seven, eight, nine, ten . . .

DAMN IT.

As I bumped along the pavement, my body went from ice-cold to subarctic, and it wasn't only because of the machine. The new rule of the night replayed in my mind.

The game will reset if no team scores.

We'd have to do this whole thing again. We'd have to face this thing *again*.

No.

NO. NO. NO.

I lost it.

I ripped my dagger from its sheath, twisted around, and started filleting the machine. Hunks of metal went flying. I shouted incoherently. Even I don't know what I was saying. The machine glitched and contorted, its arms twisting into impossible angles.

This was my berserker mode.

After several more stabs, the machine seized a final time and powered down. It faded from view.

I braced my hands against the pavement to keep myself from collapsing. My ankle throbbed, my head pounded, and my skin burned from dragging along the road. Rooke hurried to my side in a stumbling gait. Blood soaked his pant leg, starting at a gash in his upper thigh. More blood dripped from his nose, and his right eye was already turning black.

"Derek's out," he said as he slipped my arm around his shoulder and pulled me up beside him. "Ascension's out. It's just us."

Yeah, just us. *And* the robotic spawn of Satan.

Together, we started limping and stumbling toward the base. Between all our injuries, we must have looked like we were competing in a drunken, three-legged race. We closed in on the base. Three feet. Now two.

Metal footsteps pounded behind us.

"Target acquired."

Fuck!

The robot lunged for me and grabbed both ankles. I went down hard, slamming into the pavement. Pain detonated in every cell as my body cracked against the road. My vision swirled. Rooke latched onto my wrists. The machine had my ankles. They both pulled, like I was a toy and they were two dogs playing tug-of-war. I felt like I was being ripped apart. I glanced over my head, where Rooke was straining with my arms. My fingertips were two inches away from the base, if not less.

"Pull it out," I screamed. "Pull my arm out of the socket."

Rooke glanced between me and the base and furiously shook his head.

"Do it!"

Instead, he let go.

Argh. I'll kill him next.

I slid away from the base again, my body bumping along the pavement. But what was that I'd said about machines? They're predictable, and it looked like I wasn't the only one who realized it.

I slid to a stop when the robot released my ankles and reared back to deliver the final blow. Rooke instantly snatched me back, dragging me by the arms. The robot scrambled after us. I backpedaled, pushing my feet into the pavement, propelling us even faster toward the flag's home.

We closed in on the base. The machine closed in on us.

Three feet away.

The machine swiped its hands through the air, missing me by an inch.

Two feet away.

Its claw sliced through the bottom of my boot.

One foot away.

Its eyes were all I could see.

Rooke's leg gave out, and he collapsed three inches from the base. I lunged.

Reached.

Strained.

And slammed my hand home.

A glowing outline of the flag appeared. The horn echoed overhead.

Victory.

I collapsed and rolled onto my back, just in time to watch the machine descend on me. I froze. My throat constricted, and I sucked in a raspy breath as it reached for me. Then the outline of the machine wavered and grew transparent. Moonlight cut through its image. Then the stars appeared. And the night sky, more and more, until the machine faded from view completely. A phantom wind whispered along my neck, as if its claws had passed right through my skin.

I shuddered.

Rooke's heavy breaths next to me brought me back to reality. Or, at least, as close to reality as we could get in this place. We lay on the pavement together, the rain drenching our battered bodies. Breaths heaved from our chests. At some point, out of the absolute absurdity of the matchup, I started laughing.

Rooke glanced at me. "You're laughing?" He shook his head. "You're fucking crazy."

"And what happened to you?" I pointed down at his leg and pouted, mocking him. "Do you have a boo-boo?"

He chuckled. "Wanna talk about getting a boo-boo? I nearly swept you off your feet and carried you to the flag."

I gave him the side-eye. "Oh, I would have hurt you. Very, very badly."

"I would have enjoyed that." He winked.

And, for a second, there he was. My friend. A glimmer of the person he used to be. My heart just about exploded, and I would have let it. In that moment, everything was aligned. Rooke was at my side, and he was smiling. Hell, even I was smiling. We'd worked together. We'd won together. Real or virtual, for just that fleeting second, all the things in my life were right where they belonged.

My vision went black, and I felt the insides of the pod. I blinked away stars as my senses adjusted to reality. My chest heaved, my hands shook, and it had nothing to do with plugging in. I braced my hands against the sides of the pod, gasping for air. We barely made it. Just barely.

And that thing. That machine.

I shuddered. I'd dream about it tonight, whatever that was.

I wriggled my foot. No pain. It was fine. Of course it would be. None of the pain or injuries I'd endured in the game were real, and just like the matchup, once the pod stopped sending signals to my nerves, everything virtual vanished in an instant. Still, my heaving breaths took a while to subside.

The speakers around me crackled as the real-life audio cut into the pod.

"Wow, wow, wow," Marcus said and repeated it several more times. "What a match. What a show by Defiance. They earned every inch of that map."

"This is why they're calling it the all-star tournament. That was the most insane thing I've ever seen," Howie chimed in, adrenaline pumping through his own voice. "And with that, Defiance advances to the next round."

The next round. What the hell would be the next round?

CHAPTER 14

The press conference after the matchup didn't go as planned. I sat with my teammates in front of the sea of people and pointed at a reporter. He stood and turned toward Rooke.

"Rumors are you're headed for rehab. Any comment on that?"

I cut Rooke off before he could answer and spoke into my mic. "We're not going to be discussing that at this time."

Before I could point to another reporter, one stood on his own and looked at Lily. "Given that your girlfriend recently came out as straight, how did that make you feel?"

I glanced at Hannah. Her face was blank. On most people, I would have taken that as a good sign, but I knew for Hannah, a lack of cheer and a stony expression meant she was really feeling this.

Lily stuttered. "She's not—"

The reporter pressed onward. "Are you still together?"

"Well, yes—"

He scoffed. "So, you're standing by her?"

She glanced at me, her eyes pleading for help. I pressed my lips to my microphone.

"Do any of you have questions about our gameplay?"

Silence answered. I think someone sneezed.

I fought the urge to sigh. Really, people? After a matchup

that intense, the concern was on the gossip and rumors circling my team?

"Fine," I said, my voice stern. "I think it was interesting how the VGL introduced NPCs into the arena. It's a nice shake-up from the norm, and it really challenged us as a team."

No one said anything. No one even raised a hand.

"Isn't the game more important to you than our presence in the tabloids?" I asked the crowd.

Someone at the back answered me. "Then stop creating gossip."

A few people laughed.

I placed my hands down on either side of the mic. "If none of you have questions pertaining to the game, then this conference is over."

The conference was over.

The following week, the media had yet to let up on my team. On my tablet, I flicked through the covers of nearly every tabloid.

Rehab for Team Defiance?

Hannah O'Leary's secret straight life revealed.

Exclusive photos of Jennifer Talen's baby bump.

I shook my head. I knew it was best to leave it alone and not even read these headlines. If we weathered the storm long enough, they'd find someone else to go after. Still, every instinct inside me was screaming to call out the lies and protect my team. For my own sanity, I left my tablet in my bedroom as I headed down to the kitchen for breakfast. It was practically pointless. When I walked into the room, Hannah was hunched over the table, an untouched breakfast at her side and a tablet gripped in her hands.

"Bringing your tablet to the breakfast table now?"

She failed to look up at me. "I would have brought my phone, but someone took it away."

Ouch. Well, somebody was cheeky this morning.

I grabbed a coffee and a plate of my perfect proportioned breakfast, and sat down across from her. Three bites into my meal, and Derek walked into the room

"We can relax," he announced, sitting down at the table. "I finally got ahold of Jennifer. The rumors aren't true, and it's not her fault, either."

I let out a heavy breath. Thank God. Derek wasn't leaving the team, and he didn't have this huge responsibility before he was ready for it. It must have been a load off his mind, too.

"How do you know it's not her fault?" I spooned a mouthful of blueberry yogurt into my mouth.

"Apparently, she had her identity stolen by an AI bot. The person smearing us all over the Internet isn't even a real person. It's a program pretending to be her."

I thought about that. "How would an AI bot know about you two sleeping together?"

He shrugged. "A thousand ways. A blog. Instant messages. A hacked online journal. If someone had a one-night stand with a pro gamer, do you really think they're not going to tell their friends about it?"

Hannah pointed at Derek and nodded vehemently. "He has a point. If I slept with someone famous, I'd tell everyone I know."

"You are famous."

"You're missing the point, Kali," Derek said. "People put their lives online. Even the best antitheft software can't stop every AI program from taking their identity."

Decades ago, the general public had worried about other people stealing their identities. So they were a little blindsided when computers started doing it, too, taking over their social-media accounts, getting them fired from their jobs or disowned by their families for comments that weren't even real.

Derek took a breath. "Here's the thing. I don't think the target of the attack is Jennifer. The bot hasn't touched her bank accounts, online profiles, or anything else. This is only about our one-night stand. I think someone is using her to target me."

I tried to follow his line of thought. "Basically, you think someone created this AI program just to make you look bad?"

"And, by extension, the team."

"Who would do that? A kid, or somebody with no life hoping their name would end up in the news?"

"Could be. Or . . ."

"Or?" I prodded.

He sighed. "Maybe this is crazy, but we all know who specializes in artificial intelligence programs."

I frowned at him. "Come on. Tamachi is not behind this."

Derek didn't look certain. "Maybe not Tamachi, but it could be someone inside his organization. Or it could be a marketing ploy. I'm sure even Tamachi has to agree to the VGL's seedy brand of advertising."

"He invited us into this tournament. He brought me to the meeting at the VGL. Why would he do any of those things, then try to destroy our reputation?"

He shrugged.

"I don't know. Maybe I'm wrong."

"More good news," Hannah piped up, gripping her tablet. "Looks like the media has a new target in the tournament. Our team's problems will be old news soon."

A strange mix of relief and guilt churned inside my gut.

"Well, that's . . . kind of terrible, actually. To think of someone else getting hit like that."

"I know," she said. "But if it gets the heat off us . . ."

True. As much as I hated for someone else to suffer, we needed the break.

"Who's the victim?" Derek asked.

"Apparently, they've got an Asian team in some sort of dating scandal, and one of the European players is secretly an heir to a billion-dollar fortune."

"So, that's how it evolves," I said with a sigh. "From the world's greatest competition and a nine-figure grand prize to dating scandals and family dramas."

"Uh, Kali . . ." Hannah's voice trailed off. She glanced at me, and bit her lip.

"What?"

She flashed her tablet at me. On it was a photo of me and Kim Jae together at the club. The caption read:

Defiance and K-Rig: Enemies with Benefits?

I went numb. You'd think after dealing with this bullshit for years, I wouldn't be surprised by this kind of thing anymore, but the media always found a way.

"There's commentary," Hannah said. Her finger hovered over the tablet. I sighed, and nodded.

"Let's hear it."

She tapped the PLAY button. The hosts of Hypnotized popped up on the screen.

"Are we serious about this? Kali Ling and Kim Jae actually hooked up at a club? K-Rig doesn't associate with anyone."

"He's certainly associating with her."

They laughed.

"First her own teammate and now the enemy. Can't Kali Ling keep her legs together?"

My teeth gritted together so hard, I thought they would crack.

"You're screwed," Derek said to me. "Do you have any idea how the Korean fans are going to react to this?"

I knew exactly how the Korean fans would react. When it came to the portrayal of relationships and affairs in the gaming world, the East was the complete opposite of the West. While Americans practically squealed over a new gamer-celebrity couple, the Korean players portrayed themselves as eternally single—and, hypothetically, available. My mind flashed back to the fans at the all-star dinner reveal and the women literally throwing themselves at K-Rig. Now they'd be diving at me— probably with knives.

"Wait a minute," one of the hosts continued. "This is why Rooke failed a drug test? He couldn't handle seeing her with another guy? How long has this been going on?"

"Does that mean he relapsed because she left him, or did she leave because of the drugs?"

"Either way, she's a bitch."

My hands morphed into trembling fists. Hannah hit the PAUSE button before I could hear more.

"Maybe it'll be okay," she said, making a calming motion with her hand. "They still have another scandal. It could trump yours."

"It'll probably be about us, too," I said. "The media has latched on, and they're not letting us go anytime soon. They're bleeding us dry and loving every minute of it."

Hannah frowned at me. "How could the next scandal be about us? It's a European player who's the heir to a billion-dollar fortune. Is that you?"

I scowled at her. "Fine."

Hannah tapped the screen a few times. "A new feed just popped up. Looks like the announcement."

She hit the PLAY button again. The traditional hosts of Hypnotized cut out, and were replaced by a breaking news segment by the same network. Celebrity gossip as breaking news. Oh, how far we've come. A single man sat behind a news desk. After introducing himself, he got right down to business.

"We've just confirmed this, so we're bringing it to you live. So, who is this disenchanted heiress worth a cool thirty billion? That would be Defiance's Lily Collins."

WHAT?

I nearly jumped out of my chair, and everything inside went numb. No, that had to be a mistake. They were just making things up now. Had to be. My gaze flicked up to Hannah. I'd never seen the expression of someone being shell-shocked before, but it was the only way to describe the look on her face. My eyes fell shut. Holy shit. Either it was bullshit, and she couldn't believe it, or it was true, and she had no idea. On cue, Lily walked into the room and started grabbing her breakfast from the counter. Hannah slammed her tablet down on the table.

"You're an heiress?"

"I don't want to talk about it."

"So I find out in front of Kali and Derek?"

"I said I don't want to talk about it."

I sat in my office, pretending I couldn't hear them shouting through the walls as I hunched over my computer, investigating Lily's background. Apparently, she'd moved to the States and changed her surname a few years ago. But given that I had no idea what her original name was, I was having trouble tracking down who her family really was.

As for me, the death threats had already started, mostly directed through the team's online sites. People saying things like they'd kill my mother, or cut out my uterus—all because I might or might not have been dating another gamer. Lovely.

A door slammed upstairs. Heavy footsteps pounded through the house, heading straight for my office. Hannah stormed into the room, and I quickly closed out the information on my computer.

"She holed up in her room," Hannah said, sitting down in a huff. "She doesn't want to talk to anybody. Even me. I knew her family was a real sore spot for her and that she'd changed her last name."

"But you didn't know—"

"About the money and who her family really is? No. I didn't have a clue."

Who her family really is? Looks like Hannah knew now. I nearly asked, and bit my lip to keep the question from slipping out.

"I feel like I don't even know her," she said. "Am I being selfish about this?"

"I don't think so. I don't think you should have to tell each other everything, but the big stuff, yeah. And that was pretty big." I rested my arms on my desk and leaned toward her. "Look, I have a favor to ask you."

She nodded. "Yeah?"

"It's just . . . first Rooke's relapse, then Derek's controversy, and everything else that's happened, we can't afford to look any more broken than we already are. Can you just pretend that everything is okay between you two until the end of the tournament?"

She tensed and narrowed her eyes at me.

"Sure," she said slowly. "Do you want us to kiss in the middle of a match?"

I bit my tongue. It was something Rooke and I had done in our first tournament, to prove to the media that we were a couple, when we actually weren't.

"That's not the same thing," I told her.

She frowned. "It's exactly the same thing."

"I'm just asking—"

She stood up from her chair and stomped toward the door.

"I'll be in the training room," she muttered.

She slammed my door shut, too.

Damn it.

I let my head roll back against the chair and drew in a slow, careful breath. There had to be a way to fix this. She wouldn't talk to Hannah, but maybe she'd talk to me.

I made my way to Lily's room and knocked on the door. No answer. I pressed an ear against the door and heard the faint, muffled sounds of techno-metal music. She was wearing headphones.

I tried the knob. It wasn't locked, so I nudged it open a little.

"Lil?" I called through the crack.

I edged the door open a bit more and peeked around the room. The walls of Lily's bedroom were painted a deep, dark blue, like the depths of the ocean. Every so many feet the deep blue was interrupted by oversized, spray-painted depictions of blossoming flowers, graffiti-art style. Lily had done the artwork.

Speaking of, the artist herself stood on the far side of the room, facing away from me, head bobbing to the death-tech metal blasting out of her cordless headphones. Brush in hand, she swiped across a canvas propped up on an easel.

I walked up behind her.

"Hey," I said, tapping her on the shoulder.

She jumped and whirled around, brandishing her brush like a sword. Still, she would have looked fierce if it weren't for the paint smudged on her nose. I grabbed her wrist.

"It's me."

She blinked, and her face softened as she recognized me. She pulled her earphones out, and the techno metal cut off.

"I'll be down for practice in a little bit. I just need time. I swear."

I sat down on her bed. "I came to talk if you want."

"Oh." Her face fell. She set her paintbrush down and sat on her bed. "Yeah, not really. I just want to be alone."

"Look, Lil," I pressed, "it's none of my business what's going on with you and Hannah and your family, but just make sure it's worth it."

Stoic, little Lily just looked at me and blinked.

"I won't let it affect the team," she finally said.

My heart twisted. Relationship troubles, and she was worried about the team. "Let me worry about the team. You just take care of yourself. Did you want to talk?"

"I really want to be alone. I just need a little time."

I understood that. Lily was deeply introverted and needed space to process her feelings.

"Okay," I said, standing from her bed. I walked up beside her. "But first, I'm doing this."

I wrapped my arm around her back and pulled her into a side hug, until her head rested against my shoulder. She chuckled.

"Thanks."

As we stood there, her head resting on my shoulder, my sights landed on her half-finished work of art, a sugar-skull painting of a woman wearing a hood. Purple flowers outlined the woman's eyes while black curlicues adorned her nose, mouth, and cheeks. A hood pulled low on her forehead cast dark shadows down her face, transforming the colorful painting into something both gothic and eerily beautiful. The curls of her hair and texture of her skin looked so real, like I could have reached out and touched her. I half expected her to wink at me.

"Damn, Lil. You really have a talent there."

"Thanks, but it's not about that," she said, lifting her head from my shoulder. "I do it because I enjoy it. I think art does the same thing for me as meditation does for you. I lose myself in it. But, somehow, I find myself in it, too."

"Lily," I began, "whatever you do, don't quit painting." I glanced between her and the artwork a few times. "I'll give you space."

I started to cross the room, but she called out to me when I reached the door.

"Kali?"

I turned and found her standing in front of the painting again.

"Yeah?"

"Thank you."

I smiled. "Of course." I watched her for a minute, as her brush stroked and curled around the canvas. There was something mesmerizing about watching an artist at work. It really did have a meditative quality to it.

"Hey." I took a step back into the room. "I've been meaning to ask. You froze up during the last match."

Her paintbrush quivered against the canvas. She slowly lowered it to rest in the tray below the painting.

"I don't like machines," she admitted.

I sputtered. "But, Lil, they're everywhere. Machines mow people's lawns, they clean their houses, they—"

She held up a hand. "I know. My family had an army of them. But, when I was a kid, I just always had this fear that one would attack me. I even had nightmares about it. And strangely . . ." Her voice trailed off, and her eyes grew a little distant.

I leaned into her point of view and waved a hand. "And strangely?"

"This one reoccurring dream, the worst one of them all, had a machine that looked a lot like the one in the game. So, when I saw it, it was like I was living inside my own worst nightmare. That's why I locked up."

A chill shot through my veins and up the back of my neck. Living your own worst nightmare. Having it brought to life in a simulation that feels anything but fake. That was terrifying. Truly terrifying. No wonder Lily had locked up.

"I'll be in the training room," I told her. "Just come down when you're ready."

She nodded, picked up her brush, and turned back to her painting. I closed the door, and the muffled sound of her music started up again.

Lily. I doubted I'd ever truly know her, and that was okay. Some people wore their hearts on their sleeves, and some people were Russian nesting dolls. As soon as you opened one, there was another hiding more of what was inside. And Lily was a Russian nesting doll, inside a safe, inside a bank vault. Still, it added a certain harmony to the team. Out of all of us, Lily and Rooke were the most alike. Both were quiet and stoic. Both kept to themselves more than they shared. Derek and Hannah were the outgoing ones. Loved the spotlight. Loved talking with anyone. I was somewhere in the middle. Together, we were balanced.

I lingered outside Lily's door for a moment and rested my head against the frame. The relationship between Lily and Hannah wasn't the only one on the rocks. Rooke and I hadn't been an item for months, and things between us had been tempestuous at best. There were moments when I felt close to him, like during the matchup the previous night, after we'd scored and shared a laugh. For the most part, he'd been cold and distant. But I hadn't been the greatest friend, either, and he was going through a hard time. I couldn't entirely blame him for our current friendship status or lack of one. On top of it all, I wasn't sure how he'd react to the news of me and Kim Jae even though it was a lie.

I went straight to the training room and saw him at the bench press, standing behind it as he adjusted the weights. I crossed the room to his side.

"It's not true," I said, cutting right to the chase. "I'm not with him."

With his back turned, Rooke paused for a second and started adjusting the weights again. He didn't look at me. "Who?"

"Kim Jae."

He shrugged. "I don't care. Be with whoever you want."

"I will," I told him. "But it's not him. I wanted you to know."

Rooke paused again for so long I wondered if I should just leave. Then he turned to face me, and my mouth hit the floor. His cheeks were sunken, his eyes were dark, and his skin was so pale he looked like he'd just crawled out of a cave.

My heart pounded so loudly the trainers across the room should have plugged their ears. Then my throat grew thick, and tears stung my eyes. I never thought I'd break down just from the sight of one of my friends looking so unwell, but I knew Rooke wasn't just under the weather.

Please don't tell me he relapsed again.

I forced my mouth to move and eventually convinced it to form words.

"Are you okay?"

I wasn't sure what to say. If I straight out asked him about anything to do with drugs, I doubted he'd open up.

"My drug test will be fine," he said, "if that's what you're asking."

Or he might tell me directly.

I stood there blinking for several beats. I wasn't sure if I was shocked that he'd been so uncharacteristically blunt or if it was because I wasn't sure if I could trust his answer.

I moved closer to him and lowered my voice. "If you're lying, I need to know right now. For the team."

He snorted and shook his head. "I'm not lying, Kali, but how am I supposed to prove it?" He flashed me the insides of his elbows, which were clean of any marks. "Do you want to look up my nose next? Or search my room?"

"Okay, okay," I said, holding up a hand. "I believe you." A flash of heat crawled up the back of my neck, and I turned my gaze to the floor. I shouldn't have doubted him, and I was embarrassed that I had.

"What do you need?" I asked, forcing myself to meet his gaze again.

He pushed past me and headed for the door, but not before uttering a single word.

"Space."

My heart sunk as I watched him walk out the door and disappear into the house. I started after him, but a hand grabbed my arm and held me back.

"Let him go," Hannah said, dropping her grip. "He doesn't want to talk to you."

Nobody wanted to talk to me. I was surprised Hannah had at all. I turned to her. "It doesn't matter if he wants to talk or not. He can't be alone right now."

She glanced between me and the door a few times. "I'll talk to him."

She headed for the exit, following Rooke's path.

"I don't get it," I called out to her as she walked away. "Aren't you mad at me?"

She turned back.

"Yes," she said simply. One word, and it still stung. "But we're a team, and one of my teammates needs me."

"Hannah, you don't have to—"

She stepped up to me again and lowered her voice. "You talked to Lily for me. You looked after someone I care about. Now it's my turn. Okay?"

Eventually, I nodded. "Okay."

Hannah left the room, and I watched her go. As strange as it sounded, the way we were sticking together despite the fights and setbacks made me feel like the team was becoming something more. More than a team. More than just friends.

I surveyed the training room. Derek was running on a treadmill, and the trainers were gathered in the corner, planning out today's exercises. Might as well warm up. I climbed onto the treadmill next to Derek, but before I could start my run, my cell buzzed. I glanced at it.

Digital Revolution Apparel

Another sponsor, this one specializing in athletic clothing for gamers. I sighed. Maybe it was good news.

I pulled the cell from my wrist and pressed it to my ear. "This is Kali Ling speaking."

"Ms. Ling, we need to talk."

That's usually why people call. Somehow, I managed to keep

my lips pressed together to prevent that little comment from escaping.

"What can I do for you?" I asked, trying on my best professional voice.

"This is Suzanne Lockhart, CEO of Digital Revolution." She paused. "We believe you're in breach of contract."

I went numb. You've got to be kidding me.

I forced an even tone to my voice. "How's that?"

"Your sponsorship was for the coming RAGE tournament, but that's not the tournament you're participating in."

"Yes. We were invited to play in the all-stars. I figured—"

"You figured?" She scoffed. "But you never discussed this with us. We never agreed to sponsor you in this tournament."

"But the opportunity here—"

"Are you saying you spent the funds we provided on the all-stars instead of the RAGE tournaments? Because that would violate our terms. The terms you yourself agreed upon."

"This tournament is giving your brand worldwide attention—"

"Attention that needs to be managed and monitored. We weren't prepared to deal with a worldwide backlash if the athletes sporting our brand perform poorly."

I scoffed. "Did you not see our last matchup? The crowd loved it."

"You barely survived. How many more are you going to make it through?"

Did the whole world think we weren't ready for this level of competition?

"And what's this nonsense in the media? Drug relapses. One-night stands and pregnancy rumors. Can't you control your team, Ms. Ling?"

Derek slowed in his run and looked over at me. I tried to ignore his stare and attempted to salvage the conversation.

"My team is fine, and we can make it through all the matches. We wouldn't have been invited into this competition if we didn't stand a chance. And if we win, you'll be dealing with a different kind of worldwide attention."

"Then you'd better hope you win, or you'll be sued for the full amount."

My mouth fell open. "How can you even—"

The dial tone answered.

Argh.

I chucked my phone across the room. It smacked the wall and tumbled to the floor. How the hell was this happening? Every time I picked up the phone or turned around, somehow things got worse.

I felt Derek staring at me for a minute, before he got off his treadmill and left the room. I didn't even ask him where he was going, and at that point, I didn't care. God, I needed to pound on something. I marched straight for the punching bags and just started ramming into one with my fists. Fucking sponsors. Fucking VGL. Stupid, fucking life, and everything in it.

I wrapped one arm around the bag, bringing it to me, and assaulted it with my right. I pounded the bag so rapidly, my movements practically blurred. My arm screamed, and my lungs burned, but I kept punching, harder and harder, until I physically collapsed and hugged the bag for support.

"Wanna fight something that punches back?"

I followed the tough, feminine voice to Lily, standing beside me. She nodded at the bag.

"You do realize you can't kill something that's not alive, right?"

I released the bag and backed away a few steps, knees still wobbling with exertion. Heavy breaths panted through my mouth while beads of sweat gathered around my hairline.

"It's not going to make me feel better," I said.

"Yes it will." She started walking across the training room. "Get on the mats."

I met her on the mats, and we squared off.

I moved first, throwing a punch. Too weak, too slow. Lily slipped under my arm and swept her foot under both of mine, sending me face-first into the mats. She followed me down, locking my arm against my back. Then she twisted my wrist. I yelped.

"Couldn't quite hear you there," she said. "But that sounded like a tap out."

"Fuck you."

She twisted harder. I yelped again, writhing beneath her.

"What's that?"

I tapped out.

We faced off again. She pinned me twice more.

Now I was pissed, and strangely, more focused. I took up a stance and waited for her to attack first. She did, striking at my face with both hands. I blocked both blows and wrapped my arms around hers. We locked up. It became less of a practice fight and more of a grappling match.

She kicked at my knees, trying to knock me off balance. I held my weight low and quickly found a pattern in her movements. She lifted one leg again to kick, and I promptly attacked her other. She went down. I followed through, my weight on top of hers, and locked her in a choke hold. She gasped and clawed at my arm.

"What's that?" I shouted, mimicking her tone from earlier. "It sounded like a tap out."

She swore at me, and I pulled my arm tighter around her neck.

She tapped out.

I let go and collapsed on the mat beside her. We both lay on our backs, gasping for air, feeling the bruises blossoming from head to toe.

"How did you know I needed that?" I asked her.

"Because I did, too." She glanced across the training room at Hannah on the treadmill, and her eyes went soft. After a minute, she cleared her throat and looked back at me. "Well, you already know why I needed to fight, but what are you so upset about?"

I relived the phone call from our sponsor and dropped my head into my hands. "We might have to drop out of the tournament."

Lily froze for a minute, then leaned toward me. "Why?"

I glanced around at the others in the room and lowered my voice.

"I might have to pay the sponsors back."

Her eyes bulged. "What?"

"The agreement with them was for the RAGE tournaments, not the all-stars. I didn't realize that it mattered. I thought they were just our sponsors, period."

"We've been in the all-star tournament for weeks, and they never said anything until now?"

"It didn't look like we'd lose until now. We're barely scraping by, and that's not how they want their brands represented. They want to see us dominating, not barely surviving."

She snorted. "Typical. If we were doing well, it wouldn't be a problem. But because we're struggling, suddenly, they're not really our sponsors."

"And if that happens, if they really demand their money back, I can't afford to pay the trainers, or Dr. Renner, or anything else. We're finished." I held up my fingers and pinched the smallest space between my thumb and index finger. "We're this close to being done. We're hanging on by a thread."

Lily went quiet for a minute. "Is there another way you could make money?"

I considered it. "At the club the other night, the owner offered to pay us to make appearances there."

Lily glanced around the room. "Well, I think the team would be willing to do it if it keeps us together."

"I know. I was just hoping to avoid that." I glanced at Rooke. The last thing he needed right now was to be surrounded by drugs and alcohol every single night. "I don't want you guys to have to do that. I want you to be your own people."

"Is there anything else we could do?"

I brought a bottle of water to my mouth and paused, thinking it over.

"I don't know," I finally said, noting the exasperation in my own advice. I took a swig of the water. Lily watched me drink, eyed the bottle, and smirked to herself, as if she was the only one who understood some secret joke.

"You know that water you're drinking," she began.

"Yeah?" I asked, taking another swig.

"That's where the family fortune came from. They were one of the first to start mining water from asteroids."

I nearly choked and had to cough a few times to clear my throat. Holy shit. If that was true, then her family really was loaded.

Lily tilted her head toward me, and a chunk of hair fell over her eye.

"Almost forty years ago," she said, "my grandfather started a company to develop the technology. There were dozens of competing firms, but his was the first one to reach success in trial runs on Earth. Once the program actually launched, and production began, the company became an empire."

I swallowed down another gulp and felt it gurgle in my

stomach. I believed her, but it was still hard to process. If Hannah hadn't told me that Lily had forsaken her family's fortune and wanted nothing to do with them, I would have thought she might have been offering to help the team financially. Still, Lily had shared something with me. This was progress for her. For some reason, I felt like I should reciprocate.

I leaned toward her.

"You wanna know something?"

She nodded.

"I don't have a fricking clue what I'm doing," I admitted. Since she was sharing secrets, I thought I'd contribute. "With the team and everything. Not. A. Clue."

Lily was quiet for a minute. "Familiar paths end at the edge of your comfort zone. So, if you don't know where you're going, you're already headed the right way."

I sat half-up, propped up by my elbows, and peered down at her. Wise, insightful Lily. Her soul as endless as the midnight blue in her eyes. Still, this was a declaration deeper than I'd ever heard her say before, and Hannah had surprised me just the same a few weeks earlier. Had they stumbled across Rooke's philosophy books when he'd moved into the house? Or maybe we were all just getting further and further away from our teenage years. Suddenly, our choices had consequences, partying wasn't half as fun as it used to be, and adulthood had snuck up to whisper in our ears.

You have insurance and utility bills. You're a grown-up now.

I sighed and slid back down to the mats.

"Yeah, but it's you guys that I'm tugging along behind me."

"We wouldn't be here if we didn't believe in you."

Everyone kept implying that, but for some reason, it just wouldn't sink in.

"Thanks for the fight," she added.

I shrugged. "Coming in here is better than plugging in and trying to escape in the virtual world."

"I don't think plugging in to escape is wrong once in a while."

"Sure, games are fun, and that's what they should be. But not as a way to escape from dealing with real life. Not every time shit gets tough."

"That's not fair," she said. She sat up, and looked me dead in the eyes. "Sometimes you can't control everything in your life. Sometimes people die, or someone you love leaves. The only thing that really heals something like that is time, and games can make that fucked-up, miserable time just a little more bearable."

I sat up and swiveled to face her, so I could look her straight on.

"Look, I don't want to get nosy, but are things that bad between you and Hannah?"

She was quiet for a few beats. "It's just making me think that maybe we're not right for each other. There were always a few things that bugged me about her."

"Like how she flirts with men?" I asked.

Lily snorted. "Hannah would flirt with a statue. So, no. She doesn't mean anything by it, and I know that." She was quiet for a long time. So long, I didn't think she'd say something more, until she did.

"Sometimes I feel like she doesn't have any depth."

This was the most Lily had opened up since I'd known her. I nodded for encouragement, didn't say anything else, and just waited for her to continue.

"I know that sounds harsh," she said, "but most of the time, it's all clothes, shoes, and hair with her. I mean, I love that she's girly and all. But sometimes it feels like there's nothing else beyond the superficial."

I had to stop my face from reacting to the irony in her statement. Instead, I laid it out for her as neutrally as I could. "I realize I'm not the best to give relationship advice, but did you ever think that maybe she's holding back because you are, too?"

Her eyes flicked to mine, and her mouth opened slightly as if in shock. She hadn't thought of that before, and as her gaze grew distant, I knew my words were sinking in. Finally, she blinked and looked to the ceiling.

"I don't understand why the situation with my family is such a big deal to everyone. Sometimes, families have falling-outs. Just because they're rich doesn't make it any different."

"You can't see why it's a big deal because to you it's normal. And I don't think Hannah's upset about the money. She's upset that you hid a big chunk of your life from her. Everyone else cares about the money, but Hannah cares about you. Doesn't that alone make her less superficial?"

Lily sighed. "I suppose. I just don't get why it's a scandal. Does it really matter that much to most people?"

"Of course it does. To them, your family is the one percent, of the one percent, of the one percent. Most people would wonder why you don't want a part of that."

It was her turn to sit up and face me.

"Most people think money is important because they don't have it. I had money. I had it handed to me. You know what I felt? Empty. So, I gave it up. Started a new life."

"And now?"

"Now I get to spend my days doing the thing I love with the people I love," she said. "That's what I call the one percent."

Damn.

"The people you love," I repeated. "Does that include Hannah?"

She turned her gaze to the ceiling and shrugged.

"I know I told you this before," I began, "but make sure it's really the end. If the relationship is beyond repair, and you're really happier apart, then go your separate ways. But once it's over, that's pretty hard to come back from. Don't let her be the one that got away."

She glanced at me out of the corner of her eye.

"Sounds like you're not just talking about Hannah."

Okay, that probably didn't take a lot to figure out.

"How's he doing?" she asked, referring to Rooke.

"He's . . . working through it."

"And how are you doing?"

I drew a deep breath. "I'm working through it."

She took my hand and squeezed. I squeezed back.

"Thanks for the talk," she said.

I pushed up to my feet. "You, too. But I'm not the one you should be talking to."

"Speak for yourself," she called out, as I started to walk away. I glanced over my shoulder and grinned.

"Touché."

I continued to walk away, then I paused and turned back at her.

"Just a question."

"Yeah?"

"Would your family be interested in sponsoring an eSports team?"

She showed me what her middle finger looked like, and I laughed. I started to walk away again when she called out to me.

"Kali?"

I turned back again.

"I didn't want to say anything, but you look tired."

As she said it, my shoulders sagged, and my eyelids felt heavy, but I smiled anyway.

"I don't have time to be tired."

"Kali?"

I turned around to find Derek standing behind me. His arms were crossed, and a stern expression masked his face. That couldn't be good.

"I need to show you something."

LIARS.

That's what was painted on the wall next to the front gate of the house. I stood in front of it, arms crossed, blinking a few times.

"When did this happen?" I asked Derek. He shrugged.

"Recently, or we would have noticed before now."

I tried to tell myself it wasn't a big deal but couldn't ignore the growing pang in my chest. If people weren't afraid to come up to the house, what would they do next?

"There they are!"

I turned to find a group of hecklers rushing toward us. One of them pointed at me.

"Hey, Ling. Fuck any more Koreans lately?"

Derek's eyes went wide. "Shit."

He grabbed my arm and started backpedaling. We retreated into the confines of our property and slammed the gates closed just as the horde descended on us. Their limbs poked through the bars, and they banged against the gate like some undead mob.

Derek and I backed up several steps as the shouts continued.

"Have any other kids you don't know about, Cooper?"

"Go back to the RAGE tournaments, Defiance. You were shit then, and you're shit now."

"Where's that other bitch? The one that's straight."

I gritted my teeth and shouted back, "She's not straight."

"Kali," Derek warned under his breath. "Do not engage."

"Bullshit. She's probably screwing the rest of K-Rig in there right now."

Derek still held his grip around my arm. I wasn't sure if he was doing it instinctively to protect me or to hold me back.

"The famous Kali Ling hides behind a gate," some guy shouted. "If you're really so tough, come kick my ass yourself." He placed his hands behind his back. "Here, I'll make it easy for you."

I wasn't falling for it and didn't even take a step toward him, but Derek's grip tightened on me anyhow.

Sadly, this was expected. You gain fame and money, and with it comes the haters. But I'd never experienced the backlash quite so directly. Last year, when Defiance was Clarence's team, we were kept inside his facility and shielded from the hate. Playing games for the tabloids had still been a big part of our jobs, but I'd never had to deal with anything like this before. Maybe the way Clarence had run things wasn't as bad as I had thought. He had tried to spin the tension on the team, specifically between Rooke and myself, as some hot-and-cold romance for the media to gobble up. But by doing that—putting a good twist on a bad situation—maybe he'd protected us from stuff like this.

I shook my head. I never thought I'd find myself agreeing with Clarence.

"There's more," Derek said.

I pointed at the gates. "Of this?"

"No. Something else."

Derek led me back inside the house to the pod room.

"What am I looking at?" I asked, as he tapped the screen behind my pod, bringing up the maintenance menu. He pointed at a window of data.

"There's something going on here."

Derek had taken programming in school before he left for a career as a pro gamer, so I knew he knew what he was talking about. I took a step toward the pod.

"What do you mean?"

"Well, these pods are designed to understand us. It's like they're . . . evolving."

Evolving? Well, that explained how the practice matchups were getting harder.

"You mean, so it can challenge us inside the game."

He stared at me for a while. "No. Not just inside the game. It's learning everything it can about you. About all of us."

Something cold slid through my stomach. "How can it do that?"

"By evaluating your physiological responses to different stimuli. If it presents you with a situation in the game, it monitors your breathing, increase in sweat—"

"Are you saying these pods aren't safe?"

"In terms of virtual addiction, I think they're fine." He went quiet for a long time, and crossed his arms. "I think this is how the media is finding out everything about us."

"Oh, Derek. Come on—"

"Think about it. Hannah hates stereotypes, so the media creates one about her. I grew up without a father, then it's implied I got a girl pregnant on a one-night stand. Lily hates her family, and so—"

I held up a hand. "Okay, okay. Even if someone is accessing these pods to find out our dirty laundry, what are we going to do about it?"

He shrugged. "I can't alter any programming on the pods. That'll get us banned from the league."

"At this point, I don't care. If it's between my team and the league, I'm going to choose you guys every time. If that gets me banned, so be it."

"If we get banned and can't compete, then there's no point to having a team."

I sighed. "So, what?"

"Either we drop out of the tournament—"

"Or?"

"We keep going and bear the brunt of whatever they throw at us next."

I realized then I couldn't just drop out of the tournament. I'd risk getting sued. I had sponsor contracts to fulfill. Plus, it would only further damage our reputation and show the VGL that they had won. I took a deep breath, released it, and shoved my emotions to the side. I wanted to do right by my team, and unfortunately, doing right meant taking a stand. Not backing down.

Earning our namesake.

Defiance.

"We keep going."

CHAPTER 15

Saturday Night Gaming.

It was the staple of American virtual sports. Every Saturday night, most of the continent tuned in to watch the best players in the league duke it out in various virtual arenas. But now, with the international teams participating, *Saturday Night Gaming* was rivaling the Olympics in terms of worldwide popularity and viewership.

As I stood inside the game that Saturday night, it didn't feel like a billion people were watching me. The air had no scent or movement. Instead, it was suffocating, thick and heavy. The streets were empty and brimming with absolute silence. Unlike the RAGE arena, basked in golden tones and rich scents, this place was devoid of sensations. Instead, it felt mechanical. Barren. Lifeless. This was a pocket reality where nothing else existed. Just me, and the game.

Tonight, we were up against Inner Sanctum, a newer team from England. Derek, Hannah, and Lily had all run for the flag. Lily was a decoy tonight, running straight through the open streets, while Derek and Hannah stuck to the rooftops and alleyways. The hope was that Sanctum would pounce on Lily, leaving their flag open for Derek and Hannah to take with ease.

Rooke and I were left to guard our base.

I stood three feet from our flag, sword drawn. My gaze

flicked from street, to street, to rooftop, and everywhere between. Movement caught my eye on one of the rooftops. Three blocks down, a shadow leaned over a roof's edge and disappeared again. They were canvassing the area, preparing to attack.

"They're on the roof." I pointed with my sword to where I'd seen the shadow. "Ready?" I glanced over my shoulder and found empty space. "Rooke?"

I whirled around. He stood twenty feet away, back to the flag, in front of a glass storefront of one of the buildings, staring inside.

"Rooke!" I shouted.

He didn't move. I darted over to him, and tugged on his arm. "Come on. What the hell are you doing?"

I followed his gaze to the glass, except it wasn't really glass. It was a mirror. In the reflection, he was lying in a coffin, dressed in a plain, all-black suit. His cheeks were sunken, eyes closed and dark. Lined with gray satin and made of black wood, the coffin looked like something he'd actually choose to be buried in.

Like it was real.

I stepped back and nearly stumbled as all the feeling in my body evaporated.

"Shit."

The reflection's eyes opened and locked on Rooke. A chill shot through me, and I scrambled backwards. Rooke didn't move.

The reflection crawled out of the glass and materialized into the game. It looked like him, except its cheeks were too sunken, and its eyes were soulless. Rooke stared at himself. Unblinking. Unbreathing.

Paralyzed with absolute fear.

My initial shock solidified into resolution. My teeth gritted, brow furrowed, and I felt my own expression morph into one of pure vehemence.

I drew my sword and charged. The reflection remained locked on Rooke, even as I raced toward it and reeled back, preparing to slam my blade home.

In a blink, its arm moved in a blur of black smoke. An open palm slammed into my chest, launching me into the air. I flew back several feet until I smashed into the ground with a sickening smack. A groan escaped my lips as the pain blossomed in every corner of my body. My head throbbed. My ribs and sternum ached, feeling like I'd been hit with a sledgehammer instead of an open-palm strike. Despite it all, my hand instinctively groped around for my sword. About a foot away, lying in the street, my blade glimmered in the moonlight. My fingers closed around the hilt, and I smiled.

A horn rang out overhead.

Oh, damn it. The flag. The game was still in play. What the hell was I doing?

Two members of Sanctum stood right next to our base, one of them glowing with our flag. Their eyes were squinted and locked on Rooke's ghost, like they didn't understand what was happening. I stumbled to my feet, sword in hand. We locked eyes. Theirs widened. They both turned and started to run.

So did I.

"Rooke!" I screeched as I took off down the street. I didn't look back as I pursued Sanctum, but no footsteps followed from behind.

Great. Alone.

Again.

I chased Sanctum down the street, gaining with every step, the flag carrier just out of reach. His teammate abruptly turned to attack, unsheathing his weapon as he rotated. I slipped under his arm and pounced on the flag carrier, stabbing repeatedly into his back. He cried out and crumpled to the ground. The glow faded from his body, and our flag reset.

Footsteps echoed down the street. Two blocks up, Hannah and Derek were running our flag in, their pursuers close behind.

We had a chance to score.

I stood.

A blade ripped through my side, slicing deep into my abdomen. So stupid. The player who had been guarding the flag was still in the game. I'd let myself get distracted by the sight of my own team and the taste of victory drawing near.

I dropped to the ground, closed my eyes, and went limp, faking my demise. Footsteps sounded away from me, headed for the rest of my team. After a few seconds, I opened my eyes and patted the pavement around me as I lay on my back. Blood puddled against my left side, growing brighter with the passing seconds. It was funny, really, when I thought about it. Rooke had faced his own death, and now I was the one bleeding out in the middle of the street. Was that irony? Or just tragedy?

Darkness pooled around the edges of my sight and wavered, threatening to close in and swallow me whole. I grunted and strained against it. I shook my head and kicked my feet, whatever it took to keep conscious inside the game.

The fight played out in my peripheral vision.

Rooke still stood in front of the glass. Lily was nowhere to be seen. She must have been out of the game. It was down to Hannah and Derek. Their cries and commands reverberated in my ear as broken, muffled sounds so only their voices were recognizable, not their words.

They scrambled around the flag. A clash of swords. A spray of blood. It was chaos. They were struggling.

I had to fight. I had to help.

I rolled onto my side. Pain coursed through my entire body, blurring my vision and grinding my molars together. A sound left my mouth, a bitter, gurgled wail. It was a warning.

My body was about to give out.

I braced a hand against the pavement and fought the darkness closing in, the crushing hand of unconsciousness.

No.

Stay. Awake.

I slapped a hand against the pavement and grunted, hoping it would help in my struggle. As the sound escaped my lips, I realized something.

Maybe it wouldn't just help my struggle.

I smashed my hand on the pavement and started yelling as loud as the air in my lungs would allow. I must have looked like a flailing idiot, but maybe I could distract one of our opponents. Even just a head turn could give my team the advantage. And it worked. Except, the head that turned was not the one I'd expected.

Rooke jerked back to life. Drawing the pair of short swords from his back, he spun and sliced right through his reflection. The blades slid through nothing but smoke, but the reflection screamed a horrifying scream, one that sounded like a thousand voices dying in agony, all at once. It dropped to its knees and faded out of the game.

Rooke stared at the spot where his reflection had been. Then he turned, and his eyes landed on me. They went soft, then hard. Really hard. I'd like to say that he raced into the fight, but really he forced himself into it, like he was straining against his own soul-consuming rage. Whether he was mad at the game or himself, I wasn't sure, but he was about to take it out on Inner Sanctum.

He dropped his swords and headed into the fight bare-handed. He marched straight up behind Hannah's attacker, cocked back his fist, and bashed the back of his skull. The attacker went down, and Rooke followed him, whaling on the guy's neck. Another attacker pounced on Rooke's back. His elbow jabbed back, catching the guy in the ribs. He stumbled, coughing, gripping his side. Before he could recover, Rooke retrieved a discarded dagger from the pavement and plowed into him, driving the blade up from navel to sternum.

Damn.

Hannah stood there for a minute, stunned.

You've got a blocker, I mentally screamed at her. *Go for the end zone.*

Did I just make a football reference?

Hannah bolted.

Someone slammed into her, knocking her off balance. Rooke ripped him off and tossed him to the side. Literally tossed him, like he was a bale of hay, and started pounding on him, too, just like the first guy. Hannah hesitated for a second, still gaping at Rooke. Then she scrambled to her feet and crossed over to our base.

There. We'd scored.

We'd won.

I heaved a final breath, and gave in to the darkness. My eyes snapped open, and I was looking at the shimmering interior of the pod. We'd made it. Another victory. Another step up through the tournament.

Just barely.

My pod doors opened in sync with everyone else's, but Derek burst out of his pod before the doors were even fully open.

"What the hell happened there, defense?"

His head swiveled back and forth between me and Rooke several times. Rooke said nothing. He sat on the edge of his pod, staring down at the floor. The look on his face was so distant, I wasn't sure if he even realized where he was or that someone was talking to him.

I ignored Derek, crossed the room, and knelt before Rooke. "Are you okay?"

Rooke still stared at the floor, his eyes full of everything and nothing.

"Hey."

I placed a hand on either side of his head and forced it up until his gaze met mine. I dropped my hands to his shoulders and squeezed.

"Are you okay?" I repeated, emphasizing every word.

He still said nothing. Just gave me one shake of his head before he stood, pushed past me, and left the room.

"What happened to him in the game?" Hannah asked, as the door whooshed shut behind him.

"He . . . saw something."

"What?"

I looked to the door, where Rooke had just left.

"His future," I said. "If he's not careful."

His bedroom door was shut.

I wasn't sure if he'd talk to me, but I had to check on him. After seeing *that*, after seeing himself in a coffin, who wouldn't be disturbed? And what kind of friend would I be if I didn't at least try?

I knocked on the door. The sound echoed and was answered by silence. *Please just open the door.* But it remained shut.

After several seconds of silence, I sighed and turned away.

"Come in."

I halted. He was letting me in. I opened the door.

Rooke was pacing at the foot of his bed again, the way he usually did when he felt trapped or was confronted with too many emotions. But this time, his brow was furrowed, and his steps were purposeful, as if he was deep in thought.

I took two steps into the room and stopped, keeping several feet between us. I wasn't going to bombard him, but we needed to talk.

"Look," I said slowly, calmly. "I don't know if you want time alone, but I think we need to talk about—"

"It's challenging us with things we fear."

I blinked. Not what I was expecting him to say, but at least he was saying something. He stopped pacing and met my eyes. The emptiness within was gone, replaced with certainty. I had no idea what he was talking about, but I wasn't about to tell him that. He was talking. That's what mattered.

"What do you mean?" I asked.

"The new pods. They're using our fears to challenge us inside the game."

"So," I began, trying to follow his line of thinking, "you think the pods are finding things that every team is afraid of, then realizing those fears in physical form, all inside the game."

"No, not all the teams. Just us."

I slowly shook my head. "Last week every team faced off against that machine. And I bet if you watch this week, every-one will face . . . what you saw."

"Every team is facing these things," he agreed, "but they're based on our fears. Not theirs."

I blinked and drew a slow breath. Was this some sort of paranoia from the drugs and his withdrawal? But I didn't want to discourage him. This was the most he'd talked in weeks.

"Lots of people fear machines," I said, keeping my voice neutral. "Lots of people fear death. That's not specific to us."

"It is." He started pacing again. "I know it is."

"Okay," I said, playing along. "Why would the game do that? Why would it target us and no one else?"

"I don't know." He tossed his arms up. "Maybe they're trying to knock us out of the tournament, or make us feel like we shouldn't be here, so we end up losing."

"Why would they invite us in if it was just to knock us out?"

"To lower our morale. To embarrass us. To bankrupt us."

I considered that. I still didn't buy into it, but I wanted to keep him talking. "You think the VGL doesn't want us competing?"

"I think they don't want *you* competing." We locked eyes, and he took a step toward me. "You're not afraid to challenge corruption or the problems in this sport. That could hurt their ratings. Their stock." He cleared his throat. "Their image."

He was talking about the VGL, but I had a feeling that last comment was a stab at yours truly.

"Okay, I'll admit that this is all very suspicious, but I have no proof. Besides, why would they be so afraid of me? I'm one person."

"Sometimes that's all it takes. One person who doesn't back down. They know you won't, so they have to do something about it."

I scoffed and crossed my arms. "So, they create an entire tournament and invite teams from around the world just to set me up?"

"No, I think the tournament was legit. I mean, they're making plenty of money from it. Bringing you into this was just a bonus."

I deflated a bit. "So, if it is true, we really don't deserve to be in this tournament." I sat on the edge of his bed. "Doesn't matter. We don't have any proof of anything. Besides, what are we going to do? Whine about it?"

He sat next to me on the bed. "I don't know what to do, but that doesn't make it fair."

"Life isn't fair." My voice went up several decibels as the words left my mouth. "You can complain about it, or you can toughen up and own it."

I immediately clamped my lips shut. Damn it. I'd said that because I meant it—because I was passionate about tackling problems head-on. But, technically, I'd implied that he was whining, and the last thing I wanted to do was shut him down.

He studied me for a long time, then the floor, then the walls, then finally he turned back to me. "Maybe you're right. Maybe the NPCs in the game are just there by coincidence. They are common fears."

"Either way, it's still a good challenge."

He chuckled. "Only you would consider looking death in the face a challenge."

I laughed, and we locked eyes again. Something passed between us, a weird feeling that I could only describe as someone striking a chord inside my soul. Whatever it was, it was warm. Comforting. Not the standard hostility that had existed between us over the last several weeks.

I kept talking, in the hopes of keeping him talking.

"To be honest, I almost didn't come here. I wasn't sure if you'd want to talk with me."

"For a while, I didn't." His voice was tight.

"Can I ask why?"

He met my eyes. "You want the truth?"

I nodded.

"I was pissed."

Well, that was obvious.

"Because I reported the test?" I guessed.

"Because you cared more about what other people thought

than what I did. You had to know what the press was saying, but you didn't ask me what I thought about it."

My stomach sunk. He'd been so shut off and snappy, I figured he didn't want to talk to me about it. But really, he was my friend. I shouldn't have assumed, and I should have put him first.

"I know it seems shallow to watch the gossip channels," I began, "but I was trying to protect—"

"I know what you were trying to do, but you can't control the crowd. People are going to say whatever they want. They'll love you today and hate you tomorrow. You shouldn't care what other people think, but if you do, make sure it's the ones that matter. Your teammates matter."

I nodded, letting the words sink in. "How do I do that? How do I show that you guys are more important to me?"

"Just listen. You don't even have to agree with my opinions, but a little respect goes a long way."

"Okay," I said slowly. "Then what's your opinion?"

"You need to stop caring so much about image."

I sighed. "This is the biggest tournament in the world. Look at the all-star dinner. Look at K-Rig—"

He stood up from the bed. "They didn't become all-stars because of the color of their eyes, Kali." He was yelling, but not really at me. More like he was just trying to drive the point home. "They became the best because they worked and ground for every fucking inch. I used to know a woman who was like that, too."

I pulled back. *Used* to know?

"Image is a part of this sport, I get that," he said, much calmer this time. "It's a part of life, too, as stupid as it is. People will care more about what you look like than what kind of person you are or what you're capable of."

"I agree, but you just said it. Image is a part of this sport. I can't ignore that."

"You don't have to ignore it. You can even have fun with it. But do you really want image as a priority? Over the game? Over your teammates?"

Had I really gotten that caught up in everything? For a second, it felt like someone had hit the PAUSE button on everything in my life except for me, so I was able to step back and look at the situation from a neutral standpoint. I was trying to do what was best for the team, especially him. I'd been trying to make us look whole. Instead, I'd asked Hannah to pretend her relationship with Lily was fine for the cameras. I'd dressed them up like little dolls. Then there were Rooke's problems, and how I'd focused on the media's opinion of him. I'd cut out our nightly practices together just to stick him in front of the cameras. I took away the thing he probably needed the most and gave him what he needed the least.

I'd worked for months to take over this team, to give them a place where they'd be safe. All that, just to do a pretty shitty job of taking care of them? I don't think so.

No. That ended tonight. Right now.

"How's this for starters?" I began. "We've got fifteen minutes until the press conference. If you can't make it, we'll cover for you. I won't give a shit what the press thinks. If you need time, take it."

"It's okay. I'll be there." He stared at the floor again, his new best friend, apparently. He shifted his weight a few times, rubbed the back of his neck, and moved in a way I could only describe as fidgety. It seemed like he had something to say, but the words wouldn't pass through the lump in his throat.

"It started on New Year's Eve," he finally said, chewing through the words like they were stuck in his teeth.

I froze. This was it. The moment I'd been hoping for. He was really going to open up now.

"What started?"

"That's when I first slipped." He paused again, but not for as long this time. "I went to a party. I know I shouldn't have, but the team was going out, and I didn't want to be alone. So, I went. That's when I started hitting HP again. When I sobered up and realized what I'd done, I was so ashamed of what had happened, I left and didn't tell anyone. I tried to hide. You don't deserve that."

"It doesn't matter what you did. I'm here for you."

"Why?"

"Because what happens to my team, happens to me. Derek, Hannah, any of you. Whatever you guys go through, I'm going through it with you. No matter what. Because you're my team, and that's what we do." I took a step toward him, and that was when I noticed how much I was trembling, partly from hope that I was finally getting through to him and partly from the thousand other emotions bubbling up inside me. Emotions over my own addiction the previous year. Everything over his breakdown and how much he was struggling.

The team. Especially the team, and how much I loved them all.

"Where you are right now," I said, "I've been there, too. You know that. So why was it so hard for you to tell me?"

He looked down at the floor again, much longer this time.

"It's embarrassing."

I reeled.

"You're embarrassed?" I scoffed. "Last year, when I was detoxing, do you know how many times I nearly threw up on you? When we used to sneak out of those clubs to train together and the withdrawals would hit me, and you'd sit beside me all sweaty and shirtless, all I could think was 'Please don't vomit all over his perfect abs.' Okay? That was embarrassing for me, but did you care?"

He was quiet for a minute before he finally said, "No."

"Then why is this any different?"

"I didn't want to disappoint you."

"Disappoint me? Why would you think I'd be anything other than supportive?"

"Because you're Kali Ling."

Well, that stung.

I frowned. "So, being Kali Ling means I'm not there for my friends."

"No, no," he said, shaking his head. A smile flashed across his lips, and for a split second, he was himself. It wrenched my heart a little. "It means you're *the* Kali Ling. First female captain of RAGE. Youngest team owner in history. You set your mind to something, and you just do it. No matter what. So, how could I come to you with a fuckup as big as this?"

He sat on the edge of his bed again. I knelt in front of him, pressing my forehead against his.

"Because you've seen the parts of me no one else has. You've seen my scars. My darkness. You know I'm not invincible, and neither are you. Stop expecting to be." I took a breath, and my voice was shaky. For once, I didn't try to force it to sound strong. I didn't try to hide from him. Because, sometimes, showing weakness is the biggest strength of all.

"I'm not going anywhere," I told him. "But you have to let me in."

Being this close to him, I noticed everything that seemed a bit off when he first showed up at the house. The paleness of his skin. The bags under his eyes. It had context now. He was tired.

No, he wasn't just tired. He was shattered. In that moment, my heart felt about the same.

"Whatever is going on between us," I whispered, "whether

we're in a relationship or not, doesn't matter. I'm here for you. We'll get you through this."

He swallowed thick and pushed the words out of his mouth.

"I almost got high again."

My chest went tight. "When?"

"Earlier this week."

I thought back to the morning when he looked like he'd been hit by a bus. "Because of the reports that I was with Jae?"

He slowly nodded. "I just didn't think it would bother me so much. I mean, you and I aren't together, and you can be with whoever you want. But even if it wasn't true, it made me realize that you had moved on, and I was barely holding it together."

"You got through that day, though."

"That day," he repeated, and shook his head. "Every day. It's every fucking day. I feel like I can't stop."

Despite how he felt, he was in more control than he thought. He hadn't done a single hit since he'd failed his first drug test. But I knew what he meant. The temptation wouldn't stop. To him, that was as bad as hitting up. Maybe worse. Because, for Rooke, self-discipline was everything, and craving the drugs meant he didn't have control over his impulses and had failed at his most highly regarded virtue.

"You have," I assured him. "You've already stopped. You're so much stronger than this. And we're all here for you." I rested a hand on either side of his face. "You're home."

His eyes fell shut, and his face relaxed. He looked relieved. Strangely, the words were as much of a realization for me as they were for him. This wasn't just my home. It was the team's, and I hadn't exactly been treating them as such.

"Kali." He gripped my hands where they rested against his face, pulled them down to his lap, and squeezed. Just once. But it told me something that was so clear, he might as well have spoken the words.

He was ready to make amends. He was ready to atone for his sins.

I cleared my throat. "Can we practice together in the garden again? I miss that."

Slowly, he nodded, and the joy I felt instantly spread across my lips.

"We have to go," he said.

What? Oh, yeah. The press conference. Right. I blinked a few times, and my cheeks felt wet. I wiped away tears. Funny. I hadn't even felt them fall.

We stood from the bed and headed for the door, but Rooke paused halfway across the room.

"What about after the press conference?"

I smiled and gave him the same advice he'd given me when I'd been in his place.

"You need to take a shower. Stay in there until the water turns cold."

He smiled back, and it was the first genuine, lasting smile I'd seen from him since he'd rejoined the team.

"And what about you?"

"Me?" I paused, knowing exactly what was coming next. "I have changes to make."

CHAPTER 16

Nathan's picture.

I stood directly in front of the life-size, digital poster of him hanging in my office. He was the reason I'd started this. His death had brought me down this path. After he'd overdosed, and our former owner didn't give a shit, I was determined to take the team from him and give them a better place to live and play.

A better place.

Instead, I'd turned into another version of Clarence. Caring more about image, photo shoots, and what the media thought than the team itself. I'd taken away their phones. I'd asked Lily and Hannah to fake their relationship in front of the cameras.

What the hell had I become?

I gathered the team in the living room. The four of them sat on the couch while I talked. I also gave everyone their phones back.

"If I pushed too hard, it's because I know how talented you all are. I got too caught up in everything. If you have problems with the things I've been doing, I want you to come to me. I'm here to listen. *But*—" I emphasized. "You'll have to put up with my demanding schedule for one more night."

They all sighed.

"More photo shoots?" Lily guessed.

"Interviews?"

Hannah held up a hand. "Club appearances?"

"No," I said simply. "It's game night."

They erupted with hoots and cheers.

Soon, the living room was filled with laughter. Popcorn overflowed bowls and littered the coffee table. We took turns playing, tossing the controller around the room. We teased each other, blocking eyes or parts of the screen.

Classic video game night was something I'd started when we first became a team, for many reasons. It gave us appreciation for the classics. It brought us together as a team for fun outside of the competition. Most of all, it reminded us that this was all just a game.

As I looked around the living room, watching my teammates battle through Halo 3 on four-player co-op mode, I knew this was what it was all about. Playing games. Having fun.

A good time with friends.

In that moment, there was no tournament. No sponsors or VGL. No corruption. Just me and my team. And really, that's what mattered.

While the rest of the team dominated the couch, I sat on the floor in front of Hannah and Lily. I leaned back toward them and asked, "What classic video game scared you the most?"

"Resident Evil 4," Hannah said.

"Silent Hill 2," Lily chimed.

I thought about my answer for a minute.

"Japan's The Grudge."

They both shuddered.

"Good one," Hannah said.

Across the couch, Derek spoke up.

"Super Mario 64."

Did he just say what I think he said?

"You mean, the first 3-D Mario?" I asked. "Like, the little kid's game?"

He paused the game and turned to us.

"The underwater level," he emphasized, making a snake motion with his arm. "That eel thing!"

I traded glances with the girls and wondered if my face looked the same as theirs. Staring, dumbfounded, blinking.

Derek waved us off. "Whatever. I was traumatized."

During her time-out from playing, Lily found a stuffed-animal version of the eel from Super Mario on her tablet and ordered it. It was delivered to the house by drone within the hour. At 4:00 a.m., long after Derek had gone to bed, we over-rode the lock on his door—strictly for admin purposes. When his high-pitched shriek echoed through the house the next morning, we knew he'd woken to his new bedmate.

After that, Unagi the Eel became a staple in the house, often woven through the stair's banister or sitting atop the couch's headrest. On the better days, he'd find his way into Derek's virtual pod or pop out from a cabinet upon opening, like a snake in a can.

In the early evenings, I practiced in the garden with Rooke, every night without fail. No matter what was going on, I put everything else aside for those few hours of the day. No excuses. It was good for him.

It was good for me, too.

We were working with the knives now. They were shaped like two crescent moons facing toward each other, overlapping about two inches in from the corners, with a small gap in the middle. Your fingers fit through the gap in the center and wrapped around one of the blades, protected by a leather grip. Holding one in each hand turned your fists into double-bladed, four-cornered weapons of death.

With the sun setting around us, we'd pivot and twist in unison. Slow moving, fast moving, sudden bursts of energy, like flags flapping in a restless wind. I watched him more than our virtual instructor. He was focused. Controlled. His eyes were narrowed, and the movement in his muscles was both fluid and strong.

He caught my eye and realized I was watching him.

"Maybe one day we could spar with these," he said, nodding at the knives in his hands.

"Technically, I don't think they're meant for sparring. Besides, I'd slice you up like a sushi chef."

"Could you cut off my ears first? Then I wouldn't have to listen to you talk before I died."

If I weren't so relaxed, I might have tomahawked one of my blades into his eye right then. Speaking of relaxed, the mood in the entire house was different. There was constant laughter, whether from the corners of the training room or gathered in front of the television for another classic video game binge.

Online was a different story. The death threats continued. Whether because of my supposed hookup with Kim Jae, Hannah's secret sex life, or everything else the media had claimed about us over the last few weeks, we were hated around the world. People were posting videos of us, montages of our RAGE tournament days, including every fight where we were either gutted, stabbed, or had our throats slit. They looked like horror movies with all the gore and none of the story line. We were laughing about that, too. No one was going to stop us now. Either we could bow down to the people who had nothing better to do but spend their days slamming us online, or we could keep going in the face of adversity and achieve our goals anyway. That sounded like Defiance to me.

Even the tabloid gossip settled down to a low simmer.

Without our going out every night, there were no new pictures to flood the market.

Soon, the sponsors noticed our absence from the media.

"We've been working hard," I insisted with my cell pressed to my ear. I sat in my office, straining against my fist not to break something. "We can't be out every night and still be rested enough for the tournament."

"The other teams are out every night," said Suzanne Lockhart, the CEO of Digital Revolution Apparel. The same one who'd threatened to sue me for entering the all-star tournament was now upset that I wasn't promoting it enough.

Derek walked into the room. I glanced at him and returned to the call.

"If you're so impressed by the other teams, why don't you go sponsor them?"

She hung up on me.

I groaned and slapped my cell down on the desk.

"Sponsors?" he asked, sitting down across from me.

I nodded. "They're giving us grief for staying in." I rested my arms on the desk and sighed. "I don't know what to do. We stay in to rest and have some fun, and they scream. We go out, tire ourselves, and don't perform as well, and they scream."

He studied me for a minute. "Look, you said we could come talk to you about problems with the way you manage the team."

I did, didn't I? But I wasn't someone who was super open to criticism. I pushed my emotions aside. Handling criticism was the only way to get better.

"Okay," I said slowly. "Go ahead."

He slid his tablet across the table. I glanced at it. A virtual money order was on the screen.

"What is this?"

"One million. It's my winnings from the RAGE tournament last year. Think of it as an investment in the team."

I balked. "I can't accept this."

"You can."

I shoved it across the table. "Absolutely not. I can't let you do that."

He sighed and leaned forward in the chair. "Maybe I'm not saying this right. I want to buy part of the team."

My brow furrowed. "You want to be . . . co-owner?"

"You need the help," he said frankly.

I glanced between him and the tablet and bit my lip. "Is that a polite way of saying I'm a bad team owner?"

"No, no. You're fighting for the right thing. You've stuck by your convictions even when things got rough. But there are some things about being team owner that just aren't your strong suit."

". . . like?"

"Kali, let's be honest here. Between you and me, who has the charisma for dealing with the sponsors? You tell it like it is, and I respect you for it. But that's not what the sponsors want to hear. They want sugar, and I'm damn sweet."

I glanced between him and the tablet a few times. "And the money is because . . . ?"

"The sponsors aren't going to listen to me unless I'm a team owner. This is so I have authority."

I sat back in my chair, considering his offer. "So, you think you're sweeter than me? Prove it."

He grinned. "Watch this. Give me your phone."

I hesitated for a minute before I handed it over to him. He started flicking through my contact list.

"Who's the one giving you the most grief?"

"Lockhart at Digital Revolution."

He tapped her name and pressed the phone to his ear.

"What are you doing—"

He raised a hand and gave me a face that simply said, *I've got this*. He tapped his foot as he waited. I heard the line click.

"Yes, Ms. Lockhart, please," he said.

There was a pause.

"Ms. Lockhart? This is Derek Cooper. I'm the new co-owner of Team Defiance." As he said it, he slid the money order back across the desk. "Ms. Lockhart, let's talk for a minute. I'm not sure if I understand something right. I hear you're considering taking legal action against us, and I'm concerned for you. Do you have any idea what that will do to your image?"

My mouth dropped open. He was getting them at their own game. Derek paused as he listened to her speak.

"Listen, people love athletes. They hate big business. I don't want you to come out of this deal looking like corporate over-lords. Do you?"

Another pause.

"I didn't think so. Look, we're proud to promote your products. We believe in them. So, let's work together on this. Tell me what we can do to make you happy."

He winked at me.

Damn, he was sweet.

"Now, that sounds completely reasonable to me . . ."

With the cell pressed to his ear, he pushed himself out of the chair and sauntered out of my office and down the hall.

My phone went with him.

Not a bad trade for one million. Derek Cooper, you just bought yourself a team.

Maybe officially delegating more of my team-owner responsibilities to the rest of the team wasn't a bad idea, especially if their talents naturally suited the task. With Derek handling the sponsors, I wondered if he'd mind my being captain again.

That's what everyone wanted to see. Scratch that. That's what I wanted and what felt best for the team.

I called Hannah into my office next. I'd already involved her in the team's image. Might as well take it all the way.

"We need to talk about our image," I told her.

She slowly lowered herself in the chair. "Am I doing a bad job?"

"No, no. You're doing an amazing job. So, I'm wondering if you want to be our full-time Image Coordinator. On top of coordinating our look, you'll need to monitor our presence in the media. Stay up-to-date on the latest gossip and figure out the best ways to counter it if it's even worth the attention. I'm not going to try to control what the media thinks, but we still need to be aware of what they're saying."

"Where is this coming from?"

"I can't be watching the gossip channels anymore. It's too much of a distraction. But it's still something that needs to be managed, and I think it's a role you're well suited for. I'll need to sit down with Derek and go over our finances. But you'll have a budget somewhere in the high six figures, maybe seven. You'll have to manage that, too."

Hannah had no reaction, at first. Eventually, she sat back in the chair, her face a blank slate. Was she insulted?

"Thank you," she said solemnly.

That didn't sound like a genuine thank-you.

"Hannah, if you don't feel—"

"No one ever takes me seriously," she said, and I immediately shut my mouth. "They think I'm all hair and shoes, all about the superficial. That I'm just here for show."

"I don't think that—"

"A few times, I thought about changing to suit everyone else. Especially when those rumors about me started in the tabloids.

But, really, I love who I am. So, I thought, fuck changing. If people don't even try to see what's below the surface, why should I do the work for them?"

Is that how she thought I viewed her? Of course she did. I'd just offered her a job that revolved around clothes and celebrity gossip. Oh God, what had I done?

"Listen, I'm sorry—"

"You're sorry? No one's ever thought of me as capable of something more. They treat me like I'm just another pretty face. But now you're offering me a job that actually combines everything I love and tests my strengths? Kali Ling, I could kiss you."

I blinked.

Uh, what?

Hannah brimmed with so much excitement, she could barely sit in the chair.

"Coming up with the newest, hottest looks before the other teams do," she gushed. "Outmaneuvering the press at their own game. Managing a seven-figure budget." Her voice got higher and more excited with every sentence. "I think I could be good at this. Really good."

I smiled. Not because I was happy but because of how happy this was making her.

"You will be. Own it."

"I better get started, then. Thanks, boss." She bounded out of the chair and headed for the door.

"You know what's nicest about exciting news, like job promotions?" I asked. She turned back to me and shrugged. "Sharing it with someone."

She pressed her lips together and crossed her arms.

"I'm not the one who doesn't share."

"You sure?"

She looked down at the floor and scuffed her foot against it.

"Look," I began, "I know what it's like dealing with someone who doesn't want to open up. *Trust me*. But if you take the first step, maybe it'll make things easier for her."

She considered that for a few minutes.

"Okay," she said reluctantly. "But if she doesn't reciprocate . . ."

"Walk away. You've been more than fair."

Hannah nodded and headed for the door again. When she reached the doorway, I called out to her.

"One piece of advice."

She turned back to me again. "I'm starting to think you don't want me to leave."

"Be patient. If she doesn't open up, don't get mad. That'll just push her further into her shell. Just accept it and leave."

"I will." She lingered in the doorway for a minute. "And Kali?"

"Yeah?"

"Thanks. For everything."

I smiled at her and kept smiling long after she left. All along, I'd been trying to do things right, ever since I took over the team. Now that I'd finally stopped trying and just relaxed, I could see what needed to be done.

Later that evening, when I went to the kitchen in search of dinner, I found Hannah and Lily sitting at the table together. They talked and giggled, and linked hands, playfully stroking one another's fingers.

I held back in the entranceway to the kitchen, out of sight, watching them for a minute. Though they both looked like they'd cried recently, their smiles were genuine and their eyes were soft with love.

Footsteps walked up behind me.

"So," Rooke said quietly, looking over my head at the scene

in the kitchen, "instead of telling them to be together in front of the cameras, you help get them back together in secret."

I glanced up at him over my shoulder.

"They look happy. That's what matters." I went quiet for a minute. "I've realized that if I'm going to be team owner, I have to give up some of my responsibilities. Managing the team on my own has been empowering in a way, but trying to do everything all alone is just stupid."

He went still. "Are you not going to play anymore?"

"No, no. I'm divvying up the work. Derek is handling the sponsors. Hannah is taking over our image. And I'm going to talk to Lily, see if she wants to manage marketing, advertisements, and design, like our logos. I think it'll appeal to her creative side."

Plus, it tied her responsibilities in with Derek and Hannah. Marketing and design went hand in hand with the sponsors, and with our image. Maybe if I could get her working with other members of the team on things other than just training together, she'd learn to open up some. Even more, it further integrated the team, made us more tight-knit and dependent on each other. It would make us stronger. A win-win situation.

"I think that's a great idea," Rooke said. "Look at you, delegating."

I turned to face him. "I was wondering if you wanted to manage our training."

He squinted at me, like he wasn't following. "The trainers manage that."

I shook my head. "The trainers know fitness. You know martial arts. Plus, you could keep an eye on the team. Watch out for our health, and if anyone slips."

He hesitated. "With these new pods, I'm not sure that's really an issue anymore."

"That doesn't stop us from partying too hard or working ourselves into exhaustion."

He didn't look sure. "Kali, I'm the last person who should—"

"You're the best person for it. You've been there. You've picked yourself back up more than once, and you know the signs more than anyone." I took a step closer to him. "You saw it in me when no one else did, and you knew exactly what I needed to come back from it. You've even taught me a few things. That couldn't have been easy."

He considered that. "True. If teaching you things is the benchmark for becoming a training instructor, then I should be a sensei by now."

I reeled back to punch him in the gut, but he blocked my attack, locked his fingers around my wrist.

He grinned. "Is that part of my employee evaluation? Because I think I just passed."

I gritted my teeth and shook him off. "You'd have to work with me."

His head tilted. "How's that?"

"I'm going back to being team captain. So, I'll be studying the other teams and planning our strategies. Your input on our strengths and their weaknesses would be helpful."

He considered that.

"Being captain is where you belong," he said simply. "It's where you've always belonged."

"How do you figure?"

"You balance us out. When it's the five of us, it's something more than a team. I don't really know how to describe it."

I did. I knew exactly what he meant.

We felt like family.

I turned back to the kitchen, watching Hannah and Lily talk and giggle with each other. I smiled. Maybe watching them was making me sentimental or something, but suddenly I missed having that kind of connection with another person. One where you felt free. Where you could touch, laugh, and share without hesitation because that person seemed like they were just an extension of yourself.

I leaned back until my shoulders pressed against Rooke's chest. He went still for a beat, not moving at all, but he didn't back away, either. As we stood there together, I focused on his breaths, and the way his chest expanded out against my shoulders. I smiled. His breaths were steady. Strong. Like he was at peace.

So was I.

"If I'm watching out for the team's health," he began, "does that mean I can trade out your morning coffee for a protein shake?"

"Only if you want to know what it feels like to be my alarm clock."

He chuckled against my back. "I don't know. I think I could—"

"Don't be a hero."

He laughed again. Though I had my back pressed against his front and couldn't see his face, I had a feeling he was smiling. I sighed. Lily and Hannah were back together. Derek had the sponsors wrapped around his finger. Rooke was doing well.

The stars were aligning.

At least, until later that night when I sat down at my desk. A random e-mail sat in my in-box from someone simply marked as GuestUser. The subject line read:

You need to see this. Do not reply.

I clicked my nail against the keyboard. The e-mail had made it into my in-box, which meant it hadn't been marked as suspicious. That didn't stop my own internal filters from questioning the message. Open. Don't open.

I opened it.

The e-mail contained several screen captures from a chain of messages traded between two people. The names had been redacted, but the more I read, the more I suspected they were exchanges between Diana Foot and Tamachi.

> You said they'd be out of the tournament by now.
> They better be out this round.

> They will. They'll be bankrupt soon anyway.
> Really, what does Ling think she's doing?

> You told us these pods would put them up against
> challenges they can't defeat. That's why we
> allowed them into the tournament.

> Stop worrying, Diana. They'll be out soon.
> And then they'll be done for good.

A chill flooded my whole body as I read over the words. The realization left me in such complete shock, all I could do was sit at my desk and blink. I had my proof. There was no denying it now.

They were trying to kick me out of the league.

don't know how long I sat in front of my computer screen, trying to process the words I'd just read. My mind was a clogged drain. The information was trying to come down the pipes but wouldn't pass through.

They were trying to kick us out.

I repeated it to myself over and over, but it still wouldn't sink in.

My computer chimed again. Another e-mail appeared in my in-box. I hovered over it as my pulse rose another ten beats a minute. Shallow breaths panted through my mouth and my stomach churned, but I pushed my finger down and forced myself to read it. In this e-mail, the screen captures were dated from a few weeks ago.

She cost us millions in PR damage control.
I want her to pay as we did.

She is. She's putting everything she has
into this tournament.

A tournament that she's still in.
You said she'd be gone by now.

She will be.

Next round, I'll be sure of it.

Bankrupting her is not enough.

She still has the public on her side.

By the end of this,

her name will mean nothing.

If this message really was from a few weeks ago, then this must have been when they started to turn the media against us. And now it was coming true. We were going under, both financially and in the public eye.

In that moment, I knew only two things. One, they really were trying to kick us out of this tournament, and the whole thing had been a setup. Two, someone inside the VGL had access to these e-mails and was forwarding me the screen captures.

Three, the VGL was shit.

Four, they'd really pissed me off now.

We'd been invited to this tournament for no reason other than to destroy us. We never should have been here. We weren't ready, and they knew it. Worst of all, they weren't just doing it to me. They were messing with my team. Their careers. Their futures. For what? For ratings? Just so I'd shut up and go away?

They'd done it now. They'd found my breaking point.

They'd screwed with my team.

My. Team.

I gripped the edge of the desk, tighter and tighter, until I was trembling, and the desk groaned in response. Everything inside me burned. I stood and was shaking so hard I had to steady myself against the desk. There were plenty of places I could go in the house to work this off. The training room. The garden outside. Dr. Renner's office. But one place kept coming to mind again and again, and I could only ignore it for so long.

I marched through the house to Rooke's door and knocked, straining against my own hand to keep it from pounding.

"Come in."

When I opened the door, he was lying on his bed, on his side, book in hand. He looked like . . . well, him. And I hated it because it tugged at my heart a little.

I wanted to tell him everything. The e-mails from the VGL. The conspiracy against the team. But when I opened my mouth, all that came out was, "You were right."

Rooke closed the book and grinned. "It happens sometimes." When his gaze traced over my expression, his grin disappeared, and he stood from the bed. "What's wrong?"

"I have these e-mails . . ." I panted between breaths, tears brimming in my eyes. "And the VGL is . . . And now the team . . ."

He grabbed my shoulders. "Whoa, slow down. What's going on?"

I closed my eyes and forced a few slow breaths through my mouth. Any attempt at clearing my mind or my temper was futile at the moment, but I managed to dial it back a bit.

"Someone inside the VGL forwarded me a series of e-mails. You were right. They're trying to kick us out, and it's not just with the game. They're trying to discredit us through the media, too. They know bankrupting us won't be enough. They have to find a way to destroy our popularity and reputations, too."

Rooke stared at me for a minute while he processed that.

"Who sent the e-mails—"

"I don't know. But someone inside the VGL wants me to know what's happening." I swallowed thick as the realization hit me. Numbness took hold of my insides, and my knees went a little weak. "They're doing this because of me. I never thought about how everything I was doing could hurt all of you. I'm a terrible person."

He shook his head. "Kali, you're not—"

"Yes, I am," I exclaimed. "After I didn't falsify your drug test, I cared more about what the media thought than how you were handling it. I bought out the team to create a better life for them, then I paraded you around like little dolls for the cameras. And now the VGL is trying to destroy our careers and livelihood just because I spoke out about corruption and tried to make the game safer. I try to do the right thing, and it doesn't matter because I just mess it up anyway."

"You're being too hard on yourself. You're going to make mistakes. It's learning from them that matters. Life's not black-and-white."

I sat down on his bed and dropped my head into my hands. There was no way this was really happening. It must have been a dream, or a simulation, like the game. Come on, Tamachi himself had brought me into that meeting with the VGL . . .

"Holy shit," I gasped, rising from the bed. "That's why Tamachi brought me with him to the VGL. It wasn't for my opinion on the game. It was to show them he'd roped me into this." I started pacing around his room and smacked the side of my head with my open palm. "I'm so stupid."

"You're not stupid."

His words were distant as all my senses filled with rage. How could they do this to my team? Were they really more worried about money and ratings than us? I punched the wall, hit a stud, and cried out when the jolt of pain shot up my forearm.

"Fucking stud." I punched the wall again with my other hand. "See? I can't even punch the wall right."

Rooke grabbed my wrists. "Stop."

"I'll hurt myself if I want to."

"No. I won't let you."

My temper flared, and I reeled.

"You won't let me?" I roared.

In a blink, he spun me around, locked his arms over mine, and crushed my back against his chest. I struggled against him, locked in his vise grip. After a minute of failed escape attempts, I glared up at him, breathing hard.

"I'm so close to punching you in the dick."

He glanced down at my pinned upper half and chuckled. "I can see that."

I squirmed against him, snarling. "I swear to God, I hope you're wearing a cup."

He gripped me tighter. "Drop the bullshit, Kali. If it was reversed, you wouldn't let me do this, either."

I snorted at him and ignored the fact that he was probably right.

He pulled me toward his bathroom. I kicked my legs.

"Let me go."

"Break my arms."

I went rag-doll limp against him like a three-year-old child, dragging my feet as he dragged me. He cursed my name under his breath, but kept going. He pulled me through the bathroom and into the shower, turned it on, and held me under the stream. Water cascaded down. He kept me there, under the water, his front pressed against my back.

My hair plastered against my face, my clothes against my skin. The stream flowed over me and down the drain, and my emotions went with it. I turned to jelly in his arms and slumped against him. Water seeped into my eyes and back out. I stood there with him, listening to the raindrop prickling of the stream hitting the tile.

I knew what he was doing, holding me under the water like this. He was pulling me into the present moment, reminding me that nothing can stop the flow of water. It doesn't resist. It doesn't protest. It just glides around whatever is in its path and continues on its way.

"This doesn't fix anything," I said. My voice sounded tired and defeated.

"Nothing's really broken."

With his chest pressed so tightly against my back, his voice sounded as if it was reverberating straight through me.

"That doesn't make any sense," I said. "You said yourself that things need to get better in the industry and that I'm the one to bring it about. Every time I try, it slaps me in the face."

"The industry is broken. You're not. You're perfect. Just being yourself is more than enough. The VGL knows that. Why do you think they're trying so hard to stop you? They wouldn't do this if you didn't pose a threat to them. They're afraid of you."

"They're afraid of the truth. Not me. I'm one person, and I'm not enough."

"You're enough the moment you realize you're already enough. You're strong enough and skilled enough to deal with this."

"I can't. It's too big."

"The whole is too big. Just work at it one piece at a time. Change one person. One team. One tournament." He took a breath deep enough that his chest expanded against my back. "How do you build a wall?"

I thought it over.

"Program a drone to do it for you."

He sighed, and his arm tightened around my waist.

"No." His voice was stern. "How do you build a wall?"

Now it was my turn to sigh.

"One brick at a time."

I turned to face him. The front of his clothes were spotted with water, and some of his hair was damp from the shower. He'd never gone completely under the stream but had gotten some backsplash from holding me there. He looked like he'd been standing on a curb's edge and had a puddle sprayed up on him from a passing cab.

"Don't try to be anything more than yourself," he said, taking my face in his hands. "Just be Kali Ling. That's all you can be. And really, that's all you need."

I let out a breath that came from deep within and left me feeling a little more fulfilled on the inside. Not completely better, but a little closer to center than I had been.

Rooke rested his hands on my shoulders and looked over my expression.

"Better?" he asked.

Mostly. The VGL could do whatever they wanted to me. I'd still have the things that mattered. I had my team—my friends— and the determination to make things the best for them. Rooke had always been something more than a friend, though. He'd been everything from a confidant to a pain in the ass, and usually exactly what I needed in my life. And I was finally ready for it to be something more again.

I met his gaze.

"Yes, but we have another problem."

"What?"

"Your clothes are all wet."

His jaw set, and his eyes darkened. His expression went from serious and concerned to something far more primal. I knew that look, and I liked it.

I gripped his shirt and tugged him farther into the shower.

"Oops. Now they're more."

My hand trailed down his shirt, flicking buttons open, one after the other. He watched my eyes the entire time. I spread his shirt wide as the water slipped down, flowing through the recesses in his chest and stomach. I pressed my lips to his chest, tasting skin and water, inhaling the scent of him.

I pulled my own shirt off and pressed against him, until we were skin to skin and nothing else. He grabbed my chin and tilted my head up until our eyes met. I gave him one look, of ferocity and need. One look was all he needed.

He swept me into his arms and slammed me against the shower wall. A moan escaped my mouth as my back hit and my legs instinctively wrapped around him. He ravished my neck as he pinned me there. More clothes came off, some sticking, too heavy and slick from the water. It fueled us. Made us desperate for each other.

Things got rough.

He took me there, pinned against the wall, under the shower's stream. He pressed into me, deeper every time. Our lips brushed together, whispering things between gasps. We shared everything. How good it felt, how much we needed each other, why we were so stupid sometimes to deny that what we had could be beautiful.

When we'd finished, both shaking and sated, clinging to each other as the water poured down over us, he kissed my forehead and murmured against my skin.

"See? Water really does make things better."

CHAPTER 18

"The VGL is trying to kick us out."

I met with everyone in the training room, including Dr. Renner. Everyone stared at me, blinking, like they couldn't quite process my words. Rooke stood behind everyone else, leaning against the wall. Since he already knew what was going on, he was the only person in the room unsurprised by the news.

"Someone forwarded me a string of e-mails," I continued. "All the harassment by the media, everything we've faced inside the games, it's all specifically designed to knock us out of the tournament and ruin our reputation as a team."

Everyone exchanged looks with each other. Derek looked a little more certain than the others, given he'd already suspected something was going on with the pods. The girls weren't entirely buying it.

"You really think they're targeting just us?" Hannah asked. "I mean, the paparazzi has had a field day with us, but that's what they do."

"Lily saw the machine from her childhood nightmares inside the game," I pointed out. "That's awfully specific. Plus, Rooke faced his own death."

Everyone looked at Lily and Rooke. They both nodded.

Hannah turned back to me. "But why would they try to kick us out?"

I cleared my throat. "Apparently, I cost them a lot of money."

Dr. Renner took a step forward to address the group. "It's like the football-concussion controversy at the turn of the century. Ever since Kali spoke out, research into virtual reality and addiction has tripled. Most studies have shown that the pods and programs the VGL was using were detrimental to psychological health. Suddenly, the VGL has to explain why ratings and money have been more important than the players' safety. They're scrambling, and they're trying to punish her for it."

I knew Dr. Renner was saying that for the rest of the team, but her words hit home. I sat down on the mats and hugged my knees to my chest. This was all happening because of me. The rest of the team didn't deserve it, didn't ask for it, and now their careers and reputations were being destroyed simply because of my actions.

I hugged myself tighter, feeling the tears sneaking up.

Hannah knelt in front of me.

"Kali," she said softly, stroking my arm. "What's wrong?"

"I fucked up for you guys. I never thought when I spoke out that it would affect the rest of you this much. I was trying to do what was right for Nathan. But this isn't just about me and what I think is right. These are your careers, your dreams, and I'm ruining them."

She smiled. "You're not ruining—"

"Yes, I am. It's not just me who's being punished. It's the team. What they do to you guys, they do to me. They hurt any of you, and it hurts me." I buried my face in my knees. "I know I screw up a lot, and it must not seem like it sometimes, but you guys are more important to me than anything. And now to think that they're screwing over all of you because of something I did—"

My voice caught against the growing lump in my throat. Hannah wrapped her arms around me. I lifted my head to meet her eyes, and she rested her forehead against mine.

"It's not just you they're going up against. It's all of us."

I sniffled, rubbed my nose, and pushed back the tears. "So, what do we do? How do we take on something as big as this?"

She smiled again.

"Simple. We win anyway."

I laughed. It would be the solution to everything. Our sponsors would be ecstatic, if we'd even need them anymore. We'd have our choice. With that hundred-million grand prize, we'd never be reliant on anyone else again to keep us afloat. And there was a chance that a victory that sweet might win back the hearts of the crowd.

Hannah offered her hand. I took it and pushed up to my feet.

"Dr. Renner, I'm asking you to work with each of us individually to uncover our fears and how to face them." In the corner, Dr. Renner nodded in agreement. "Hopefully, it'll help us get through the rest of the matches."

Derek stepped forward and crossed his arms. "But that's only half the problem. If their plan was to break our reputation through the media, they've done it. We're the most hated team in the league right now."

"That's true," Hannah said, turning to me. "What do you want me to do about that? I don't think designer clothes and showing skin are going to change people's opinions about us."

I had no idea what to do at this point. Celebrities facing scandals and controversies was nothing new, and oftentimes, they rebounded and came back even stronger than before. But this was different. I had entire corporations working against me, controlling the media and what was printed about us. Anything we did could be twisted, misconstrued, and made ten times worse.

"I think it's best if we try to stay out of the spotlight as much as possible. It won't fix anything, but it won't give them any new fodder, either."

Derek didn't look sure. "That's not really enough—"

"It's all we can do for now." I sighed. "Let me think about it, okay?"

Reluctantly, they all agreed.

Later that day, I met with Dr. Renner. While sessions with the doc were never a bad idea, I'd mostly been thinking about the team's opening up about what scared them. But as I sat down across from her for my own session, I realized I would be opening up as well, and I wasn't sure there was much to tell.

"So, can you tell me what you fear most, Kali?" Dr. Renner asked, as she made a few notes on her tablet.

I stared down at my feet. "I . . . don't know. I'm afraid of losing the tournament and not being able to fund the team."

She nodded. "Okay, anything else?"

"Letting down my friends?" I tried.

"That's not really what I'm looking for. It has to be things that can actually manifest in a virtual world. Otherwise, how will they use it against you?" She tapped a fingernail against her tablet a few times. "How about childhood fears?"

"Nope. My dad says I used to ask him to check the closet for monsters, so I could have something to wrestle."

My answer was rewarded with a rare burst of laughter from Dr. Renner.

"How do you treat fears?" I asked.

"Usually through desensitization." She smiled. "Ironically, most therapists use virtual reality to help people conquer a phobia. If someone is terrified of heights, for example, it's much easier for them to stand on top of a building when they know it's not real. After enough sessions, the patient gains confidence, and it transfers over well to the real world."

Dr. Renner studied me for a minute and adjusted her glasses. "You really love your team," she said. "I think more than you even realize."

My heart swelled at the thought. "Of course. I mean, we live together. Train together. Our lives and careers are so interconnected, if we didn't love each other, this wouldn't really work."

"And you'd do anything not to see them hurt."

"Well, of course not—"

My voice cut off in my throat even though my mouth dropped open. The hair stood up on the back of my neck.

"You think I'm going to see them hurt inside the game," I concluded.

Dr. Renner pressed her lips together. "I think it's a possibility."

The air in my lungs went tight. "I can't. I can't deal with that."

Dr. Renner made a calming motion with her hand. "You see them hurt inside the game all the time. You fight to the death right beside them. That's what you do every week."

I started pacing around in front of my chair. "This is different. If it's about my fear, Tamachi will find a way to make it so much worse than that. You know it."

"Kali. Sit. Down."

She didn't just say the words. She commanded it in such a fierce and uncharacteristic way, I immediately sat.

"If you can't calm down," she began, "you're letting them win. You realize that, right?"

I took a breath and realized it, but it did nothing to quell my racing heartbeat. "What do I do?"

Her lips curved into a smile so wide it took up half her face.

"You already have the tools. You're ahead of the rest of your teammates by miles. You meditate. You practice handling your emotions and letting go all the time."

Not with this. I hadn't been meditating nearly as much lately, unless the nightly Baguazhang sessions with Rooke counted. Maybe they did. The deep concentration required by the art was close enough.

"How's it going with the rest of the team?" I asked. She gave me a stern look. "I know you can't tell me about their actual sessions, but how are they doing with talking about their fears?"

She nodded. "Well, actually. Most people aren't very in tune with their fears. At least, not their truest ones. Most will admit that they fear spiders or heights, for example. Few will dig deeper and talk about a fear of failure or not living a full life. Issues like those can take several sessions to root out. But the team is already looking at it that way. I think it's because of the game. It's already on their mind, and they're quick to put their fears out there, so they can figure out how to win."

I had to grin. "That sounds like my team."

"They're approaching this with a 'bring it on' type of attitude. I think you're rubbing off on them. I'm not sure if that's a good thing."

I chuckled. Whether it was a good thing or not, during the matchups, their fearlessness showed. After the next matchup, I sat in my office, watching highlights from the previous night on the television screen.

Inside the game, Hannah hurried down an empty street, racing toward the enemy's flag. The power cut out to the streetlights and lanterns surrounding her, plunging the street into darkness. Hannah gasped and ground to a halt. I could practically hear her heart beating through her armor. Darkness. This was her fear. Only the glow of her battle-axe gave any indication where she stood. Watching this as a highlight after the fact made me realize how cool this looked to the audience.

The smoky-gray glow of her weapon smoldered in the shadows, and her heavy breaths came through the audio. Eventually, her breathing slowed, until she was taking deep, meditative breaths. Nice, Hannah.

The outline of two opponents appeared at the end of the street. They charged into the darkness. Hannah raced to meet them. Her axe swirled and chopped, streaking through the black backdrop. Her opponents cried out, and one after another, dropped to the ground. Faint moonlight creased the edges of her face as she looked up at the sky and shouted, "Is that all you've got?"

Yup. Definitely enjoying this. The audience would think she was just putting on a good show, but really, it was a subliminal taunt at the VGL.

The weeks started clicking by, faster than I could count. Derek faced his fear. Not surprisingly, snakes. His apprehension of Unagi the Eel suddenly made a lot more sense. But that only caused our teasing about it to triple.

I still hadn't seen mine. I didn't know what the game would prepare for me, but nothing triggered my fears over losing the team or seeing them hurt, other than by the hands of our opponents. But the game itself remained stoic on that front.

The winners' bracket of the tournament played out. K-Rig won the first slot into the championship. The second went to Eon, the Swedish team I'd met at the all-star dinner.

Pretty soon, the game had nothing left for us to face. The matchups were only between us and our opponents. Either we'd mastered our fears, and the pods couldn't sense them anymore, or the VGL had realized we'd figured out their plan and backed off.

The week of the semifinals for the loser's bracket, I sat in front of my computer, waiting for the announcement that would reveal our opponent. Derek sat beside me, leaning against the desk. I wasn't sure where the rest of the team had taken off to, but they disappeared after supper, and Derek had insisted on waiting for the matchup announcement in my office. He hunched over my shoulder, watching the screen as intently as I was.

My e-mail chimed, and I immediately tapped it open. I leaned across the table so Derek could read the message as well.

Legacy vs. Epoch

Defiance vs. Oblivion

Rounds: Best out of three

We traded looks with each other.

"Best out of three," Derek said. "Looks like that's the new element for the semifinals. So, we'll have to win twice."

"Against Cole's team," I emphasized. "He knows things about us. Weaknesses."

"We know things about him, too," he pointed out.

"But he knows our whole team. We don't know his."

He considered that. "I know I'm not in charge of strategy anymore, but I think you and Rooke should go for the flag this round. The chemistry between you is back."

So was shower sex.

"We could debate strategy against Oblivion all night," I said.

"In that case, I'm grabbing a drink." He nodded toward the door. "Come with me."

"Can't even get a drink by yourself?" I teased, standing up from my desk. "Don't let the game know that."

He frowned at me until I bumped shoulders with him and skidded past him toward the kitchen.

"Everything's going really well with the team," he said, hurrying to catch up.

I glanced at him as he reached my side, and grinned. "Can I tell you something?"

He nodded.

"I think we can make it."

He grinned back.

"Me, too."

We walked into the darkened kitchen together, and the lights popped on.

"Surprise."

The chorus rang out from the rest of my teammates, who were all gathered around the kitchen table. Their tablets projected holograms of virtual balloons. There was a pile of gifts on the counter. A cake sat next to it. Judging by the pink frosting and floral design, Hannah had ordered it.

"Whose birthday is it?" I asked.

Lily laughed. "It's yours, dumb-ass."

What? No. It couldn't be mine . . .

I counted the weeks in my mind, thinking back to the first day of the tournament and going forward. It was April 21. Holy shit, it really was my birthday. I'd been so caught up in training, working with the team on our fears, and prepping for the next matchup, I'd completely lost track of time.

I glanced between the cake and the stack of gifts.

"Which first?"

"Oh, I think we'll start with this," Hannah said with a grin, picking up a knife to slice the cake. She placed a piece on a plate and handed it to me. I studied it. Chocolate cake glistened, all moist and dark, and the thick scent of sugary frosting wafted up to my nose. I eyed Hannah over the dessert.

"If it's sugar-free, I'm going to hurt you."

I shoved a forkful in my mouth, and it melted the minute it hit my tongue. Definitely not sugar-free.

Hannah quickly sliced pieces for everyone else. Derek helped himself to seconds, then thirds. The rest of us followed his lead. This was the first junk food we'd had since the start of the tournament. Hell, I was surprised we didn't rip the cake apart and eat it with our bare hands like one-year-olds.

Next came the gifts. The first few were a series of gag gifts, including a hat and scarf for Unagi the Eel. The first serious present I opened came from Hannah, who got me a gift certificate for massage and acupuncture.

"I figured you could use some relaxation time after the tournament," she said, and kissed my cheek. I laughed, and nearly kissed her back. With all the chaos of the tournament, relaxation sounded just about perfect.

When I grabbed the next box and popped it open, my mouth dropped. Inside was a three-foot-by-two-foot bamboo canvas. Painted on the canvas was the team. Done in a black and white graphic-novel sort of style, only the shadows of our faces were colored in with black ink, so the wood-colored bamboo showed through to make up the highlights. We were encircled in swirling puffs of smoke. In each corner was one of the four Chinese symbols from my jacket inside the game. Harmony, balance, nature, and peace.

"Lily," I gasped. "Did you make this?"

She blushed a little and nodded.

"Thank you."

It seemed like a meager thing to say for a gift so personal, but the smile on Lily's face was all I needed to know it was enough. I pulled her into a deep side-hug, and she squeezed me back.

When I reached for Rooke's present, the rest of the team did a drumroll against the kitchen table. I ripped off the wrapping to reveal a PlayStation 5, the first PlayStation with a VR headset included in the box set. Rooke had also added a stack of games and adapter plugs for modern TV screens. But before I even set my hands on the box, my teammates snatched it up.

"Now we can play Tekken 9 on the original system," Derek said, as he carried the box over to the living room. "Me versus anyone who wants to die."

Hannah followed him with the stack of games in hand. "It's Kali's gift, and Rooke gave it to her. They should play first."

Derek pulled the system from the box and attached the adapter unit to the cables. "It's her house, too. She should be a good host and share with her friends."

"Hey, guys," Lily called, interrupting the argument. She had pulled on the VR headset that came with the system. It was solid black, somewhat sleek but still ridiculously oversized, taking up a good third of her face. She grinned. "Look, it's cordless!"

The room erupted in laughter. Both Derek and Hannah fell on their backs, gripping their stomachs.

"Holy shit," Derek squeezed out. "It's so advanced."

As I watched my teammates kill themselves laughing over the archaic technology that was my birthday present, I leaned toward Rooke.

"Are you sure this gift is for me?"

He laced his fingers through mine. "I have something to show you." He nodded toward the back of the house.

I glanced at my giggling teammates on the floor. "But everyone else—"

"They already know."

He tugged on my hand. I resisted.

"Where are we going?"

"Do you really think all I got you for your birthday was a classic video game console?"

Interesting.

Really, the console was more than enough of a gift. The PS5 had been released more than three and a half decades ago, so to find one mint-in-box couldn't have been easy. Still, I grinned. "I get a second present? Why can't you give it to me in front of everyone else?"

"It can't be wrapped."

How interesting, indeed. What kind of present couldn't be wrapped? Okay, I'm down for it. I let him lead me into the pod room. It was empty, other than the pods, and hummed with the buzz of machines and electricity. In other words, same as usual.

"So," I began, rocking on my feet. "What are we doing?"

He walked toward his pod. "Derek helped me create a special program just for us."

Oh, a *special* program. Just for us. If it was anything like what I was already thinking of, there were plenty of "special programs" in the back rooms of strip clubs.

"This is my birthday," I told him. "Not yours."

He grinned. "Get changed."

Fine. I wasn't going to ruin the surprise. The expression on his face told me this meant something to him. So, I stopped resisting, changed into my pod suit, climbed into my pod, and closed my eyes, with no idea what waited for me on the other side.

Pure silence.

The deafening kind of silence that swallows any other sound, even your own thoughts, leaving behind nothing but a sense of peace.

I didn't open my eyes. Not at first.

I took a breath. Thick mountain air expanded my lungs and made me feel whole. Then a bubbling sound broke through the quiet. A stream? No. A river or a small lake, flowing effortlessly over rocks and around bends. Everything was still and moving. Bustling with noise, and somehow still quiet. Birds chirped, leaves rustled, and water bubbled. And yet, the air held an omnipotent weight of calmness and tranquility.

I opened my eyes.

I stood on a dock, which wound its way over a shallow body of water. Its surface shimmered in the sunlight, reflecting that above it while still revealing what lay below, like a translucent mirror. Where the dock ended, stone stairs and paths broke off in several directions. All around me, mountains rose from the ground. As they climbed higher and higher, rock and vegetation wrapped around one another and became one. Stone walls and trails led the way up into the mountains. Every so often, there was a plateau, where small villages of stone structures, statues, and temples had been built, their bright red walls and jade-colored roofs gleaming against the mountainside. Wisps of mist slithered through everything: the lake, the stones, and the mountaintops.

My heart beat just a little softer then, and stronger. I knew this place. The Wudang Mountains. The birthplace of Baguazhang, several other martial arts, and one of the most sacred places in the world for Taoists.

Footsteps walked up behind me.

"I know it's not as good as the real thing," Rooke said, "but we can't actually get on a twenty-hour flight in the middle of a tournament."

I turned to face him. He stared into my eyes, his expression stoic and warm, like it always was when he was at peace. I opened my mouth to speak, but nothing came out. The words snagged in my throat and refused to ascend any higher.

Because, really.

What do you say to the man who built you a mountain?

I crossed my arms as I looked up at him. "You're still an asshole, sometimes."

Apparently, that's what I say.

He grinned. "And you're still stubborn."

I grinned back. "Proudly."

He offered his hand. I studied it for a minute, tapping my foot against the dock. Then I laced my fingers through his, and he led the way. Together, we walked along the dock to the stone steps. We passed through a gate to a small group of buildings and courtyards. In one of the courtyards, nine monks stood in a three-by-three formation. They moved together in perfect synchronicity, performing Bagua circle walking.

"You can interact with them," Rooke told me. "Since the pods have artificial intelligence, the programming isn't limited to what the programmer created. It can tap into the Internet or any electronic source, extract information, and channel it through a virtual teacher." He paused, and chuckled to himself. "Turns out these pods are good for something."

"So I can discuss Taoist philosophy with them? Don't I have you for that?" I nudged him playfully. He smiled.

"It's more than that. You can study every style of martial arts specific to the Wudang school. Plus, I'm not so familiar with the religious side of Taoism. If that's something you'd like to know more about, you can talk to them."

He took my hand again. We left the practicing monks behind and kept climbing. Pine, cypress, Chinese maples, and gingko trees framed our path while camellias bloomed the color of sunsets after storms. We wandered through some of the villages, where monks nodded at me as I passed.

In the center of one of the villages was an eight-sided fountain approximately fifteen feet in diameter. It rose three steps, each level slightly smaller than the former. In the center was a stone platform with a yin yang symbol embedded in the stones. The bagua.

"We took a little creative licensing," he told me, motioning at the water feature. "Not everything here is exactly the same as at the actual Wudang Mountains. But whenever you need some time to yourself, you can come here. Stay for minutes, or for hours."

I glanced up at him. "Is there hours' worth of content in here?"

He turned his gaze to the mountains. "Days' worth, technically. The whole mountain range is accessible. There are steps all the way to the highest peak. You can climb over fifteen hundred meters to the Golden Hall. Plus, there are over a hundred palaces, temples, and pavilions you can visit from different dynasties throughout history."

We started climbing up the mountainside again. Midway up the steps to the next collection of temples, I stopped at an overlook. It stretched out several feet and ended in the shape of a dragon's head. I placed a knee against the perch and leaned over it a little, taking in the deep ravine. Below was nothing but green treetops and brush, with streams of water running downhill. The air smelled sweet and dense, the way only mountain air could.

At the next cluster of pavilions, Rooke led me inside the closest one, which was obviously used for studying martial arts. Several classic Chinese weapons lined the walls, including dao glaives, hook swords, and ji polearms. In the center of the room, a pair of men sparred bare-handed, while a semicircle of monks clustered around them, watching their techniques. As we approached, they halted their fight, turned to us, and bowed deeply. Then they motioned for us to take their place.

I surged forward. Good idea, boys. But when I reached the center, my fighting partner hadn't followed. Rooke walked over to the wall, retrieved two sets of deerhorn knives, and handed a pair to me. I gripped them tight in my hands, feeling the subtle leather grips rub against my palms. I rested my weight on my back foot and swirled through a few sharp movements from the Baguazhang poses. The knives slid through the air, feeling both weighted and fluid. The knives, my movements, everything felt the same as real life.

Rooke took up a pose opposite me, like he was preparing for a duel. I had to smile.

"I told you before. These aren't really meant to spar with."

"That doesn't sound much like the warrior to me." His grin spread from ear to ear. "Unless you're afraid to lose."

My expression set. I slid back and struck a pose. "I'm going to take your ears off last, so you'll hear my rants the entire time."

He got into his position and grimaced. "I might just stab myself in the eardrums."

It went quiet between us, and throughout the entire room. I felt nothing but the air on my skin and the intense stares of the monks around us. I locked eyes with Rooke, each of us waiting for the other to move. When we finally did, it was in perfect synchronicity.

The whole thing was a dance. We moved like one. Like the entire routine had been planned out and rehearsed.

We spun around each other, growing closer with each turn.

When the blades started wisping across each other's skin, Rooke suddenly surged forward for a final move. We locked up. The tip of his blade dug into my back, and the edge of mine pressed into the soft spot under his jaw. He glanced down at me, keeping his head high.

"I guess that's a draw."

"Only because you stopped."

He dropped his weapons to the floor, and with his arms still wrapped around me, crushed me against him. I burst out laughing and dropped my own weapons.

"Death by asphyxiation," I squeezed out between gasps of laughter. "That's cheating."

He caved.

The second he loosened his grip, I wrapped my ankle around his and threw my shoulder into his upper body. He lost his balance and fell back. I landed on top of him, pinning him on the floor.

He laughed, and I watched the movement rumble in his chest. That wasn't manufactured laughter, not simply a response to the situation. It was genuine. Whatever anger he'd been holding when we first started practicing was gone.

It made me happy. Happier than I expected. I pressed my lips together as my throat grew tight. I didn't feel quite connected to my body in that moment. Not because this was the virtual world. But because this was the virtual world *and* what I felt was so real. But instead of fighting it, instead of separating what was real and what wasn't, I just let them mingle. Constructed or organic. Digital or real. It didn't matter. Together, they left me breathless.

Together, they made me who I am.

I realized something right then. Virtual or not, life is only as real as you make it.

"I can't believe you did this," I told him, taking another look around the pavilion and to the mountains beyond. "It's . . . unbelievable."

He simply looked into my eyes, and smiled. "No, Kali. You're unbelievable."

Oh. No.

That's when the tears started.

I blinked rapidly, trying to contain them. They spilled over and down my cheeks. He wrapped me in his arms, and I fell into him, pressing my ear against his chest. His heart beat soundly, and his breaths were deep. I could have stayed there. Forever. Not because of the pleasures of the virtual world. Not because of the beauty of the moment.

Because of us.

Because of everything we'd gone through. Individually. Together. And as a team. We each had our weaknesses and strengths. But somehow, we balanced each other out. Just like the team, we were strong individually but even stronger as a whole.

I turned my face to rest against his neck, and pressed my lips against his skin. Once. Twice. He whispered against my forehead something that had me yearning for the knives again.

"I told you we should practice this virtually."

CHAPTER 19

y whole body was electric.

I gathered with my teammates in our virtual base, waiting for the countdown to begin. The shield shimmered in the doorway. Rooke and I stood ahead of everyone else, preparing for our run for the enemy's flag.

Cole flashed through my mind. Right now he'd be doing the same as we were—gathered in his base with his team, hoping they'd win and make it to the championship. For the next few seconds, anything was a possibility. But in the end, either he was going home or we were. I thought about his kind smile, his calm and friendly personality. Even on different teams, he'd treated us as both allies and friends. But now he was the enemy. He stood between us and the ultimate glory.

The countdown began.

"Everyone stick to the plan," Derek said behind me. "Only deviate if you have to. Just get through tonight, and we're in the championship. We practiced hard. We're ready for this."

This was it. The final matchup of tournament play. Whoever won this would be in the championship and competing for the hundred mil. No NPCs. No tricks. This was just team on team. Player on player. The best wins.

"It's best out of three," I reminded them. "Make the first round count."

The shield dropped. We ran.

Rooke and I bolted ahead while the others remained behind to guard our flag. Our feet pounded the pavement as we raced down the street.

"Rooftop?" Rooke asked through the mic, nodding at an upcoming fire escape.

I nodded. "Go."

He reached it first and propelled himself up the ladder. I followed close behind. We hit the rooftop and bolted across the map. The sky glowed with shades of charcoal and midnight blue, and the full moon was a smudge against the dark canvas, shrouded in heavy clouds. In moments like these, it was easy to understand why a gamer might get lost inside the virtual world. The moon wasn't real. The air wasn't real. Hell, I wasn't even really looking at a night sky. But the wires and electrodes stimulating my body, nerves, and brain told me it was real even when it wasn't.

We reached the final rooftop, knelt in the shadows, and peered over the edge. A single member of Oblivion guarded the flag. There must have been more of them, hiding in the darkness. I scanned the rooftops.

"There," Rooke said, nodding at a rooftop the next building over from the flag. Against the midnight sky, the faintest outline of a silhouette shifted in the darkness.

Rooke glanced at me through the shadows of his hood. "You ready?"

I grinned. "Always."

We backed up on the roof together, drew our swords, and charged. As we hit the edge, we pushed off. Our blades streaked through the air, cutting against the midnight sky with flashes of gray. I reeled my sword back as I flew. Together, we smashed into the guard on the flag, driving our blades through his body.

He landed on his back, eyes wide, gasping. His hands absently grabbed at the blades protruding through his body, leaving thin cuts along his fingers. Blood pooled around him. He gurgled twice, convulsing, and went limp.

I dove for the flag.

The attacker on the roof slammed into me, knocking me to the side. I hit the pavement with a hard smack, and the air whooshed out of my lungs. I lay on the ground, gasping, trying to force myself to take a breath. The Oblivion attacker appeared above me. He grinned, gripped his sword tight, and slammed it down.

Inches from my face, Rooke's sword caught his. The sharp clang of metal echoed through the street. My attacker turned his attention on my teammate, swinging with all his strength. Rooke blocked two of his attacks, knocked his arms open, and punched him hard across the jaw with the hilt of his sword. Oblivion stumbled back several steps. He spat blood.

Now it was my turn to grin.

As I got to my feet, another member of Oblivion jumped down from behind us.

Surrounded.

The flag shimmered just feet away.

Rooke and I exchanged glances. We didn't even need to communicate.

We went back-to-back.

Well, this felt familiar.

We'd fought like this before, the first year we were on the team together. It was sort of a specialty of ours. We moved like magnets. When one moved, the other perfectly countered. Derek was right. Our chemistry was back.

I pressed my shoulders against his back, feeling his own muscles tighten, ready for the fight. Our attackers closed in. We moved. Together.

Sword met sword as our attackers swirled around us, trying to break our defenses. We moved as one, bowing in, stepping back. Our arms became a blur as we fended off our opponents.

Then a sound called out into the night that ground my heart to a halt. Rooke had howled in pain. The muscles in his back went slack, and he dropped to his knees. I whirled around. A blade had impaled his chest, dead center. I watched him fall.

No.

That's not what was supposed to happen. We were supposed to win. Together.

A blade ripped straight across my arm, slicing my right tricep open. My arm went numb, and my sword clanged to the ground. I scrambled to retrieve it with my other hand.

Amateur move.

His blade plunged into my left side. I gasped, my whole body going rigid as the hot steel pierced through my body. He ripped it out again. Blood spattered down my legs and all over the ground. I dropped to my knees, clawing at the wound in my side as the nausea rolled through me. He cocked his fist back and released, delivering a hard blow across my jaw. Bones cracked and crunched, and my brain felt like it had been punted fifty feet away. My eyes rolled back, and I collapsed onto the pavement. Everything went black.

Stupid, stupid, stupid, stupid.

Maybe it was nerves, or maybe we were vastly outmatched, but I was playing like it was my first matchup ever. *Get it together, Kali.*

For a few seconds, I hung in suspended animation. I had no body, no feeling. There was only darkness, and the ever-present game breathing all around. Not really alive, but still there, cloaking me in its darkness, like shadows closing in on a single, flickering flame before snuffing it out.

When I reloaded into the base, I slammed into my body like I'd jerked awake from some horrifying dream. Except this wasn't a dream, and something wasn't right. The side of my face pounded. My stomach ached, like I was about to vomit, and my arm stung, as if I was still cut. I grabbed at my arm, but nothing but smooth skin slid under my fingertips. The churning feeling in my stomach went cold. The wound was gone, so why wasn't the pain?

Beside me, Rooke leaned against the base wall, hugging his arms to his chest—exactly where he'd been stabbed. I leaned toward him, covered my mic with my hand, and lowered my voice.

"Are you still hurt from that last round?"

He met my eyes and gave a curt nod.

"Do you think it's on purpose?" I asked. "They said no tricks for this matchup."

"No tricks for Oblivion, maybe. I doubt they're hurting right now."

I went cold. "It's a setup?"

"Hard to say."

The rest of the team materialized in the base, panting hard and grimacing. Damn it. We'd lost the first round, and it looked like their injuries were lingering, too.

The thirty-second countdown flashed across the map's screen.

I moved to the middle of the base. "Guys, huddle up." I wrapped a hand around my mic again. "Cover your mics. Drop your voices."

Once they'd each wrapped a hand around their mics, I lowered my voice to a faint whisper.

"Everyone else still feeling the pain from the last round?"

They nodded.

"Looks like this is the final attempt to take us out of the tournament. That pain you're feeling right now isn't real. But the kind we'll show Oblivion will be. Remember that. We have to win this one, or it's game over. So, just win. There are no other options. Push through the pain and show this game what you're made of."

"Even if we win and push it to three rounds," Derek began, his voice quiet yet strained, "will our injuries from this round carry over?"

"And compound with the injuries we already have?" Lily concluded.

The coldness in my gut went subarctic. If it did, would we even be able to stand on our own feet? I shook my head.

"Don't even think about it. Just kick ass." I glanced at the timer. Seven seconds. "New strategy. All of us guard the flag. We'll bring them to us, take out as many as we can, then go for their flag. If we're hurt, then it's best to fight as a team. As one."

Everyone agreed.

When the shield fizzled out, we walked out onto the street and surrounded the flag. All five of us. The air was silent. The game hovered all around us, that omnipresent feeling that never left. I looked up to the sky and realized that, with all its emptiness, there was still beauty to be had in this digital world. The moonlight glowed, catching highlights in the windows and across every hint of glass. The Japanese lanterns dotted the street like hanging poppies. It hit me then. Part of me was going to miss this place.

Then another realization hit, and I pushed this one as far away from my mind as I could.

This could be my last time inside the game.

Three members of Oblivion appeared through the closest alleyway and charged. We held our ground, bringing them to us. Their feet pounded the pavement in a steady thrum. Twenty yards, now ten.

We smashed together. It was a messy fight. Swords clanged. Fists bashed heads and ribs. Somewhere in the chaos, a foot slammed into my chest. I stumbled back, and surged forward again, ripping my sword through anything that wasn't a teammate. Blood sprayed across my face, speckling my skin with red dots and splotches. Yelps and screams rang out, along with moans of pain. Male or female, my team or not, I wasn't sure.

A back turned toward me, marked with the white highlights in Oblivion's armor. I pounced, wrapping my legs around his waist and my arms around his neck. He flung around wildly, trying to knock me off. Gripping my dagger, I slashed it through his neck. He went rigid, dropped to his knees, and collapsed to the ground. I followed him down, landing hard on his back.

It went quiet. The fight was over.

Breathing hard, I stumbled to my feet and surveyed my surroundings. The flag still shimmered in its place. Lily and Hannah were helping each other up. My male teammates hadn't fared as well. Derek and Rooke were on the ground, pools of blood around their bodies. Slowly, they faded from view.

I sighed. It wasn't a bad scenario. Oblivion had two players left, and we had three. Not a guaranteed win, but we were on our way. I surveyed my remaining teammates. A deep gash tore through Lily's calf muscle. She could barely stand. Hannah was in better shape, but her complexion was pale, and she breathed slowly through her mouth. Her injuries from the previous round must have been rough.

"You go. You're the least injured," she said. "We'll guard. Just get the flag."

I nodded and took off running. The pavement pounded

beneath my feet. I should have taken to the rooftops, but the ache in my gut and the dizziness in my head told me that jumping between buildings was not going to happen right now. Running on compounded injuries felt like mile twenty of a marathon. Every cell in my body was begging, pleading with me to stop, but I pushed myself onward.

The farther I crossed through the map, the more my stomach prickled. Oblivion was nowhere to be seen. I reached the edge of the map and peered around the corner where their flag stood twenty feet down the street, in front of their base. There was no one else. At least, no obvious guard. I surveyed the rooftops and alleyways for a movement in the shadows. The air remained silent and deathly still, the way it always did inside this game.

I went for it.

I pumped my legs as fast as they would go, every nerve on full alert. Nobody came for me. Looked like Oblivion was scrambling, too, or setting a trap for us. My suspicions were on the latter. We outnumbered them three-to-two, but that would only motivate them to come up with a more desperate, ruthless plan.

I zipped through the flag, and sprinted back for our base. I became a blur, a streak of white-blue against a background of gray.

"I'm coming in," I said into the mic. "Oblivion is nowhere to be seen."

Only silence answered.

"Hannah?"

A few grunts cut through the audio.

"Got one here—" Hannah's voice cut out into a scream. Then it went silent again.

"Lily? Hannah?"

Nothing. Uh-oh.

"Guys?"

A horn rang out. Shit. Someone had picked up our flag. Only a faint, static hum buzzed in the comms. I was alone. It was two on one, and I had to take their flag carrier out in order to score. On my own. With injuries from both rounds. And if I didn't score, we were out of the matchup and the tournament. What was that I usually said about liking a challenge? This time, my stomach swirled.

Now my best bet at finding him was from the rooftops. I spotted a fire-escape ladder. I grasped the first rod and started to pull myself up. A blinding pain shot through my side and I collapsed back to the pavement. Damn it. With my compounded injuries, there was no way I was making it to the roof. With no other choice, I started my search on the streets. My sides ached, my head pounded, and only adrenaline and sheer determination kept me pushing onward.

The pavement clacked under my feet as I darted around corners and through alleyways. I could run right past him, but he wouldn't be able to score as long as I had their flag. Right now the hunt was for each other.

Somewhere around the middle of the map, a white-blue glimmer caught my eye a hundred feet out.

Gotcha.

I slipped into an alley and peered out. The glow took on the outline of a man as he raced down the street, heading directly for me. The flag carrier. I'd found him, and he appeared to be alone. Given the possible scenarios, he was probably running our flag to his base, where he'd wait for his remaining teammate to take me out, leaving him open to score instantly. But his teammate was nowhere to be seen. Probably split up to search for me.

It dawned on me then. Did they even know I was alone? At the beginning of the match, three of their players went for our flag and were taken out. Maybe the remaining two didn't know that Rooke and Derek were already out of the fight. Maybe they thought there was more than one left on my team. Either way, the advantage was mine, and now I just had to take out their flag carrier with as little conflict as possible, and I was on my way to scoring and taking the match.

I backed up several feet and knelt, listening carefully to the pounding of his footsteps. Thirty feet away. Twenty.

I bolted.

I ran full speed toward the alley's mouth and, once I hit the street, slid into a dive, feetfirst. I slid right into him as he passed and twisted my legs through his. He tripped and sprawled face-first onto the pavement. As he lay there groaning, I pounced on his back, fisted a hand through his hair, wrenched his head back, and slid my dagger through his neck. Blood sprayed out and pooled on the pavement. He went limp, and the glow faded from his body.

I did it. Our flag had reset, and I still had theirs. Now all I had to do was run it in and either avoid or take out my final opponent.

I released his head, stumbled back from him, and caught my breath. Every part of my body ached. Injuries from the last round throbbed with my newly acquired scrapes and bruises. All I wanted to do was curl up and rest my head. But I had to keep moving. If I made it back, I'd score and push the matchup to a third round. It was down to one versus one now, and my final opponent was nowhere to be seen.

I pushed up to my feet and took off for our base. My legs pumped as I darted through the map, zigzagging between the narrow alleyways and the open roads. I rounded the corner to our street, where our flag shimmered brilliantly. My heart rate rose ten notches. There was fifty feet between me and the flag.

Fifty feet to victory.

Movement caught my eye from above, and a shadow appeared on the rooftop above me. The last of Oblivion. I took off running toward our base, just feet beyond the flag. So did he, along the rooftop's edge. I crossed half the distance before Cole jumped down and landed on the street, blocking my path. I skidded to a stop, and so did my heart. The final fight of the matchup was coming down to me and the guy who was on my team just weeks ago.

We both looked at each other, then at the flag, and back again. What was his plan? He could go for our flag and try to stop me from scoring. If he got to the flag before me, I couldn't score unless I took him out of the game.

Or would he try to take me out first and go for the fight right now?

Cole grinned, took a step toward me, and drew his blade. The fight. He was going for the fight. I drew my sword and took a stance. Silence settled between us. We didn't move but let the scene build itself. We both knew what we were doing. Build the tension. Put on a show. But judging by the grin still tugging at Cole's lips, the crowd weren't the only ones enjoying this.

I could just picture the announcers.

"Here we go, folks. In a bold move, Cole Wilkinson is going for the fight and will try to take Kali Ling out of the matchup. This could decide who moves on to the championship and whose tournament run ends. Will Kali Ling push the matchup to a third round? Or is Team Defiance going home right now?"

I knew my team, and we weren't going home.

We took off running and soared toward each other, two freight trains on a collision course. Our bodies, our swords, everything smashed together, and exploded apart in a blast wave, like we'd torn through the sound barrier. Both swords went flying. We went flying.

I hit the ground rolling.

I tumbled over myself again and again until I landed on my back. Hard.

I lay there, not moving, soft breaths whispering through my mouth. Pain radiated through my entire body. Bruises formed like mini fireworks. A burst of color, a jolt to the senses, then they faded in with the numbness I already felt everywhere else. Then my higher functioning kicked back in, like someone had hit the reboot button on my brain.

Get up.

Where's Cole?

Find your weapon. Now.

I rolled to my stomach, pushed up to my hands and knees, and groped around the pavement. My sword. Where the hell was my sword? Shadows stretched and roiled between the star-filled puddles and neon rays of light. Cole was on his side, breathing heavily. He tried to push himself up and collapsed again.

There. The soft glow from my sword glinted in the darkness, several yards away and in the opposite direction from the flag.

I left it.

I pushed to my feet, gritting my teeth against the screaming protests of my body, and started running, arcing a curve around Cole. He lunged, sticking out a hand that caught my leg. I tripped and slammed into the road. The impact sent my brain somersaulting while my insides played pinball against my rib cage. I skidded across the pavement, collecting gravel and road burn until I slid to a stop. Shallow breaths whispered out of my mouth as I did a mental inventory of my injuries. Half of my face was on fire, like I'd pressed it against a furnace grate. Everything hurt. Every muscle I had, and even ones I didn't. With a groan, I turned onto my back, and Cole appeared over me. Suddenly, the fire wasn't just on my face, but churning in my gut and chest.

I backpedaled.

He clamped down on my ankle, and I snapped a kick across his jaw. He rolled to the side, unsheathing the dagger from my boot as he went.

Goddamn it, Kali. You fucking idiot.

I'd forgotten about my dagger, and now he had it.

I scrambled to my feet. So did he. My weapon was in his hand, the only weapon left between us.

I bolted.

He dove for me.

His hand caught my knee, and I hit the ground again. Hot pain shot up my leg as the blade sunk into my calf and twisted, shredding nerves, muscle, and bone.

I screamed.

With my free leg, I kicked the dagger from his grip and smashed his face with my boot.

Repeatedly.

His head rocked back each time, snapping harder with every kick. Blood inked his teeth and collected in the crevices. I halted my attack, retracted my leg as far as I could, and slammed down. The final, deafening crack of his bones snapping under my foot could have triggered an avalanche.

He collapsed. Shallow breaths expanded his rib cage as his breaths whistled through his busted mouth. He was down but not out of the game.

I turned to our base.

I crawled, a limping crawl, dragging my leg behind me. My arms shook. Breaths screamed through my lungs. Bile burned at the back of my throat. Every nerve inside begged me to stop, roll over, and play dead. But I pulled myself along. An inch at a time.

The pavement scraped at my hands, knees, everything. My

leg burned, and I stifled the grunts trying to pry their way out of my mouth. Despite the blood, sweat, and tears in my eyes, the flag shone clearly in my view. Less than a foot away now. I was there. It was all mine.

Fingers latched onto my ankle, and a chill shot through my body.

No. NO.

I'm there.

Cole pulled himself up both my legs with my dagger gripped in his mouth. Blood leaked from his gums and nose, snaked across the blade, and dripped from the edge. As he passed the open wound just below my knee, his fingers dug in and twisted.

The scream that ripped from my mouth nearly shattered the streetlights.

Unyielding, soul-splitting pain shot up from my leg and erupted through my whole body. I rocked and contorted under the unbearable agony. Tears burned in my eyes. My brain felt like it was rupturing through my skull.

Cole pulled himself higher.

My hand formed a fist. I turned and reeled back to deliver a blow when he slammed me down, pinning my shoulder blades with his forearm.

Oh shit.

I struggled beneath him but couldn't budge his weight. My hands, arms, everything strained, as my fingers brushed against the edge of the base. So close.

The world stopped.

The neon lights danced against the dark background, like rainbow stars winking out before the sunrise. Cool air whispered empty promises of victory across my tongue. The pavement was damp against my cheek, like the street's tears had replaced my own.

The dagger squealed against Cole's teeth as he ripped it from his mouth. His weight lessened for a split second, like he was reeling back. Then he plunged the blade straight into my spine.

I spasmed.

Gurgled.

Went limp.

And everything faded to black.

CHAPTER 20

Oh, God.

No. No. No.

What just happened?

I slammed back into the pod though my insides still felt hollow, like my soul hadn't come back with me. Like a piece of me had died in the arena. My hands clawed at the pod's interior as the cords detached from my skin and retreated. No. Let me back in. I can fix this.

I have to fix this.

The speakers crackled around me.

"What an amazing fight."

The announcers were still reeling. The excitement from their voices overflowed the audio feed until it sounded like it was straining against the speakers.

"Kali Ling is out. That's it, folks."

My clawing hands turned to my own face, tugging at my skin. Quick, panicked breaths panted from my mouth.

Was this real?

"What a close match. Great show by both sides, but with that, Defiance is out of the all-star tournament."

I curled in on myself, cradling my head in my hands. Hot tears singed my eyes. We'd risked it all, and we had lost. The sponsors would pull out. The money would dry up. What the hell were we going to do now?

I took a breath and pushed the emotions away before I faced my teammates. As I shoved down the lump in my throat, the pod doors opened.

My teammates sat on the edges of their pods, all with the same bewildered looks on their faces. Finally, Derek looked up at everyone else.

"What the hell happened in there?"

"It was Tamachi's final effort to push us out of the tournament," I said simply. "It's smart, too, if you think about it. Compounding our injuries like that nearly guarantees our loss, and we can't say anything to the public. Who's going to believe us?"

Lily's hands gripped the edge of her pod tightly. "I can't believe we're out. It's not fair. They cheated."

I shook my head. "It doesn't matter. If we go public, the VGL will crush us. It's my fault, anyway," I admitted. "I lost it for us. I almost scored. I was right there, and I lost."

Hannah tsked at me. "You didn't lose it for us. We're a team. We win together, and we lose together."

"We won't be together anymore," I reminded them. "We can't maintain the team now."

"The house is paid for, right? It's not like we don't have a place to live."

"Yes, but that doesn't include the cost of the staff, maintaining the pods, everything else."

"So? We'll figure this out together. If we have to do a bunch of ads and marketing and club appearances, we'll do it to keep the team together. The team isn't just your responsibility. We're family now. We lean on each other."

My heart melted. And really, at the end of the day, they were what mattered to me most. Not winning. Not championships.

My team.

My friends.

Hannah smiled. "But tonight, let's just relax. Let's go get the press conference over with. Then I vote for seventy-two hours of classic video games, junk food, and sleeping in."

"I second that," Lily chimed in.

"Third," Derek added.

"Junk food," Rooke began. "Does that include pizza?"

Hannah shrugged. "Sure."

"I'm in."

Everyone turned to me. Despite the loss and getting kicked out of the tournament, they were smiling now. Because Hannah was right. We were family.

I smiled with them. "One condition: Whatever we play, Hannah has to be the princess."

At the media pavilion, a crowd had gathered, larger than I expected. Reporters sat in the chairs while fans gathered around the edges. Most looked disappointed, even those in the media. Despite our damaged reputation, at least we still had some admirers in the audience.

I leaned forward and pressed my lips to the mic. "Thanks for coming. We'll begin the questioning now."

I pointed at the reporter in the front row. She stood.

"How did it feel to lose against a former teammate?"

"Cole deserved to win," Derek said. "The whole team deserved it. They were right on top of their game. We wish them luck in the championship."

I nodded to another reporter. He shouted his question from his seat.

"How does it feel to be kicked out right before the championship?"

I spoke, straining against the tightness in my throat. "We had a lot of fun, and we're grateful for the opportunity to compete in this kind of tournament. It was an honor."

I scanned the crowd again for another reporter to call on when I noticed a fan at the edge of the audience. His foot was tapping a thousand miles a second, and he was chewing on his bottom lip like it was gum. I pointed at him.

"You look like you have something you want to say."

He glanced around, like he was making sure that I was pointing at him. "Uhh, I'm not a reporter."

"So? The floor is yours."

He looked around him again and found all eyes on him. Arms folded, he turned back to me and fired off his question.

"How come you didn't kick ass?"

The crowd laughed. Great question. Probably the one everyone wanted to hear. I took a breath and spoke into the microphone.

"Some days, that's how it goes. When you're pursuing greatness, you're going to lose. A lot. But losing doesn't represent weakness. Quitting does. Losing just means you have an opportunity to get better. To push harder. And we'll never quit pushing."

The crowd erupted. Heavy applause and a few cheers resounded back at us, until they felt like they were reverberating on my insides. Rooke leaned toward me and whispered against my ear.

"For someone who's not afraid to speak her mind, that might have been the best thing you've ever said."

I whispered back against his ear. "Like you said, I was just speaking my mind."

He grinned a grin that told me he was impressed, and a little turned on. He glanced down at my lips, and for a second, I thought he'd kiss me right there in front of everyone.

Another reporter stood and addressed the entire panel.

"So, does that mean we'll see you in the RAGE tournaments this fall?"

Everyone looked at me.

After our loss tonight, our sponsors would probably bow out. Even if the VGL made a permanent switch to these new pods and I didn't have to pay for programmers, I didn't have enough money for the trainers, security, and other personnel. But my teammates had agreed to do whatever it took to keep us together. Now we just had to figure out exactly what that was and where we were going next.

"We love the game," I said simply. "And we'll always keep playing."

After the press conference, we planned to do exactly what Hannah suggested. Seventy-two hours of sleeping in, junk food, and video games. Hannah was right. Sometimes analyzing our weaknesses and what went wrong right after a matchup wasn't the best strategy. Giving ourselves a few days to veg out, relax, and be normal people would clear our minds and give us better insight into fixing our problems and figuring out this hole we'd dug ourselves into.

And really, we needed the break. After the insanity of the tournament, where every moment of our lives, awake or asleep, revolved around the game, we needed to unwind. Laughter and good times with friends was the best way to do that.

As the rest of the team set up in front of the living-room television, debating classic video games and pizza toppings, Derek and I ducked into my office to take calls.

One by one, our sponsors bowed out.

Can't have a team that goes too big too fast. Can't have a team who fails their drug tests. Really, it didn't matter what they said. They'd only signed on for one season, and our season was finished. Some demanded their money back. I barely listened to them. Maybe I should have been worried, but I'd since become numb to the demands of the sponsors. If they tried to get their money back, they'd have to take us to court. The process could last for years. I could always mortgage the house. Do more appearances at the clubs. Whatever it took. I'd told that fan at the conference that Defiance didn't quit, and while I had my doubts and weaker moments sometimes, I meant it.

When the last call ended, I pressed myself into my chair and stared up at the ceiling. We had no sponsors, no money, possibly no future, and yet I couldn't get over how lucky I was. Honestly. I got the chance to pursue my dreams. I had a roof over my head. I had my health.

I had my friends.

Really, that made me more fortunate than most.

"You okay?"

Speaking of friends.

Derek sat in the guest chair across from my desk. His arms were crossed, and his eyebrows were raised, like he was waiting for me to respond.

"I'm fine."

He shook his head. "Kali—"

"Really, I'm okay. We did what we could, but with those odds stacked against us, we were never going to make it through the tournament."

Derek stared at me. "You're just accepting defeat? That doesn't sound like Kali Ling."

I had to smile. "There's standing up for yourself, then there's knowing when to move on. And we will. We'll move on from this." I pressed my hands against my desk and breathed deep. "I just need a minute."

He looked me over a few times, and even though he didn't look sure, said to me, "All right, but if you need me . . ."

"I'll find you."

After he left, my cell buzzed on my desk. I sighed. Probably another sponsor calling to chew me out one last time, or the VGL with their follow-up call about our exit from the tournament.

We appreciate your efforts and we're sorry to see you go . . .

Yeah, right.

I grabbed the phone off my desk and didn't even glance at the caller ID as I pressed it to my ear.

"Kali Ling speaking."

"Kali? It's Jessica."

I sat up straight in my chair. Jessica Salt was calling me. Say something, stupid.

"Uh . . ."

Smooth, Kali. Smooth.

"Sorry to see you're out of the tournament," Jessica said.

My eyes fell shut. Not only had I failed the team, but in that moment, I realized I'd failed my idol as well.

"We're out, too," she added.

Somehow, I sat up even straighter. "What?"

"Epoch won."

I blinked several times, unable to process her words. I had completely forgotten about their matchup. With our loss, the press conference, and dealing with the sponsors, I hadn't even thought about the results of the other matchup of the night.

"Are you still retiring?" I asked.

There was a pause. "Maybe. I don't know. I was hoping to retire on the championship, not out in the losers' bracket." She paused again. "No matter what I do, I hope you'll carry on and keep playing."

Of course she did. She thought I was supposed to take her spot. Have this great career and be an inspiration for the people coming up behind me. I wasn't sure how we'd even compete now, but I wasn't ready to admit that to Jessica.

I rubbed a hand across my forehead. "Yeah." I cleared my throat. "I really should get back to my team."

"Can we talk again sometime?"

I wasn't sure what she'd want to talk to me about, probably the future of my nonexistent career, but I answered her anyway. "Sure."

I tapped the END CALL button, placed the phone down on my desk, and pinched the bridge of my nose. I was fortunate to have gotten this far, to have competed in the biggest tournament in the world. But I'd shot for my dreams and missed. Some people thought remaining positive in dire situations was optimistic. Others, naïve. Either way, I had to accept that I'd failed, and the only thing I could do now was pick up the pieces and try to keep going.

I started to push away from my desk when I noticed that the top drawer was slightly ajar and something bright and red was peeking out. I pulled it open and found *The Tao of Pooh* tucked inside. With a hard cover and made from real paper, it wasn't hard to surmise who'd left it there for me. Thumbing through the pages, I had to smile. No matter what creed, religion, or faith I believed in, or not, all I really knew for sure was that I have this life. Maybe there would be no bonus round. No respawns. But when I finally get to the end and see that game-over screen, I hope my score represents how many times I leveled up as a human being, and how many lives I changed along the way. Not how big my bank account was.

I closed the book, wrapped my cell around my wrist, left the office, and joined the team on the living-room couch.

"Work's done," I announced, plopping down next to Hannah. All four of my teammates were strewn about the living room, controllers in hands. Need for Speed was on the screen. Lily had Unagi the Eel wrapped around her shoulders as she played. Every once in a while, she'd lean toward Derek until he yelped and drove off the road.

Beside me, Hannah leaned toward the coffee table and nudged a pizza box my way.

"Try it."

I flipped the box open to find a fresh, steaming pizza with extra cheese. I picked up a slice and sunk my teeth in.

Oh, dear Lord. It was beautiful.

The cheese was delicious and gooey, and the crust was crisp. I devoured the entire piece. Hannah laughed and dropped a controller in my hand. I grinned and started tapping buttons, customizing my vehicle of choice. I was halfway through the first lap when my cell phone buzzed. I glanced at the ID.

The VGL.

It was nearly midnight, a somewhat unseemly time to call, but it was expected. This would be our condolence call. *Thanks for participating in the tournament, and we're sorry . . .*

Yeah, sorry. This is exactly what they wanted. Team Defiance out before the championship round.

Hannah grabbed my wrist. "Don't answer it."

"Team owners don't get nights off." I passed her my controller. She frowned but took control of my car and joined the race with my other teammates.

I pulled the phone from my wrist, clicked the ACCEPT button, and pressed it to my ear. "Kali Ling speaking."

"Hello, Ms. Ling. This is Farouk Nasser. I hope I'm not disturbing you."

Ah, the New Games Coordinator. I put on my business voice.

"Not at all. What can I help you with?"

"I'm calling to offer my condolences."

Knew it. I had to smile. "People lose. It happens."

He faltered. "Not about the tournament, Ms. Ling. About Cole Wilkinson. He was your former teammate, wasn't he?"

I stood up off the couch. "Yeah, why? What happened?"

"You don't know? It's all over the news."

The news. We hadn't tuned in for hours. With technology nowadays, that might as well have been for days.

"What's going on?"

"Cole was in a car accident. Both teams from tonight were involved."

I tapped Hannah's tablet and opened the television remote app. The in-progress game cut out to the local news station. My teammates erupted in protest, dropping their controllers.

"Hey!"

"What the hell, Kali?"

A scrolling newscast popped up. The whipping blades of a drone filled the speakers as a reporter spoke over the background noise.

". . . as you can see here, the site of this horrific accident . . ."

The camera hovered over a pile of black fiberglass, warped metal, and popped tires smoldering against the stretch of highway.

". . . virtual gaming stars from teams Oblivion and Epoch were airlifted to a hospital earlier this evening. It is believed they were out celebrating tonight's win, possibly joyriding, when they crashed into each other . . ."

The living room went silent, along with Farouk on the phone. He must have heard the news stream coming through. I stared at the screen, blinking. The wreckage. The warped fiberglass. Judging by that scene, there was a chance he wasn't . . .

My bottom lip quivered as I forced myself to ask, "Is he alive?"

Farouk paused for what was probably just a few seconds but felt like an hour. "Yes. He's in serious but stable condition. Both teams survived."

I nodded to my teammates.

"Alive," I mouthed to them.

They collectively sighed with relief.

Farouk cleared his throat. "Preliminary investigation by the authorities shows that alcohol and drugs were factors in the crash." He paused for effect. It had one. My stomach dropped through my toes. "Now, if both teams were high, how were they going to compete in the championship in two weeks?"

"I can't really answer that for you."

"Of course not. But we pulled every drug test from Teams Oblivion and Epoch. Most of them have been tampered with."

I knew that. I'd seen them partying hard at the clubs. I just never expected this.

"I want you to know I urged the VGL to ban both team owners from participating in any VGL divisions effective immediately."

"That's good," I said, hoping my snarl wasn't coming through the phone. "I'm glad you've made that decision."

"I realize this might be a lot to handle at once, but as the New Games Coordinator, I have a strong say in what happens next. My opinion is that the last two teams knocked out should be put back into the tournament."

Though I knew what he was saying, it wouldn't process. He was talking about the tournament while two of the teams were in the hospital. I ignored my disgust and forced my brain to trudge forward. If the last two teams out took the slots, we were back in, alongside Jessica's team, Legacy.

I cleared my throat. "The championship slots belong to Epoch and Oblivion. Not to us. We didn't earn it, and I'm not about to take it away from them."

Farouk was quiet for a minute. "I understand your perspective, Ms. Ling. But regardless of the accident, Oblivion and Epoch would have been disqualified for drug use. The accident only brought it to light."

A light the VGL couldn't ignore. They had to ban the team owners and replace the teams in the game. But was it right for us to take Cole's spot? He was a friend. Now he was lying in the hospital, and we were going to take over his dream. My stomach churned. No, that just didn't feel right. Besides, why would the VGL work so hard at kicking me out just to bring me back in again?

Was Farouk the one sending me the e-mails? Or was this all just another setup?

"Given what happened with the other teams," Farouk continued, "we'll be conducting a full review of all drug testing before officially allowing any team back into the tournament."

"We had a failed test earlier in the season," I reminded him.

"Yes, but you reported it and took the penalty. Did you have any other failed tests we don't know about?"

"No."

"Well then, your choice to report that test might have just earned your team another shot at the championship."

A shot at the championship. A shot that was supposed to be Cole's. I sat on the couch and pressed my free hand against my forehead. My brain felt sluggish. There were thoughts swimming through it, but nothing was processing.

"Oh," Farouk added, "also, I feel it's important to inform you that some e-mails from within the VGL were leaked to a couple of team owners. We're not sure if you received anything, but I'm asking that you delete it if you haven't already."

I picked up on his slip of the tongue instantly. *We're not sure if you received it*, speaking in third person for the VGL. *But I'm asking that you delete it*, speaking first person, directly from him. It was sounding more and more like he was my mysterious whistle-blower.

I took a chance.

"I'll be sure to do that." I cleared my throat. "Thanks for the pointer on what was going on . . . with the e-mails, I mean."

"Of course." It went silent on the line for a minute, like he was trying to tell me telepathically that he was on my side.

He broke the silence. "We can't go public with this change in the tournament until our examination of your records is complete. It will take us at least twenty-four hours. Please keep the news to yourself until you hear the official announcement from us."

"Of course. I understand."

"I'll be in touch regarding the results," he continued. "But I'm fairly confident when I say, welcome to the championship."

I ended the call.

I sat in my chair for a few minutes. At least, my body was in my chair. My head wasn't quite attached. We had a new shot at the championship because Cole and his team were lying in hospital beds. Now, that didn't seem fair at all. Should we even take it?

Was that the right thing to do?

I sunk down into the couch, staring at nothing in the distance.

"Kali?"

I blinked and turned toward the rest of the team.

"What is it?" Hannah asked, and I realized she was the one who had called my name.

"Both teams crashed because they were high. Looks like their owners were tampering with their drug tests. They've been banned from the league."

"That's good," Derek said. "That's what should happen."

"I hope you realize that's because of you, Kali," Rooke added. "A year ago, the VGL would never have banned them."

I nodded. "I know . . ."

Hannah leaned forward, tilting her head. "What's wrong?"

I swallowed and pushed the words out of my mouth.

"We have a second chance at the championship."

Everyone shifted to the edge of their seats, though I wasn't sure they were even aware of their actions. It was silent in the room for several seconds. Finally, Derek spoke up.

"What do you mean?"

"They need teams to fill their spots in the championship. Since we're last out, we're first back in."

"Does that mean Legacy is back in, too?" Hannah asked.

Technically, yes. They would be the ones to fill Epoch's spot. Which meant Jessica had another shot at one last championship before retiring, and I had one last chance to face my idol inside the game.

Lily stood from the couch and started walking away. I squinted as I watched her leave, wondering why she'd walked away so abruptly.

"Lil," I called. "Where are you going?"

She turned back to me and blinked.

"The hospital."

I didn't even have to say anything to the rest of the team. In an instant, we were all moving through the house and heading out the door.

CHAPTER 21

The five of us gathered outside Cole's hospital room. The entire wall between the hallway and the room wasn't really a wall but a translucent screen that could be programmed to tint, darken, or display images on command. Currently, the screen was clear, leaving Cole completely visible to anyone walking past, probably so the doctors and security could keep an eye on him.

Speaking of security, there were plenty in the hallway, with two guards at every door and a few more patrolling the corridors. Probably there to keep the fans or the paparazzi from snapping pictures of the teams in their current state. None of them made a move to remove us, though, and one of them even nodded our way. Sometimes, being recognizable had its advantages.

"He looks so small," Hannah said, pressing an open palm against the glass. "How does a guy that big look so small?"

He did look small, and alone, lying in that bed. Needles poked out of both arms, and exoskeletal casts covered his right leg and foot, and his left wrist. With that many broken bones, there was no way he'd be competing for the rest of the year. Maybe even the next. In an instant, his dreams of becoming a champion had been shattered. I couldn't imagine what that felt like, let alone the pain he must have been in.

A doctor strolled up to us, making notes on his tablet. "Friends or family?"

"Friends," I said. "Is he okay?"

"He's got several broken bones, severe whiplash, and a lot of bruising, but nothing too serious. He was lucky. He'll be in casts for a while and will need some physical therapy, but he'll recover."

"How is the rest of the team?"

"Two are currently in surgery, but everyone survived."

I nodded at Cole through the glass. "Can we see him?"

"Normally, we'd only let family in, but they haven't arrived yet. I think only one of you should—"

Four sets of hands pressed into my back and pushed me forward.

Okay, I guess it's me.

The doctor slid the door open for me, and I walked into the room. My shoes clicked along the floor until I reached his side. Cole's eyelids fluttered, and he peered up at me, squinting, like he was trying to focus on my face.

"Hey," I said softly.

He groaned, but managed a smile. "Hey."

"Are you in a lot of pain?"

"Some." He pointed at the IV bag, which I assumed was administering morphine. "I like that." He looked back to me. "Are you here to buy another team? I've heard we're for sale."

I saddled my hip on the edge of the bed. "Sorry this happened to you."

He shrugged. "Shit happens."

Shit happens. He was full of broken bones, and his career might have been over. To me, that demanded a stronger reaction. I glanced at the IV bag. Maybe it was the painkillers talking.

"You're taking this rather lightly," I told him. "When you're off the morphine, I'm not sure you'll feel the same way."

"Morphine doesn't change anything. I could've died, but I didn't." He waved a hand at his body. "This just sets the stage for an epic comeback story."

I guess if you had to go through a painful, months-long recovery, a positive attitude was the best way to handle it.

I twiddled my thumbs as I pushed the next words out of my mouth. "The VGL called me. They want us to take your spot. You were in this horrific accident, and they're concerned about who will be in the championship."

Cole chuckled to himself, then coughed and gripped his side. He winced. "It's a business. None of us are going to be able to compete for a while. Somebody has to take our place." He studied me for a minute. "You are taking our spot, right?"

I made a face. "Well . . ."

He sat up a little, grimacing as he did. "Kali. You have to take our spot. You deserve it."

"We don't," I said simply. "You do."

He glanced down at his body. "We made some stupid choices. Maybe that means we don't deserve it. What if becoming a champion isn't just about how you play the game? Think about it. No one sees all the prep we do. The endless training. The insane diets. Early mornings. Late nights. All they see are the matchups and whether or not we win. To them, that's all it takes. Talent and luck. But you and I know it's a lot more than that. It's an endless grind to reach the top; and then you have to work twice as hard just to stay there. So, being a champion isn't really about winning. It's about how you choose to live your life and how hard you're willing to work for it. By those standards, you deserve a shot."

I rolled my bottom lip through my teeth as I considered his words. "But how is that—"

He held up a hand. "If you don't take our place, I'll be pissed."

I sighed. "I'll, uh, talk it over with the team." I pushed off the bed and shoved my hands in my pocket. "You take care of yourself."

"Take care of myself?" He scoffed. "Why? I have a cute nurse."

I laughed.

"I'll see you in the arena sometime."

He scoffed again. "Yeah, if I recover."

"Like I said, see you in the arena."

We shared a smile. He would be back. His attitude and determination were too strong not to. Gaming wasn't just a career. It was a passion. A calling. I'm sure when we were all in our eighties, while most were enjoying their retirement, we'd still be playing the games we loved, albeit, slower.

Much, much slower.

I turned away from Cole and headed for the door.

"Hey, Kali?"

I turned back.

"That last round, you looked like you were struggling. Were you guys just having an off night?"

This time, I chewed on my bottom lip so hard I nearly bit it off. If I told him the truth, that the game was working against us, it would be petty and take away from their victory—if he even believed me.

"No, we weren't having an off night," I said, and a smile slowly spread across my face. "You were the better opponent. We were really feeling it."

He considered that and nodded, and we shared one last smile before I walked out.

"Good luck in the championship," he called, as the door slid shut behind me.

The championship. Even with his blessing, it still didn't feel right.

When we arrived back at the house, I broke away from the team.

"I need to be alone for a while."

I went to my office and closed the door. Much to my surprise, and a little to my disappointment, no one followed me. I sat at my desk, trying to process the night. What time was it? Three forty-five in the morning. I wasn't even tired. Numb, maybe. But wide-awake. Learning one of your friends had almost died was like combining an entire pot of coffee, a bucket of ice water, and a handful of amphetamines. I'd be lucky if I slept well in a week.

The television was off, my computer was on sleep mode, and the kind of silence that only comes in the dead of the night was pressing up against me. Like the game. I shuddered. If there was one thing I didn't like, it was being alone. It was important at times. Meditation. Reflection. But this house was always so full of people, so full of my friends that more than a few minutes of it was suffocating.

I pulled my cell from my wrist and hit REDIAL on one of the more recent numbers. A voice answered.

"Hello?"

I cleared my throat. "Jessica? It's Kali."

We'd talked just hours before, but with the events of the night, it felt like a month. Scientists like to think time is constant, but really, it's completely fluid. Ten years can go by in a blink, or a single day can feel like a lifetime.

"I guess you've heard the news," I said. "Were you offered Epoch's spot in the championship?"

"We were."

"Are you taking it?"

There was a long pause.

"Yes. Are you taking Oblivion's?"

I fumbled with nothing on my desk. "I don't know what I'm doing."

Did I ever? Hell, ever since I took over Defiance, I'd been flailing around. I'd had drunken pin-the-tail ventures that had been more successful than my attempt to manage the team.

"Why aren't you taking the spot?" she asked.

"It just . . . doesn't feel right."

It went quiet again, but I could hear her tongue clicking against her mouth, like she was thinking.

"When you were offered the captaincy, was it for the right reasons?" she finally asked.

"Well, I guess—"

"You were marketable. A female RAGE captain. Genius. The sponsors will love it. It'll drive ratings and sales. Am I right?"

"Pretty much."

"But you still did it, and made it into your own career-defining moment."

I shook my head even though she couldn't see me. "I'm not sure this is the same—"

"Kali, listen to me. You're just getting started in your career, so it's hard for you to see the big picture here. Yes, there's corruption in professional gaming. There is in any sport, and any business, for that matter. At some point in nearly everyone's life, they'll be offered an opportunity under questionable circumstances just like these. It's not pretty, but it's the way things go. Bottom line: There's still an opportunity in front of you, and it's only going to sit there for so long before someone else takes it. The VGL is pushing ahead with this tournament either way."

"So, you think I should do this?"

"Absolutely."

"How do you know it's the right thing to do?"

She chuckled. "It comes with experience. This championship will be my last game. Ever. I know for you it must feel like your entire career is in front of you, but you never know where life will take you. What if it's your last game, too?"

I leaned back in my chair as if the weight of her words had pushed me back. What if it was? I didn't know if we could survive much longer. The media was destroying us, and the sponsors had left. My bank account was two withdrawals away from growing a middle finger and showing it to me. There was a good chance this would be our last tournament.

Most of all, if it hadn't been for the VGL's tricks, we might have made it on our own. We would have done better in the tournament, the media wouldn't have been hounding us, and the sponsors wouldn't have been breathing down our necks. Maybe it was the right thing to do.

I pressed the phone to my lips. "Thanks for the talk."

"Will I see you in the tournament?"

"I don't know. It's not up to just me."

"Of course. Say hi to the team."

"I will."

I hung up the phone and left my office. As soon as I opened the door, some god-awful, greasy smell assaulted my nostrils. I followed the stench to the kitchen and found my teammates. Eating, of course. Half-empty Chinese take-out containers littered the table. I nearly gagged.

The team froze when they saw me in the room.

"Uhhh," Hannah began. "We didn't think you'd want to eat, and the rest of us wanted Chinese food."

I glanced at the table. My lip curled.

"Chinese food," I repeated. "Is that what you call that?"

Lily pointed across the kitchen with her chopsticks. "I think there's some leftover pizza in the fridge."

I held up a hand. "It's fine. I'm not hungry."

I sat at the table, trying to breathe through my mouth. Hannah pushed her take-out box under my nose.

"The rice is pretty good."

I didn't even look at it.

"Did my father make it?" I asked.

She glanced between me and the box a few times. ". . . no."

"Then it's not good rice."

She frowned and pulled the box away.

I waved a hand at the table. "Is this really what you guys chose as your last meal?"

Derek stopped plowing food into his mouth long enough to ask, "Last meal?"

"If we're back in the tournament, then we're back on our diets, too."

Now everyone stopped shoveling food into their mouths to stare at me. Derek swallowed down what was in his mouth.

"Are we back in?"

"I want to talk it through, at least. Legacy is taking Epoch's spot, and Jessica Salt thinks we should do the same."

Rooke leaned in. "Then what's making you hesitate?"

I sighed. "Part of me feels like we didn't really earn it."

Derek shook his head as he reached for an egg roll. "Tamachi threw everything he could at us to take us out, and we're still standing. We didn't whine. We didn't complain. We just took it and dug deeper. I think that means we deserve to be in the championship more than any other team in the tournament."

I shrugged. "Maybe. But we're only getting a second chance because of the car accident."

"That's not entirely true," Lily said. "Oblivion and Epoch should have failed their drug tests all along. They shouldn't have even been in the competition."

I tapped my fingers on the table as I considered that and pushed out a heavy sigh. "I guess."

Rooke studied me. "What's really bothering you?"

"What if it's a setup?"

Everyone stopped eating and just stared. Apparently, no one had an argument with that, so I kept going.

"They worked the whole tournament to kick us out, to get us to the point where we are right now. No money. No sponsors. Nothing. Why would they just let us back in unless they've cooked up something ten times worse."

The room got so quiet, the only noise was the hum of the refrigerator in the background. Everyone traded looks with each other. Though no one said a word, the bleak expressions on their faces told me everything. They were worried I was right.

Finally, Derek cleared his throat. "The VGL wanted to kick you out as punishment. You spoke out about corruption, and it cost them millions. But the industry can only silence people for so long. Maybe with this crash, they're realizing that. If the police investigating the accident are reporting that drugs were involved, the VGL can't hide it. It forces their hand."

"That still doesn't stop them from doing the same things they've been doing to us all season. NPCs specifically targeted for us. Injuries that compound as the rounds go on. If we enter that championship, who knows what they'll come up with?"

Rooke grinned. "I think the warrior would say that's nothing more than a challenge."

I grinned back. That was certainly true.

"We've gone up against everything they've thrown at us," Derek said. "We're ready for whatever they have next."

"We could be plugged in for hours," I pointed out.

Lily shrugged, like it was nothing. "That's just hours to kick ass."

I smiled. "Against K-Rig, Legacy, and Eon, three of the best teams in the world."

Hannah rested her elbows on the table and winked at me. "And now we're about to be one of them."

We were all smiling now. I looked around the table.

"You really sure you want to do this?"

They all nodded. Vigorously.

"Then we need to prepare," I said. "For anything."

LEVEL 3:

THE CHAMPIONSHIP

We had two weeks until the championship. We were the lowest rated team by far. We were hated across the board. None of us cared. We'd been given a second chance, and we were going to make the most of it.

Really, all the teams were at some disadvantage. No one knew what the course would be until we were inside the game, and no one had ever played a game that ran this long.

Going up against K-Rig, you have to tell yourself things like this.

We trained. We jogged for hours, preparing our bodies for the endurance haul of our lifetimes. The trainers specifically redesigned our workouts to match those of marathoners. Squats, dead lifts, and core workouts. We sprinted in place. Thirty seconds. Stop. Sixty seconds. Stop. Two minutes. Stop.

Should have hired freaking drones.

Going into the championship on the losing side meant we'd have a handicap. The winning teams got five respawns. They'd have to return to a starting point, but they'd keep coming back. Again and again. The losing teams got none. Once we were dead, it was permadeath, and we'd be out of the game.

I sat with Rooke in my office, going over strategy. With such an important matchup, it was better if we worked together on it. The screen across the office rolled through footage on our opponents. The arena would remain a mystery until we were on the inside, but at least we knew who we were facing.

Eon.

Legacy.

And K-Rig.

"Apparently, Derek has been scoping out the illegal betting sites." He nodded at the Koreans on the screen. "They're the favorites to win by a margin of ten."

My eyes closed. "Don't tell me Derek put money on the matches. We don't need to be kicked out again."

"I think he was just checking out our odds. I hope."

"What are they?"

"What?"

"Our odds."

He grimaced. "Better not to ask."

I knew it. We were going up against three megastar teams, and we were like the dorky little brother trying desperately to keep up.

Jessica Salt flashed across the screen. I cringed as a pang hit my stomach. She'd talked me into this. Had been there when I needed a mentor, someone more experienced to guide me along my path. Now I was about to face her in the arena. She'd gone from confidante to opponent in a blink.

Rooke noticed my apprehension.

"How do you feel, going up against your idol?"

The pang in my stomach became a thunderbolt. I tapped my foot against the desk. "Well, if someone else takes her out, I won't have to face her at all."

Rooke grinned. "That's a good way of avoiding the question."

I took a breath and tried to push the feelings of trepidation away. "If I get to fight her, it'll be an honor."

Please, someone else take her out.

"What's your advice?" I asked him. "What do I do if I have to face her?"

He considered it. "She has experience, but you have youth. If you can keep the fight going long enough, she'll get tired, and you can take her."

"You seem pretty sure about that, as if you're not talking about Jessica Salt."

"Kali, she's just a human being. Yes, she's amazing. She set records. Won championships. But that's how half the world looks at you, too. At least, before all the media bullshit in this tournament."

I'm sure he said it to make me feel better, but my heart did flip-flops instead. Jessica herself had said she felt I was the one to take over her spotlight. Though I still didn't really agree, suddenly I understood just a little more why she felt that way.

"I feel a little lost over all this, to be honest," Rooke admitted, motioning at the tablet in his hands. "Without a map or objectives, it's hard to plan and come up with tactics."

"All we can do is focus on our strengths and minimize our weaknesses."

Soon, the entire team started working on strategies. We'd gather in my office, or around the kitchen table, debating over our meals.

"K-Rig has no weaknesses," Lily claimed as she stuffed a forkful of steamed vegetables in her mouth.

"Yes they do," Hannah said. "We've faced off against teams like them before, and they're all the same. They fight as one. Knock them out of sync, and they fall."

Rooke swallowed down a gulp of protein. "We're focusing all our attention on K-Rig, but there are other teams in this game."

The whole week went like this. Even while we played games in the living room, we were discussing the other teams. Eon's incredible run through the tournament. Legacy's ten-plus years of experience. K-Rig's raw talent and immense dedication.

"We're the lowest ranked team going into this," Lily pointed out, as we blasted our way through Gears of War 3 in a four-player battle. Hannah was sitting her turn out and stroked her fingers through my hair as she sat beside me.

Derek shrugged as he thumbed the controller in his hand. "Someone has to be."

Hannah smiled. Not a practiced smile, but a soft grin that curled up the corners of her mouth. She leaned toward me and lowered her voice.

"We have heart," she said. "We have natural chemistry. K-Rig is manufactured. We weren't raised from childhood to do this. Hell, three years ago, I was modeling, and you were in high school. Look at everything we've accomplished, and we don't have half the practice and support they do. We built this together because we love the game and each other."

I had to smile. She was right. It was something we had above the other teams. A sort of family. No matter what happened, how much we fought, we always seemed to come back together stronger than before.

The Friday before the championship, we trained in the morning, stretched, and prepared ourselves. For the rest of the day, we relaxed. Played console games. Downed bottles of water to stay as hydrated as possible.

"Maybe we'll piss ourselves in the pods," Lily said. We all laughed, then worried it would come true.

Sometime in the middle of the day, our phones beeped. All of them.

This is a message to all VGL players: Please tune in to the VGL's home channel at 7:00 p.m. this evening for a special announcement.

At 7:00 p.m. that evening, we congregated in front of the television. A crowd of reporters had gathered inside the media room of the VGL headquarters. At the front of the room was a platform with a podium. A row of VGL executives sat behind the podium, and beyond them was an oversized screen taking up the entire wall featuring the VGL logo.

Diana Foote stepped up to the podium.

My best friend.

"Good evening. Thank you for joining us this evening. On the eve of the championship of virtual gaming's first all-star tournament, we have a special announcement. Here to make this announcement, please allow me to introduce the President of the VGL."

The crowd erupted with applause. Jonathan Kreger stepped up to the podium, smiling and nodding at everyone. The President of the VGL. Given the amount of media attention and security around him, you'd think he was President of the United States.

"Thank you," he said into the microphone, and the crowd calmed itself. "The VGL has been proud to host the world's first all-star tournament. However, it has brought to light some of the oversights in virtual gaming.

"There has been a lot of discussion, and after many debates, the participating countries in the all-star tournament have agreed. Tonight, we are happy to announce the formation of the International Association of Virtual Gaming."

He motioned to the screen behind him. The logos for each

gaming league participating in the all-star tournament appeared under a huge banner, the International Association of Virtual Gaming, or the IAVG.

It was sponsored by Tamachi Industries.

Something cold slid through my stomach.

On-screen, people clapped and cheered. Inside my house, no one was clapping.

Hannah glanced around at us. "Anyone else feeling a little sick?"

Yeah. We all were.

"What the hell is going on?" Derek asked, voice wary. "What does Tamachi Industries have to do with the formation of an international association?"

"Because it's not really about an international association," I said, as my chest went tight. "Tamachi must have planned this from the start. He wanted to bring these countries together so he could consolidate the leagues under one name and get his pods into every gaming league in the world."

Lily snorted. "He's gonna make another hundred billion."

The cold feeling in my stomach turned to ice as the realization of what was happening sunk deeper and deeper. The VGL controlled vast sources of media, like Hypnotized and *Pro Gamer Weekly*. I'm sure the gaming associations of other countries weren't much different. Tamachi Industries had stakes in mobile devices and now virtual pods. Soon, they'd all combine under one international association if that's really what it was.

Conglomerate, anyone?

A multinational association that controlled the media. Tamachi's cyberpunk game was becoming reality. Or had he fashioned the game around what he'd already had planned? It didn't matter. Virtual or real, those two worlds were merging more and more every day.

Long after everyone had gone to bed for the night, I sat in my office watching the VGL nightly feed. Marcus and Howie had been joined by two others as they debated the upcoming championship amongst themselves.

"I don't think anyone would argue that K-Rig is the number one overall favorite heading into the championship round."

"These guys have been together for nearly eight years now. Rumor is they practice up to fourteen hours a day. I think they breathe in sync even in their sleep."

"Then you have to consider Team Legacy. Eleven years strong, nine championship wins. They have the most experience in the competition."

"Don't discredit the Swedes, here. They aren't nearly the best team in the competition, but they've had a hell of a run. Everything is just jibing for them. Let's see if they can continue their streak tomorrow night."

"You know, the dark horse in this competition has really been Defiance. They've only won a single championship, they're the least experienced team in the pack, and it's Kali Ling's first year as team owner. No one knows what to expect from this team."

"Whatever happens, we can know one thing for sure. This will be unlike anything we've seen before."

I clicked the television off, stood, and turned to the wall beside me. Our former teammate Nathan glowed on the electronic poster hanging there. Footsteps walked up behind me. Rooke wrapped an arm around my waist and pressed his front to my back. I sighed and leaned back against him, conforming my body to his.

"I thought you were in bed," I told him.

"Couldn't sleep." He breathed deep, and his chest expanded against my back. "Anxious about tomorrow?"

"I still have a hard time believing all this. I don't know what the VGL is going to hit us with tomorrow when we step inside that game. I'm not so sure being on the VGL's shit list makes me a great team owner."

"You are. Even people inside the VGL are starting to take your side. You're inspiring people."

"I inspired people to create those new pods, too. If this international association goes through, and gaming leagues around the world make the switch to Tamachi's pods, thousands of programmers will lose their jobs."

"There's a negative side to everything," he said. "There will always be people against you, no matter what you do. And I think there will always be some corruption in gaming. All you can do is to try to make things better, the best way you see fit. That's all you can do."

I turned to face him. His arms slid around me, keeping me securely against him. I rested my chin on his chest, stared up into his eyes, and sighed. "What if at this time tomorrow, we're out of the championship?"

He smiled. "And what if at this time tomorrow, we're number one in the world?"

The crowd roared.

I stood backstage with my teammates in the Riot Games Arena in downtown L.A. Thousands of fans filled the seats. Hundreds more were gathered in the parking lot. They'd even renovated and reopened the old Staples Center across the street, transforming it into a secondary viewing area for the matchup.

Inside the main arena, the seating was divided into four major sections. Each section glowed with a team's color; red for Legacy, ice blue for K-Rig, gold for Eon, and dark gray for us. A single seat in the nosebleed sections cost five grand at the minimum and went up from there. Some of the best seats were going for a record-breaking six figures. There were more than enough people willing to dish out that kind of money for a one-night-only event. Billionaires. Rock stars. Actors. L.A. had more than enough of them. Virtual gaming had become what boxing was fifty years ago.

The VGL theme music started up, and the noise from the crowd rose several decibels. Marcus Ryan and Howie Fulton walked out onstage, waving at everyone. Their images were projected onto screens behind them that stretched nearly fifty feet high, facing all directions, so everyone in the audience could see.

"Welcome," Marcus boomed into his mic, "to the VGL's first international, all-star championship."

The audience cheered.

"That's right, Marcus," Howie chimed in. "We're about to see the best teams in the world fight it out in the longest match in tournament history."

They brought us out one at a time, presenting the teams to the crowd. The whole thing became a blur to me. Even when I led my team onto the stage, I felt numb to it all, not quite connected to the moment. How could I be? I was on a stage with the top gamers in the world, and I was one of them.

As the announcers continued, their voices became an echo in the background. The audience was a blur, a painting left out in the rain. But as I stood there, I spent the time thinking one thing.

Thank you.

I wasn't sure who I was saying it to, but I felt it in every nerve. I got to play the games I loved with the people I loved. Whatever happened tonight, wherever we'd go from here, I'd never forget this experience.

"The next time you see these teams, they'll be on the inside. Join us after the break. The world's first all-star championship is about to begin."

As the live stream cut to commercial, we were ushered toward our set of pods. Each set on the stage faced out in a different direction, with an enormous, oversized screen above for airing the gameplay. As Derek climbed into the pod next to mine, he winked. "See you on the other side."

I grinned.

I climbed into my pod, and the doors shut. The sound of the crowd cut out, and a hollow emptiness filled the pod, like I'd suddenly been dunked fifty feet under water. The wires started scuttling across my skin and attached to my suit, face, and arms. I pushed a slow, deep breath out from between my lips. The moment had come. No more preparing. No more waiting. The VGL's championship round and a shot at the nine-figure grand prize was happening right now. The next few hours would decide the rest of my life.

All our lives.

I closed my eyes and disappeared into the game.

CHAPTER 23

I t was night.

I loaded into the base with my team. It looked the same as any matchup: a shield across the door, a map next to it, and weapons all around us. Currently, the map was blank. My throat went a little dry, and I hoped that didn't mean we'd have to play the whole game without a map.

I reached to grab my standard weapons and froze. Next to my sword was a pair of weapons I'd never seen offered in the game before, and yet, I knew exactly what they were.

Deerhorn knives.

The weapons from my training with Rooke. The same from his virtual program.

I tentatively reached for them and quickly jerked back. If I touched them, I wasn't sure if they'd become my permanent weapon. I leaned in close to examine them. Their silver edges and older style weren't exactly fitting in a game that was filled with ornate, glowing blades. So, what the hell were they doing in here?

Derek nudged me.

"Load up, Kali. Quit stalling."

Casting one last glance at the knives, I picked up my standard sword and dagger duo and shook the thought from my mind.

The map of the game loaded onto the screen near the door,

flickering a few times before going solid. There were four bases off the edges of the map, one for every direction. Ours was in the south, Legacy to the north, Eon to the east, and K-Rig in the west. Eight flag locations popped up on the octagon-shaped map. A bagua symbol. The map was a bagua symbol. I went cold and had to admit the irony. At first, I'd been worried we wouldn't have a map of the game. Now we had it, and suddenly, I was wishing we didn't.

I backed up until I hit the far wall. I felt numb to everything, even as I watched Lily, Hannah, and Derek cluster around the map. None of them noticed me.

"It's not that big," Hannah said, tracing an outline of the flags with her finger. "It's only triple the size of the standard round."

"That makes for more conflict," Derek said. "Putting four teams together in an arena not much bigger than standard means we'll be running into each other all the time. It's what the crowd will want."

Their voices were distant. My vision blurred a little until they were just hazy images in the background. The map was a bagua symbol. Why would Tamachi do such a thing? Whatever his reason, I doubted it would bode well for us.

"We don't have to run the flags to the base," Hannah said, and I barely heard her. "We just have to collect them all."

"I don't think that's all." Derek's voice resounded next to hers at the edge of my hearing. "Looks like there's a second part to the game in the center."

Footsteps walked up to me, the sound rippling like I was underwater.

"Kali?"

I blinked and looked up to find Rooke hovering over me, his arms crossed. Beyond him, my teammates had finally noticed my shock and were staring at me as well. While everyone else seemed confused, Rooke had a knowing look in his eye. He dropped his voice to just above a whisper and covered his mic with his hand.

"Why would Tamachi structure the final map of the game to be like a bagua symbol?"

"I-I don't know," I stuttered.

The rest of my teammates left the map and formed a semicircle around me, concerned looks on all their faces.

"Maybe he knows you'll recognize it," Rooke continued, "and thinks you'll follow it blindly the whole way."

My chest tightened. "You think it's a trap somehow?"

"Could be."

Great. On top of figuring out the solution to each flag and fighting against the top teams in the world, I now had to be on guard at all times for a trap.

"Wait," Hannah began, pointing back at the map. "You know this?"

"It's an ancient Chinese symbol."

That was all I managed to say before my throat swallowed up my own voice. If Tamachi had expected me to be unnerved by this turn of events, he'd succeeded.

Derek shifted his weight. "Well, that could be good, right? I mean, you'll know the game."

I shook my head. "I don't know what it means."

The shield dropped on the door. I kept my back pressed against the far wall. Lily started walking toward the opening. "It won't mean anything if we don't get moving."

Derek and Hannah followed Lily's lead and headed for the exit. I didn't move. Rooke watched them go and shoved his hands in his jacket pockets. "She's right."

I watched my teammates filter out the exit. "They don't seem to be taking this seriously."

Rooke leaned toward me. "They don't know what this means to you or how unsettling it is. They haven't been practicing with us every night. They haven't been in the program I created. But there's nothing we can really do about it except be careful."

Inside, my stomach still churned, but I knew I couldn't spend the entire game inside the base. Rooke offered his hand, and I swiped it away. A grin spread across his entire face.

"There's the warrior."

He turned and headed for the exit. I trailed behind him. When I reached the doorway, I paused, threw one last glance at the map, and set out into the game.

The first flag was only a few streets away, directly north of our base. It stood in the middle of a dead-end alley, open space all around it. Five monks stood in front of it, all holding ancient Chinese weapons.

They were the same monks from the Wudang Mountains program.

My stomach dropped. I turned and nearly marched straight out of the alley. Nope, not doing this.

Rooke grabbed my arm and turned me back. "Kali."

"What the hell?" I pointed at the monks. "What. The. Hell."

The rest of the team traded looks with each other but said nothing. Rooke simply shook his head. "You have to face this."

I met his gaze, hoping to stare him down. He stared back with nothing in his eyes but firm resolve. I sighed.

He released my arm.

Fine. Let's deal with this.

I drew my sword and marched up to the monks. My teammates followed suit, drawing their weapons around me. The monks mirrored us, taking up a stance directly opposite us. I lunged, and my teammates moved with me in nearly perfect sync. So did the monks. They moved with us, step for step, countering every strike with ease.

I slammed into my attacker, knocked his arms open, and swiped for his shoulder. My sword slid through nothing, as if the monk was merely a ghost.

I pulled back.

How was I supposed to defeat an NPC that didn't take damage?

I backed away from the fight.

Derek glanced at me. "Kali?"

This didn't make any sense. First, the deerhorn knives. Then the monks from the mountain.

What did it mean?

Then it clicked. This was the southern flag, and that meant Earth.

"Back up. Drop your weapons," I told everyone, and placed my own on the ground. Everyone listened to me and backed away but kept their weapons in their hands.

"Lay them down," I repeated.

They traded looks with each other but eventually placed their blades on the ground. The monks started coming toward us.

"Don't move," I instructed.

My team stood strong, but their breaths quickened. The monks picked up speed. Their blades glistened in the moonlight.

"Kali?" Hannah's voice wavered.

"Hold."

The monks charged us and reeled their weapons back.

"Kali!"

"Hold!"

The monks reached us and swung through, one for each of us, aiming straight for our necks. I didn't move. The blade came to a sudden halt at my neck, the blade pressed against my throat.

I smiled.

The monks backed up a step, bowed to us, and moved aside.

Beside me, Hannah blinked.

"What was that?"

I walked up to the flag and wrapped my fingers around it. It shimmered for a second before it disappeared and consumed me in a greenish glow that slowly faded from my skin.

I turned to the group.

"It's Earth," I told them.

Derek took a step forward. "What?"

"The map isn't just a bagua. Each flag represents a different element within the symbol." I glanced at the monks. "And I'm guessing each one will have a challenge to pick it up based on what it represents. Earth represents passive energy. That's why we couldn't attack the monks even when they attacked us."

A voice called out behind me, and it didn't belong to one of my teammates.

"Speaking of being attacked."

My insides congealed to ice at the sound of the Korean-accented voice. I turned to find K-Rig standing behind us. In front of them all, Kim Jae narrowed his sights on me and smirked.

"Thanks for showing us how to get the flag."

Then he signaled to his team, and they charged.

CHAPTER 24

Kim Jae slammed right into me.

I went flying back, landed on the alley floor, and skidded along until I hit the far wall. My back whacked the bricks hard, pushing a full breath out of my lungs. I gasped for air as Kim Jae descended on me. I kicked up, knocking him back. He stumbled and surged forward again.

Out of his sight, I gripped the dagger in my boot.

Kim Jae swiped for my head. I ducked under the blow, tumbled forward, feigning a fall, and drove my dagger through his foot. He cried out and tumbled to the ground. I pounced on him, reeled back, and slammed the dagger through his eye.

He froze instantly.

A final breath rushed out of his mouth, and his head lolled to the side.

I retrieved my dagger and looked up. My mouth dropped at the scene in front of me.

All five members of K-Rig were on the ground.

All four of my teammates were standing.

I leapt to my feet and screamed at the sky. "Is that the best in the world? Bring it on."

"Kali." Derek's voice sounded empty. I turned my gaze back to the team. For the first time, I noticed Hannah. Her face was blanched, and a dagger was sticking out of her stomach. Blood pooled out and dripped on the ground. She stumbled back and collapsed.

We rushed to her.

Lily and I ended up on either side of her while the guys hovered over us. Hannah smiled up at me. "Don't think I'll be helping you much this game."

She started to chuckle and seized with a cough instead. The dagger in her stomach jerked and twisted. I gripped the hilt.

"It'll go faster if I pull it out," I told her.

She nodded and braced herself against the pavement. Lily pressed her hands across Hannah's shoulders. I tightened my grip on the hilt and ripped it out. Hannah gasped, and her whole body went rigid, until her back lifted off the ground. Then she collapsed, jerked a few times, and a breath rasped from her lungs. Her eyes glazed over. Tentatively, Lily reached with her fingertips and shut Hannah's eyes. Then she hung her head. I did the same.

First flag, and we were down a teammate.

Rooke's hand came down on my shoulder. "It's going to be a long game, Kali."

Hannah's body dematerialized and faded out of the game. I watched her go and scrubbed my eyes with my palms.

"K-Rig's not going for the flags," I said. "They're aiming to take everyone else out first. That's why they got here so fast."

"They thanked us for showing them how to get the flag, though," Derek pointed out.

I shook my head. "I think that was to throw us off. They're going after the teams. That's why they came after us. They thought we'd be easiest."

Derek grinned. "Well, we proved them wrong."

I pointed back at the alley floor, where all that remained of Hannah was a small pool of blood. "We just lost a teammate. Why the hell are you grinning?"

"Because we just sent K-Rig back to their base and cost them one of their respawns. Maybe they'll think twice about their strategy."

"Or they'll double down. Maybe we just angered the beast."

He tossed his arms up. "Okay, so what are you saying? That we're not supposed to fight the other teams?"

"No. I'm just saying to stay alert."

"Why? Because we wouldn't be alert anyway?"

"Shut up!" Lily bellowed.

My lips instantly clamped shut. So did Derek's. Neither of us were used to having Lily shout commands, and the shock was enough to shut us both up.

She stepped up to us. "We're only one flag into the biggest game we've ever played, we've already lost a player, and you three are just standing there arguing. If you're going to fight, at least walk at the same time. Otherwise, I'll be waiting at the next flag while you three figure things out."

Lily turned and started to march out of the alleyway. I chased after her and grabbed her arm.

"Lil, wait. Sorry."

She halted and met my eyes.

"What do you think we should do?" I asked.

She answered immediately. "We have to split up."

I took a step back. "What?"

"Our best chance is getting the flags as quickly as we can."

I shook my head. "No. Absolutely not."

Derek crossed his arms. "Lily isn't wrong. It's a good idea. If we split up, we could collect the flags much faster than the other teams. If they're really going after each other, the flags should be ours for the picking."

"We're Defiance," Lily said simply. "We go big, or we go home."

I glanced between them. Derek and Lily had made up their minds. I wasn't so sure. In fact, everything inside me opposed the idea. I glanced at Rooke. He said nothing, but his expression was grim. I couldn't tell if he agreed with it or not, but he wasn't happy.

Still, I couldn't bring myself to say no to the idea, either. It was as good a plan as any. If they were right, collecting the flags while the other teams battled it out was the best thing to do.

"Okay," I sighed. "How do we divide the team?"

Lily nodded at me. "You and Rooke shouldn't be together."

Well, that was awkward.

"I mean, you two know what the game is about," she clarified. "You'll be able to figure out the flags."

I considered that and realized she was right. I linked my arm through hers. "Okay, you're with me." I tossed my head over my shoulder and grinned at the guys, trying to ignore the sinking feeling in my stomach. "Think you can handle yourselves, boys?"

They grinned.

We set out in opposite directions, Lily and I to the west and the boys to the east. Now we were only two each, against the other teams, and the game.

We made it to the next flag without running into any NPCs or other teams. The flag itself stood alone in the middle of the open street. There was nothing around it other than the buildings towering overhead and the lanterns strung from rooftop to rooftop. Strangely, it looked peaceful. Unlike my stomach, which was a roiling mess.

Lily walked around the flag, looking it up and down.

"What's this one?" she asked, sounding as suspicious as I felt.

"It's thunder. It represents movement."

She glanced around the street and back at the flag. "I don't get it. There doesn't seem to be any trick to it."

That didn't mean there wasn't one.

"What's going on?" Derek's voice sounded in my ear.

"We're at the next flag," I explained, pressing a finger to my mic. "Nothing else is here. Just the flag." I swallowed thick, trying to keep my mind calm. "Where are you guys?"

"Closing in on the next flag. Not quite there yet." He paused. "Does it bother anyone else how quiet it is?"

It always bothered me how quiet it was in this game.

"It makes it easier for the other teams to find us," Rooke said.

I shut my mouth. If we were split like this, communication would be key to winning. But it could also be the thing that got us killed and out of the game.

Lily reached for the flag. My stomach clenched, and I lunged for her.

"Wait," I said, locking her hand inside my own. She looked at me and sighed.

"We can't just stand here the whole game, Kali." She glanced up the road again. "Another team could show up at any minute." She placed her free hand on top of mine. "Relax, okay? Being this much on edge isn't going to help anything."

I sighed. She was right.

"You stand guard," she said. "I'll pick up the flag."

I released her hand and backed up several paces. I nodded at her. Lily wrapped her fingers around the flag. It shimmered and burst, wrapping her in a bluish glow.

I held my breath.

Nothing happened.

The street was silent and still. Shadows lurked in the alleyways, and dark corners remained where they were. The flag flashed and respawned, ready for the next team. We waited, not moving, my hand itching for my sword. But only the weighty presence of the game surrounded us.

Finally, Lily shrugged.

"Maybe that's it. Maybe there won't be a trick for every flag."

I released my breath, and my shoulders sunk with relief. Still, a nagging feeling pulled at my gut. This wasn't over.

"Okay," I said reluctantly, backing away from the flag a few more paces. "Let's go."

I turned, and took half a step forward when Lily grabbed my arm. Her brow was furrowed, and her lips were slightly apart. She looked confused.

"Did you hear that?"

I hadn't heard anything. I cocked my head, listening. Something rumbled in the distance. Together, we took a step toward the noise. Thunderous pounding marched toward us, growing louder every second. Then I heard two words that turned my stomach inside out.

"Target acquired."

Oh, no.

No, no, no.

Not again.

Monstrous footsteps pounded the ground until the pavement shook with the impact. The robot appeared from the mouth of an alleyway and streamed toward us. Its massive claws swung from side to side like meat hooks. As it neared, I realized this was not the same machine we'd faced before. This one was at least twice the size, claws double in length, and it had eyes. Tiny, little red eyes that flicked about. And those beady, little, devilish eyes zoomed in on Lily.

"Target acquired."

Lily stood frozen in fear, her mouth a gaping hole.

"Run," I screamed.

My voice ripped through the mics, knocking her from her dazed state. She turned and bolted down the street. I followed.

The guys were going ballistic in our mics.

"What's wrong? Kali? Kali?"

"What the hell? What's happening?"

"Not right now," I shouted as I raced alongside Lily.

"Plan?" she managed to ask me, her voice huffing.

"Just run. Let me handle this thing."

"Got it," she managed.

Handle this thing? What the hell did I think I was going to do? Killing it didn't work. Cutting off its limbs didn't work. The only way I'd survived before was by outrunning it to the base, and now we were on the opposite side of the map.

With Lily at my side, we sprinted down the open road. The machine closed in.

"Turn," I commanded into the mic.

We cut into a narrow alleyway, too small for the machine to follow. But that thing, that *beast*, simply smashed through it, its massive arms and claws ripping apart the surrounding buildings like wrecking balls. My stomach went to knots and twisted in on itself.

We'd never outrun this thing.

We exited the alley and raced down the new street. Pounding footsteps echoed behind us, crushing the road beneath as they landed.

We were dead.

I glanced at Lily. Sweat poured down her face, and she looked like she was two seconds away from a panic attack. Then, suddenly, she slowed her pace, and stumbled to a halt in the middle of the road. A distant look filled her eyes, and she turned to face the machine, planting both feet firmly against the pavement. I went streaming past her and nearly tripped over my own feet as I reversed directions and rushed up to her.

"Lil!" I shouted, tugging on her arm. "What are you doing?"

She kept her gaze locked on the machine, and her eyes narrowed with determination. "I'm going for it."

She stepped forward. I grabbed her wrist and held her back.

"It'll respawn," I warned.

She turned to look me dead on. "I've been afraid of this thing since I was a kid. I'm done running. I need to do this."

One look at the determination in her eyes told me there was no talking her out of this. I released her grip and backed up a few steps.

"I'll guard your back," I told her.

She nodded at me and turned to face the machine. Lily gripped her axes and charged, letting out a ferocious scream as she streamed toward the machine. My eyebrows went up. It's a little scary when something so small goes into rage-fueled ninja mode.

The machine swung its massive hooks at her. She zigzagged through the strikes, dodging each blow. One blade came down beside her head, catching the very edge of the cheek and shoulder. Skin split and blood trickled out. Lily recoiled to the side, instinctively guarding her wounds. Then she wiped away the blood and dove back into the fight.

She wound her way through the machine's legs to its back and latched onto its spine. She climbed. The machine spun and grappled to reach her, but Lily held on and ducked beneath the grabs as she ascended the machine. When she reached its neck, she reeled back and repeatedly hacked away. The machine spasmed and jerked, and stumbled across the road. With a final blow, its giant head clanged to the ground and rolled a few times.

The rest of its body dropped to its knees and fell forward. Lily somersaulted off the machine and landed safely a few feet away.

I gripped my own weapons and waited for the machine to dematerialize and reappear.

It never came.

The machine simply lay against the pavement, little sparks fizzing out from the severed connection that used to be its neck. I walked up to the head and kicked it. It lolled to the side and never moved again.

Lily walked up to me.

"What did you do?" I asked her.

She looked at me and simply shrugged. "I faced my fear."

"But I've taken out that machine before—"

"It wasn't your fear to face. It was mine."

Fears exist until we face them. After that, they can't come back. The machine wouldn't respawn. At least, not for us, because it was no longer symbolic of the greatest thing Lily had ever feared.

"Come on," Lily said. "We've got more flags to get. We're not even halfway through this thing."

Though she sounded serious, I didn't miss the expression on her face.

She was grinning.

We set out for the next flag and started working through the rest of the game.

I talked the guys through their first flag, mountain. It represented both a great obstacle and remaining still within oneself. Soon, we'd figured out they needed to scale a four-story building, moving as slowly as possible, or the building would start to rumble.

Lily and I hid from Eon in a dark alley as they walked past on the open street.

On the other side of the map, the guys did much the same thing as K-Rig passed them by.

"Seems like K-Rig and Eon are all over the map," Derek said once it was safe to talk again.

Lily pressed her lips to her mic as she walked along beside me. "They're hunting. They're more focused on getting everyone else out than collecting the flags."

When we arrived at the next flag, it sat at the top of a three-level structure, each level rising a foot higher than the next and growing smaller as it moved inward, much like a water fountain except there was no water.

Tentatively, we approached. As soon as my toes touched the edge, ten-foot-high flames shot up in my face. I stumbled back. "O-kay."

Lily smirked at me. "I'm gonna guess this one is fire."

I approached the fountain again. The second I got within a few inches, a wall of fire blasted into the air, blocking all paths to the flag.

"Great," I muttered. "Now what?"

Lily backed up.

"Maybe it's testing our fear again," she said, taking a sprint stance. "Maybe we have to charge—"

"Lil, no—"

My heart jumped in my throat as she pushed off and soared toward the fountain. Her feet touched down right before the first level, and a barricade of flames shot up in front of her. Lily slammed on the brakes and nearly toppled in. The fire singed the ends of her hair, and her eyes went wide. I grabbed her arm to steady her, and the fire cut out.

The fire cut out even though we were within an inch of the fountain. I glanced around the fountain, then back at Lily. I let go of her arm, and the fire shot up again.

"That's it," I said. "We have to do it together."

We wrapped our arms around one another, her right with my left, and locked ourselves together up to each other's elbows.

"On three," I said. "One, two, three—"

We stepped up. Fire shot up around the fountain's edge but halted on either side of us. I pushed out a heavy breath. "Next step. Now."

We stepped up.

The flames closed in around us but stopped within an inch of our skin. The heat burned, turning my leather armor hot. I squirmed, trying to remain calm, but my heart slammed repeatedly against my chest.

Lily raised her foot. "Next."

I mimicked her, and we stepped up together.

Same level as the flag.

The flames closed in, blasting heat against our faces. Fire crackled around us until it was all I could hear. I drew slow, careful breaths through my mouth, but soon I was gasping for air in the immense heat. My vision swirled, and I thought I'd hyperventilate.

The flames swallowed the flag, engulfing it completely in shades of yellow and ochre.

"We have to reach through the flames," I shouted over the sizzling blaze.

In unison, we stretched our free hands toward the flag. The flames receded around our fingertips. Together, we wrapped our fingers around the pole. It burst and consumed us in a reddish glow.

The flames cut out, gone as quickly as they had appeared. The air around us faded back to the void-like emptiness it always was. I let my eyes fall shut. My heart still knocked against my rib cage, but relief flooded my body.

"Count one more, boys," I said into my mic, as Lily and I descended the fountain. "Where are you now?"

"Far east, closing in on the flag," Rooke said. "That'll make five. Where are you?"

"Far west."

Rooke paused for half a beat. "So, you're near K-Rig's base?"

"Yup. And you're in front of Eon's."

"Relax," Derek piped up. "No one is going to show up unless they respawn. The bases don't mean anything, otherwise. K-Rig and Eon could be anywhere."

"He has a good point," Lily said, as we wandered away together. "I wonder who even still needs this flag."

"We do."

I heard Lily gasp, and my breath caught in my throat. Slowly, we turned together, white-knuckled and ready to attack.

Legacy stood behind us.

CHAPTER 25

L egacy simply stood there, staring at us, making no move to attack. At least, with what was left of their team. I recognized them all in an instant. Damon Mercier, their leader and team captain. Joe Davids, a hulk of a man and their enforcer, for lack of a better word.

And Jessica Salt, who needed no introduction.

They had three players, one more than us.

The breath caught in my throat wheezed out.

We stood opposite each other with a five-foot gap between us. Breaths were heavy. Knuckles were white, gripping hilts. Tension was hair-trigger thick, where one twitch from either side would have sent us straight to war. But nobody was moving. The space between us was no-man's-land.

The audience must have been on the edge of their seats. Given that Legacy still had way more experience, not to mention more players than us, there was a good chance they could take us out, and only Rooke and Derek would be left to try to take the championship on their own.

But Legacy still wasn't moving, and I realized what they were thinking. Each of us stood a better chance with the other in the game.

"We'll walk away if you do," I said.

All eyes were on me, including Lily's. Jessica glanced up at

Damon. Their eyes met for a few seconds, as though they were speaking telepathically. They'd been together for over ten years and spent more time in each other's presence than most married couples. I wouldn't be surprised if they could read one another's thoughts.

Damon nodded behind us.

"We need the flag."

I stepped to the side, keeping a five-foot gap between us. Lily followed suit. We circled each other, step for step until we were on opposite sides as before, Legacy now closer to the flag. They backed up a few steps, now a ten-foot gap between us. But they kept facing our way and made no move to retrieve the flag. My heart hammered against my rib cage.

Damon stood at the front of the group, arms crossed against his chest.

"By the way, Eon is already on their third respawn."

I nearly choked, and I wasn't sure if it was because Eon had already been killed three times, or if it was because Damon was offering me insight into the game.

"Third?" I repeated.

He nodded. "K-Rig's been hunting them, trying to get them out of the game. Eon is their biggest threat since they have respawns."

They were going after each other, just as we thought.

"What about K-Rig?" I asked. "How many respawns do they have left?"

He shrugged. "We haven't taken them out. As far as we know, Eon hasn't, either."

I traded looks with Lily.

"We did," I told him. "We took out K-Rig. Once."

"Bullshit."

It was my turn to shrug. "It's your choice to believe it."

Damon crossed his arms as he studied us, trying to discern the truth. As he stared through the thin slits of his eyes, I realized what he was thinking. If we could take out K-Rig, we could take the whole game. My heart rate rose ten beats. Maybe they weren't going to back away.

"How many flags do you have?" he asked.

I pressed my lips together. I wasn't sure if we should tell them the truth. We had four. Five, if the boys had reached it on the other side of the map. For now, they were being silent.

"We have—" Lily began.

"Three," I stated, taking a step forward. "We have three flags."

If they bought it, we'd look like less of a threat.

Legacy traded looks with each other. Damon's gaze turned back to us, flicking between me and Lily.

"Is this all that's left of you?"

They were sizing us up.

"No," I said, hoping my voice wasn't quivering as much as the rest of me. He took a step toward us, and my hand twitched for my sword.

Easy, Kali.

"But," he began, "you're all that's here right now."

He said it more as a statement than a question. My gaze floated between the rest of Legacy. Jessica was staring at me with a neutral expression, and Joe looked like he was one twig-snap away from charging us.

Damon took another step. "You're all that's here, aren't you?"

Behind me, gravel crunched on the road as Lily shifted her weight. Her breaths quickened. My own pulse beat against every nerve. I glanced down. Damon's hand gripped the hilt of the dagger sheathed at his waist. Joe moved up behind him. Jessica did nothing.

Damon's sights narrowed on me, and he slid the dagger out an inch until I saw metal. Fuck it. If they were going to attack, we were going down fighting. I grabbed my sword and charged. Lily's footsteps followed right behind me.

Legacy bolted for us. We streamed toward one another on a collision course. No matter what happened, one of us would go down right now.

Jessica threw herself between everyone.

"Enough."

Her voice ripped through the air, grinding everyone to a halt. We all stared at each other, mere inches apart. Breaths were heavy. Weapons were in everyone's hands. I watched Jessica's movements, making sure this wasn't some kind of trick to catch us off guard. Instead, she turned to Damon and pressed an open palm against his chest.

"We should get going. We've wasted enough time."

Her voice was firm. Damon kept his sights fixed on me.

"But—"

"You know it's best to leave them in the game for now. We can take them out later if no one else does."

Damon stared down at her a long time. It felt like minutes, maybe hours, had ticked by as they stared at each other. Finally, Damon nodded at me.

"Back up," he told us, pointing to the distance. "And keep walking."

We did.

We backed up several yards, our feet moving as rapidly as they could without tripping. Legacy held their ground as they watched our retreat. We hit a crossroad and turned, breaking their line of sight. Just before I turned my back, I caught eyes with Jessica. Her expression said one thing.

Good luck.

Yeah. You, too.

I disappeared around the corner and trotted down the street beside Lily. A shaky breath passed through my lips.

"What's going on?" Derek's voice came through the mics. "You guys okay?"

"We ran into Legacy," I explained. I pushed out another uneven breath, my heartbeat still thrumming in my ears.

"Legacy?" He sounded panicked. "Did you take them out?"

"No. We held a truce. It's for their benefit if they keep us in the game. If you run into them, remind them of it."

"Got it."

It went quiet then. Not just between us but across the entire game. It always felt so empty in here, but realizing how close we'd nearly come to being out of the game, the emptiness felt peaceful. Comforting. It was a reminder that we were still here, still pressing onward, still with work to do.

Lily looked at me.

"What's next?"

"Marsh."

"What the hell is that thing?"

Lily blinked several times as she stared down at the scene below us, as if her brain wouldn't register what she was seeing. I stood next to her on a rooftop, overlooking the next flag; we were tucked between the rooftop's corner and the building's oversized generator. Down on the street, all five members of Eon were locked in battle with some kind of swamp monster. Dripping with moss and standing well over twenty feet tall, it swung its massive fists into Eon's chests and stomachs, sending them catapulting across the street. Behind it, the flag shimmered in the center of a small pond.

Yup, definitely a swamp monster.

Just minutes before, the guys had retrieved their latest flag, Water, where they had to wade through a pool, sinking like quicksand to reach the flag. While it was a test of nerves, they certainly hadn't faced anything like this.

We watched as the monster pulverized Eon. All five of them attacked the monster together, but none got any closer than ten feet to the flag before the monster swatted them away. Lily was right. What the hell were we going to do?

A distant noise snapped my attention away from the monster and across the rooftop behind us. It sounded like someone talking, and they weren't speaking English. I stopped breathing.

Lily kept her gaze on the fight below and opened her mouth. "What are we supposed to—?"

Lily's words became a muffled mess as I pressed my palm against her lips and shook my head. She understood immediately. Her eyes went wide, and she went silent.

Footsteps echoed across the roof. They were only a few feet away.

My stomach dropped out.

Together, we scrambled away from the rooftop's edge and pressed our backs to the generator, trying to shrink down in the shadows. K-Rig rounded the generator's corner and approached the rooftop's edge, muttering things in Korean to one another. I pressed myself harder against the generator as a silent prayer slipped between my lips. How could they not see us? Kim Jae stood within inches of me. I could have reached out and touched his leg.

As his teammates surveyed the fight, Kim Jae took a step to the side, and his foot brushed against mine. My heart jumped into my throat. Kim Jae glanced down with a curious look on his face.

Oh shit.

Lily's hand gripped her axe. I wrapped my fingers around hers and shook my head. She froze.

He started to kneel, moving closer to the shadows. I released Lily's hand, and my own went for my sword.

I prepared myself for the attack.

"Jae."

His head snapped around to his team, and he answered them. There were a few, sharp exchanges between them, and they started rushing to the edge of the roof. Kim Jae threw one last glance at the shadows and followed his teammates down.

A rush of air passed through my lips, and I let my head fall back against the generator. Relief flushed through me until I felt like I was melting into a puddle out of my toes.

Beside me, Lily scowled. "We should have taken them. We could have knocked half them off the roof in a second."

I pushed up to my feet. "They'd just respawn and come after us again."

Lily followed my lead and leaned over the roof's edge again. "They'd come after us anyway. At least then they'd have to trek across the map again to pick up this flag."

"Or, we could just let Eon and K-Rig take each other out." I pointed down at the flag. Below us, Eon, K-Rig, and the NPC were locked in a messy, three-way battle. Despite already going up against the monster, Eon fought against K-Rig with determination, slamming strike after strike into their swords. Swords plunged through K-Rig's abdomens and necks, spraying blood, inking the pond with droplets of red. I blinked several times, and shook my head. I couldn't believe it. Eon was winning.

Lily gasped, and grabbed my arm.

"We should take the flag."

"What?"

"Right now. It's our chance. We could sneak up from behind. There's so much chaos, there's a chance we'd never be seen."

I hesitated. "That's not really sportsmanlike, is it? Stealing the flag like that?"

Lily frowned at me. "What part of this competition has been sportsmanlike for us?"

Good point.

"Fine," I said. "Let's go."

We jumped down from the roof's edge, landed on the street, and crept through the shadows. The sounds of the battle cries and clanging swords filled the air. We waded into the water behind the fight and ducked down up to our noses, just enough to breathe and keep our eyes on the attraction.

We neared the flag.

It stood tall on a small, circular platform just out of the water. The waves lapped up its sides. A body went flying past us and splashed into the water. We froze and submerged into the water up to our eyes. The body floated and didn't move again. No one else entered the water.

We surged forward, the flag shimmering within reach. Lily grabbed the flag. It flashed and consumed her in an orange glow. Then it faded.

We had the flag.

There was an enormous moaning sound. The swamp beast wavered, stumbled on its feet, and collapsed to the pavement. The ground shook with the impact. With the beast down, the rest of the battle revealed itself. All five members of K-Rig were on the ground, and three from Eon. The remaining two stood in the center of the fight, blood smeared across their bodies, gasping for air.

My eyebrows went up. They'd survived. They'd taken out K-Rig and defeated the swamp monster.

Then their eyes landed on us. Their expressions grew fierce, and they shouted things in Swedish. I had no idea what they were saying, but I doubted they were nice words.

They charged.

Lily backed away from the flag, but I grabbed her arm.

"We make our stand here. It's our best chance."

Lily nodded and drew her short axes. I did the same with my swords, gripping them tight in my hands. We clustered around the flag's tiny platform. Eon hit the water, which slowed their assault. They continued to charge us, driven more by anger than reason.

They neared us.

Once the closest one was less than three feet away, I leapt from the platform, aiming both swords directly at his torso. I slammed home. My blades slid straight through his chest and out the other side. He seized, eyes wide, and collapsed to his knees. I ripped my blades out, and he face-planted into the water. Red clouds pillowed out beneath him, slowly turning the entire pool red.

Lily appeared at my side. Her opponent floated in the water next to mine.

"We need to get out of here." She nodded behind me, where the swamp monster had faded from view. "Before that thing respawns."

I followed her and started wading over to the side of the pond. Behind us, the water began to ripple.

"Go," I shouted, shoving Lily out of the water.

A massive hand closed around my foot, and I started sliding back down.

"Lil!" I screeched.

Lily grabbed my wrists and yanked hard. The grip tightened around my foot, and I slipped deeper into the water. A monstrous cry echoed from beneath the surface, morphing the ripples into churning waves. I slid lower. The waves slapped at my mouth. I coughed and gurgled.

"Pull hard," I shouted, wrapping my fingers around her wrists. "As hard as you can."

Lily heaved.

My foot slipped out of the mossy hand. I scrambled onto land, and we took off running down the street. We didn't stop running until we were several blocks away. Eventually, we slowed, panting hard. I pressed my lips to my mic.

"You guys there?"

"Yeah," Derek answered. "What the hell happened to you?"

I pushed the words out of my mouth, between my heavy breaths. "Count number six. We're heading north now."

"Cool. We're—"

Derek's voice cut out, and there was a commotion on their side of the comms. I pressed my fingers to my ears, trying to hear more.

"What's wrong?"

Derek's panicked voice came through the audio. "Eon's here."

I went cold. We'd sent Eon back to their base, same side of the map as the guys. We'd screwed them over.

"Kali, they've got Rooke. They're going to—"

The audio cut out.

I pressed my finger harder against the mic, nearly driving it into my ear. "Derek?"

Dead silence.

"You alive?"

Nothing.

Then a voice came through Derek's mic, but it wasn't his voice and had a heavy Swedish accent.

"This is for that last flag, you bitch."

"Next time I see you, I won't be quick with my sword. I'll rip out your throat with my bare hands, you fucking coward."

There was a snort, like he didn't believe me. A cry echoed in the background. A woman's scream. Not my teammates. There were shouts in English and Swedish, and clangs of swords, but it all jumbled together in an inaudible mess.

"Guys? Anyone there?"

I had no answer.

The radio cut to white noise, then nothing at all.

CHAPTER 26

"We don't know for sure if they're out."

Lily trudged along behind me, trying to keep my spirits high. We headed north, sticking to the edges of the streets, surveying the shadows and sharp corners for the other teams.

"Why wouldn't they answer if they were still in the game?" I countered. I glanced back at her, and she shrugged.

"Maybe their mics got damaged."

Or maybe they were out of the game.

"We have to be realistic," I told her as I pressed my back against another corner and peered around it. Clear. "If they're gone, we'll still have an extra flag to pick up."

"But if Derek and Rooke took out Eon," she continued, rounding the corner with me, "then that was their final respawn. They'd be out of the game."

That was unlikely. A victory with two against five wasn't unheard of, but with Eon's respawns, they'd be coming back into every fight injury-free and fully stocked with weapons. The chance of my teammates' survival was minimal at best.

I glanced at the map in the corner of my visor. A red dot blinked two blocks ahead in the north. We were closing in on the final flag.

When we arrived at the spot on the map, we were met by a

single-story, flat platform, a perfect square, running a hundred feet long on each side. A single set of oversized stone stairs led up to the platform. In each corner was an angel, cast in stone. Each was cloaked in a heavy hood to hide its face, and each was kneeling as if to pray. Wings spread out from their back and wrapped around them in a semicircle, each angel so large it could swallow you whole.

Gripped in each of their praying hands was a sickle.

"Maybe we should wait it out?" Lily offered, eyeing the angels. "See if another team shows up. Let them handle it first?"

I shook my head. "I don't know. Our advantage in the game is speed. We need to stay ahead of the other teams. If we keep waiting around, they'll catch up to us."

She considered that and nodded. "Okay, then. What do we do?"

I sat on the alley floor and buried my face in my hands.

"I have no idea," I murmured against my palms.

The sound of leather armor crunching together filled the air as Lily knelt in front of me.

"Hey," she whispered. "I'm tired, too."

I pulled my palms away from my eyes. "It's not that . . ."

My voice trailed off before I said anything more. I was tired, but that wasn't the point. Doubt was creeping in, leaving a sinking feeling in my gut. All along, I'd thought we'd have a chance. Just a glimmer of a chance at making it through this game, maybe even winning. Once we were kicked out, we'd be right back in reality: where everyone hated us, and our dream of playing the games we loved would be over. No sponsor would touch us. No fan would follow.

We were done.

I met Lily's eyes and felt my own begin to water.

"We're not going to make it."

Her expression went soft. "Don't think like that. The guys could still—"

"Cut the bullshit, Lil. They're out, and you know it. We're alone in here. It's just me and you against K-Rig, Legacy, Eon, and the game. Nobody could survive those odds."

Lily blinked a few times as she processed that, and her shoulders sagged. She thought so, too.

I covered my mic and pressed my lips to her ears.

"The VGL wants us out," I whispered. "They purposely set up the game like a bagua symbol, and I haven't seen a trap yet. This is the last flag before the finale. Whatever they have planned, it'll be on that platform."

Lily's jaw went slack, and her shoulders sagged even more. She glanced between me and the platform a few times.

"Well," she began. "Whatever it is, let's go down fighting. Let's show the world Defiance one last time."

She offered her hand.

The doubt I felt inside turned to resolve. If this was our last fight in front of the world, we would give it our all. Go out with glory. Down to the last breath.

I took her hand and hauled myself up. Lily turned her gaze to the platform.

"What are you thinking?"

This flag was Heaven, situated directly north and opposite of Earth. For the Earth flag, we had to be completely receptive, lay down our weapons and refuse to fight. I surveyed the stone angels in each corner and had a feeling who our opponents would be.

"This will be the battle," I told her. "We'll have to fight with brute force. Whatever comes at us, don't back down."

She nodded.

I edged up to the end of the alley and checked up and down

the street. Empty. I nodded at Lily and drew my sword. She gripped her axes.

"Charge on three," I told her, planting my feet on the ground to push off. She did the same. "One, two—"

A hand wrapped around my arm and yanked me back.

"Want some help?"

I whirled around and followed the hand gripping my arm up to a pair of soft brown eyes.

Rooke.

I didn't remember moving, but suddenly, I was hugging him. He wrapped his arms around me and crushed me against him, burying my face in his chest until I couldn't breathe. I didn't care. He could have squeezed the life out of me, and I would have smiled for every second of it. My hands gripped his back, feeling the leather of his jacket, and the way his muscles moved beneath. He wasn't real but real enough.

Rooke pulled back, and I sucked in some much-needed air.

"I thought you were out," I breathed.

"Almost, and I had to drag him along."

He nodded behind us.

Derek stood five feet back with his arms wrapped around Lily. He glanced over her head at me and flashed his movie-star grin. He released Lily and limped up to us, grimacing whenever he put weight on his right leg.

"Legacy showed up," Derek explained. "With the three of them, and the two of us, it was five on five. Eon was surrounded."

My chest tightened. "Legacy's still in the game?"

"Jessica is. The rest of their team went out in the fight."

Lily stepped up to the group. "That was a pretty big gamble on their part."

Derek shrugged. "They wanted Eon out and us in. It's the way the fight went."

That was when I noticed their visors and mics were gone.

"What happened to your mics?" I asked.

Derek grinned at that. "When Eon first attacked us, they went straight for our visors. Ripped them right off our heads." His grin grew wider. "To be honest, I think it was to disorient you two. They seemed pretty pissed. By knocking out our mics, you wouldn't know what happened to us."

I probably would have done the same thing in their circumstance. We'd screwed them, and they'd done it right back to us. It didn't matter now. All that did was that our plan worked. Now we were together, and ready to fight.

"So, Eon's out," I said, though I was more thinking to myself out loud. "And Legacy is down to just Jessica."

I traded looks with my teammates. They all grinned and nodded at me. We were thinking the same thing. We could win this. If we beat K-Rig to the center of the game, we could take it all.

First, the eighth flag.

Derek swung his arm out, as if presenting the flag to me.

"Lead the way, captain."

I glanced down at his leg. "We'll have to charge."

He shrugged. "I'll manage."

I knew he would. We'd all done it, played on injuries. I'd outrun that machine thing on a broken foot several matches ago. We'd gone through the semi's respawns battling the same thing.

I checked the street again, the buildings overhead. Empty. No movement. I led my team across the street. At the bottom of the steps, we paused and drew our weapons.

"Go in hard," I told them, gripping my sword tight. "Don't slow down. Just attack whatever comes at you."

Everyone nodded. I planted my feet and set my sights at the top of the stairs.

"Ready," I shouted. "Go."

We charged.

We took the steps two at a time and bounded up the stairs. The second our feet touched down on the platform, the stone statues in the corners came to life, like angelic gargoyles. They raced toward us at blinding speed and halted in front of the flag, forming a single line across and blocking our path.

We never slowed down, and behind them, the flag grew brighter with every step we took.

We crashed into them.

A giant sickle swung down, and I dove to the side, dodging the blow. I scrambled forward, attempting to squeeze between the statue's legs. It swung back again with its weapon, caught me along the flat side, and slammed into me with a sickening smack. I tumbled away and rolled across the platform several times before coming to near the stairs. I groaned as pain shot through every inch of me. Coughing, I spat blood. It splattered against the stone platform, red on beige, like a red, wax seal on a centuries-old letter.

I pushed up to my hands and knees. The sound of metal clashing on stone drove my eardrums into my brain as my teammates fought against the line of angels. Beyond it all, the flag was fading.

Had to get back into the fight.

As I pushed up to my feet, footsteps pounded up the steps behind me. I turned in time to see K-Rig step onto the platform and rocket toward the center.

My heart went into my throat.

As they drove across the platform, the flag glowed so brightly it seared against the dark, grayed background of the game. A realization hit me then. The brute force required to capture the flag wasn't toward the NPCs. It was toward the flag itself. The NPCs were merely a distraction.

"Charge the flag," I screamed.

I broke away from my angel, just as a member from K-Rig lunged for me. The angel slammed into him instead and knocked him to the ground. They locked in battle.

I was free. Mostly.

The platform became a war zone. My team, K-Rig, and the NPCs all clashed together in battle. Screams punctuated the air between the thunderous smashes of stone against stone as the statues toppled or crashed into one another.

This was chaos. Pure, utter chaos.

In the middle of it all, I took a breath, calmed myself, and set my sights on the center of the platform until all that existed was me and the flag.

I bolted for it.

With every step I took, the flag glowed a little brighter. Ten feet from it, a pair of hands grabbed my ankles and I slammed to the ground. Refusing to look back, I kicked out hard. My foot connected with something solid, and there was a whooshing sound, like the air rushing out of lungs. I'd hit a rib cage or a sternum. Didn't matter which. The tension around my ankles released.

I scurried forward.

A body landed next to me. Blood sprayed out of its neck and splattered the side of my face. Stone crumbled beneath my palms and dug into my skin. I never took my sights off the flag.

It was within my reach now.

My fingers wrapped around the pole. It flashed, and consumed me in a grayish glow. Relief rushed through me, like a gulp of fresh air at the bottom of the ocean. The eighth flag was mine.

A weight jumped on my back. I went with it, twisting as I collapsed. The weight rocked sideways, and I flipped onto my back. Kim Jae appeared over me.

In his hand was a dagger.

My throat tightened.

I reached for my own weapon tucked in my boot. Kim Jae knocked my hand away and pounced on me again, pinning me to the platform. He reeled back with the blade. As he swung down, my forearm shot up and blocked his wrist. The inside edge of the blade dug into my arm. I grimaced through the pain. A trail of blood snaked down my arm and dripped onto my neck.

The dagger lowered. I recoiled, pressing myself tight against the ground. Kim Jae pressed his weight into it. The blade neared my eye. I squirmed beneath him, unable to budge. Inside, I knew it was over. I wasn't getting out of this one.

So, this is how Kali Ling goes out of the fight. Almost at the end, but not close enough.

At least we'd given them a good show.

Kim Jae grinned down at me and leaned in more, preparing to thrust the knife home. Then his mouth split open into a silent scream, and his body went rigid. I glanced down. A sword had driven through his stomach and nearly impaled me as well. I sucked my gut inward as the tip pressed against my belly. Kim Jae gasped a few times, spasming, and his body rolled to the side.

I collapsed against the platform as relief flooded through me for a second time. Breaths wheezed through my lungs. My vision swirled, then cleared as I stared up into the night. The ominous presence of the game pressed around me, as thick as morning fog, and I'd never been more thankful for it.

I was still here.

Still in the game.

I looked up to see which of my teammates had saved me. A shock of red hair hovered over me.

Jessica Salt offered her hand and smirked at me lying on my back.

"Taking it easy, Ling?"

I pushed up to my feet without taking her hand. I still didn't trust her. Not entirely.

I surveyed my surroundings. Eight bodies littered the platform, interspersed with hunks of stone from the shattered angel statues. The smaller bits, like gravel, crunched beneath my feet. Of the eight bodies, five were K-Rig. They slowly faded from view.

The other three were my team.

I stood tall and swallowed thick as they slowly dematerialized out of the game. My heart almost went with them. One mistake, one stupid misinterpretation of the puzzle, and it had cost me my team. After they faded from view, I retrieved my weapons and kept them gripped in my hands. I wasn't alone up here, after all.

"You're all that's left," Jessica said, as if I couldn't see it for myself.

Something immensely bright flashed in the distance. A golden sunburst exploded from a skyscraper's rooftop in the center of the map. Then it collapsed in on itself until all that was left was a tiny spark of light, like a star in the night sky.

The final flag.

Jessica and I locked eyes again. We stood there, looking at each other for a few seconds. The eighth flag respawned behind me. Jessica moved toward it, walking straight to me. I kept my breaths steady, but every nerve was on edge, waiting for her to make a move. I could go up against my idol right here, on this platform, in front of the entire world. The sword in my hand suddenly gained ten pounds.

She slid past me.

Nothing happened.

She made no move to attack. Instead, she gripped the pole, and a burst of color consumed her.

"You have all eight flags, don't you?" she asked. "That's why the final flag went up."

I nodded again. She turned back and studied me for a minute.

"That was a bold move, splitting up your team. I still need one more. So does K-Rig."

My brow furrowed. "How do you know that?"

"I've been keeping track." She nodded at the one next to her. "If I'm right, that's the last they need, and you stopped them."

I scoffed at her. "You stopped them. If you hadn't shown up, I'd be out of the game right now."

"Well, you're not. You're the front-runner now." She pointed to the final flag, hundreds of feet away in the center of the map. "That's all yours if you can make it there before the rest of us."

Why was she telling me this?

"Make no mistake, Ling," she said, as if she could read my mind. She walked along the platform, heading toward the east. "As long as K-Rig is here, we're still of use to each other inside the game. But if it comes down to me and you, I'm not holding back anymore. I hope you won't, either."

I grinned. "I wouldn't dream of it."

She reached the edge of the platform.

"K-Rig will be coming back for this one," she said, nodding at the flag behind me. "I'd get out of here if I were you. Like, now."

She backed up a few steps and prepared to jump.

"Hey," I called out. She halted and glanced back to me. "Thanks. For everything."

She stared at me and kept her expression neutral. Though, I swore I saw a hint of respect in her eyes. "Sometimes in these tournaments, you aren't dealt a fair hand. The press tears you up and fans turn their backs. But, in here"—she pointed down at the ground—"it should be an even playing field. The game should be fair. But I don't think it is anymore. Not for everyone."

I blinked several times, unsure of what to say. Jessica knew what had happened to us in this tournament. Or, at least, had a sneaking suspicion. That must have been why she was helping me. She wanted me to have an equal chance at winning, despite the VGL's working against me.

"Get to the center, Ling. Maybe I'll see you there."

With that, she jumped off the platform's edge and bolted down the street. I watched her go, then turned toward the center of the game.

The final flag.

It was down to me now.

Jessica was still in it and had seven out of eight flags. Despite their delay at the start, K-Rig had seven flags—not much of a surprise there. Eon was out.

Then there was me. I had all eight flags.

I was alone to make the trek to the center of the map, survive whatever the game and my opponents threw at me, and conquer the final flag.

I looked up at the sky and felt the ominous presence of the game all around me.

It's just me and you now.

I gripped my sword tight, descended the platform, and marched toward the center of the world.

didn't even make it a full block before something whizzed past me.

Inside the narrow alleyway, I stopped dead. My hand instantly went for the hilt of my sword, currently sheathed at my back. Shallow breaths slid through my mouth as I surveyed the area around me. The alleyway was empty. At least, it looked empty. But that creepy feeling of being watched snuck up the back of my neck, and I knew it wasn't just the game itself. Some*thing* had just brushed past me. I took a cautious step forward, then another, watching, listening, every nerve on alert.

It could be K-Rig, I thought, *playing some kind of trick.*

I halted and backed up a few steps, distancing myself from the alley's mouth. Another whizzing sound whipped past the end of the alley behind me. I froze. My heart beat in my throat. The air around me was deathly silent and emphasized the thrum of my pulse and sound of my shoes crunching against the pavement. If it was K-Rig, and they had me surrounded, I could be toast. But waiting around in the alleyway for them to close in wasn't doing me any favors, especially if they were on the rooftops. If they came from one direction, the narrow passageway would work to my benefit and funnel them in only two at a time. But chances were, they were in front, behind, and above. Not good for me.

I silently drew my sword, gripping it tight. With a breath, I pushed off running. When I reached the alley's mouth, I slid down, feetfirst, hoping they'd swing high and miss me. I skidded along into an empty street. No K-Rig. No soul in sight.

I stood, blinking, as I looked around. I swear I'd felt something, saw something whizzing around the alleyway. I shook my head. Was I losing my mind? Was this a side effect from being plugged in for too long?

Then, on the street in front of me, a team materialized out of thin air, like they'd stepped into the game through black clouds of wispy smoke. My stomach bottomed out. It wasn't K-Rig.

It was my team.

At least, they looked like my team. They were completely monochrome in color, like gothic imprints of the people they once were. Black armor, gray skin, eyes so dark, the entire socket, from eyebrow to cheek, looked hollow and sunken in.

They all held weapons in their hands.

I took half a step back, and my mouth went bone-dry. All this time, I was afraid to be alone. Afraid to be without my team. Afraid to fail them. Now they were here with me, and I would have done anything to be alone again.

Lily charged me, her axe drawn back to strike. I spun around as I ducked under her swing, drew my dagger from my boot, and drove it deep into her stomach. Black liquid pooled around my blade and slithered down her body in thick goblets, like wax melting down a candle. Her mouth opened, and more blackness spilled out from her lips. She leaned in close, until I could almost see a hint of midnight blue behind the shadows of her non-existent eyes. A single word rasped from her mouth.

"Why?"

I reeled back. It was Lily's voice, Lily's face. Tears streamed dark trails down her chin. My stomach twisted so hard, I thought I'd vomit. I wrenched my dagger out of her and scrambled away, running on numb legs as I bolted down the street.

This isn't real. They're not real.

A whooshing noise came up behind as my teammates chased me. They moved like phantoms, surfing on black clouds of smoke.

I ran faster.

I darted in and out of alleyways and narrow roads, trying to lose my tail. Every step I took, every time I sped up or changed direction, they were on me, matching every move. Breaths wheezed through my lungs, and my legs ached. I'd never outrun them, and I was wasting time and energy trying.

I slowed to a stop and rested my hands on my knees as I caught my breath. The whooshing behind me halted a few feet away. They were waiting for me.

Waiting for me to attack them.

My heart beat in my throat. The game was forcing me to face my fear, and it wasn't what I had expected. I thought that being alone or failing the team would have been it. But the game knew me better than I knew myself, and it had discovered the one thing I loathed above all else. What was truly my greatest fear since I'd taken over ownership.

I wouldn't just see my friends suffer. I'd have to do it myself.

I'd have to sacrifice my own team to win the game.

Hannah walked up first. The others remained behind. Looked like they'd attack me one at a time. It made sense. They weren't here to take me out of the game. The point was to punish me, slowly.

I drew my sword from my back and my dagger from my boot. Hannah casually tossed her massive battle-axe back and forth between both hands as she closed in on me, smiling her sweet smile.

She spun. Gripping the axe tight in her hands, she twisted around, cutting the blade through the air. I slipped under her axe, came back up, and slammed both of my blades into her gut and ripped them out again. Her eyes went wide, and her whole body went rigid. The weapon dropped from her hands, and she clawed at me as she collapsed.

"Kali, help me. Please."

Her hands slid down my body, clutching me with desperation. I closed my eyes and turned away. My stomach threatened to expel itself.

This was a horror show.

Hannah went limp at my feet, and a puddle of black blood pooled out around her. She gurgled twice, and her head lolled to the side.

Derek came at me next.

He raced toward me with his sword drawn back, preparing to strike. I held my ground. His sword met mine as he swung.

We danced.

Metal hit metal, sparking smoky-gray fizzles between us. I feigned a strike to his right shoulder. He twisted to block, leaving his lower half open. I sliced through his thigh with my dagger. He cried out and dropped to his knees. His sword clanged to the ground and out of reach.

I walked up to him. He held up his hands.

"No, Kali. Don't. Oh God, don't."

I wrapped an arm around his head. He started screaming, pleading with me. My own muscles started convulsing with disgust. I closed my eyes and made my hands move. I cocked his head back and slid my dagger across his throat. His screams cut off into gurgles, and he seized violently as he crumpled to the ground. His whole body spasmed as the blood streamed out of him. He clawed at the cut in his neck and at my own feet. I turned my gaze to the sky and swallowed the acid burning in my throat until his sounds were no more.

Rooke walked up last.

Every nerve inside me shook. He was smiling, calm. He looked at peace. Inside me was anything but peaceful. We'd worked the entire tournament to get him to that point. Where he was tranquil. Safe from his own demons.

Now I was about to kill him.

I closed the gap between us and thrust my sword halfheart-edly. He easily deflected the blow. Two more swipes of my sword were also parried with ease.

He smirked.

"Come on, warrior," he said. "Where's that mouth of yours now?"

My heart nearly wrenched itself apart. Tears stung my eyes, and my bottom lip quivered. I shoved down the lump in my throat and gripped my weapons tight.

"It's right here."

I rushed him.

He crossed his swords over his chest. Pointing the tip at the ground, I swung my sword up, knocking his arms open. With-out breaking stride, I slammed into him and drove my dagger right into his heart, down to the hilt. He gasped, dropped to his knees, twisted as he fell, and landed on his back. He lay there, blinking, with a stunned look in his eyes.

"How could you?" he rasped.

Black tears poured down his face. His fingers reached for me.

"Kali," he whispered. "Look at me."

His fingertips brushed my lips. I shut my eyes and swallowed thick. It looked like him. Sounded like him. Dying was his big-gest fear, and something that he could have faced in reality this tournament. And now I'd done it to him myself.

I gripped my dagger and pulled it out. He spasmed. A last, gasping breath escaped his lips, and he went still.

I knelt and gripped my stomach. It roiled and somersaulted. Sweat beaded along my hairline. With a deep breath, I closed my eyes and pushed out my anxiety. It was over. I did it. I took out my own team. While my hands shook, and my stomach threatened to expel itself, it didn't feel like I'd truly resolved my fear. But still, I had faced it head-on. Now I just had to get to the end.

The game was mine for the taking.

Was it worth it?

There was a nine-figure grand prize at the end of this thing, but Lily had told me herself that money was empty without the people you love. The people I loved had gone through hell this tournament, from the media gossip to Rooke's relapse to the haters, and even the VGL's conspiring against us. Even more, I'd spent too much time worrying about money and image instead of enjoying the tournament and appreciating getting to play in the greatest competition in the world. I did what I had to do to get through it, even taking out my own team inside the game. When I thought about it, the whole thing made me a little sick. Maybe once this was over, it was time to take a step back and reevaluate what I was doing with the team and whether battling the VGL was even worth it. A horn rang out overhead, so loudly it shook my soul, and it kept resounding, like I was trapped inside a church bell. I slapped my hands over my ears. I had a sinking feeling I knew what that horn meant. If Jessica had been telling the truth, then both she and K-Rig had one flag left each. The horn could mean that all eight flags had been captured by the remaining teams, and I was no longer ahead.

The horn suddenly cut out, and the game returned to its usual deathly silence. I pulled my hands away from my ears. For once, I was thankful for the emptiness pressing in around me.

The ground started shaking.

A rumbling filled my ears, and vibrations shot up my legs. I spread my feet to balance myself. My head whipped around as I tried to grasp the situation. Was this another giant NPC? Or something different?

The ground cracked up, as if a lightning bolt were streaking through the pavement. The road split open right between my feet. The crack widened, and chunks of the road started to cave in and sink.

Definitely something different.

I ran.

I darted through the street as it ripped itself apart, pushing off. Buildings around me trembled violently and collapsed. Debris whizzed past me in all directions. Dust choked the air.

The game had become a war zone.

My heart thrummed in my ears until it was all I could hear. Massive hunks of the road broke apart and slid down into the earth. Molten lava seeped up through the fissures, painting red streaks through this monotone gray world. As I ran, my boot clipped the edge of a bubbling lava puddle and the heel started melting instantly. Great. If I fell or touched this stuff, I'd be dead.

Several circular platforms, approximately three feet across, splintered off the pavement and started rising. The rest sunk lower. The lava pools. I set my sights on the closest platform and pumped my legs as fast as they would go.

I was fifty feet away.

Lava continuously seeped in through the cracks until there was more red than gray on the road. More of my boots melted, hissing beneath me with every step. The platform kept rising. Four feet high now.

I ran faster.

The ground beneath began to crumble, as if my own feet were causing it to cave in on itself. Every step I took, more of the road melted away. Heat burned my legs. My armor felt as though it would melt and sear into my skin. My consciousness wavered. Black spots crept into the corners of my vision.

No.

I'm not done yet.

I shook my head, reached inside, and pulled out all the fight I had left. I focused inward and zeroed in on the platform, ignoring the outward sensations. The burning heat, the lack of air in my lungs, all of it disappeared, until there was just me and that platform.

It reached six feet high.

I closed in.

The ground beneath shook so violently, I nearly stumbled and fell. I zigzagged through the crumbling road, pushing off whatever bits of pavement my feet could find. Five feet from the platform, I leapt just as the final chunk of road broke away beneath me and was swallowed up by the raging molten storm.

I flew. My hands clawed at the air until one latched on. I gripped the edge and dangled from the platform as it continued to ascend. Magma gushed up in spurts and licked at my feet. I kicked my legs. My arm strained from the movement and my own weight, and threatened to give out.

Come on, Kali. *Push.*

I gritted my teeth and grasped at the edge with my other hand. It caught. With a grunt, I pulled myself up. My muscles shook so hard, it nearly made my teeth chatter. My head rose over the platform, then my chest, and my waist. I leaned across it, gripped the far edge, and heaved myself onto the platform.

I made it.

Panting hard, I knelt to catch my breath. Soon, my gasps for air turned to laughter, and I didn't stop laughing until there were tears running down my cheeks. I'd made it. I'd made it to the end of the biggest tournament in the world.

This was the endgame.

CHAPTER 28

pushed up to my feet and surveyed the world around me. At least, what was left of it.

The game was ripping itself apart.

The sky had turned black. Not a soft, nighttime black offset by stars and moonlight, but an impossible black as if the entire sky had been replaced by a gaping abyss. It glowed red at the horizon, reflecting the rolling waves of lava beneath it. The entire sea was now one swirling mass of hot yellow and red that fizzled and hissed until the air filled with white noise. A charred stench assaulted my nose, and a deep, smoky taste bit at the back of my throat. Still, I took a deep breath and let it out. This was the first time in this game I'd felt my senses engaged. Taste. Smell. Sound. All along, the game had felt like a machine, thinking but not aware, present but not really alive. Now it had a soul. And it was angry.

Once every few feet, there was another platform like the one I was standing on, leading to the middle of the game. The center few blocks of the city were still intact, and at the very core of it all, a single building stretched tall, taller than all the others and completely untouched by the raging storm. Atop it, a golden beam shot up to the sky. The outline of a flag phased in and out of my view.

The final flag.

I scanned the rooftops and other rotating platforms. There was no movement, no sight of the other teams. Just the crumbling buildings and the lava creeping ever more inward. Despite the immense heat, a chill slid under my skin.

I could be alone in here. The championship could be down to me. All I had to do was jump from platform to platform and make it to the middle of the game.

I flexed my legs, preparing to leap. Just as I started to push off, a geyser of hot lava shot up between my platform and the next, blasting my face with heat. I skidded to a stop. My toes slipped off the edge, and my arms pinwheeled backwards to keep my balance. I scrambled back a step and sighed with relief.

The geyser shot up again, lasting four seconds before disappearing for four, and shooting up again. Four on, four off. Soon, geysers were shooting up between all the platforms and buildings, turning the sea of lava into a volcanic symphony.

I let my eyes fall shut. This was becoming more and more like an actual video game by the minute. I steadied myself on the platform and counted the timing. *One, two, three, shoot. One, two three, off.*

I jumped and landed on the next platform. The geyser shot up behind me, and between every other platform. I steadied myself, and prepared to leap again.

The platform began to sink.

In a matter of seconds, it had descended several inches and kept getting lower. The next platform was rapidly becoming out of reach. The geysers shot up again.

Are you kidding me?

I leapt, scrambling for the platform. I gripped its edge and hauled myself up. The geyser shot off. A flame caught the edge of my armor and licked up my leg. I slapped the fire repeatedly with my hand, singeing my palm as I smothered the flames. My jaw went tight as I surveyed my hand. Blisters were already forming.

The new platform started to sink.

I rocked on my feet as I gauged the timing and leapt to the next rocky edge. Bits of the platform crumbled away. Not just the one I was standing on, but all of them leading to the center of the game. The geysers shot faster, with less time between.

It became a race.

I started darting across platforms. Heat engulfed the air around me. My hair clung to me, sticking to the back of my neck. Geysers shot off within inches of my skin. The platforms were getting smaller by the second. Soon, I could only touch down a single foot as I vaulted from step to step.

In the center of the game, a single skyscraper remained, stretching so tall, it looked like it pierced the sky.

I was three jumps away.

The middle of the game. I was almost there.

The geysers were almost continuously on now, with only quick blinks of open space between. The platforms kept sinking, more by the second. I dashed between it all. I'd stopped counting. Instinct was leading me now. It was more of a dance than anything. My knees shook, and my head swam, but I pushed myself onward.

I landed on the final platform.

No more than a few inches wide, I teetered on the ball of one foot. The skyscraper was within my reach.

The platform sunk, touching down into the lava. It splintered apart immediately. There was nothing left to stand on.

I leapt.

I flew toward the building, my arms desperately seeking any ledge to grasp. I slammed into the wall with a thick smack. The world spun, and I started sliding down. As I passed a window, three fingers snagged the windowsill, and I snapped to a halt and dangled in midair. I closed my eyes and breathed deep.

I'm there, I told myself.

I'd reached the center. Three inches below my feet, the lava storm raged. I clung to the wall, wishing I could wrap my arms around it entirely, but the final building took up the entire city block on its own. I looked up. I couldn't really see the top from where I hung, but a beam of golden light shot up into the sky from the skyscraper's rooftop.

The final flag.

Now it was just a matter of the climb. Up a skyscraper. With nothing but window ledges to get me there. This was like mountain climbing without a net or a safety line. If I fell, I would be dead and out of the game.

Unless I could get in through the windows.

As soon as I steadied myself against the wall, I pounded a fist against the glass window to see if it would shatter. The glass thunked under my hand. I boosted myself up on the windowsill and kicked the glass with my foot. Nothing. Harder. Still nothing. The glass made a deadened sound as my foot pounded against it, like I was kicking concrete instead. Looked like the interior of the building was off-limits. Up the exterior, then. As I reached toward the next window, the wall rumbled under my fingertips. Oh, what fresh hell was this? Another earthquake? Wall climbing during an earthquake. The primitive part of my brain that refused to believe this was all virtual sent buzzers through my brain.

Warning. This is counterproductive for your general health.

The building started to spin.

Each floor of the building spun independently from the others, at different speeds, some in the opposite direction. This one ten miles an hour, this one twenty. Then a shuddering sound came from the walls, like the building itself had groaned, and ledges suddenly protruded, one every few feet up the side of the building. All were five feet long and three feet across. One extended out below my feet. I touched down on it and surveyed the scene above me. It was like an actual video game, where I'd have to time the leaps to ascend up the side of the building, as each one moved at a different speed and in alternate directions.

Wonderful.

The message playing in my mind changed to a new one as I spun around and around the building, watching the ledges above me whip by.

Don't throw up. Don't throw up. Don't throw up.

I closed my eyes and steadied myself. I was not going to throw up. I was going to own this whole building. The flag was at the top. The championship, the hundred million, the answer to all my problems was only a few stories away. All I had to do was take my time, concentrate, and kick ass. I would not let myself be intimidated.

When I opened my eyes again, movement below caught my attention. Five pairs of ice-blue eyes cut through the shadows, staring up at me. K-Rig. Right below me. My stomach went to knots. Now I had no time.

Okay, I got slightly intimidated.

I started racing up the side of the building, timing my jumps between the ledges as they whizzed past me. I glanced down. K-Rig was two levels down, each on a ledge, so they were staggered against the side of the building.

I kept climbing.

They were faster. The closest one was only a story below me now, and gaining. I looked up the building. At least fifteen stories towered above me. There was no way I'd make it. I couldn't outrun them.

I had to fight.

I steadied myself on my ledge, drew my sword, and gripped it with both hands, pointing it downward. I waited, poised on the ledge as it circled the building. One pass. Then another. When the highest member of K-Rig lined up directly under me, I jumped down.

Bull's-eye.

I landed on his shoulders, and my sword slid straight down though his body, from his neck to his navel. He went instantly rigid. I ripped the sword back out, jumped off his shoulders, and kicked my feet into his back. Straight as a board, he toppled off the ledge.

One down.

Another member of K-Rig jumped for my ledge. I gripped my sword again and spun like a whipping blade. The tip sliced through his face, chest, and abdomen in three quick passes. Stunned, he stumbled back and fell into the darkness below.

I knelt, braced myself against the ledge, and breathed deep. That's two.

I surveyed the side of the building. Another set of icy eyes was down one level, twenty feet over.

I counted, waiting for him to get close, and jumped.

I missed.

I got the timing wrong, missed the ledge he was standing on, and started sliding down the side of the building. Damn it. The rough surface burned against my clothing and skin as I slid. I glanced down. The lava was coming up fast. Gritting my teeth, I drew the dagger from my boot and ground it into the wall. My descent slowed and started to curve. Instead of plunging straight down, I was skating diagonally across the building's exterior. I pushed harder, grinding the dagger deeper into the wall, aiming for a slow-moving ledge. The tip of the dagger broke off in the wall and I started free-falling.

Oh shit.

Shit, shit, shit.

I pinwheeled my legs, trying to guide my body toward the ledge. It came up fast, as if it was racing up to meet me. My upper half smacked into it and slid off. My fingers caught the edge, and I dangled from it.

I did it.

I was down a weapon, clinging to a ledge for dear life, and three-on-one against the best team in the world.

But I was still in the game.

I hoisted my lower half up onto the ledge and lay against it for a minute, panting, hugging myself to it. The wind whipped around me as the ledge continued to whisk around the building. I braced my hands against the ledge and slowly pushed myself up to a crouching position.

Two down.

Three to go.

I steadied myself on the ledge and prepared to jump when one of them came flying at me. I was knocked to the side as a body hit mine. Fists gripped my jacket and I swayed from side to side. All I saw was a pair of ice-blue eyes, and they were angry.

I didn't resist the throws of his weight and instead went with them. I leaned to the right with him, slid my foot against his ankle, and swept it out. His feet slipped off the edge. As he fell, his hands kept their grip on my jacket and pulled me forward. I toppled over the edge and started racing toward the bottom.

No, no, no.

Ledges whizzed past me as I picked up speed. I had no way to slow my fall. Even if I caught a ledge now, the impact would probably kill me.

My shot at the championship was over. I was out of the game.

I clamped my jaw shut and braced for death.

Three stories from the bottom, a hand wrapped around my wrist in midair. I arced in a curve, swinging like a pendulum, and my descent suddenly ended. My shoulder jolted. Pain like I'd never felt before shot through my body, and I cried out. I looked up, blinking through tears and black spots from the pain. A set of fingers were still wrapped around my wrist. I followed them up to find Jessica hovering over me, leaning over a ledge.

"How many times am I going to save your ass?" she asked.

She hoisted me up. I screamed again as she lifted me. On the ledge, I stumbled to my feet, trembling violently. Pain enveloped my entire shoulder, and it was so intense, I nearly blacked out right there.

"I think my shoulder's out," I told her.

Jessica folded up my left arm against my chest. "Hold it there."

I gripped my wrist with my other hand.

"What now?"

"Now we just—"

She slammed me sideways into the wall. I screamed as pure agony convulsed through my body. Then I felt a jolt, and after that, nothing at all. I blinked and opened my eyes.

"How about now?" she asked.

I rotated my shoulder a little and flexed my fingers. A dull thudding radiated through the joint, but most of the pain was gone.

"Better," I said with a nod.

"Good. Now, get your ass in gear."

She turned and leapt to the next ledge. I followed.

Jessica moved like an acrobat as she jumped and flipped between the ledges, racing up the side of the building. I struggled to keep up.

Two levels from the top, Jessica reached the lowest K-Rig member on the building. I scurried up the ledges, trying to keep an eye on her as I passed the fight. She grappled with him on the ledge. She spun. In a blur, she drew her dagger from what seemed like nowhere and slammed it into his gut. He crumpled to his knees and tumbled off the side of the building.

Damn.

She had moves.

I looked above me. One left.

Kim Jae.

He was on the top ledge and reaching for the roof. I was one ledge below. He was within my grasp.

I leapt.

I slammed into him, my front to his back. I wrapped my arms around him and dropped my weight. His grip slid off the roof.

We grappled.

It became a wrestling match as I stayed at his back, throwing my weight in either direction, trying to knock him off the narrow platform. He elbowed me hard in the gut. I gasped, lost my balance, and slipped off the ledge. I smacked into the ledge two levels down and landed hard on my back. My head cracked against the concrete. My vision went a bit hazy, and I blinked several times, trying to focus on the events above me.

Kim Jae and Jessica Salt fought for the ledge. He shoved her sideways, into the wall. Jessica lost her balance, slipped down the side, and caught the edge of the platform with her fingers.

She needed my help.

I pushed myself up. My head reeled, and I slid back down. Damn it.

Jae stomped on her fingers. Jessica cried out, losing her grip with one hand. With her dangling arm, she pulled a dagger from her waist and stabbed Jae repeatedly through his foot. He screamed, scrambled backwards off the ledge, and plummeted to the bottom.

I released a breath.

Was K-Rig out now? I couldn't remember if they had lives left at this point. Since the bases were gone, I wasn't sure where they'd respawn, if they would at all. Even if they did, they'd have to get to the center of the game and mount the building again.

We were almost there.

The haziness in my head cleared, and I pushed myself up, to the next level, one below Jessica. She held out a hand as we spun around the building. I held my better arm up and as my ledge passed under hers, she scooped me up. Then she pushed me toward the wall and stuck her knee out, so I could use it to boost myself up. I gripped the top edge, used her body to push mine up, and heaved myself over the edge.

I nearly face-planted against the roof as heavy breaths heaved through my entire body. I could have given in right then. My head was so heavy; my limbs were filled with pain. I could have curled up and stopped right there.

Instead, I lifted my head. In the center of the roof, the flag shone like a golden star in the darkness. A wire cage protected it from all sides except the top. It was set up higher than everything else, five steps up from the rooftop. I'd have to climb the steps, mount the cage, and drop down inside to claim the flag. But there it was. Twenty feet from my grasp. Everything the team had suffered through over these past months. All the gossip and bullshit. It had all been to get us here, to this moment.

Can't stop now, I thought. *Just a little bit farther.*

I pushed myself to standing. I swayed, but managed to stay on my feet. As much as my head was still spinning from the climb, the rooftop was stationary. Only the levels below it were still moving. There was no edge or barrier to this roof. Just the end, and a twenty-story drop. One wrong step, and you were toast.

Jessica had mounted the roof's edge a short distance away, panting just like me, slowly pushing up to her feet.

"Is K-Rig out?" I asked her, resting my hands against my knees as I struggled to catch my breath.

Jessica placed her hands on her hips and glanced down the roof's edge. "They've got one more respawn, by my count." She glanced at the center of the roof, where the flag sat within its cage. "I hope you realize I'm not going to hold back anymore."

Despite the breaths gasping through my mouth, my lips spread into a smile.

"Good."

We locked eyes. We'd made it. Together. Now it all came down to a fight between me and her.

She bolted. I bolted.

In the middle, we clashed.

CHAPTER 29

Halfway to the flag, we slammed together and tumbled to the ground, rolling over each other several times. I landed on my back and she pinned me down. She swung for my jaw. I dodged her blow and slammed my forehead against her nose. She tumbled to the side, gripping her face. As she pushed herself back up, she grimaced and wiped blood.

Round One: Kali Ling.

I pulled myself up, unsheathing my sword. Jessica drew her own. We circled each other, each reeling back. Swords smashed together in rapid succession, sparking and fizzling with each hit. Gray and red ribbons swirled around us, trailing from the weapons as we swerved and dodged each other. For a Special Ops gamer, she was good with a blade.

She came at me, again and again, smashing with more fury and strength with each hit, as if she was gaining combo points from the attack. She swung, backhanded. I slid back, narrowly avoiding the blow. She came back again.

I blocked her swing, knocked her arms open, and lunged forward, smashing my shoulder into her chest. She gasped and stumbled back several steps.

Her foot slipped off the edge of the roof.

Her balance teetered as her foot desperately swiped at the

edge for purchase. Her sword tumbled from her hand and into the darkness below.

No, no. You don't get off that easy.

I ran for her, just as she slipped and started falling backwards. I reached the edge, grabbed her arm, and heaved. She tumbled forward and fell to her knees on the rooftop, panting hard. She looked up, eyes wide and glazing with bewilderment.

"What the hell are you doing?"

"I'm not done kicking your ass. If I'm going to beat you, it'll be because I actually beat you. Not because you slipped off the edge. Now get up."

They call me the warrior for a reason, and I prefer to earn the name.

Every. Damn. Match.

I took a stance across from her, sword raised over my shoulder. Jessica pushed up to her feet and brought up her hands in defense. I swiped through the air. Jessica ducked and dodged my blows. We twirled around the roof as I sliced and she dodged, a close-cut game of cat and mouse. I halted my attacks and glanced down at my sword. This wasn't really fair, was it? I could toss my weapons aside and fight her hand-to-hand. The audience would love the show. But for me, it would mean something so much more: facing my idol on even ground. If she wanted to pass me her torch, here was my chance to prove I deserved it.

I smiled and tossed my sword over the roof edge. It toppled through the air until the shadows below swallowed it. My dagger followed shortly after.

Jessica watched my blades tumble over the side, looked back at me, and grinned. We had no weapons. The only thing that stood between us and the championship was each other. Barehanded. The best wins.

I brought my hands up.

Let's dance.

We circled each other again, step for step. She lashed out first, throwing a right hook. I blocked and snapped my foot against her ribs. She grunted.

She attacked again, faking twice, throwing me off, and landed a clean swipe across my jaw. My head rocked to the side, and I stumbled back.

Damn, that girl can pack a punch.

My vision reeled. I spat gore. Blood, teeth, whatever had collected in my mouth. The rooftop became a blood-spattered battlefield. Footsteps pounded away from me as my vision cleared. Jessica was on the stairs and climbing.

The flag shimmered from behind the cage, inches from her reach.

I scrambled after her and latched onto her ankle. With her free foot, she stomped down on my hand. Hard. Holy Mother. I bit down on my scream as my hand jerked back, instinctively. I instantly shot my arm back up, wrapping my fingers around her ankle again, and pulled with my weight. She crumpled, tumbling down the steps.

On hands and knees at the bottom of the stairs, we grappled. Our arms wrapped around each other's, heads pressed together, both grimacing and grunting. We were matched again. Dead even. I focused on her weight. Instead of fighting against her movements, I went with them, violently rocking her back and forth with her own momentum until she lost her balance, and I tossed her to the side. She rolled several times before catching herself. She slapped the roof, spewing and swearing, and started pushing up to her feet. Her breaths heaved. Her hands shook.

She was getting tired. Experience versus youth.

Youth was winning.

I scrambled up the stairs, listening for her following footsteps. When the metal clunked behind me, I whirled around, gripped the railings, pushed off with both feet, and slammed a double kick into her chest. She went careening back and crashed into the roof with a sickening smack. She landed on her back, arms out. Soft grunts escaped her lips, but she made no move to stand.

I knew right then I'd played one too many fighting games because the words echoed in my mind.

Finish her.

I bolted up the last of the steps, turned, and leapt, propelling myself into an arcing jump above her. Time slowed again as I sailed through the air. I straightened out so my back faced the roof and my front, the ceiling. As I descended, I lifted both arms into the air, cupping one fist around the other, and brought it down, driving my elbow into her sternum as I landed.

The rooftop rumbled with the impact.

Jessica seized, as if she'd been cut in two, her head and feet lifting a few inches off the ground. Blood spewed from her mouth, and she gasped like it was her last, heaving breath. Then she went limp.

I kept a hand on her chest. Shallow breaths expanded her lungs, pushing up against my hand. Her heartbeat throbbed under my palm until I could practically hear it. Blood trickled from the corner of her mouth and out her nose. Her eyes glazed over for a few seconds until she blinked and looked at me, a hint of fire still dancing within them. She wasn't done. Not quite yet.

I backed away, giving her a chance to get up. I wasn't going to end the fight with her on her back, like an animal. She deserved a dignified death, to go down fighting.

Jessica pulled herself up in slow motion, grimacing, gripping her stomach. Her face was tight with pain. More blood trickled out of her mouth, and her knees trembled violently. Still, she took up a fighting stance across from me. But even then, she couldn't hide that her whole body was shaking.

I was shaking, too, but for a different reason.

I was winning.

I was about to defeat my idol.

I was about to take the all-star tournament.

Number one in the world. One hundred million dollars. My team would be set for life.

I positioned myself between Jessica and the stairs, and glanced behind me. The flag shimmered just feet away. *I'm coming for you next.*

A grin twitched in the corners of Jessica's lips. She knew, and she was proud.

She raised her fists. I raised mine. This was it. The finale. I was one solid hit away from victory.

And then, with Jessica in front of me, me standing tall, ready to take the match and the game, and the entire world watching, K-Rig mounted the rooftop and charged for us.

CHAPTER 30

K-Rig was coming. All five of them.

I looked at Jessica. We were two on five, against the best team in the world. We had no weapons. Jessica could barely stand. K-Rig would destroy her.

Time stopped. It often does in the moments that define your life.

I glanced back at the flag. I could make it before K-Rig caught me, take the steps two at a time, climb the cage walls, and claim the flag. I could take the entire championship right now.

My gaze flicked back to Jessica. She wobbled, barely standing, blood oozing out the side of her mouth. Still, she smiled at me. She could see what was happening. She knew I'd leave her to K-Rig and take the flag for myself. But I wouldn't have made it this far if it hadn't been for her. How many times had she saved my ass, and not just in the game? I didn't deserve the championship.

She did.

This was her final year. Her last tournament. Her last game. And I could either take that from her or turn it into the single greatest moment of her life and thank her for everything she'd done for me.

Besides, I preferred a good fight.

I grabbed Jessica's arm, pulled her past me, and shoved her toward the platform.

"Get the flag. I'll give you time."

She stumbled up two steps. As she gripped the railing to steady herself, her head snapped back around, eyes glazing with bewilderment.

"GO!" I shouted, shoving her again.

She did, using the railing to haul herself up the stairs. Stumbling up the steps, fighting against her fatigued, battered body, she'd need time to reach the flag, and I'd give it to her. I turned around to face K-Rig alone.

I charged.

They charged.

Jessica climbed.

My footsteps smacked against the rooftop as I streamed right for K-Rig. They mirrored me, weapons poised for attack as they closed in. Five feet. Three feet. I brought up my fists and we collided. I slipped under an arm and slammed my full weight into someone's chest. As he stumbled back, I twisted my hand around his, and his sword became my own. I rammed a shoulder into him, and he lost his step and tumbled off the roof. He screamed as he descended into the darkness.

Kim Jae swung for me next.

He moved like lightning, his blade a metallic blur through the air. He knocked my arm to the side and plunged his sword through my stomach. I gasped and went rigid, gripping the blade where it disappeared into my body. I stumbled back, and Kim Jae lost his grip on the sword.

Hey, now I have another weapon.

I gripped the hilt and bit down, preparing for the pain. *It's not real,* I told myself.

I pulled.

A mewling groan escaped between my clenched teeth as the blade ripped from my stomach. My vision swirled as the world swam, and my abdomen and legs grew warm with my blood. I trembled violently and more blood bubbled up the back of my throat and lurched out of my mouth. But I stayed standing, a sword in each hand, ready for more.

"I told you to make it count," I said.

K-Rig just stared. Kim Jae uttered something in Korean that I'm pretty sure translated to: *This bitch is crazy.*

Behind me, Jessica climbed the cage.

K-Rig came at me again, Kim Jae with his fists, the other three with their swords. I raised mine. We slammed together. I knocked Jae's arms open and drove my twin blades through his stomach. He halted, his mouth dropping open with a gasp. I grinned. My stomach, now yours. Tit for tat. He grinned back at me and collapsed to the floor.

His teammates' swords speared through my sides. Hot pain ripped through my nerves, and my back bowed to the onslaught.

Jessica hauled herself over the edge and jumped down. The flag consumed her in a burst of golden light.

A horn rang out.

I fell to my knees. The ground shook violently beneath me. Metal clanged and smashed together. Sections of the ceiling buckled, caved in, and collapsed. Everything was breaking apart, ripping into blue-and-white code.

My body went numb, and I collapsed onto my back. A sharp, bitter cold slunk through my veins, slithering through my extremities up to my chest. As death closed in from all sides, smothering me in its icy darkness, it wrapped around my heart until all that existed was my steady, thumping pulse and the cold hollowness threatening to crush the last beat.

It closed in.

My heart stopped.

I smiled.

Dying had never felt so good.

CHAPTER 31

The applause was deafening.

I sat inside my pod, doors still closed, alone in the darkness. I covered my eyes and just listened to the sound, like the beat of a hundred rainstorms pounding together. This had been the tournament of a lifetime. I'd fought my idol. I'd participated in the first all-star tournament in VGL history.

It was glorious.

Third. We were third in the world. It wasn't first, but it felt like it.

Rooke was on me the second the pod doors opened. He drew me into a deep kiss, and even when he pulled back, he kept his hands on either side of my face. He was shaking.

"I can't believe you did that."

He sounded shocked, not upset. The rest of my teammates stood behind him, staring at me, completely stunned.

I shrugged.

"Did what?"

Rooke opened his mouth, but nothing came out. Eventually, his open mouth spread into a smile, and he wrapped me tight in his arms. My teammates joined him, smothering out the sounds of the arena and most of the air in my lungs.

When they finally released me, I peered through the crowd onstage, to where Jessica stood. The announcers had her arms raised.

"Jessica Salt takes it for Team Legacy."

The crowd roared even louder.

Even with all that chaos and noise swirling around her, Jessica's gaze wasn't on the cameras, or the audience, or even her own teammates. It was on me. Her expression was a mixture of shock, elation, and a bit of gratitude shining through. Could I have taken the flag? Sure. But I'd have plenty more chances. Jessica? That was it. Her last championship.

She turned back to the audience and smiled.

"Team Legacy is your first all-star champs and the number one team in the world."

They presented Team Legacy with the championship trophy, one specifically designed for the all-star tournament. Jessica and Damon raised it together, each with one hand on either side. The roaring of the crowd reached a decibel level never before recorded by man.

One day, there would be another name on that trophy. Defiance. Not this year, and maybe not the next. But before my career was over, the name Kali Ling would be etched forever into that cup. I knew because I wouldn't stop until I made it happen.

When the cameras clicked off, security started pulling the teams offstage, Legacy first. As they passed by us, Jessica halted the procession in front of me, and stared. She said nothing, but I could see the question in her eyes. I leaned in, acting like I was just patting her on the back. Instead, I whispered in her ear.

"If you're going to pass the torch, I want it shining brighter than the fucking sun."

She pulled back and studied my face again, this time with admiration instead of bewilderment. Pride filled my chest and stung my eyes. Third in the world was a grand title, but impressing my idol? That was worth ten times more.

———

"Team Defiance. You got knocked out of the tournament in the semifinals and were given a second chance when you took over Oblivion's spot in the championship. How did that impact your mind-set going into this?"

As the cameras flashed, and the crowd bustled with energy, I sat with my teammates at the press conference, addressing questions from the media. They were doing follow-ups with all four teams, Legacy being first and getting the most attention for obvious reasons. Still, everyone wanted to hear from all the teams inside the championship match.

Derek leaned toward his microphone. "It made us appreciate the opportunity more and focus on what really matters."

"Kali." I turned my head to a reporter in the front row. "At the end there, it looked like you gave Jessica—"

"I did nothing."

The room went silent for a few seconds, minus the camera clicks and general murmurs.

Another reporter spoke up from the back. "Jessica announced her retirement at Legacy's press conference. Did you know anything about that beforehand?"

"There are always rumors. Some the public doesn't hear, and some we hear from the public first." The crowd laughed. "But we wish her well in whatever comes next for her."

"So you didn't decide to help her—"

I smiled. "You're hunting for a conspiracy where there isn't one. Legacy won the tournament. That's all."

A few reporters nodded, and several others frowned, like they didn't believe me. But they let it go.

Another reporter stood. "Considering that Defiance won its

first year in the RAGE tournaments, what did it feel like to lose this time?"

I shook my head. "We didn't lose."

He faltered. "But, um . . ."

"We spend our days doing the thing we love with the people we love," I said, paraphrasing what Lily had said to me just weeks ago. "Most people will never get as far as we have. So, getting to play in the greatest tournament the world has ever seen is never a loss, whether you place first or thirty-second. And I'd take third over first in a heartbeat because it means I still have something to learn. Placing anything other than first is not losing. It's a challenge to come back stronger."

I looked directly into the cameras and winked.

"That's what makes a real champion."

CHAPTER 32

"So, I've been getting calls from companies all around the world wanting to sponsor us," Derek said when I walked into my office the next day. "They say they want their name on a team that stands for something more important than winning."

I smiled as I sat down behind my desk. "Sounds like the right kind of people to work with, doesn't it?"

Derek studied me for a minute and shook his head. "You can act all innocent as much as you want. Everyone knows what you did, Kali. "

I waved him off. "It's not that big a deal. Besides, I wouldn't have made it that far in the game if it hadn't been for her."

"You still gave up a nine-figure prize to honor someone else. Not everyone would have done that even if Jessica really did deserve it. People think that was . . . heroic."

No, people who saved lives were heroic. I played games. But there was something in the way he'd said that. The tone of his voice was hinting at something more. He wasn't talking about other people. That was the way he felt about it, too.

"You fixed it," he said simply. "People hated us before the championship, and you changed their minds with one move." He leaned toward the desk, resting his elbows on it. "What made you do it? Was it because of the crowd?"

"No, no." I shook my head. "Jessica feels like I'm the one to take her place. But she's amongst the best in the league. I just feel like I should have to earn that status, not have it handed to me."

He smiled. "And you don't think taking the biggest tournament in the world would have proven that?"

"Being the best isn't about how much you win. It's how you play the game. Besides . . ." My voice trailed off. Nah, it was too corny to say.

He quirked an eyebrow at me. "Go on."

". . . I was in there for a while after you guys were out."

He shrugged. "So?"

"It just . . . didn't feel right."

He sat back in the chair and blinked a few times. "What do you mean? Were you plugged in for too long, or did something happen to you in there?"

"No. It just made me realize something I never want to do."

"Which is?"

"Play without you guys," I said simply. "I know we've had moments where we go off by ourselves inside the game for strategy or whatever. And in the first championship, I did the final fight by myself. But that was no more than a few minutes. Anything more than that without you guys by my side just doesn't feel right. Winning isn't worth it. Playing isn't worth it. Not unless we're together. All of us." I paused, clicking my fingernails against the desk. "So I let Jessica have her final tournament. But the next one? We'll take together. Side by side."

An indescribable look filled Derek's eyes as he processed my words. He laced his fingers across his chest and was quiet for a long moment.

"Aww, Kali," he finally said, and pretended to blush. "You love me."

I frowned. "I'm trying to be serious here."

"All this time I thought it was Rooke, and secretly, it's me you want by your side."

I held up a hand. "Enough. I get sentimental, and you start acting like an asshole."

"Okay, okay. I'll stop." But he cracked another smile and shifted his hands so they rested over his heart. "A part of me always knew how you felt."

I pointed at the door. "Fuck off, and get out of here."

He pushed out of his chair and headed for the exit, laughing at me as he went. But, at the door, he paused.

"Hey."

I looked up. His lips twisted into a crooked, half grin.

"I don't want to play without you, either," he said, and slipped into the hallway before I could reply. I smiled. As much as he acted cool, somewhere inside, Derek was a big, old softie.

When I finished my paperwork, I left my office in search of the team, half expecting them to be getting ready for the after-party celebration downtown. Instead, I found them on the couch in the living room, a controller in each hand, and Diablo 4 on the screen. I caught more than a few elbow jabs and hands covering eyes, but was far too entertained to play referee.

Rooke was sitting beside Derek, his eyes narrowed in concentration. He looked good. Healthy. He'd always have to be careful. But then again, we all did. And if any of us fell, for any reason, the rest would be there to pick up the pieces. I was sure of it.

Hannah was right. We were family now.

As I watched the quartet on my couch elbow each other and shout at the screen, the tablet in my arms pinged. I glanced down at it and found a new message from Jessica Salt blinking on the screen. I tapped the message.

Did they really do this? CALL ME.

Attached to the message was an article. I opened it.

TEAM DEFIANCE BANNED.
Under allegations of cheating in the all-star tournament, the
VGL announced just moments ago that Team Defiance has
been banned from the league and stripped of their championship titles . . .

I leaned against the closest wall for support. Suddenly, I felt like
I was falling down an endless, black hole. I blinked several times
and forced myself to reread the article again and again. They'd
actually done it. Found a way to kick me out of the league. I'd
pushed too hard, and now the whole team would pay for it.

Laughter echoed from the couch. My teammates had no idea.
When their game was over, I'd have to tell them.

I forced myself to read on, despite my churning stomach.

. . . a program found on the virtual pods inside the Team
Defiance home points to proof that they knew the outline of
the championship course weeks before . . .

My birthday present. The program Rooke had designed for
me. Tamachi must have accessed the information from our pods
and used it to redesign the final course. Rooke was right. It had
been a trap all along. But not in the virtual world.

In the real one.

I closed my eyes and rested my head against the wall behind
me. My mind drifted back to everything we'd been through
over the past several weeks and all the times I'd said in one way
or another exactly how to get to me.

What you do to my team, you do to me.

And he did. He'd just kicked me out, times five. Took away my hopes and dreams, same for everyone else on my team.

My. Team.

Tamachi knew exactly what to do to crush my soul. Whether he'd picked up on it through the pods, or just assumed because I'd taken ownership of the team, or even because of my crazy protective streak over them, he knew.

And now my insides were ripping themselves to shreds.

We were finally back together again, acting as one force. We finally had the right sponsors, we had the crowd back, and we'd earned a championship and a finalist title in the biggest tournament in the world.

It was all gone in a heartbeat.

All of it.

"Hey."

I looked up to find Rooke standing over me. His gaze was locked onto my face, and I knew he could tell something was up.

"What's wrong?" he asked.

I said nothing and handed him the tablet to read for himself. After his eyes scanned back and forth a few times, they shot up to meet mine.

"They can't do that."

"They just did."

"But—" he sputtered. "We can disprove it. I created that program for your birthday. Tamachi was the one that used the program to change the final course."

I stepped up to him and took my tablet back. "And who do you think the public is going to believe, huh? Tamachi, a businessman and founder of the International Association of Virtual Gaming? Or a former . . ."

"Drug addict," he finished.

I sighed. "I didn't mean it that way."

"But it's true." He glanced down at the tablet in my arms. "What are we going to do about this?"

My churning stomach solidified to steel. This was far from the end. The VGL could do anything they wanted. I'd never stop fighting, in or out of the arena. If there was anything I had learned from this tournament, it was that video games aren't the only thing that can be an open-concept world. Reality is what you make it, and it can be as empty or full as the digital domain. True, our lives wouldn't be the same without the virtual world. But video games weren't inherently bad or evil. Some people used them as a substitute for real life. Others used them to make friends. To build families. Across countries and continents. Living in this house right now were the four most important people in the world to me. Games had given me that, and it was something worth fighting for. Until the very end.

"I'm going to do what I do best," I told Rooke. "Kick ass."

He grinned. "I wouldn't expect anything less."

"Kali," a voice called.

I glanced around the corner into the living room. Hannah had turned on the couch to face me. She held out a controller and grinned.

"It's your turn."

Damn right it is.

PERCENTAGE OF GAME COMPLETED: 100%

THANK YOU FOR PLAYING

ACKNOWLEDGMENTS

To Anne Sowards for your patience and persistence. If it wasn't for you, I'd still be writing chapter three.

To Leon Husock for your advice and support so far and, hopefully, for many years to come.

To my family. Throughout everything, you've been there. Special thanks to my sister for being my first co-op gaming buddy.

To the wonderful team at Erie Architectural Products, especially Ron and Nellie Stronks, for encouraging me to chase this crazy dream.

To the developers of Pokémon Go. Thanks for giving me a reason to leave the house that qualifies as "research for my books."

To Carrie "CrazMadSci" Day for your experience and input. I bow to thee, oh great lady gamer.

To Eric. I've spent hours wondering what to write because there are no words. Your creativity is inspirational, your mind is sexy, and your understanding is unbounded. Thanks—for everything.

Lastly, to all the gamers out there. Whether it's your hobby or your career, your dedication to the game continues to inspire me every day.

Play on.

Photo by Timeless Photography & Design

Holly Jennings is a lifelong gamer who has spent innumerable hours playing World of Warcraft and Call of Duty. She is the author of the Arena novels, including *Gauntlet* and *Arena*. She lives in Canada.

CONNECT ONLINE

authorhollyjennings.com
twitter.com/HollyN_Jennings
facebook.com/authorhollyjennings